Conflicted

a novel by

M.M. KOENIG

Heather ~ Thank you so
much for your support. I appreciate
the pimping of my series so much!!

M. M.

Edited by tgh writing services
Cover Design by L.J. Anderson - Mayhem Cover Creations
Formatting by L.J. Anderson - Mayhem Cover Creations

DEDICATION

This is for the best friends we have in our lives that help shape the people that we become. I wanted to thank my best friend for her unwavering belief in me in all our years of friendship. Thank you for giving me the best advice.

"We are our own genie."

I had heard it time and time again but never truly got the meaning behind it. I get it now. The power to make your wishes and dreams come true lies within you.

CONTENTS

CHAPTER ONE
No Plan

"*What's my plan?*" I stared at my ceiling taking in the rays of light as the sun slowly began to rise. I was awake with no chance of falling back to sleep. Every day began with the same thought – "*What's my plan?*" Life changed. Shit happened. That much was obvious. I definitely had a firm grasp on that fact. I wasn't *that* naïve. If your plan changed, you readjusted your course. I was, without a doubt, on a new path – but I had to say that the path was leading me and not the other way around. I kept hoping that one of these days, I'd wake up, and everything would be clear again.

My head turned towards the light breathing next to me. It had to be nice to be able to sleep more than a few hours. I was having difficulty recalling if it was Braden or Brandon. Their shaggy blonde hair fell the same way. It was just the right length and sexy as hell for pulling when ... well ... you know. I needed to make a better effort at remembering their names or at least branch out to other letters in the alphabet. I was going through a crazy string of guys with names that began with the letter 'B'.

My life had changed so much in the last year. I was living with my closest friends in an amazing house. It was a far cry from the types of places I'd lived in before, but that was probably because it was in an uppity part of Chicago. Then again, everything was the polar opposite of the streets on the south side. This place was a testament for me though because I actually liked it here. In twenty-one years, I had never felt at home anywhere, but living here gave me that sense of home – it was a first. When this house opened up, Jackson jumped on it. The problem was that it ended up being bigger than he anticipated, so he needed to recruit roommates. After several rounds of 'Mia, it's going to be epic', I caved to his charms. I convinced Bri, Trey, and Shane to make up the numbers.

The house was gorgeous. Situated in a swanky neighborhood a couple of blocks from the upper lakeshore, it was the perfect location and a short drive to the campus that everyone attended. The Victorian structure matched the rest of the neighborhood. It was a fine white with black shutters and heavy oak door. It came finished with a feature we all adored – a huge wraparound porch. A set of stairs divided it, and the right side of the porch had stairs that led into a side door that took you into the kitchen. On that side of the house, there was another deck on the second story that led out of the master bedroom. We fought for that room and the alcohol-induced shenanigans that we pulled to get it left us in rough shape. Jackson got it in the end. Shane and Trey took bedrooms near the stairs while Bri and I selected rooms at end of the hallway. Our rooms were next to the enormous bathroom that came with the house. The boys demanded the sizeable den for their man cave so we claimed the bathroom as ours.

My thoughts broke when his arms reached for me. My flight instincts kicked into high gear. Our arrangement had always been casual sex. Spooning was not on the menu. I tiptoed towards the door. On my way downstairs, my eyes widened at the scene below.

Unfuckingbelievable.

I saw red wine peeking back at me from every part of the surfaces that were visible at this angle. Jackson and Shane were nothing but trouble when left alone during our parties. The result was always the same – disaster. Thank God the entire house had hardwood floors – it made it easier to clean.

When I hit the kitchen, it was horribly wrong of me to assume I'd seen the worst. There was red wine everywhere; the counters, the island, the stools, the table, the cabinets – even the door leading out to the porch had a coat of it. It was confirmation that we had thrown another kickass party, but the mess staring back at me was less than desirable. Blocked by rows of kegs, the door to get outside was out of commission. On the island, there were enough empty bottles to make any bar envious at the end of the night. Everything else in the kitchen was its normal self: dirty dishes, to-go cartons, and plenty of empty pizza boxes littering the countertops and island. I peered around the landing for something to cover my feet from the sticky mess beneath me. Shane's sandals were at the bottom of the stairs and sufficed for the short trip to the stainless steel fridge. With his flip-flops on, I hopped through the wine puddles to grab a bottle of water.

"I've got to reconsider getting a small fridge for my room," I muttered under my breath.

Scanning the living room, I got my second confirmation that last night was a real hit – ten or so people passed out on the couches and chairs. I couldn't point out any of them in a line up if you paid me. I hit the porch and glanced at the open couches covering it. We got several old couches and mixed them in with other normal porch stuff. If these couches could talk, they could pen a best-selling novel. With parties every other weekend, they were in use more than the furniture inside the house.

I took a seat on the nearest one and opened my water. I welcomed the cool air as it blew across my face. The birds chirped a quiet tune, so I shut my eyes to enjoy their song and the temperature.

In a few hours, the humidity would make it unbearable to be outdoors.

"Why the hell are you up so early this morning?" Jackson yelled.

He was strolling towards me from the long driveway that curled around part of the house. It was nice, considering all five of us had cars. Jackson rounded the corner of the house looking fresh in his ripped jeans and black V-neck shirt with his backwards baseball cap. Seeing the stubble lining his face, I fought the urge to lick my lips.

"Look who's talking? Do you ever end the night here or is it second nature to make sure you end up in whatever random girl's bed?"

Jackson was – for lack of a better phrase – smoking hot. His jet-black hair was long enough to fall into his eye line. He had thick eyebrows that framed his deep blue eyes with a perfect nose. The chiseled nature of his cheekbones matched the definition that ran from his muscular arms, which had plenty of tattoos plastered upon them. I met Jackson freshman year. After he stopped hitting on me, we became great friends, bonding over our shared major in journalism.

He settled on the couch next to me and lit the cigarette in his hand. He flashed a crooked grin before playfully punching my arm. "Someone's on the feisty side this morning? Mia, I know your MO. You're down here to drum up an excuse to get last night's guy out of your bed."

I rolled my eyes. "I don't need any excuses. The difference between my rendezvous and yours are that I at least stick to the same couple of guys. With you, there isn't a tracking system made for human kind that can calculate the amount of women you've had in bed."

Jackson took another drag and puffed smoke circles. "Touché. You have to admit that it's easier to walk out in the morning than giving someone the kick to the curb."

I snorted. I hated admitting it, but he was right. With his looks, it was no surprise.

"I can't say that I'm not intrigued to know how you manage to kick them out and then get them to come back all too willingly," Jackson mused.

I gave him a flirtatious wink. "Now that would be telling, wouldn't it?"

Sometimes I can't help myself. I like messing with him.

Jackson finished his cigarette and stretched his arms as he let out a loud yawn. He eased himself up and headed for the door.

"I'll see you around six tonight when you roll out of bed," I called over to him.

He glanced over his shoulder with a sleepy smirk. "Ah, you know me all too well. Good night, Mia" he said on his way into the house.

I leaned back, absolutely loving my living situation. We had been here since last May. It had been a great summer, but now the beginning of August was upon us. It meant most people were back to school. They went back, but I was the exception to the group. I wasn't sure if I would. This meeting displayed promise. My advisor had an upbeat attitude when he requested it. It was enough for me to feel somewhat hopeful that something positive would result from it. I needed to do something other than watch everyone else move forward while I remained stuck in the same spot.

I wrestled myself out of my daze because my boy of the week would be waking up soon. With my water in hand, I went into the house. I paused after entering the door to veer left into the living room. We circled the living room off on one side with two different couch and recliner sets. They had a perfect angle to the seventy-inch flat-screen affixed to the far left wall. Between each couch set we situated coffee tables. They came in handy since we never used the dining room. The furniture and most of the floor had sleeping strangers covering them. I announced that it was time to leave. I received some nasty glares, but they shuffled out of the door.

I took the stairs two at a time on my way to the bathroom that Bri and I shared. The bathroom was astonishing, with a huge tub situated in the right corner complimented by a spacious tile shower and a vanity holding two sinks. The window above the whirlpool brought in the light and made soaking with the jets feel like a relaxing retreat to the spa. We had fun decorating it with a Zen-like charm.

We had been inseparable since we met in junior high. The best thing with us was that we never worried about hurting each other's feelings by being honest. We fell into an easy rhythm and became best friends fast. We were as opposite in appearance as you could get. We stood at an average height of around 5'6", but that was where the similarities ended. Bri's body resembled that of a model. She had the perfectly thin figure and flawless skin that every girl wanted to have. To top it off, she had a movie star smile. Her long brown hair changed to match the latest hair fads and her makeup always brought out the sharpness in her emerald eyes. I was a shade paler than her, but not albino white. I usually curled my dirty blonde locks or pulled them into a ponytail. I had curves that men tended to appreciate. They complimented my toned legs and arms that were the result of years of playing sports. My deep brown eyes were set evenly apart. They were the only things I liked on my face besides my lips. I had full lips that had made kissing boys another extracurricular activity for me, once I had learned how to kiss.

I tied my hair into a messy bun before brushing my teeth. On my way to my room, I pulled off my pajama shorts and tank top. I crawled into bed and snuggled into my flavor of the week.

It's not as if what I'm doing is horribly wrong. I mean, I like sex. Who doesn't like to be woken up with sex? It's a great way to start the day.

He was lying on his back, so nestling into him just the right way didn't take much. I started to run my fingers up and down his chest while letting my lips explore his neck, until settling on an earlobe. I gave it a gentle bite then slid my tongue down around his jaw line to get him to turn his face towards me. He rolled to his side, bringing his muscular arm around my waist. As my body inched towards his, there was no doubt he was ready by the hardness pressing into me. A soft moan found its way out when his lips captured mine as his hands slid over my breasts. What started as a slow kiss quickly became an intense exploration of each other's mouths.

He pulled away and rolled me onto my back while giving my jaw tender kisses, as he made his way down my throat to my breasts. He picked up with the wicked suckling and biting that he had done last night. I shifted my hands from his ass to his hard length and gently stroked him.

He certainly does know how to use his hands well. Pity I can't remember his name.

While his lips tormented my breasts, his other hand slid between my legs. His fingers settled into a rhythm on my hot spot. Eager to move things along, I pushed him back onto the mattress and positioned myself on top of him. He grinned with satisfaction and grabbed a condom. He entered slowly and dropped his elbows to the bed.

He started to rock, satisfying the hunger flowing through me. He kept to a pace that was slow, but I urged him with my hips to go faster. His eyes burned into mine with more care than I preferred during casual sex. I closed my eyes as his body pressed on at a steady pace. As the beads of sweat increased between us, he rolled onto his back to put me on top. I moved much faster with each thrust. I ran my lips down his neck to keep down the moans. As our lips traveled across one another and our bodies moved together at a relentless pace; we reached our climax.

Just for a moment, the numbness faded from me. It probably

made me a horrible person to use someone else like that, but I just didn't have it in me to care anymore. After everything over the course of the last year, I had stopped opening up. I was numb all the time and preferred it that way. I sought out sex to feel something physically, enough to ease the deadness temporarily.

When we caught our breath, I kissed him lightly on the cheek. He gave me a shy smile and ran a finger delicately above my eyebrow to rid it of sweat. It was far too intimate a touch for me. "As much as I would love to do this all day, I have to get ready for a meeting I have this afternoon," I said, rolling on to my back.

His smile faded as his eyes looked for more than I could ever offer him. "I guess I better get going. Thanks for inviting me to your party. I had fun last night."

I smirked at the tone in his voice, because he made no effort to hide his amusement. "Well, you didn't seem to mind too much once we were upstairs."

He grabbed his shirt from the end of the bed and slipped it on with a wide grin. "You have a way of making everything else fade away. Can I call you this week and maybe we grab dinner?"

I sat up and tossed on my clothes. "Let me give you a call. If this meeting turns into something, my current schedule could change," I replied, forcing a smile.

He finished dressing and waited for me to exit with him. As he went down the stairs, it hit me that I should have let him call me so that I could figure out if he was Brandon or Braden.

Shit. Oh well, next time.

I turned to go to my bedroom. The slam of a door, followed by an irritated huff, made me stop. Knowing exactly who was behind me, I wheeled around to face her. Bri leaned against the door with no reservations in displaying her disappointment in me.

"Don't think that I didn't overhear that exchange."

I gave her an exaggerated roll of the eyes. "It's early. Do you want to get into this now?"

She folded her arms across her chest with her eyes narrowed at me. I rested against the wall to brace myself for the debate to come. I stifled a laugh while taking in her morning attire. She had on Trey's boxers and T-shirt, with her clothes presumably strewn across his bedroom floor.

"Stop being stupid and I'll quit being a bitch about it."

"What in particular am I being stupid about this time? I don't think you're one to talk considering you've slept with Trey again. He has yet to declare that you two are in a relationship with each other."

"I may not have a definition for whatever this is," Bri shot back, gesturing her hands in the air. "But at least I've been sleeping with the same person and not a different guy every week."

"It's not like it's hundreds of guys. I'm seeing a few guys at the same time. Why is that a crime? Guys get away with doing it all the time," I grumbled.

Bri stared at me, unmistakably annoyed. "They aren't running from their feelings. You are. It's to keep everyone out because of what happened with Micah."

"Don't go there. We're not getting into that shit. I'm enjoying having no strings. There's no shame in that. It's not like I'm not safe about it," I snapped, glaring at her until she backed off.

Her shoulders sagged on her way to her bedroom. Stopping short of her door, she turned around visibly concerned. "That isn't what I was implying. You aren't being honest with these guys or yourself. You've got to start letting people back at some point."

My face flushed and my next words flew out with more bitterness than I intended. "Just stop. I have my meeting later today. This is the last thing I want to discuss. I let you in so I'm not shutting everyone out."

I walked towards my room. Her eyes became more sympathetic as she followed me into my bedroom.

"It's not my intention to make you feel like shit. I just worry about you."

"I know. Let's put that worry to good use. Come help me find something to wear."

We looked through my clothes for a few minutes before I turned to her with a grin.

"It was your turn to keep Jackson and Shane in line so that they didn't trash the place. I hate to be the bearer of bad news, but you're going to have your hands full after class."

"How bad is it?" Bri asked.

Her head shot out of the closet as her eyes grew in alarm.

"Let's just say it gives seeing red a whole new meaning," I teased.

She grimaced before focusing back on my wardrobe. I scanned the clothes in front of me. My eyes zeroed in to my black pleated mini skirt and a red V-neck halter-top.

"You're going to help me right?"

I smiled. "You know I will. We have to stick together with these crazy boys. This one is going to take forever. I wouldn't be opposed to hiring someone to clean for us."

She groaned and grabbed the clothes that I was just considering. "Yup, this is the outfit for today. I know you're nervous. This will definitely help."

I cocked an eyebrow. I wasn't sure how showing a hell of a lot of skin would help me.

Bri rolled her eyes. "You really don't get how hot you can make yourself."

I shook my head in disagreement and went for another outfit. Not liking that one either, I let out an agitated huff. It wasn't the clothes that had me irritated. "It's going to be weird to be back on campus today," I admitted.

Bri nodded as the sympathetic look from earlier emerged in her eyes. "Do you have any clue what your advisor wants to talk to you about? I mean they expelled you with no eligibility to return. So what gives?"

I shrugged. "I'm not sure. Academically, I'm pretty much ruined, but maybe he has something I can take that will get a toe towards journalism."

Bri gave me a slight smile, but I could tell that she didn't want me to get my hopes up. I don't understand your field but you know I try."

"I know and I appreciate it. All the in-depth conversations on the topic are for Jackson," I said, stifling my amusement. Her forehead wrinkled with her wheels spinning. "What?"

"What's going on with you two? We've all noticed the amount of time you're spending with each other these days," Bri interrogated.

She flopped onto the bed. My back remained in her direction mostly so she couldn't see the aggravation on my face.

"I'm getting to know him better now that we all live together. We've been friends for ages but being roommates is different," I said while fumbling around with my shirts.

"He's a playboy. He doesn't do the girlfriend thing. I don't want to see you get hurt again," Bri cautioned.

"You know I'm not in the market for a boyfriend. I know who he is. Half our conversations are joking around about all of his women. What's the big deal if we hang out more? I hear that's what roommates do when they get along. What the hell Bri?"

I pulled away from my clothes to face her. My neck flushed as my temper started to climb. Taking a huge breath, she sat up. "I don't want to fight about this with you. I'm just making sure you know what you're doing. I know how crappy things have been after what Micah did to you."

"If you don't want to fight, then stop pushing things that aren't issues. First, it was about who I was kicking out of my bed this morning. Now, it's about how much time I'm spending with

Jackson. Do you realize how judgmental you're being?" I bit back.

Bri scooted to the edge of the bed with her eyes on her magenta-painted toes. She shifted her gaze back to me with a half-smile. "Maybe I'm being a little too hard on you. I can't watch you fall apart again. Mia, I know that you were hurting, but it tore me up to witness it," she said quietly.

"You're looking out for me. I get it. I need you to understand that there's nothing there with Jackson. Is he attractive? Of course. Do we flirt? Yes. I enjoy his company, his friendship, but I don't want to be with him."

Bri tried to maintain her smile, but the uneasiness stretched across her face. I sat down next to her and gave her shoulder a nudge to ease the tension. She grabbed the outfit that she had selected earlier. "This is the outfit hun. It's smart and sexy all in one package. Plus, you rock in it. If you want help with your hair and makeup, I'm all yours," she offered.

I grinned. "Yeah, it would be great if you could help me get all girly. It's one skill I never acquired being around so many boys growing up."

She shuffled to the doorway. "True. I'll meet you in the bathroom in twenty."

I had to give Bri credit. If you wanted a makeover, she was the person to see. Bri weaved intricate braids in my hair and tied them into a sophisticated bun. She gave me a final touch with smoky eyes and mascara. By the time she finished, I felt a lot more confident. I strolled into my room to finish off my ensemble. I rarely changed my diamond earrings. I secured my long silver necklace around my neck before grabbing my black leather studded cuff. I slid it over the scar on my right wrist that always remained covered.

CHAPTER TWO
Offers

I was a nervous wreck getting into my car. It had been close to nine months since I had set foot on campus. I almost dropped the phone the day my advisor, Derrick, called to ask if I had time to meet with him. My expulsion from school after being set up with falsified information was the second most painful thing I had ever experienced. Finding out that it was my boyfriend that did it to me slid into first place. I backed out of the driveway and drove through the side streets to get to the interstate. Flying down the freeway, I wondered what he had for me. It seemed a little odd to be taking a meeting with him on campus, but whatever. Given the circumstances, I couldn't be picky about his lack of details.

I started going through my portfolio in my head. I had done plenty of great work my first three years of college. My writing always hit with my target audiences. Before that, I had been the editor of our school paper in high school. I was grateful to have this meeting with him. Journalism was a huge part of my life. I needed to get that part of me back.

Before I knew it, the exit for campus was upon me. I steered over to the side that housed all the journalism buildings to park my car. As I walked towards the building with his office, the stares from students didn't go unnoticed. A few people stopped when I went by them. My stomach churned the entire walk. People were gawking from all angles. It was like being on exhibit at the damn zoo.

I'm still the big gossip around here. Fan-fucking-tastic.

I picked up my pace to get into the building. Thankfully, his office was on the first floor. I swiftly opened the door and greeted the elderly receptionist that handled all the appointments for the advisors.

"Hello, I'm here for an appointment at two with Mr. Smith."

She gave me a bored glance. "Name?"

"Mia Ryan."

She gasped. "Oh yes, here you are. I have to admit that it surprised me to see your name on the calendar."

Yeah, I'm sure it did.

"Derrick is running a bit behind in his schedule," she said, motioning me to take a seat.

I went over to the old wooden chairs that lined the wall by the door and sat down. My entire body was on edge. My nerves led the pack of feelings swarming through me. I thought about my decision to attend Eckman University. It was a brilliant school for those pursuing a career in journalism. It was elite in its ranking and one of the best private schools in the country. There was also the added benefit that it was a smaller college. It made it easier to develop relationships with the students and faculty.

Eckman had a mixture of old and new to it. The journalism buildings were in the older part of campus where the buildings date back to the early nineteenth century. Their dated appearance had been a quiet comfort to me. I always thought about all the excellent writers that had walked the same halls. It pushed me to do my best in my classes and on the paper. The paper published by the university was one of the oldest-running prints in academia. Being on it was a privilege. When I became editor as a junior, I strove for nothing but the best.

Before I could dwell any further, Derrick popped out and signaled for me to join him. I got up and strode to his office; it hadn't changed since the last time that I was in it. A chill ran down my spine as that particular memory flashed through my mind. I blinked and shook my head to get rid of those thoughts. With that evening out of my head, I glanced around the room. The same accolades decorated the walls along with inspiring art pieces of the last century. As I sat down in front of his antique walnut desk, the chair facing me whirled around and I was face to face with Harrison Reynolds from the magazine *Inside Out*. I gasped.

Harrison was similar to Derrick in appearance. They were in their forties but aging well. Their hair had that salt and pepper touch to it. They kept their hair trimmed short but not quite a buzz cut. Derrick had a clean-shaven face while Harrison sported a trimmed goatee. They both had a casual dress sense, wearing designer jeans with button-down shirts and an unbuttoned sport coat.

Derrick settled into the chair next to mine and let out a soft chuckle. My cheeks flamed in embarrassment. *Inside Out* was on the rise. Serious journalists dreamt of working there. The articles in the magazine pushed the limits and kept readers engrossed by the sharp content. It didn't print fluff pieces. They ran an article last year that linked the Jersey mob to a series of local murders and crimes plaguing our metro area.

Derrick shifted in his chair so he had a better view of me. "How have you been Mia?"

"Umm ... I guess OK, given the circumstances. It shocked me when you called." My eyes drifted over to Harrison, who was assessing me with a finger fixed on his chin. "And now, I'm a little confused," I admitted, with my nerves on the rise.

Derrick glanced at Harrison. "Mia, this is my good friend Harrison Reynolds. I believe you're familiar with his magazine."

I nodded as Harrison extended his hand to me. "It's nice to meet you Ms. Ryan. Derrick has told me a lot about you," he said, giving my hand a tight squeeze.

"The pleasure is all mine Mr. Reynolds."

Derrick gave me an encouraging smile. I stared at him, completely puzzled by Harrison's presence.

"I can understand why you're confused Mia. After your dismissal from the university, I tried to appeal their decision to expel you. Unfortunately, they're set on making you an example. It's my understanding you've elected to take a semester off from school."

"Yes, I'm researching the best avenues to gain admission to a new school and to reevaluate the direction to take my degree in should I get in somewhere."

My focus shifted from Derrick over to Harrison. He wasn't a guy that met with simpletons like me. He seemed far too invested in making a certain impression with me. It had my guard up.

"You can't be considering leaving the field of journalism, Mia – you're a natural. You create stories that inform and inspire readers. This incident may have happened, but it didn't take your talent!" Derrick exclaimed.

His high-pitched tone grabbed my attention away from sizing up Harrison.

I feigned indifference. "I haven't decided on anything yet. It's safe to say that my credentials are nonexistent after my expulsion. I'm not saying it's what I want. I'm taking a realistic perspective on matters."

"It's a very logical approach to take with your situation. However, you can't throw away what you've accomplished. You have the type of talent that's worth fighting for, which is what I've done for you," Derrick argued, crinkling his eyes.

I tilted my head to him, wholly baffled. He fixed his eyes onto mine before continuing. "I gave Harrison some of your work when we were out for lunch a few weeks ago. He has an excellent eye for talent. He's the reason you're here today. Harrison believes that you're a perfect fit for a story he's been working on."

Someone pinch me. Actually don't; if this is a dream, I don't want to wake up.

Harrison rolled his fingers across the desk. The hard look in his eyes had me on edge. He appeared to be a man that got what he wanted regardless of the cost.

"I've been piecing together evidence surrounding the financial institutions in our area. White collar crimes have increased within the last five years. Interestingly, they link to other crimes similar to the Jersey piece I printed last year. I've come to find some intriguing leads by sources in the field. I believe that you are the best candidate to help wrap up my investigation."

"My knowledge in that area is limited at best. Research for school work is all I've done," I replied warily.

"Ms. Ryan, the job I have in mind for you is nothing that you'll learn in a book," Harrison answered condescendingly.

I narrowed my eyes. "Why do you want me? What's setting me above the thousands of people that have degrees in the field?"

Harrison constricted his cold eyes. The inflexibility behind them freaked me out. He folded his hands together before taking a deep breath. "The company I've been researching has risen in the financial industry, with remarkable links to the crimes that have been occurring throughout the metro area. The financial institutions that raise red flags are those that are owned without any true connection to mainstream institutes."

He raised an eyebrow to verify I was still following him. I nodded for him to continue. "There is one privately owned financial company in our area that has been on the upswing for quite some time. It's curious they can remain solvent given the financial crisis and the state of the current economy without collaborating with larger institutions."

And I just got a headache.

I held my hands up for him to stop. My head was spinning. There was a reason I went into journalism and not business. Derrick sighed as Harrison took a deep breath.

"I understand but I'm missing the part of how I'm a fit. I know next to nothing about the industry," I said skeptically.

Harrison became rigid, clearly he had little patience for people that questioned him. "The company is F. F. Sweeney & Company."

The light bulb in my head went off. It became glaringly obvious why I was the best candidate. Their location was in the south side of the city, which happened to be where I grew up. They had been in business for as long as I lived in that neighborhood and probably went further back than my thirteen years there. It was common knowledge you didn't mess with them.

I'm missing something. I can't be the best candidate based on where I grew up. It doesn't add up.

"Yes, I'm familiar with them," I confirmed.

The nervousness from earlier left in a flash as tension settled throughout my body. Harrison smirked. He was really starting to rub me the wrong way.

"I'd like you to become an inside source for me. A mole. You can get a look at their operations from the inside," he requested.

"Why? Apart from having grown up there, I have no ties," I countered.

He started cracking his knuckles as his face flitted between irritated and amusement. "It's all timing. You aren't in school. It wouldn't be that farfetched for you to go back to your roots to gain some perspective. Why can't you get a job in the old neighborhood while you gain that perspective?" he said breezily.

I frowned. "Let me get this straight. You want me to secure a position with F. F. Sweeney & Company to find as much information as I can from the inside."

"That's the nuts and bolts of it. The information that you're going to obtain will be more by the relationships you build than any file you find. I'm not discouraging you to look for any data, but I doubt that information would be readily available," Harrison answered patiently.

"I realize what you're saying but I'm still not clear on how this will work. Are they even hiring? How can you guarantee that they will pick me out a pool of candidates?"

Harrison gave me another amused look forcing me to bite the inside of my lip to keep from scowling. His proposition was insane any way you sliced it.

"Mia, you underestimate me. I've confirmed that they're in need of an entry-level candidate that exhibits up-front potential. You're the ideal applicant. Your past connections to the neighborhood will more than likely seal the position for you," he assured.

Now I'm Mia all of a sudden? Why does it seem like I'm being charmed by the serpent to take a bite out of the tasty apple?

"I still don't see how I'm supposed to pull this off," I disputed.

Harrison leaned over the desk and looked me in the eye. The hardness I noticed earlier was present again. I ignored his rigidness. I wanted a better explanation.

"Mia, all bullshit aside, I believe in you because of the exemplary work I've reviewed. You are shrewd, sharp, and salacious in your approach to writing. You're the type of person I need as a source. I'm sure the thought of being an inside informant is scary but is that any reason to walk away."

If I became a source, I wasn't at liberty to receive any credentials and that left me at square one. Not to mention the whole idea was extremely dangerous. It was similar to being a snitch for the FBI, or espionage. It didn't seem ethical either.

"At the risk of sounding rude, I have to ask the obvious. What's in this for me? How will this help me stay in the journalistic field?"

I glared at Derrick. He could have given me some warning about what this meeting was going to entail. I had gone from nervous to on edge. My sweaty palms were telling me that this was *way* out of my league.

Harrison stroked his fingers along his goatee. "I reward people that prove they'll do whatever it takes to get a story very generously. I can guarantee you a job with *Inside Out*. We've expanded our operations overseas. If you can assist as a source, the position of editor and chief will be yours. You'll have full control over the European circuit."

My jaw dropped. I glanced at Derrick for feedback. He raised an eyebrow with a smile.

Did he just make me an offer I can't refuse? This is unrealistic. It's the kind of crap you read about in the happily-ever-after world of books.

I shut my eyes and pinched the bridge of my nose. I had to think about this before jumping into it. What he offered was amazing but the danger of what I'd be doing couldn't be ignored. Opening my eyes, I focused in on Harrison's stone cold expression, trying to read anything behind the man. Unable to, I settled my eyes into a firmness of their own.

"I'd like to think about it for a day or two," I requested.

"That's fair considering the rigorousness that this will entail. F. F. Sweeney & Company will be taking resumes until next Friday. I'll give you until Monday," Harrison conceded.

"If I agree to do this for you, can we have a contract put into place so I have something in writing guaranteeing me the job?" I asked hesitantly.

I was pressing my luck with the guy, but I didn't trust him. I wanted insurance.

Harrison's lips slipped into a snake like smile. "You're smarter than I expected for someone your age. I'll have my lawyers draft a legal agreement for you."

"I mean no disrespect Harrison. It's my nature to protect myself at all costs which is the only reason I want this deal to be in writing," I explained.

Harrison indicated no hard feelings in his barely-there smile. "I hope you take this opportunity Mia. I've always had an eye for raw talent and you have it. This chance will give you everything you ever dreamed of having in journalism."

Apparently, I'll be charmed until I'm out the door.

With the meeting over, I walked out more than confused with Derrick behind me. He paused at his door to let Harrison know he'd return in a minute. I stopped in the reception area. I gazed around the room to verify it was empty before lashing out.

"Is he for real because I feel like I just got hustled?"

Derrick seemed surprised by my reaction. He leaned against the receptionist's desk. "I've known Harrison my whole life. He understands what he is asking of you and that's why he is offering such a generous reward," he stated.

I sighed. "Derrick, I don't want you to think I'm not grateful for this meeting. I'm sorry if I offended you or Harrison by taking some time on this decision. I can't take this lightly."

Derrick nodded before backing towards his office. "I don't doubt you'll make the choice that is best for you. You're smart and resilient. You'll take the path that you feel is best."

My head was in a fog while walking to the parking ramp. After finding my car, I sat in the driver's seat and replayed the entire meeting. As I contemplated what happened in that meeting, my phone buzzed with new text messages. The first was from Shane.

Hey Mia, I hope your meeting goes well. I'm planning to shoot some hoops after class if you're up for a game.

I went on to the next without answering him. Jackson's message was after his.

I hope you got good news today. Give me a call or text if you want to grab a late lunch to recap. I'm on campus all day.

I skimmed past that one. It was more than obvious that people remained curious about my departure from the university. I wasn't about to let people come up to me to air out those questions. I opened the next text from Trey.

Bri said you had a meeting today. Try to make an effort to check in with her when you're done.

I grimaced before going for the last message from Bri.

I hope you consider staying down here. Please text me so that we can talk about how everything went.

I tossed my phone in my purse. They were all worried about how I'd handle being here. I was positive they all assumed I had gone bat crap crazy by now, which was understandable considering my past behavior after everything fell apart. As much as I loved them, I wasn't ready to talk about the last half-hour of my life. I needed to think and I knew where to go. I drove off campus going back to the interstate to head south.

CHAPTER THREE
Decisions

I gazed in awe over the horizon – it gave me the balance I needed. The beautiful lake off in the distance always brought me a sense of peace that I could never find anywhere else. It was one of the few places a person can view everything between downtown and the suburbs. The various neighborhoods seen from a distance all blended, not setting any one of them apart. The ugliness that plagued so many of them was invisible up here.

I admired the beauty while mulling over everything from the meeting. On the one hand, it was the opportunity of a lifetime. On the other, it was taking me back to the world I ran from before finishing high school. You didn't mess around on the south side.

Is it worth it?

I knew in my heart that being a journalist was all I ever wanted for myself. Then last year happened and it felt like my dreams were light-years away. This was an opportunity to get back into that world. As great as it all sounded, I couldn't ignore that it was a little dirty to spy from the inside for my own benefit. There was something about Harrison that didn't sit right with me. I had few reservations regarding the business end of what he was proposing, but he seemed to be the furthest thing from trustworthy. My gut had never let me down in the past. It was screaming with doubts about entertaining this offer.

My mind drifted to the idea of double-crossing F. F. Sweeney & Company. F and F stood for Fitzgerald and Fitzpatrick. Those families had been here for generations. The same went for the Sweeney's. They were hardcore, Irish families. The gut-wrenching feeling in the pit of my stomach forced me to consider the danger if anyone found out what I was doing there. As if to reinforce my thoughts, gunshots sounded off. It wasn't anything that I hadn't heard before, but it was rather eerie considering my current train of thought. It was a decent reminder of the level of danger that went into this offer.

My thoughts moved on to my uncanny ability to present myself well. Typically, I assimilated into pretty much any situation with ease without revealing my true colors. My guard was usually up. It made it easier for me to investigate when I did work on articles for the paper. I approached most things from a distance and didn't form any personal attachments. However, my morals would be in question by pursuing this offer. As I sat in my stupor, I heard footsteps crunching against gravel on the trail. I glanced over my shoulder to confirm the person behind those steps.

Trey is the last person I want to deal with right now. He knows me too well.

He was my oldest friend in the house. When Bri started crushing on him, I was open to it and not surprised in the least. I saw why she liked him; like Jackson, Trey was eye-catching. He kept his blondish brown hair trimmed to his mood or the time of year. I'd known him since we were four so I'd seen it from a buzz cut to long and shaggy. He typically kept a dusting of scruff on his face to personify the rugged, tough guy look that his personality backed up. The part that sucked you in the most was his mystical gray eyes. He was in pristine shape and always wore clothes that displayed the precise lines throughout his body.

He reached me but kept a short distance between us. I noted the concern is his eyes.

"What do you want Trey?" I asked crossly.

"I know your meeting with your advisor was today. When you didn't come home, I figured something was up. When you need to take a break from everything, you come here. You always have – even when we were kids. You may not like it, but I still know you Mia," Trey replied, shoving his hands into his faded jeans.

It perturbed me that every word he said was right. My strange quirks didn't go unnoticed by him. I met Trey and Micah on my first day in this godforsaken neighborhood. I was very eager to make friends. My uncle made it clear that life with him was going to be anything but pleasant. Those two were in every wonderful childhood memory I had. Trey always reminded me of Micah. It brought me more pain than I cared to admit. We were so close growing up and remained that way until last year. I spent more time at their houses than anywhere else. Their mothers treated me like one of their own. It was hard to be around Trey because it pushed all the memories of Micah to the surface.

We had been together since we were sixteen. Before we ever started dating, we were best friends. Puberty hit and feelings started to develop for Micah that was anything but friendly. After weeks of subtle touches, glossy gazes, and intense flirting, we discovered that there was something more than friendship and that it was worth exploring. Micah made me feel safe and cherished. He was protective of me growing up. He made so many of the hardships of having no parents manageable by making me feel like a priority to him and his family. Falling in love with him was inevitable.

"Yes, I'm thinking. It doesn't mean I'm going to share any of that with you. Why are you here?" I snarled, as memories of the three of us ran through my head.

His expression shifted from concerned to angry. He pulled his hands out of his pockets and clenched them into tight fists. His muscles rippled against his fitted charcoal shirt. If anyone else had been on the receiving end of his stature, they would have flinched, but I knew him so well it didn't even faze me.

"Mia, I know you see him every time you look at me. I can't change that, but I'm not him. I didn't leave and I'm not the one who hurt you!" Trey snapped.

My eyes returned to the silhouette of the city. The agonizing pain that I blocked from coming to the surface was starting to spread throughout me. I had gotten to the point of coasting along in life. I was indifferent about everything and everyone. However, there were exceptions that triggered all the emotions I suppressed on a daily basis – Trey was one of them. I existed fine by controlling each situation that I was in by never allowing anyone to get too close to me. Bri was the only person who paid enough attention to know how shattered I was on the inside.

"It's a beautiful place in a shady neighborhood. You've got to admit that right?"

Trey relaxed his fists before letting out a light laugh. I watched as he shook his head, probably having a few nostalgic memories of his own.

"You're dancing around my question. Why did you come up here?"

"My meeting went well. I'm considering the possibilities of what my options are going forward," I mumbled.

His jaw tensed as he gave me a cold stare. He wanted me to elaborate more on the matter. I pierced my eyes at him, stubbornly holding my ground. He ran his hands through his buzz cut before giving me a look not to argue with.

"Come on. My mom has been driving me nuts checking up on you. Let's stop at my house so she can see with her own eyes that you're alive and well."

Mrs. Donovan was the best. I loved her as if she was my own mother. She was a worrywart and was always fussing after us whenever she had the chance. I missed her so much. After everything that happened in this last year, I avoided most people and places that reminded me of Micah. I missed his family. I knew having dinner with them would be painful, but it would be worth it.

"Is she making her famous stew?"

"Once she sees you, she'll make you anything you want. She called on my way out here. I said that I'd drag you over to the house. I'm glad you're willing to go and I don't have to take you there kicking and screaming," Trey muttered.

I winced. "Trey, I really am sorry about how I've been acting towards you. I'm sorry it's affected your family too. You know how much they mean to me. It's still hard to be around anything or anyone that reminds me of him."

I couldn't stop the tear that formed in the corner of my eye. His face softened as he leaned over and pulled me in for a hug. He held me tight, doing his best to comfort me as he had done so many times this last year even when I didn't deserve it. He did everything he could to help bring me out of the darkness, which included staying away from me the majority of the time. I missed him as much as his family, but the pain ran so deep that the desire to push him away so I could breathe won every time. I could let that pain rise for one evening. I needed it and from the sounds of it so did they.

"It's OK Mia. I understand and so does my family. They want you to remember they are here for you and love you very much," Trey reassured.

"I know. It doesn't mean that I shouldn't be sorry, because I am," I whispered.

After a wonderful dinner, we headed home. When we pulled up,

Bri was sitting on the front steps. She was fidgeting with her brown hair while nervously biting on the fingernails of her other hand.

Geez. I wonder how long she has been sitting there. I know better than to do this to her. I sure do suck at life sometimes.

I noticed her outfit was different from this morning. She had ditched the worn skinny jeans and boho-pleated tank for a pinstriped fitted dress that flared above the knees. I felt awful. I had a feeling that I had more than likely ruined plans for her and Trey when I failed to return everyone's attempts to reach me this afternoon.

As I got out of my car, I gave her an encouraging wave. Trey was already up the steps. He towed her in for a quick kiss and leaned over to whisper into her ear. Whatever he said made her relax as she took a noticeable breath of relief. She stood on her tiptoes anxiously talking to him. He nodded, earning him a tender kiss from her. Bri focused on me. The distraught look in her eyes froze me to my current spot on the lawn.

"I'm sorry. It worried me when you didn't call or text back," Bri cried.

"Hey, I'm OK. I needed to clear my head. Trey found me and then we had dinner at his house," I replied gently.

Bri stared me down clearly debating if she believed me. She shifted her weight continuously and fiddled with her rings. Trey saw it too and grabbed her hands. He kept them still by entwining them with his hands.

"Was it horrible? Why didn't you get back to me?" Bri interrogated.

It tore me up that disappearing for several hours created this level of panic in her, but I knew why. What I put her through last winter had changed her perspective of me and I couldn't blame her for freaking out like this. My eyes skirted towards the trees that decorated our lawn. The sun was hitting that fine line between night and day. It was falling into a 'tween for the day – an in between of one place or another, not really being neither here nor there. I related to it.

I kept my face composed so she would calm down. "Bri, I'm sorry I didn't get back to you. The meeting left me overwhelmed. I sort of zoned out the rest of the world."

She tilted her head. I gave her a genuine smile hoping it would help her see that I was fine. Bri wiggled free from Trey making her way down the steps. She pulled me in for a tight hug. "I'm sorry. He went to look for you because I kept flipping out on him. I knew he would be able to find you," Bri whispered.

I sighed. "It's fine. I'm OK and it was great to spend a little time with his family," I admitted. I stepped away from her and headed towards the porch. As we walked, I gestured towards the house. "So how did it go today? I'm sorry I wasn't here to help you."

Bri stopped as her eyes darted from mine to the ground. "Well, I ... umm ... I took your advice," she said sheepishly.

I raised an eyebrow. "My advice?"

She shrugged. "I hired a cleaning service. After seeing the mess, I couldn't stomach it."

I laughed at the guilty look on her face and glanced up to see Trey hunched over the railing of the porch in his own fit of hysterics. "I hope they got the whole house. You might as well get your money's worth."

Bri flashed a sly smile. It made us laugh even harder. "They did and I'd never use my own money. I used the profits from our parties. I figured it was fine to make an executive decision since it was a step away from a chemical hazard zone."

"You know I don't care and obviously Trey doesn't either. Good luck with the other two. I'm not sure they will see it that way. I think Jackson had high hopes for that money."

She gave a dismissive wave of the hand. "Ah, who cares about Jackson? If Shane crosses me, I'll give him a titty twister. That shuts him up every time."

"True. Why don't we see what those two are up to? I'm foreseeing a house night in the man cave. What do you think Trey?" I asked.

"Shit yeah!" Trey shouted, pushing off the railing.

"Yeah, I could do with a night in The Cave," Bri agreed.

On our way into the house, we heard Jackson and Shane shouting at each other over a video game that they were playing. Trey and Bri continued down towards The Cave while I swerved into the living room to get rid of my heels and purse. I contemplated heading upstairs to change but decided against it, and headed down to join the others.

The sizable den branching off our kitchen was affectionately coined 'The Cave'. Once you walked in the door, you could turn left or right and find yourself in every man's dream play area. An eighty-inch flat-screen covered the wall off to the left. They circled off that side with leather couches and chairs. The entire room had built in shelves that lined the bottom portion of the walls throughout the room. We filled them with hundreds upon hundreds of DVDS and video games. Mounted below the flat-screen was a separate shelf with every video game console on the market along with a top of the line sound system. The wall off to the right had a wet bar that had more liquor than we ever needed in this house. We sectioned off that area with a pool table, foosball table, and a poker table. The sidewalls each contained different dartboards. The boys finished off The Cave man touch by hanging the appropriate neon beer signs, posters of naked girls, and tributes to sports dynasties.

When I got to The Cave, Bri and Trey were already shamelessly making out on one of the couches. Jackson and Shane stood in the middle of the room hollering at each other over who was cheating more. I paused to watch them playfully push each other back and forth. They were trying to knock the other off balance to get that extra edge to win the game. I was jealous of them because they were in athletic shorts and gray T-shirts from Eckman. I hated that the real world required one to dress up versus the halls of the university that allowed you to show up in your pajamas. I lingered in the doorway to watch my favorite guys interact.

Jackson had his cap cocked to the side of his head as he did a ridiculous dance after ousting Shane in the game. He didn't hold back his taunting in the least. I caught Shane rolling his eyes and bit my cheek not to laugh because he was kicking Jackson's ass. Shane was a brawny guy with a handsomely round face and soft brown eyes. His cheeks got me every time because I had to fight the urge to pinch them. He was very similar to Trey in many ways. Those two became best friends around the same time as Bri and me. His body had more definition after years of endless conditioning for sports. Trey kept up with him in that department, but Shane worked himself to the bone to maintain his physique. He kept his brown hair in a trimmed cut with an occasional goatee. I noticed his chin was garnering some fuzz so it appeared that he might be bringing it back soon.

I withheld staring at him any longer to glance over at Bri and Trey. They remained engrossed in each other's mouths. Those two flirted since the first day they met so why they drug out giving into each other until their last year of college was mind-boggling. Trey could refrain from putting a label on their relationship indefinitely, but the truth was that Bri was his girl. She had been for a long time. Trey was too just damn stubborn to say it. I knew it and so did Shane. He glimpsed over at them. Shane shook his head with a roll of the eyes. He probably felt the same way as I did. Shane went as far back with Bri as I did with Trey. Their families were in the same elite social circle. It shocked Trey and me that we fell in so easily with Shane and Bri. We had no experience with the class and wealth that went with their world.

Jackson started spouting off at the mouth again. I decided to help Shane out. Jackson couldn't see me but Shane saw me glide out of the doorway. He continued to crush his controller while extending a leg towards Jackson. He deftly maneuvered away from Shane's attempt to knock him off balance. Shane started to beat his controller even harder. I gave him a wink and pointed towards Jackson with my eyes covered. His scowl turned into a smug grin. I got up on my tiptoes behind Jackson and placed my hands over his eyes.

"What the fuck?" Jackson growled.

While he fought me off, Shane won the game. Jackson huffed and pushed me into the recliner behind him. Shane slouched into the couch laughing hysterically at the pout on Jackson's face.

"Thanks Mia," he bellowed in between howls of laughter.

"Anytime Shane," I giggled.

Jackson frowned even deeper and smacked Shane across the shoulder. "That's cheating motherfucker. I want a rematch," he grumbled.

Shane sat up threatening to pounce on Jackson if he took another swing. Jackson pulled his arm back but kept it there when Shane raised an eye in warning. I refrained from laughing again because Shane could annihilate Jackson with one hand tied behind his back. It surprised me that he put up with that crap when those two played video games together. They had become a package deal after Trey started spending more of his free time with Bri.

When I introduced Jackson to my social circle from high school, I was unsure if he would fit in with us. Jackson rounded out our group perfectly with his carefree attitude. His family was wealthy like Shane and Bri's. He had lots of stories to swap with those two about countless stuffy cocktail parties and organized events. Shane and Jackson learned fast that they liked creating trouble together. If they weren't scheming or party planning, they were in here duking out games on the consoles. Trey and Jackson bonded over music with shared interests in bands. All three boys enjoyed debating sports. Jackson and Bri spent the least amount of time with each other because of the constant jeering they did with one another. They had smart mouths that they loved to use against each other. It was in good humor though. I listened to the exaggerated huffs from behind me and turned my head towards Jackson.

"Come on Jackson, it's not the end of the world," I teased,

poking him in the side.

Before I could react, Jackson pinned me into the chair and tickled me into a fit of giggles.

"Oh, hell no! We came back here to hang out for the night as a house. Don't ruin it by pissing me off!" I yelled, squirming away from him.

Jackson stopped tickling me to see if I was telling the truth. I smiled with a nod of the head. He hauled me with him towards the bar with Shane right behind us. Jackson lined up five shot glasses and pulled the bottle of Patron from behind him. He filled them each to the brim with a slick grin.

I'm human. I do stare at him sometimes. It's hard not to fall prey to his hotness.

"Well shit, if we're going to have a house night, we better kick it off right!" Jackson shouted.

Bri and Trey pulled their tongues out of each other to join us at the bar. We picked up our shots and enthusiastically tossed them back. It burned going down, but it felt good. It took the edge off what had become a long day. We spent the rest of Thursday night in The Cave as a house. The five of us devoted the evening to drinking while challenging each other to games in pool, foosball, and tournaments on the various gaming consoles. It was the perfect distraction for me. I didn't have much time to sit on this decision. At the moment, I didn't care.

CHAPTER FOUR
Give Me A Reason

Friday morning arrived too fast. I was in bed contemplating Harrison's offer, and by the time I had gotten up to go downstairs, the rest of the house had already gone their separate ways for class. I set my laptop on the island before heading over to the half-made pot of coffee to pour myself a cup. I crossed over to the microwave to warm it up. Once heated, I situated myself on a stool at the island to sip my coffee. It was strange being in the kitchen without the mess of take-out boxes surrounding me. My eyes drifted out of the bay window above the sink. Soon, the colors of fall would grace the trees but for now the lasting moments of summer lingered bringing a smile to my face.

I brought my laptop to life. I wondered what Harrison had discovered that was intriguing enough to ask someone to plant themselves inside the company for more information. Once it had powered up, I went to my old friend Google. I typed in F. F. Sweeney & Company and hit enter. The search results that came back, numbered in the

thousands. I settled in for a morning of research.

After several cups of coffee and hours of reading, I had a better idea of their operations. It was still unclear to me what their connections were to anything that Harrison was insinuating. Bigger guns were necessary to acquire that kind of information.

Maybe Jayden can help. No, that would involve telling Jackson.

I checked my phone – I had spent a significant amount of time researching, only to find out the basics. I groaned before setting it on the counter and headed upstairs for an overdue shower. After drying off, I tossed on a pair of short jean shorts with a sky blue cami and tied my hair into a ponytail. I went downstairs hoping that someone might be home. This opportunity had appeal merely for something to do while everyone was at class.

As I hit the landing of the stairs, I heard footsteps on the front porch. I stepped out to find Jackson grabbing his cigarettes out of the mail slot. He gave me a stiff nod and sunk onto the couch. I sat next to him wondering what had him off. Jackson kept his focus forward while playing with the fringes of his jean shorts. He was sporting one of his many rock T-shirts. The tattoos on his arms and right leg jumped out for me to devour.

"So how was class? I'm surprised you even made it to a Friday class. It's got to be a first!"

Jackson scowled before blowing out perfect circles of smoke. "I go to class when I need to Mia. There is nothing in the syllabus that states we have to show up for every boring lecture."

I rolled my eyes. "You either had mandatory attendance or you had a test."

Jackson huffed. "We had a quiz."

"Ha! I knew it. How did you do? What class was it?" I asked curiously.

Jackson paled as his eyes darted out to the lawn and the cars in the driveway as if they were going to answer for him. He took another drag as he ran his fingers through his hair. Instant irritation spread throughout me.

I squared my shoulders to him. "It's fine Jackson. You can tell me about class. I'd like to hear about it."

"It was old man Kennedy. You know how he's a stickler for the Friday morning quiz. Why do you think I moved partying to Wednesday nights? It was purely selfish," he snickered.

"So how did you do on it?"

Jackson shrugged. "Meh. I'm sure I would've done better if I had my old study partner."

I sighed. "It's not like I lost the knowledge when I stopped going to school. You can always ask for my help when you study."

Jackson squinted before a subtle smile crossed his face. "Thanks Mia. I'd like to get more than a C in his class. Studying with you all these years has probably given me a better GPA than what I deserve," he said sincerely.

I beamed. "What are we doing this weekend? We should break from partying around here. We should do something epic. Any ideas?"

Jackson perked up. "I have the perfect idea!"

"Do tell."

He put out the cigarette and turned towards me with excitement in his eyes. "We should go party on my parent's boat for the weekend. There are plenty of rooms. It could be another house only occasion like last night."

"You had fun with just us didn't you?" I questioned dryly.

His smile was genuine as he answered, "It's nice to hang with your closest friends. Plus, you and Bri are gorgeous so I still fulfilled my quota of spending quality time with hot chicks."

Heaven forbid the man whore goes an evening without hot chicks as company.

"Glad we could be of service. As far as your weekend proposal, I'm definitely in."

"Let's see what the other three think when they get home. If they're up for it, we'll head out tonight. Of course, after we stop and stock up for weekend's worth of trouble."

"That's a given."

Jackson toyed with his lip ring, which was his tell. He wanted to ask me something, but was nervous about doing it. I raised both brows.

"How did your meeting go yesterday? Shane and I heard Bri shouting at Trey to track you down when she couldn't reach you."

I pulled a strand of hair from my ponytail and picked at the split ends before looking at him. "It went fine. It was overwhelming to be back there. Everyone looked at me like a caged zoo animal while I walked through campus."

Jackson huffed at that revelation. I let out a light chuckle observing the concern in his eyes. "My meeting with Derrick left me with a lot to consider. I needed a minute alone and I lost track of time."

The empathy vanished as his face-hardened. "If you want to talk about it some more, I'm always here to listen."

I knew that he was just as worried as Trey. It was heartwarming, but I had to figure this out on my own. I planned to tell Bri, but that's it. I knew those boys cared about me. With this type of offer, I couldn't share details about it with too many people. Above of all, they would scream at me for even considering it. I stood to venture into the house.

"Thanks Jackson. I'm going to call Bri. She can fill in Trey so you should call Shane. I'd rather get a jump-start on the weekend than wait for them to come home. If they confirm, we can go pick up supplies."

Jackson cocked his head to the side with a roundabout grin. "I love the way you think. The sooner we get started on this weekend, the better."

He followed me into the house. I headed for the kitchen to get my phone to call Bri while he walked past me to call Shane. I grabbed my cell from the counter, sat down at the island, and hit speed dial for her number. Bri answered on the third ring. I filled her in on the weekend proposal – she squealed in delight at the idea, and said she would meet Trey and fill him in on the plan. Jackson entered with a wide smile, confirming Shane was in as well.

"Let's hit the grocery and liquor store. Bri and Trey will be home within the hour. When's Shane getting home?" I asked.

Jackson walked to the fridge with a hungry look in his eyes. He tossed the door open and emerged seconds later with a slice of leftover pizza. He glimpsed at me with a mouthful and mumbled, "Within the hour as well."

He gazed around with what I consider his cutely confused look. His eyebrows scrunched in bringing a V to his forehead. It never failed to pop up when he was incapable of piecing something together. I had seen it many times when studying with him. "Man, this house is fucking spotless. How did it get this clean?"

My eyes dropped to the island. My fingers started tracing a pattern in the brickwork. I peeked at him through my long lashes. "Umm ... funny you ask ... Bri sort of hired some help to clean up the place. We may clean, but we don't have the capabilities of the professionals – especially Bri. You know she hates cleaning."

His face remained cutely confused. "How much do we owe her? She shouldn't have spent money on it, but I can see why she did."

"We don't owe her anything. She used some of the profits from our last few parties to cover the bill," I confessed.

His face flipped to disapproving in a second. "I thought we were going to treat that as house money. The plan was to make decisions together on how to use it."

I arched an eyebrow not caring for the disgruntled tone he projected at me. His eyes flickered from mine as he finished off the rest of the pizza. "We were. We were also going to work together to keep this place clean. That hasn't really been the case so she made an executive decision. Seeing as her and I are stuck with most of the cleaning, I back her choice one hundred percent," I replied, crossing my arms.

"Fair point, I suppose we should get a move on so we're ready to go when they come home," he said, motioning to the door.

After making the journey north to the marina, we were out on the lake. The weather report declared clear skies throughout the weekend. We were offshore getting as much sun as we could before we docked back at the marina for the evening. It was fortunate that Shane and Jackson knew how to operate the boat because I was useless. I turned my gaze towards where the boys were talking. All three had slipped into trunks and tight white tanks. Their beers were nestled in can koozies. I glanced at Bri, who was practically drooling while she carefully studied all the features of Trey from behind. I snatched her hand to drag her inside so we could put away the reserves for the weekend. She grumbled but followed me.

It's not like it's a new sight for you. You see him every day. Naked no less.

There was enough food, liquor, and beer to keep us on this boat for two weeks rather than a couple of days. Once we got everything squared away, we took turns in the bathroom to get into our bikinis. After changing, we headed to the back of the boat to soak up some sun. The boys were at the front with poles in the water drinking beers as they discussed football. We laid our towels down before lying on our backs. I pulled my shades off to let the rays hit my face. After a half hour or so of silence, I braced myself on my elbows to confirm the boys were out of earshot. I leaned to my side and put my head in my hand. Bri had closed her eyes so I cleared my throat to get her attention. She propped up on her elbows.

"I've been waiting until we were alone to fill you in on my meeting yesterday."

Her eyes encouraged me to continue.

"You have to promise not to tell the boys and don't wig out."

She squinted, clearly hesitant of the request. "I won't say anything to anyone. I can't promise you I won't freak out."

"My meeting wasn't just with Derrick. It was with Harrison Reynolds too."

Bri furrowed her brow in confusion.

"Harrison Reynolds is the founder and owner of *Inside Out*," I continued patiently.

She rolled her shoulders not following me.

"In layman's terms, it's a magazine in the city that rose to the nationwide circuit not long ago. *Inside Out* is amazing. It reports on issues that matter. It's the big time with them."

Bri sat straight up, so I followed. I brought my knees up to my chest and rested my cheek on them. She leaned back on her hands with her legs stretched past me.

"So he was there. The magazine is awesome. What happened to make you disappear?" Bri asked. She scowled, still obviously bothered about my vanishing act.

I nervously chewed on my lip. "Derrick gave him some of my work. Harrison wanted the meeting. He asked me to be a source for a huge piece that he has been working on. He thought I was the best fit for it."

She constricted her eyes. I shifted my gaze away from her out to the boys to confirm they remained oblivious. "Harrison wants me to secure a job at a company that he believes is linked to major crimes in the city. He's asked me to gather as much inside information as possible."

Bri slanted her head as her eyes told me to get on with it already.

"It's F. F. Sweeney & Company," I said and waited for her to go berserk.

Bri shrieked, "Mia, are you fucking crazy?"

Her voice raised an octave higher than I was comfortable with. I checked up front to make sure the boys were still fishing while motioning for her to take it down a notch. Thankfully, they weren't any the wiser. Bri lowered her tone but continued to freak out. Her face wavered as her nerves accelerated. She wrung her hands together and narrowed her eyes at me.

"I can't believe you're even thinking about doing this. I may not have grown up there but I know how dangerous it is if you cross the wrong people," she hissed.

"Bri, I'm not crazy. After hearing him out, I know he asked me because I grew up there. I also believe that it is how my work comes across. I'm cutthroat with my writing and that makes me a good candidate when you're trying to complete an exposé of a corrupt company. I acquire and present the truth with no reservations about whose feelings may be hurt from it. Rather than finding a source, he's creating one. It's a ballsy move, but it could pay off ... and not just for him."

Her face remained in absolute disapproval. "What's in it for you?"

"If I can get what he needs, he's offered me a guaranteed position with the magazine. It's an amazing opportunity," I answered excitedly.

Bri frowned. "It sounds a lot like bribery for you to do something stupid Mia. Why are you even considering it?"

I shrugged. "It's giving me the chance I need to get my life back on track. I'd be running a magazine in my twenties. It's unheard of. Besides, what's life without a little risk?"

Bri glimpsed over her shoulder to verify the boys were still out of earshot. "Mia, you probably don't want to look at it this way but I have to say it. What you're considering is just as bad as what happened to you last year. You're signing up to do damage to people – powerful people. If they figure out that you betrayed them, they won't hesitate to make you pay for it," she pointed out.

My eyes soaked in the horizon from our spot on the lake. The skyscrapers from downtown had become miniature Lego blocks. I looked to the sky taking in the clearness. It was a breathtaking shade of blue that breathed a wave of calmness in me.

"I have thought about what you're saying. I would be crossing some serious lines that would make me question myself. But you know what Bri...who's to judge me for being a horrible person on taking an offer like this one?"

She raised an eyebrow. I took a deep breath to continue. "I'm not above saying it's selfish of me to do something because I get a personal gain from it. I'd be just as selfish to walk away. I'm aware that there is a company out there that may be responsible for crimes affecting an entire city. They will continue to get away with hurting innocent people if someone doesn't stop them. Which side of the coin is worse? Which decision makes me less humane?"

Her expression turned soft. "I'm not saying I'd look down on you for doing it. I want you to understand that it's morally questionable."

"I've been thinking about that nonstop. If I take this offer, I'm going to have to deal with all that comes with it. That will include how I look at myself."

"Is this about Micah?"

My cheeks reddened as anger erupted through me. "It's not about him. Since you brought him up, it brings me to my other point. I'll admit that there is one thing I keep coming back to. Bad things happen to good people all the time for no reason at all and that's bullshit. Maybe to right a horrible wrong, you have to wrong a few people to make it right for that many more."

"You're beginning to sound like Dr. Seuss," Bri muttered, massaging her temples.

"All I'm saying is that this particular situation isn't black and white. It's lying in that gray area that falls between right and wrong making it easy to reason either side of it."

"I'm throwing in the towel because you're starting to hurt my head. Debating with you when you're in this mood never gets me far. There isn't any reasoning with you," she grumbled.

I grinned. "Harrison gave me until Monday for an answer."

Bri examined me carefully. "How do you plan to get a job there? Does he have magical powers that will just place you there?"

"They're hiring right now. Harrison is confident that my resume and connection to the neighborhood will get me the job. Either that or he isn't telling me something. Who knows? He thinks I'll get it."

Her face tightened. "It sounds like he could be pulling some strings. Are you really going to do it?"

"I'm not sure. I wanted you to know that I was considering it. You can't tell anyone," I reiterated. I narrowed my eyes, letting her know to keep her lips sealed.

"I won't. I promised you I wouldn't," she agreed.

Bri crawled forward and cupped her hands forcefully on my cheeks. It made me focus into her green eyes deep with concern. "Mia, if you do this, promise me that you'll walk away if it gets too dangerous. You must keep me informed. I'll go crazy if you don't. It's nerve racking enough when you disappear for a few hours."

Sharp pain spread through me. I knew how much that was true when it came to her worrying about me. "If I do take it, I promise I'll keep you in the loop. We don't need you going bat crap crazy," I answered. The whole sentence was a jumbled mess because she was squeezing my cheeks so hard.

Bri giggled. "No, I don't want to steal your crazy bitch title. I love you Mia."

I pulled her in for a hug. "I love you too Bri. You and the guys are the only family I have."

We separated and I saw that she had plastered on a supportive smile, but her eyes were full of anxiety. I rose to my feet and extended my hand to pull her up.

"Alright, enough with the heavy shit, let's go get drunk with the guys," I suggested.

She got up and linked arms with me. While strolling over to our boys, we snickered the whole time. It was always fun finding new things that we could pull with them to keep them wrapped around our fingers.

CHAPTER FIVE
Blast From the Past

Sunday night arrived and I still hadn't made a final decision. I was tossing and turning in bed. I rolled over on my stomach and punched my pillow into submission as if it was its fault I couldn't sleep. I retrieved my phone to listen to a playlist. It helped me sleep if I popped in my headphones to quiet the voices in my head. As the lyrics filled my ears, I started to fall asleep.

The final draft of the paper is ready for the printers. I sent off the file when my cell rings. I let it go to voicemail. My phone beeps so I pick it up to listen to the message. Derrick does nothing to hide the urgency in his voice as he requests me to go downstairs to his office right now. It's strange that he's even here at this hour. I'm the only one that burns the midnight oil around here, as is the case tonight with the clock nearing ten.

I turn off my computer and hit the lights. As I walk downstairs, the paranoia in my body starts to grow. After turning down the last stairwell, I can see Derrick's office with the lights on. Several voices are arguing with each other as I near the door. I can't quite make out what they're disagreeing about, but the feeling in the pit of my stomach leads me to believe I'm about to know in a minute.

"Derrick?"

"I know it can't be your work but you better be prepared to defend yourself. The evidence they've compiled is substantial and they're out for blood," Derrick hisses.

We enter his office. I'm face to face with the Dean of Students and several members on the board of directors for the university. The color drains from my face. The panic inside of me increases so much that I'm almost shaking. My palms are slick with sweat as an icy chill runs through the rest of my body. I steady my breathing to keep from hyperventilating. It's like watching a horror movie, only I'm starring in it rather than watching it.

The Dean is sitting in Derrick's chair with two board members lining the back wall. Dean Martin motions to the seat in front of him.

"Ms. Ryan, it took you long enough," he snaps.

Taken aback by his harsh tone, I stumble into the chair. "I'm sorry. I was finishing the paper for tomorrow and missed the first phone call from Mr. Smith. May I inquire what this meeting is regarding?"

His eyes pierce into mine. I cower under the wrath behind them. "Acting like you have no idea why you're here only makes this matter that much worse for you. I suggest you take this seriously."

The feeling eating away at my stomach starts to rise. "I'm sorry sir. I don't understand why I'm here," I reply.

His eyes go from fury to outrage. "Let us enlighten you. It seems that you're planning to print malicious and false content about the university and several members of the board."

I clutch my hands around my stomach hoping they'll help contain the contents that are persistently pushing their way to the surface. Seeing my reaction, Derrick stirs in his chair.

"Dean, we should discuss this further to determine the IP address those files can be traced back to. It's a public drive for the university that can easily be manipulated."

He waves a hand in Derrick's direction, effectively silencing him.

The vein in his forehead looks like it's about to burst. "Derrick, we've done the necessary research and you've pleaded your student's case. We've taken what you said into consideration. Going forward, you will not say another word – this is now up to Ms. Ryan to clarify."

I'm flabbergasted, so I finally speak up. "Sir, there's a misunderstanding. I would never print anything malicious about the university or its faculty."

Dean Martin slams his fists down on the desk so forcefully that Derrick and I jump.

"Ms. Ryan, we have hard evidence. When were you planning to print this article?"

I stare in confusion. He lets out an agitated puff of air as he turns Derrick's monitor around. My jaw drops in disbelief. I'm staring at a file that links to the folder I use for the paper. It's nothing I wrote but the final print layout shows me as the author. My stomach swan-dives into the basement as my head begins to spin so fast I think it might roll off. I take a steadying breath to keep my cool. The article is so damaging. It states the university is receiving money from illegal sources and that various people on the board, including the Dean, are seeing back-end payouts from these sources. The pressure inside my chest, coupled with the tears demanding to be set free, is close to taking over.

"Dean Martin, I know this doesn't look good but I didn't write that article. I don't know how it got into my folder. I can assure you that it isn't by me," I whisper.

"Are you accusing us of lying Ms. Ryan? Are you attempting to state that we fabricated this evidence?" he asks coldly.

I sink further into my chair. His eyes are full of so much rage that I'm not sure he even hears me when I speak. As far as he's concerned, he has all the tangible proof in the world to nail me to the wall.

"No ... No Sir, I ..."

My voice fades off in despair. My pleas won't matter.

"We've heard enough from you tonight. You can provide no

explanation as to why this is in your folder on a university drive. I'm sure you want us to believe that someone stole your username and manufactured this in your folder. We don't have time for those types of excuses."

Panicking, I begin to ramble before he can further incriminate me for something else. "Sir, you have to believe me when I say I didn't write that piece, let alone set it up to print. I'm the editor of the paper. It's my job to make sure what we present to the university is based on factual research and resources. Someone is setting me up. The computers are accessible to anyone. It's possible that someone watched me login and wrote down my username and password. Tomorrow's layout for the paper is the only document that should be in there."

Even I can hear the desperation in my voice. I want to scream that what he believes isn't true.

His finger roughly hits the monitor as he snipes, "Is this your folder?"

"Yes, it is but ..." I fade off in defeat.

My whole body starts to slip into what I assume is the shock that people experience after being in a horrific car accident. He whips the monitor around and keeps his fists clenched.

"There is no 'but' ... you have confirmed it's your folder. You have the access and authority to print an article as damaging as this without anyone being the wiser. This is a direct violation of the university code of conduct," he declares before looking at the rest of the board members.

He brings his enraged eyes back to me. "We're processing the disciplinary action for these infractions right now. The overwhelming amount of evidence going against the integrity and conduct of the university cannot be ignored. We will not undermine the code by giving you a slap on the wrist. Effective immediately, you are hereby expelled from Eckman University. Your academic transcript will reflect this matter with no eligibility to return."

Derrick lets out a disgusted breath. He clears his throat to argue, but the Dean cuts him off with an icy glare. I go numb. The tears start to drip down my face. My body and head shake nonstop. I think I hear that I'm no longer a student, but my brain is full of fuzz.

I'm still sitting there when Dean Martin dismisses me, "You're excused Ms. Ryan. Please leave the university premises."

Somehow, I shuffle towards the door. As I make my way out, immense pain runs through my entire body. My arms and legs feel like a million pounds. My head is so heavy and hazy. The tightness in my chest feels like it is suffocating me from the inside out. I almost clutch both arms around myself to keep from caving into the overwhelming pain, but hold back. I won't give these people the satisfaction of having a complete meltdown in front of them. I force my legs to move to get me to my car. As soon as I'm there, I can call the one person that can help me – Micah. I focus my thoughts on Micah to keep moving forward.

Thinking about him makes me long to hear his voice. As I approach my car, I dig out my cell to call him. The instant I hear him I'll fall to pieces, but he'll be there to pick them up. That's all I need right now. I hit his number. It rings a few times before going to his voicemail. Knowing I'm on the verge of a mental breakdown, I climb in my car and speed to our apartment. Maybe he's sleeping and that's why he's not answering. He never ignores my phone calls. I need his soothing voice.

As I pull up, our apartment is pitch black. I exit my car and go into the building. I unlock the front entrance and head to the elevators. Fortunately, it's empty when I get in and hit twelve. Once the doors shut, I release the aching sobs. The elevator makes its way to our floor. I step out in a fog and turn right towards our apartment. I open the door and my world crashes again.

Our apartment is a mess. There's stuff thrown everywhere. I don't understand. I can't even think. After taking a more careful assessment of my surroundings, I begin to see everything around me more clearly. I'm staring at an apartment of only my belongings. Then it hits me. It feels like a knife twisting sharply to ensure that every part of me shreds to pieces. Micah set me up. He's the only person that has access to my usernames and passwords.

I continue surveying the apartment, still unable to believe that his stuff is gone. No; maybe this is a robbery. I might be missing some of my own stuff. I'm trying to convince myself that I'm imagining it. The whole evening is a nightmare. I'll wake up any minute now. I pinch myself to prove that theory. I'm only welcomed with more pain.

I walk in circles like a crazy person. I notice my laptop on the edge of our bed. It exposes what he had gone in there to retrieve. It still doesn't make sense to me, but it's clear he's involved in what happened. Why? My heart and mind beg for answers – for anything – only to hear painful silence.

The masochist in me carries my legs to the closet. Sure enough, all his clothes are gone. We may have had our fights. We didn't always agree about my passion for journalism, but it's nothing that would result in this turn of events. Unwilling to stare at the reality in front of me any longer, I go to the kitchen to find the tequila. I grab a tall glass and fill it to the top. I down it in two gulps.

The compression in my chest spreads into my entire body. My heart starts to break. It shatters into a million pieces and falls into the universe. I want to cry, but I can't. Instead, I struggle to breathe as my grip on reality starts to separate me from the present. My airway tightens. I start to rasp. My brain starts to shut down. Remembering to breathe is becoming an effort. I try to put together a solid thought, but everything buzzes along with nothing staying long enough to be coherent. I'm detaching from my body, piece by piece. Waves of pain go through me like ice. I begin to feel numb.

I hope to feel something from the alcohol. Even that runs through me without feeling – not even a burn of the throat. I can't comprehend how someone that's supposed to love me could do this to me. He promised to love and protect me forever. I pour another glass and then another and then another until I lose count. The room and reality start to slip from me as my body finally shuts down. I don't feel my knees crash to the floor or myself slipping into the blackness – welcoming it – wanting to be anywhere but where I am. The last thing I feel is the unbearable pain in my chest. It's pulling me so far down that I don't know if I'll ever see the light of day again. I don't care if I ever do.

I awoke in a panic with my breaths in spurts. I hated when I dreamt about it. My fucking subconscious occasionally betrayed me. It was bad enough living through it the first time. It was even more painful when trapped in it. I had no ability to force myself awake until the end. Every ounce of pain sliced through me as it did that night.

I ran my hands against my damp tank top before clutching the comforter in despair. The hopelessness resurfaced like an old friend. It made the numbness I usually felt the best feeling imaginable. I fell back into my pillows as tears streamed down my cheeks. I hated being this broken, and for it to be at the hands of the one person I ever allowed into my heart made it so much worse. I clenched my fists to my sides, angrily hitting the mattress. I hated Micah so much. My insides twisted in anguish as the fresh pain tore through my body. I let the tears pour like a faucet. I couldn't stop them or the pain surging through my chest. The weakness and darkness that always accompanied the nightmare consumed me.

I hated this pain. I hated being numb all the time. I hated that my life's ambitions vanished because of him. I hated myself for allowing him into my heart, only to have him break it so badly that I barely found the pieces. I'd never be able to put them back together. The damage was so severe that any attempt to fix them was useless.

I remained awake for hours to force out the pain. Eventually, the pain ceased and the numbness returned. In that time, I made my decision. I was taking the offer. Morals and risk be damned. I had nothing left to lose anyway.

CHAPTER SIX
Can You Feel This

I decided to call Harrison first thing in the morning. I had been up since my nightmare. Thankfully, no one else was. I continued to pace around until it was socially acceptable to call people. When the clock hit eight, I punched in the number to Harrison's office.

"Reynolds," he answered gruffly.

"Hello, Mr. Reynolds. It's Mia Ryan. I'm calling about your offer," I replied quickly.

"Yes, Mia. What have you decided?"

"I'll do it. Do you have the contract?"

"I'm pleased to hear your decision. Why don't you come down to the office today to sign it?" Harrison requested.

"I'll be there within the next hour," I responded.

"When you arrive, tell my receptionist to put you through to me immediately."

I arrived downtown forty-five minutes after speaking with

Harrison. I parked at a meter across the street from the building that housed his office. It could have been the city, or taking this offer, but it exhilarated me. After passing several skyscrapers, I reached the JKK Building. Like its neighbors, it was tall and sleek. It demanded your eyes to admire its prestigious appearance. I entered the building and went over to the elevators to make the trip up eighty floors to *Inside Out*.

When I exited the elevator, I was standing in front of the main entrance. It was glass and allowed people to see into it. The center of the suite had two large doors with the magazine's name etched in white and black calligraphy. I opened them and approached the ultra-modern reception desk that was in front of me. I never broke eye contact with anyone that looked in my direction. The vibe I was going for was designed to convey the message that I am strong, confident, and belonged among them. In reality, I was freaking out.

Behind the desk, there were two blonde female receptionists frantically trying to keep up with the ringing phones. I waited patiently for them to acknowledge me. Five minutes passed without acknowledgment. I cleared my throat to get their attention since they failed to grasp the fact that the person in front of them needed some help. Blonde number one glared at me for my throat-clearing antic.

"I'm here to see Mr. Reynolds. Mia Ryan. He advised to have me put through right away."

She scoffed and made me wait for another five minutes. I wanted to roll my eyes but refrained. She glanced at me with irritation before picking up the phone to call Harrison. After she admitted I had been waiting, she pulled the receiver back due to his irritated voice screaming at her. I stood no chance withholding my 'I told you so' expression. Her eyes frosted over as she motioned for me to follow her. She gestured to the left for us to continue down the hallway toward a large office that encompassed the entire back wall on that side of the office. We stopped short of the doors where she knocked and waited for permission to enter.

"Yes, come in Isabella. I can't believe you kept Mia waiting," Harrison shouted.

She opened the large wooden door, indicating for me to move forward. He was behind his desk multitasking. I walked through the doorway and took in his office. The wall across from me was one large window. The view was breathtaking, displaying the heart of downtown. The rest of his office was what you would expect of any high-class executive. His glass desk was in front of the window. All of his furniture was modern and sophisticated. To me, it projected haughtiness, but that probably had more to do with my distrust for the man.

On my way to his desk, I noted the many accolades. He was beyond well-respected in the industry. Photographs lined the walls with him and many of the biggest names in TV, film, politics, and various media moguls from around the world. I took a seat in the leather chair in front of his desk. Harrison flashed a thin smile before sliding the contract towards me.

"Here's what you asked for Mia. You can take a few minutes to read it," Harrison directed.

I read it carefully, checking every word. As long as I got enough information for him to print what he wanted for this piece, the job was mine. I reread it several times to confirm that there was no escape clause. I should have been more concerned about the significance of this piece, but I wasn't. I needed this change. I signed on the dotted line and slid it over to him. He signed in his spot and handed it back to me.

I raised my eyebrows with suspicion. "Don't you want a copy for your records?"

He gave me a glib wave of the hand. "I don't need a copy Mia. I've done this for your peace of mind. I don't go back on my word. You wanted something in writing. My lawyer has a copy of it."

"He doesn't have a signed copy. Isn't that what makes it binding?"

Harrison huffed. "It's clear you trust no one, which is why you're perfect for what I need you to do. You won't allow yourself to get too close. I'm not here to hustle you. You'll get the position. I say that in confidence because I know you have what it takes to get me the information I need."

"I'll email them my resume this afternoon and let you know if I hear from them. We'll go from there," I said evenly.

"Once you're hired, we'll set a schedule to check in with each other," he instructed.

His unconcerned expression had me on edge. This guy was difficult to read. I took a sluggish breath still feeling unsure of him. He really was a charmer. I rose from my seat to head for the door. Harrison met me for a parting handshake. His hand gripped mine while his mouth morphed into an arrogant smile.

A couple of days later, my cell phone rang. It was F. F. Sweeney & Company, showing interest in me. I took the first timeslot they had open and set the interview for Thursday morning. Bri helped me put together an elegant outfit. We coupled my gray pencil skirt with a black, pleated, sleeveless shirt. She assured me it looked professional enough. I left the house that morning embracing the start of my new path.

I could get to my old neighborhood with my eyes closed and stumbling drunk, so I was on autopilot on my commute down there. The office I was heading for was impossible to miss. It was the most prominent building in a crumbling community. I parked my car in the back of their lot. On my way towards the building, I tried to ease my jittery nerves. After being buzzed inside, I confirmed my appointment with the receptionist. Ten minutes later she appeared in the lobby and raised a finger for me to proceed with her. We went down a long hallway that ended with a huge office. She opened the door but left me to announce my arrival.

"Mr. Fitzgerald?" I asked tentatively.

The man nodded and pointed to the seat in front of him. He didn't seem like he wanted to be giving this interview and did not hide it. I scurried from the door to sit down.

"Ms. Ryan, I presume," he said, keeping his head down.

He was definitely on the agitated side. His deep voice was terse.

"Yes, Mia Ryan. Thank you for your time today."

When he looked up, it stunned me. His eyes ran along my body causing his expression to change somewhat. His scowl gradually transformed to a timid smile. His eyes didn't leave mine as his brows wrinkled as if he was trying to piece something together. I didn't have much brain space to think about what was going through his mind. I was too busy attempting to contain my own impure thoughts. My body reacted in ways that I'd never experienced on the first encounter with someone. It flamed to attention as I soaked him in. Heat rushed to my cheeks while my heart started hammering loudly in my chest. I had never felt anything this strong. It was potent.

Sweet Baby Jesus! He is beyond gorgeous!

He gave God-like and beautiful a whole new definition. His appearance rendered me speechless. His detailed body alone would be enough to reduce artists and photographers to sobs as they prayed to the heavens for such an attractive creature to be amongst them. His prior irritation seemed to be gone as he sat up in his chair. Every inch of his body was within my eyesight to devour. He raked his eyes over me every so often before bringing them into my direct eye line to linger with an inquisitive stare. Tingling sensations trekked in waves throughout me. It made the draw to him more intense.

The things his appearance is doing to me right now should be illegal.

"We interview the best, and your resume is flawless, so it should be me thanking you for your time today," he replied.

His voice was commanding. My stomach tied into one large knot. I imagined what he sounded like in bed. A fiery burn coursed between my legs. I hastily crossed them.

Get it together Mia!

His black hair was amazing. It was short but not too short. It was a messy style almost like he ran his hands through it a few times without putting too much effort into it. The longer hair spiked up in all the right ways. I couldn't stop staring at his face. His cheekbones were prominent with his ears and nose annoyingly perfect upon his sculpted face. He had to be at least six-foot-two, if not taller. His shoulders were broad but muscular. I was willing to bet if I unbuttoned his finely pressed dress shirt that a defined six-pack would be staring back at me with the delectable 'V' running deeper. It was like an unspoken message to run for the door now because this could only end in trouble. He had my body revved up. I had no doubt that he was the kind of guy that could teach a girl a thing or two in the bedroom.

Jesus, focus Mia!

I readjusted my eyes from the area that led to his pant line to his dark brown eyes. They begged you to keep staring at them so he could tell you all of life's secrets. He had one of those faces that made you want to promise every possession you own just to have a chance at kissing his luscious lips. They were full and led into dimples on each side when he smiled. So far, I'd gotten him to do that a few times.

This interview has to go fast without any challenging questions because I'm not sure I can even spell my own name right now.

Knowing I had to get my thoughts out of the gutter they currently wanted to hang out in, I straightened up and set my palms on his desk. It hit me that he paid me a compliment. Perhaps, I should say something in response instead of frothing at the mouth. "I'm honored for the consideration. It's a great opportunity," I murmured.

He tapped his fingers together. "Your resume indicated you were studying journalism. I can't help but wonder why you would apply for a position with a finance company. It doesn't seem like an industry you'd have interest in if you were serious with your studies."

I gulped. "I took my studies in journalism very seriously. However, I've come to realize that to succeed it is important to have a wide range of knowledge and expertise. Since I had such a narrow focus, I wanted to expand into other areas."

"Why do you think that this position is the best fit for you?" he questioned.

His eyes burned into me, completely unreadable. My stomach fluttered at the intensity exuding from him. I prayed my heartbeat would slow down a little. It was beating so loud that it sounded like someone was hammering a board right next to us.

"I believe it's an opportunity to learn about this industry. It offers possibilities to learn skills that will benefit me in any business," I responded.

He cocked his head to the side. His long fingers went to his chiseled chin where they lingered above his mouth. My body temperature went up several more degrees as I watched his fingers trace his lips. It took everything in my power not to let my body stray to his and replace his fingers with my tongue.

God – focus Mia!

"Why are you interested in working for our company?" he asked with a thin smile.

"It's well-known throughout the financial industry that this company is the most successful privately-owned finance company that this city has ever seen. I strive to perform at my best in everything I do and your company can give me the opportunity to learn from the best."

"I don't need to ask you what your major achievements are to date. It's obvious you climb to the top in all that you do. You were the editor-in-chief of one of the most renowned college newspapers in circulation. You work history confirms you've held a variety of positions that have given you diverse skills. The 4.0 GPA is an excellent attribute. What I can't overlook is the gap from your enrollment last fall to you sitting here. Can you please clarify why you're not finishing your degree?"

His question jolted me out of the electric trance his body had me in. "There was a misunderstanding that led to my dismissal from Eckman. The entire experience brings me back to my first answer. It's imperative to have as much knowledge as you can in a variety of areas. It was an unfortunate blemish for me, but I've learned from it," I replied not showing any sign of weakness.

"What has it taught you?" he pressed.

"It's led me to believe that we can learn just as much by firsthand experience in the work force than in a lecture hall. I've elected to take time away from academics to test the skills and knowledge I've acquired thus far."

His fingers drummed on the desk. After a short pause, his eyes connected with mine. There was a hint of understanding from him as he stared at me. "I appreciate your honesty. Most people lie to cover up their downfalls. You've chosen to embrace it as well as learn from it. That's impressive. Have you decided against pursuing journalism? What I'd like to confirm is your long term goal here?"

"If I'm going to pursue a career as a journalist, there's a lot I need to learn that books can't teach me," I clarified.

"Why move towards the finance industry?" he inquired.

The fingers that were tapping his desk were now running back and forth across his perfect jaw line. He was so unreadable but definitely intrigued by everything I had to say, which made sense since this was an interview after all.

Really Mia, has your basic reasoning left the building?

"The driving force in our economy is business and ultimately the financial industry. The financial crisis is a painfully obvious indicator of that fact. Knowledge in this industry will give me invaluable experience," I said smoothly.

"Why switch focuses now?" he asked as his eyes creased together.

"I'm at an age in my life where I should be exploring as many opportunities as possible. If I'm going to become a successful professional, I want to create a resume that will allow me to assimilate myself into any field or occupation. The depth in the financial industry can do just that. If my path leads me back to journalism, I'll have gained a wealth of knowledge through this industry. It will allow me to write about a variety of subjects."

His tongue made an appearance as it licked at his lower lip. My mouth went dry. I inhaled a ragged breath. The burning sensation traveling through me was close to boiling over. I hoped that he'd wrap this up soon. I couldn't handle being here for much longer without doing something stupid.

"Why should we pick you out of the pool of candidates? What makes you exemplary?"

I squirmed before focusing my eyes to his with my last shred of seriousness. "I'm a fast learner, which I believe is an asset for any company. I'm a team player that can bring a lot to any project. I know how to multi-task and operate well under deadlines. I don't intimidate easily so dealing with difficult people and situations isn't hard for me. I'm never satisfied with learning the basics. I like to be challenged as it pushes me to perform at my best."

His face crept into a dimpled grin as he relaxed into his chair. He wasn't holding back a bit as he absorbed every feature of me. It was exhilarating and nauseating all at the same time. We stared at each other for a few moments before breaking the heated connection.

"Well, I think that about does it. We'll be in touch," he said deeply.

He rose from his chair to walk with me to the door. I collected my purse and remained a step behind him. As I suspected, he was about six-foot-two with long legs, covered in black slacks that showed every amazing detail of his fine ass. Thank God, this was over. It was even better that this position was entry-level. The less time I spent around him, the better. I liked having control over my body. I learned in this brief meeting that maintaining control around him would be problematic.

When we reached the door, he paused before turning the handle. His eyes trailed across my body. My breathing sped up at the passion behind them. My brain was working overtime to keep from moving closer to him. He opened the door and leaned against the frame as he extended a hand. I placed my hand into his and almost moaned from the pleasure my body experienced from his touch. The mass of emotions I had been feeling for the last twenty minutes bubbled over. Sparks went throughout my entire body. My heart was ready to leap out of my chest. I barely noticed that his breathing faltered as he closed his eyes. I pulled my hand out of his and cleared my throat, hoping to steady my heavy breathing. I was close to panting like a dog on a hot summer's day.

"Uh, thank you again, sir. I'll wait to hear from your office Mr. Fitzgerald," I stammered.

He laughed. "Mr. Fitzgerald was my father and sir makes me feel like a fifty-year-old man. I'm Ethan."

"It was a pleasure to meet you Ethan," I stuttered.

His laugh was doing all sorts of things to me. My stomach and everything south of me clenched together. They demanded satisfaction for the dull ache that rose to the surface. Every five minutes he was finding a new way to unleash some reaction in me.

"The pleasure was mine."

I exited his office as fast as my legs could take me without running. When I was outside, I stopped moving to take in a solid breath. The harsh humidity pressed against my face as I hunched over to gather myself. Once my heart rate slowed and my breathing evened out, I began walking again. On the approach to my car, I grabbed my keys from my purse. I slipped into the driver's seat and tossed my purse behind me. My head fell to the steering wheel where I banged it for clarity.

I had not experienced anything like that in my entire life. When I was with Micah, it was nothing like what I just went through with Ethan. I didn't know it was possible to feel this in tune to the universe. I had been using men for months in attempt to feel anything other than the barrenness inside me. Just looking at Ethan, my entire body had come out of hibernation feeling anything but broken. I had been compartmentalizing every person in my life with precision by refusing to open up or show any real emotion. He unraveled every part of me in a matter of minutes.

How is that even possible? What the hell just happened to me in there?

I was happy to see just Bri's Audi convertible in the driveway. I made my way up the front steps of the porch and let myself into the house. Bri had sprawled out her sociology books between the couch and end table for what appeared to be a long night. She was in her gray fleece yoga pants and a red off-the-shoulder top with a pencil holding her hair back. She glanced up from her textbook.

"Hey Mia, how did it go?"

I dropped my purse at the door on my way into the living room. I took a seat across from her. "Ohmigod Bri. I'm not sure I can even get the right words to describe what happened."

She set the book in her hands on the end table. "Do you think you got the job? I think Harrison is pulling some puppet strings behind the scenes and you'll get it anyway. Did you at least present yourself well?" Bri asked warily.

I flashed a wide smile. Bri raised an eyebrow at my good mood. "I got out of an interview with by far the most gorgeous man to grace this earth," I declared.

"Oh. My. God. Please tell me you haven't fallen to the point that you're moving on from frivolously screwing college guys to fifty-year-old businessmen," she chastised.

"Hell no! The man that interviewed me couldn't have been more than a few years older than us. He was the hottest guy I've ever seen in my life," I exclaimed.

"You didn't do anything stupid like offer to blow him to get the job, did you?"

"Jesus, Bri. I didn't do anything that stupid. As far as the interview, I'm satisfied with how it went, more than satisfied since his appearance practically had me catatonic," I admitted.

She rested her legs up on the coffee table. "What exactly happened to you?"

I couldn't prevent the grin that spread across my face. "I've never had a reaction to a man like that. When I saw his face, one part of my body or another went haywire. It only increased throughout the interview. It took great physical strength to not lose control."

Bri perked up at my confession as her eyes sparkled with happiness. "So you're saying the guy made you horny as hell. Nice Mia. It's about time you started feeling something for men beyond using them."

I rolled my eyes. "This is way different. I don't know how to describe it. The longer I spent with him, the harder it was for me to control myself. When I shook his hand at the end of the interview, it nearly made me convulse."

Seriousness settled upon her face. "Mia, whatever happened today, you've got to let it go. If you're going to get what you need for Harrison, you can't connect with this guy."

"I know. The universe sure has a wicked sense of humor," I grumbled.

Bri sighed. "This whole thing just got a lot more interesting. When do you find out if the job is yours?

"Tomorrow afternoon," I answered with a faint smile.

I lounged around the house until the phone rang about the job. After finishing the entertainment and world sections of the paper, I looked at the clock on the microwave to confirm the time. My phone rang with an unknown number. I quickly picked up.

"Hello?"

"Is this Mia Ryan?" Ethan asked in a husky tone.

His voice was even sexier over the phone. The sound of it had my stomach somersaulting all over itself as my heart took off.

Really? Even over the phone he does this to me.

I inhaled slowly and answered, "Yes, this is Mia."

"Mia, its Ethan Fitzgerald. We've made our decision. We would like you to fill the position. Can you start Monday morning at eight?" he inquired in a stern tone.

"Yes, Monday is perfect."

"We're looking forward to having you join our team. When you arrive, have the receptionist put you through to my office."

"Yes, sir, I mean Ethan. Ah, thanks again," I stammered.

Shit. Please tell me I'm not going to be working directly under him. Not that that would be a bad scenario. Gah! Head out of the gutter Mia!

CHAPTER SEVEN
Going Under

Monday morning came quicker than I expected. Over the weekend I went shopping with Bri to get some business attire, since my closet was severely lacking in that area. She helped me put together my outfit for the first day. It was a sensible black pinstriped skirt suit. It was on the mundane side but exhibited a professional presence. I glimpsed at the ensemble on my desk before taking a shower.

I was coming out of the bathroom when Bri shuffled past me like a zombie. Seeing her in the morning never grew old on me. She wasn't a morning person and could care even less who knew it. The only thing I could do without was being privy to the different styles of Trey's boxers. Today's were white with glow-in-the-dark dinosaurs. It was still dark enough that some of them were glowing. My lips curled into a smile as a small chuckle escaped. Between her death-like approach and the happily-glowing dinosaurs, it was impossible to hold back.

"So help me God Mia I'll make you look like a clown if you laugh again," Bri snapped.

"I wouldn't dare Bri," I replied, holding my hands up innocently.

"Get dressed so I can do my part," she mumbled, brushing her teeth in a sleepy daze.

"Who pissed in your Wheaties this morning?" I joked.

She poked her head out of the bathroom and glared at me. "Don't be a smart-ass. I think you're insane. I'm questioning my own sanity by even helping you get ready for what will probably be the stupidest thing you've done yet."

"I'll be ready in a minute," I said, putting in extra effort to tone down my upbeat mood.

She softened before rinsing out her mouth. "In all seriousness, I'm going to enroll you in weekend sessions so you can learn how to do this on your own."

I snorted. "I'll never be able to do what you do with hair and makeup."

She rolled her eyes before pointing to my door. By the time, I had dressed; she was ready to work her magic on me. When she finished, I had a sleek up-do with pristine makeup.

"Thanks Bri, for everything," I said, giving her a tight hug.

"I'd love to stay and chat, but I don't have to be anywhere for another six hours so I'm going back to bed," she declared.

"Something tells me that you aren't going to sleep much once in there," I teased.

She gave me a sinful smirk before opening Trey's door. "I might as well make use of my extra time this morning."

"Behave yourself. Don't do anything I wouldn't do," I advised, trying to stifle my laughter.

"This coming from the girl that uses sex to get rid of guys every morning they wake up next to her. I'm positive there isn't anything you don't do," Bri remarked.

I winked. "No one ever complains."

"Good luck Mia. Remember to stay away from Ethan. I want details tonight."

"I'll call you later Sass."

It wasn't long before the affluent houses of the suburbs disappeared and the hardness of the south side crept into view. It was mind-boggling that driving thirty minutes could find a person in two totally different worlds. The south side was the epitome of an urban area that wanted to catch up to its neighbors, but still displayed the remnants of a strongly-rooted culture. Rundown buildings with barred windows weaved their way in and out of more modern additions. The streets weren't nearly as tidy. On the south side, people accepted litter and graffiti as a way of life. There was never a point to clean it up because the gangs that ran rampant throughout the area would dirty it up the next day.

My uncle's bar was in the heart of the area. It was his source of pride and even he gave up on keeping the side of his building free from graffiti. Eventually, he came to an informal arrangement with one of the gang leaders to keep an eye out for his bar. In exchange, they could put whatever they wanted on the side of it. The content had to be somewhat respectable to the area and our Irish ancestry. I thought he was crazy at first, but it ended up being a wise move on his part because no one messes with his building now.

I hit the edge of the neighborhood and turned onto the road for the office. Once there, I parked in the back. After F. F. & Sweeney made it their headquarters, they spent a substantial amount of money to help modernize their area. The office stuck out amongst the grimness that plagued the south side. The building was magnificent. It took up almost a quarter of the block in space alone. It was five stories and designed in glass. Between the second and third story, the company name was in steel letters that appeared as their own floor. The modern appearance of the building made it more suitable for the luxury of the city rather than down here. The entrance appeared broad by the wide doors, but there was a high level of security. All personnel required a badge to enter. Visitors needed to be on the schedule before entering the facility.

I checked the clock on my dash to confirm the time. I still had a half-hour to kill, but sitting out here didn't seem appealing. I gathered my things and headed towards the building. I got to the front door and tapped the intercom to announce my presence. The voice on the other end confirmed that I was on the schedule and buzzed me into the main lobby area. I went up to the large receptionist desk. Sophisticated furniture and artwork adorned the entrance. It stayed true to the Irish heritage of the company and the south side community. There were photographs that showed the toughness of years past as well as those that displayed the promise of tomorrow.

I glimpsed at the receptionist, who was busying herself between her computer and phone. She held up a finger. She reminded me of the blondes that worked for Harrison. She was strikingly thin but clearly self-righteous. I shouldn't jump to that conclusion based on appearance alone, but she had a vibe about her that irritated me. After a few minutes, she wrapped up her call. I wanted to roll my eyes but refrained. My whole reason for being here was to collect information so I had to play nice with everyone.

I gave her a bright smile and sweetly said, "Mia Ryan. It's my first day. Mr. Fitzgerald directed me to report to him when I arrived."

She pierced me with her empty gray eyes before turning back to the computer. "You're early so I can't guarantee he's in yet," she sniped.

An agitated breath slipped through me at her snarky attitude. I attempted to cover it up with another contrived smile. "Could you phone him to see if he's here?"

She let out an exasperated sigh as if I had asked her to work overtime this early in the day, but she complied with my request. She stared at her computer while typing a mile a minute. "Mr. Fitzgerald is in the office. I'll take you to him."

She made her way around the desk where she waited for me to join her before we went down the hallway. As we reached his office I had to announce my own presence again. I gaped at her as she strode away. Something told me that we would not be swapping stories by the water cooler any time soon. Before knocking on the door, I gave myself a mental pep talk to try to retain some control around him.

After I knocked, I expected he'd yell for me to come in so it shocked me when he opened the door. He looked more scrumptious than the first time I saw him. He had on an Armani suit that was black with a white button-down shirt. My body stirred to life with hot flashes whipping through me as if I was going through menopause.

Lord, help me now!

"Mia, pleasure to see you again," Ethan said sincerely.

"Yes, it's good to see you too Mr. Fitzgerald," I responded quietly.

Ethan glared. I blanched recalling our discussion about him preferring Ethan.

"I mean Ethan. It's nice to see you Ethan."

Real smooth Mia.

I went straight towards his desk. I had done everything I could to avoid looking at his face for too long. I gave him a soft smile as he watched me, nothing short of amused by his expression. Our eyes caught for a small second, but I broke the connection. My mouth dried at that brief capture and my stomach tied itself together. I licked away the dryness on my lips. He abruptly looked away. After reaching the chairs in front of his desk, I exhaled deeply, praying that it would help me calm down. Ethan grabbed a folder from the corner of the desk before sitting down.

"You're punctuality is appreciated. It's sad to say, but some people don't understand the importance of it in our industry, because of which they find themselves dismissed," he said firmly.

The sternness in his voice made me squirm. I nodded before taking the file to examine it.

"We'll be touring the building so you can get an idea of what each department does here. You can sign the paperwork later today."

Without a chance to respond, Ethan was up and to the door again. I scrambled to gather my things and my bearings. Sitting that close to him, every part of my body flamed to attention. My brain was on the fritz as it tried to keep my insides from jumping all over the place.

"Leave your things here. You can collect them at the end of the day," he commanded.

It made me uneasy to leave anything personal in his office unattended. He glanced at me expressing his impatience with me for stalling. Leaping out of my chair, my teeth grazed my lips shyly. His lips curled into a smile that brought out his dimples. The burn within me was starting to settle in between my legs. I bit my lip even harder.

For the love of Christ, I need to get a hold of myself.

We went down the hall side-by-side on our way to the elevator bank. It was the most comfortable I had been since laying eyes on him. It didn't stop the heat coursing through my body or the faster pace my heart took around him, but it was bearable. Ethan hit the button before shoving his hands into his pockets. He angled his head to the ceiling. After a moment, he peered over to catch me in full-on stare mode. His lips twitched displaying his delight.

"We're going to level five. We'll do a thorough walkthrough of each floor and the departments that cover them so you can acquire a solid understanding of our operations. Once we've visited every floor, we'll discuss what your role will be. We'll be starting with the top floor to visit the other executives first."

I inhaled shakily and gave him a small nod. He must have sensed my anxiety because he couldn't contain the smirk that spread across his face. I ran my tongue across my lips before lightly biting my bottom one. I glanced at Ethan and caught him staring at me. His eyes burned as he stared at nothing but my lips. My cheeks flamed along with the rest of my body.

"It seems appropriate to meet the individuals that are responsible for such an illustrious company. After all, it's their hard work that brought this company to where it is today," I said hoarsely. I shook my head, frantically trying to pull myself together.

The elevator pinged announcing its arrival. After walking through the doors, we settled on opposite ends of it. The heat began to rise around us and the elevator turned into a sauna. It made the inexplicable draw to him even more difficult to handle. I kept swallowing to rid the drought in my mouth.

One, two, three ... oh who am I kidding. All the counting in the world isn't going to stop anything happening inside of me right now.

I couldn't take the intensity between us any longer and thoughtlessly gazed at him. He was leaning against the railing with his arms crossed and his eyes closed as softness glided over his face. Ethan opened his eyes to catch me staring again. He chuckled. My stomach flip-flopped with the sound. It was starting to make me angry that I had such a lack of control over myself when around him.

My research of the company before interviewing gave me the background of the figureheads as well as its dynamic. Liam Fitzgerald and his cousin Sean Fitzpatrick started it. It wasn't until later that Colin Sweeney joined them. Their families had been a part of the south side for generations. They were straight off the boat from Ireland. Each family made this area their home with each generation becoming more affluent within the community until they evolved

71

into this finance company.

Being a privately held company, those three men were the exclusive shareholders. Liam Fitzgerald passed away several years ago. When Liam died, his sons inherited his shares. Ethan received ninety percent while his brother Devin got ten percent. I was curious why Ethan came out so far ahead of Devin. The media took an interest in it too but eventually it faded away. After interviewing with Ethan, I researched enough to know that he never formally stepped into his rightful executive position. He chose to retain his status as senior vice president. My investigation only gave me the basics of the company and its personnel. It led me to believe that they were very cautious on what they released to the media regarding the company and their personal lives.

When meeting with Sean and Colin, it was evident that they despised being bothered with such things but they were willing to tolerate it for ten minutes. Both men were taciturn and detached while we spoke with them. The idea of being alone with either of them gave me shivers. The way they gaped at me freaked me out. I couldn't place it, but they stared me down as if I was a ghost. Their icy glares were enough to squash some of the naughty sexual desires I had while standing next to Ethan.

The meeting with Devin was much different. He didn't seem as interested in me as Sean and Colin. I focused more on the tension between those two because it was tangible. The hatred between them was alive and well. I was glad that we weren't with him for too long because Ethan became stone cold.

We spent the rest of the day between floors. The fourth floor was home to the accounting and analytical departments. The third floor housed sales and marketing. The second floor was the busiest floor of them all, with production and project management occupying it. We were back on the first floor that housed senior management and human resources. There were also several large conference rooms that bridged off from the reception and lobby area.

Ethan spent a substantial amount of time going over what each department did for the company as well as the key points to their success. This company worked with some of the most prominent people and companies in the world. Their focus seemed to be investments, but they also had lending programs. My head was starting to hurt as I absorbed all the information.

After we had covered every corner of the building, we headed back to his office. On our way, the mood shifted between us. When we were with other people, I didn't struggle nearly as much to manage my raging hormones around him. It was when we were alone that my body refused to have any control over itself.

When we reached his office, he politely opened the door. I strolled to his desk to take a seat. Ethan sat down with his palms on the desk before giving me a hard glance. I squirmed in my chair wondering what he was thinking to have such an inflexible look behind those beautiful eyes.

"What did you think of your first day?"

I smiled timidly. "I feel real good about it. The workflow of the operations is highly remarkable. What will my position entail?"

Ethan lightened up with a crooked grin. "I'm glad you asked. We do a walkthrough of the company with all our entry-level employees to find out where they'll be the best fit. Regardless of what we post in the ad, we leave plenty of room for change."

I stared at him curiously as he grazed his fingers across his chin.

"I believe you'll fit best with our team that handles all the pitches to potential clients. Connor O'Shea will give you further details on what he expects of you. You'll report to him tomorrow morning," Ethan declared.

It was obvious that he had more to say. My eyes flickered from his desk to him. "You can complete that paperwork now. I'll turn it over to HR before I leave for the day," he said, pointing at the file in front of me. "You'll need to be buzzed into the building tomorrow but we'll have a badge for you by the afternoon. The last item I want to discuss is salary. What are your expectations?"

I fidgeted in my chair as guilt consumed me. It drained some of the heat coursing through me and slowed my heart down. I could already tell that lying to him was going to make me feel like shit. He narrowed his eyes at me in demand for an answer.

"Whatever you see fit will meet my expectations," I replied quickly.

His face tightened. Ethan jotted down a figure before sliding the post-it over to me. I sucked in a quick breath at the amount. I nodded in agreement. He relaxed into his chair. I took the paperwork and started to complete it. It didn't take too long to finish. I stuffed the completed papers into the file.

He smiled. "I think that about does it for today."

Ethan rose to walk me out. I scurried past him. I doubted touching him again was a good idea, especially since my body had thrown a fiesta while I worked on those forms. If he brushed my side, I'd shed my clothes in a New York minute so his hands could travel all over me.

"Uh, thanks again Ethan. I'll see you tomorrow," I said before walking out.

"When you arrive, check in with me. I'll take you up to the third floor," he said, lingering at the door.

I glimpsed over my shoulder to see him staring at me with unwavering eyes. I faced forward and picked up my speed to get to the parking lot. I'd figure out how to deal with this bizarre attraction eventually.

CHAPTER EIGHT
Eye Opening

The following day I met Connor's team. There were six of them – Cade, Calder, Camron, Cane, Collin, and Cory. My jaw dropped when Connor rattled their names off in a spitfire fashion – it frustrated me to be on an all-male team. It was going to make getting to know the females around here a joy. I guess anything was better than working with Ethan. I'd rather suffer torture than attempt another whole day with him. It took all night to purge the dirty thoughts of him from my system.

It didn't take long for me to find my footing within the team. After a few weeks, I was like one of them. I got to know the majority of the people on our floor through the guys. They took me under their wing and introduced me to everyone. I discovered that these guys were the cream of the crop. They handled all the best marketing projects. Just by being in their presence, I had been able to snag plenty of lunch and happy-hour invitations. I found some solid ground with quite a few people. It helped to lay the foundation for finding out more for Harrison.

We worked out a schedule for updates and planned to meet face-to-face for any big news. We had a call every Friday to discuss any findings from the week. I hadn't discovered anything useful yet, but Harrison assured me that it would just take time. He urged me to focus on my relationships with people. I was adjusting into my new routine without too many issues. Even though my employment within the company was under false pretenses, I was getting a lot out of the experience. The content we marketed bored the shit out of me, but preparing the presentations was something I enjoyed. There were days I'd have to remind myself of my true purpose for being there. Waves of guilt accompanied those reminders, but I dealt with the mixed feelings; I'd made a choice to be there. As with all choices, there were consequences that inevitably followed, and guilt was one of mine.

I was an idiot for drinking the night before with the rest of the house. Since I had next-to-no sleep, I struggled throughout most of the day. It was a steep learning curve, now that I was no longer in college – slacking off in the real world did not go unnoticed. Some people gave me strange looks. The guys went out of their way to poke fun at me about it. Their blunt comments about being able to smell the alcohol from my pores continued throughout the day.

I buried myself in my work in an attempt to expel the nagging guilt that was growing by the day. I was good at separating myself from the story. My research in the past had never led me to the faces of those I was writing about. I had never had to deal with looking people in the eye while screwing them over. Most of the people here were great, but I had to remember that they were just as innocent as the people that this place may have wronged.

We had a big pitch coming up within the next few weeks, so I decided to stay late to put in some extra work for my particular part.

My assignment was finding a catchy way to lure in a potential client with words while the rest of the team worked on the imagery, but this one had me stuck. If we nailed it, the company would secure a new account that would generate millions.

And probably rip off just as many more. Oh, give it a rest Mia.

I heard faint voices coming down the hallway. A shiver ran up my spine when their cold tones registered in my mind. My spot on the floor happened to be near the exit. I was able to catch conversations that echoed off the hallway walls. Plenty of office gossip passed through my ears but nothing that would validate anything Harrison was trying to prove – until now. I listened as the chatter in the hall became crisper.

"We should be able to set up a meeting soon. My source tells me the last pieces of the puzzle are being validated now. It's rather interesting that this particular information landed at our doorstep, but I'm not going to question it," Sean said evenly.

"Are they coming here or are we flying out east?" Colin asked flatly.

"We'll fly out for this unveiling. It's something they've wanted for the better half of the last two decades," Sean sneered.

The tone in his voice made my skin crawl – I didn't think evil had an audible sound. I sensed that they might have stopped by the elevators. Their voices were no longer becoming louder.

"It may be enough to smoke them out. It'll give us the payout that we've waited for all these years," Colin responded bitterly.

"If this doesn't get them out of hiding, I don't think anything ever will. I suspect that this particular discovery is the only thing that'll do it," Sean declared.

The elevator pinged with its arrival and their voices echoed away. I curled my palms but my fingers slid all over from the sweat that was coating them. It was clear that most of what Harrison had said was the truth – they were about to get retribution against someone that wronged them. I didn't have a lot to work with in what they were talking about, but something big was about to happen soon. The pressure in my head increased. The reality of how dangerous this was for me tapped at the top of my skull screaming "I told you so, you idiot!"

"What are you doing here?"

Ethan's deep voice rang through my head. I looked up to see him standing against the doorway. His deep brown eyes penetrated mine. I didn't hear him talking with the other two, so I wasn't sure if he had been with them the whole time or if he sprang up out of nowhere. He tended to do that from time to time. My body became instantly aroused, soaking him in.

Shit. Here we go. My head is already spinning. Now he's here. I'm screwed.

"This pitch has me stuck," I answered weakly.

Colin and Sean had shaken me to the core. My voice sounded an octave above a whisper.

"Mia, you realize it's after seven. We don't expect you to be here past your required hours."

The concern in his voice made my insides warm against the chilliness that currently held me. As he approached, he flashed a dimpled grin that made me more at ease.

"I don't like the current block in my head. Sometimes my best work comes long after the day has finished."

Ethan walked around my desk to stand behind me. He leaned over my shoulder as he scanned my computer screen. Sparks zoomed throughout my body. He smelled like a summer's day, fresh after a rain shower. It was my new favorite smell. I begged myself to remain focused in spite of his proximity. I was fighting a losing battle.

"You don't fail at much do you," Ethan commented.

His breath skimmed my neck. Butterflies fluttered throughout my stomach as my chest tightened into a ball of nerves.

"Where did that come from?" I questioned.

"From what you have up on the computer, you seem well on your way to completing a perfect pitch to match the rest of your team's excellence," he praised.

My eyes zoned in on him as he continued to stare at my work. His deep brown eyes had an awe-like quality behind them as they drifted between the screen and me. I had a strong urge to press my body close to his just to satisfy the hunger he created with that look alone. I wanted to bury my head in my hands because my body and brain were in two very different places.

"This isn't finished. I was playing around with some ideas that might work but I'm not happy with any of it. I'll know when I'm there," I stuttered.

His closeness made my pulse quicken. It frustrated me not to have control over such little things. My blood boiled with the anger, but the ache for more from him was cooling it by the minute. His lips curled into small grin. The sensations between my legs started to intensify as Ethan stood there smiling at me. I rolled my chair to the side to get more breathing room. The urge to move closer to him was a step away from taking over.

"What makes you know you are there?"

"I just get a feeling," I muttered.

"Interesting," Ethan murmured.

"What's so interesting about going with your gut?"

I flinched as my touchiness slipped out in my tone. He had pressed a button that I didn't even know was there, readying me for an argument. Hell, it was probably my lack of ability to command the wayward emotions running through me that caused me to lash out. The numbness that used to hold me seemed like a distant memory because whenever he was around I couldn't seem to catalogue my feelings fast enough.

"It's not the answer I expected to hear from you," Ethan

defended.

"Maybe it *is* quitting time for me."

His eyes darkened at my mood swing. He glided his long fingers into his pockets before striding away. I started shutting down my computer. Silence surrounded me. I was thankful for the last morsel of myself that was able to keep breathing evenly, since I clearly had no control over my mouth. Ethan lingered at the door. Apparently, he was waiting for me to walk with him downstairs. The inexplicable draw to be near him pulled at every nerve-ending. I shuffled my way over to him, doing my damn best to control the wanton ache that had settled between my stomach and thighs.

"Can I ask you something?" Ethan asked as we hit an even pace, departing the floor.

"Depends."

"On what?"

"It depends on what you want to ask me."

"What? Do you have some sort of approval list?"

His tone startled me since it was out of character for him. I glanced at his perfect face and saw a hint of exasperation there. My heart pulsated at the prospect of affecting him.

"No, I don't have a list," I answered shyly.

"So I'm free to ask?" Ethan inquired.

"Fine, ask away," I conceded.

"Why are you so detached?" he questioned.

"Huh?" I stammered nearly stumbling over my own feet.

"I tend to pay attention to what happens around here. You seem to get along with everyone, but it's very superficial. I'm wondering why you keep yourself so separated."

I tensed, effectively halting all my sexed-up feelings. My breath was all but lost from the knowledge that he saw me so clearly. It downright frightened me.

"Try another question. I don't know you well enough to share something that personal," I deflected, keeping my eyes away from him.

"Why are you really here?"

What the hell? Why is he so damn interested in me?

"I needed a change."

"I assumed so, since you jumped fields. Why did you make such a drastic change?" Ethan pressed.

He tilted his head to make sure I caught his eyes. They were full of curiosity.

"I think you know the answer to that one. You seem to be a bright guy."

"Your expulsion from school," he murmured.

I nodded. "Umm ... so ... I believe this is where we say good night?"

I was mere seconds away from the blissful silence of my car.

He huffed. "I'll walk with you. This isn't a safe neighborhood."

I rolled my eyes. "Ethan, it's not necessary."

"This area is unpredictable. I'm walking with you," he insisted.

His stature wasn't worth arguing with. My stomach twisted with the hard edge that settled upon him. He despised being told 'no'. As if to reinforce his point, gunshots fired in the distance. Ethan raised an eyebrow as he opened the door. I rolled my eyes and followed him outside. I could handle a few more minutes – I enjoyed being with him. A sense of comfort wafted along with all my other sensual desires for him.

"How old are you, Ethan?"

"I'm twenty-six."

"Interesting."

"How is that interesting?"

"You seem older. It's hard to tell and a difficult detail to track down."

He squared me up with an inquisitive eye. I bit my lip. I let far too much slip out there.

Do not fuck up again. He is the last person you can make that mistake around.

"I'm not sure if I should be annoyed that you're curious about such a mundane fact or honored that you cared to know," he muttered.

"I didn't ask to annoy you. You've got a lot more going for you than most people do at twenty-six," I responded, gesturing back to the huge building behind us.

Ethan smirked. "I'm going to take that as a compliment, though the tone that accompanied it was on the sarcastic side. Is that one of your default settings?"

"Maybe," I said with a sly grin.

He laughed before his jaw tightened and pulled away his dimples. My insides mourned the loss. I loved it when his dimples appeared.

"What is one thing you're grateful for this week?" Ethan asked.

"I'm fortunate to be surrounded by great friends that are like family to me," I blurted out.

I snapped my mouth shut with that slip of the lip. I took a deep breath to reinforce the walls I have around people.

"Care to elaborate?" he asked hesitantly.

"Not particularly," I answered harshly.

His face stiffened as his eyes darkened. I offered a partial smile in apology.

"Where do you live?" I asked.

His eyes centered on me curiously. "I live downtown."

"Do you like it? It seems like it would be a hassle to get down here for work."

"I never liked living here. I moved away the second I had a chance."

"Did you grow up around here?"

"I think the answer to that is obvious," Ethan replied crudely.

"I hated it here too. I did the same thing when I turned eighteen." I said involuntarily.

Fuck. Again? Why? Where the hell is the version of myself that curbs this shit?

"I enjoy being downtown. There's a hustle to it. The liveliness seeps into you. I like the energy it gives me," he continued carefully.

It shocked Ethan as much as me. I nodded and bit my cheeks to keep quiet. My chest constricted with the fear that was rising at how very open I had become with him.

"Do you still live near Eckman?" he asked curiously.

I gaped at him. It was unnerving that he knew I lived close to campus. He detected my alarm. Ethan waved his hands back and forth. "It's not what you think. I saw your address and your academic profile on your resume. I went to the state university nearby. You keep saying you needed a change. I didn't know if that meant in where you lived as well," Ethan explained.

I softened after listening to him ramble. Despite my best efforts to prevent it, my heart swelled for him. Ethan relaxed with a shy smile. "Yes, I'm near campus. The place I'm at now is in a very nice neighborhood. It's certainly nothing like the streets around here," I said, motioning my hands around us. Ethan opened his mouth, but I beat him to the punch, wanting to know more about him. "What street did you live on? I don't ever recall seeing you while growing up."

"State and Michigan," he answered.

It looked like he wanted to kick the living daylights out of something just thinking about where he was raised. He closed the door on that subject just by his reaction alone. I was familiar with that part of the south side. It was the worst intersection of streets down here and mob central, so the crime rate was astronomical. I shivered as the conversation from Colin and Sean crept into my head.

It reinforced my thoughts that things were definitely corrupt around here. Ethan seemed to hate everything about here. It confused me because I had no clue where he fit within this picture. My mind remained captivated by that detail. It allowed for my mouth to babble against my will.

"I grew up in the opposite end."

I forcefully bit my lip. A soft smile appeared on his face that brought out his dimples again.

"Our paths must not have crossed with all those blocks between us, because I would have remembered meeting you," Ethan whispered.

Lord, he confuses me. He was irate a minute ago and now he is sweet as can be.

We had covered the distance to my car. I reached into my purse for my keys and pressed the button to unlock the doors. The headlights illuminated the dark parking lot. As the light filled the surrounding space, I caught Ethan watching me. He had calmed down – the dimpled smile still graced his face. My insides leapt at the sight. His dark irises tenderly appraised my every move as he stood there with his fists curled at his sides like he was refraining himself from moving an inch. My stomach flipped all over itself at the idea of touching Ethan again. His stance made warmth glide into my heart, attempting to crack the impenetrable walls there.

I should leave, but I wasn't ready to stop talking with him. It was the first time we had really talked to each other. I was able to ask some simple questions without losing complete control over my body. As much as I hated admitting it, he intrigued me. I leaned against my car with my eyes on him as he cocked his head with a crooked grin.

"What's one thing that you liked about growing up here?" Ethan asked.

"I was fortunate to find friends that had wonderful families who opened their homes to me and cared for me unconditionally," I responded honestly.

I had no idea how he was able to get these answers. I sure as hell didn't hand them over willingly. He had got more out of me in the last ten minutes than any guy has gotten in the last ten months. It had to be the extra effort my brain was using to control my body.

"If you were sand on the beach, what would you say to the people that stepped on you?"

"That question is even more random than you asking how old I was out of the blue," Ethan pointed out. I arched an eyebrow. His grin grew wider. "I'd say get the hell off me you assholes. I'm very selective about the people that can cross me."

I giggled. He seemed to unwind with the sound of my laughter. He uncurled his hands and crossed them over his chest.

"What beach would you be on as you cussed out all those that walked over you?"

He snorted and ran his eyes all over me as if he was trying to figure me out.

Good luck. I'm a hot mess.

"I'm not sure I want to share such intimate details with you on that one," he retorted.

Ethan was well aware of how I was handling him throughout the conversation. He was putting up his own front by refusing to answer a question. We were treading lightly with one another, but there was an ease that hadn't been present before that made it different. He wasn't too bad to be around, when I could keep my body in check. I was still using a healthy amount of brain space to control all the impure feelings surging through me; however, I was able to focus better than I had in the past. I considered it forward progress.

"What made you pick this type of car?" Ethan asked, pointing to my Mazda.

"It was in my price range," I answered but it rolled out more like a question.

He strolled around it and ran his hands along the spoiler before returning to open my door. "It's a great car. Why black for the color?"

"Because red gets people pulled over," I replied sarcastically.

I peeked at him to absorb his reaction. I never knew if he would laugh or get angry. His lips were in a thin line but quivered as he started to chuckle. "Thanks for walking with me. I'll see you tomorrow," I whispered, getting into my car.

"Yes, you will. Bye Mia," Ethan replied with a parting smile.

I got home and made small talk with Jackson and Shane, since Bri and Trey were nowhere in sight. They had hangovers, so it was a brief chat. The drain of the day had hit me too. I started thinking about Sean and Colin's conversation. I decided against talking to Harrison about it. I had no idea if what I heard would even help. It was all rather cryptic. I needed to figure out what they had attained that was so huge.

As I lay in bed, my stomach became queasy at the many possibilities of what they could've gotten to execute vengeance upon someone. The guilt subsided in light of this new information, but it was fleeting as Ethan crept into my thoughts. I wondered what his part was. He didn't strike me as someone that was cold or evil. Then again, he couldn't be oblivious to whatever Sean and Colin were up to either. I buried my head in my hands for even thinking about Ethan at all. I shouldn't care what his place was in all of it. I had issues ignoring the way he made me feel. It was becoming stronger by the day.

Our conversation flowed through my mind. I refused to entertain a discussion with every guy I had been with since Micah.

Ethan had become the exception. He intrigued me, and that scared me more than the shit-storm of feelings he aroused with his looks alone. Ethan was easy to talk to, when I was able to focus on the subject matter and not my sexual desires. I sensed we had more in common with one another than I cared to acknowledge. It was obvious he had an interest in me too.

I started tingling all over, only to become angry that he had somehow slipped in and was messing with my body, and my mind. I had little room for mistakes, considering my purpose there. Whenever he was around, I let my fascination with him dominate all my rational thoughts. Reason went out the window when he was near. I had put walls around my heart to keep people out, but when Ethan was around, the walls rattled and urged to break down. If anyone tore them down, it would be him too. I rolled onto my side and closed my eyes to banish any further thoughts about his effect on me. I hadn't signed up for this to start feeling again.

CHAPTER NINE
Bad Boys

I couldn't expel Ethan from my thoughts for very long – he poked his head in left and right. It became impossible to push him out. The harder I tried, the more he surfaced. It exhausted me to pretend like I had no interest in him. I couldn't chase him, but that never seemed to stay in my thoughts for long. They drifted to his body, or something he would say in passing. I reasoned that I couldn't be attracted to someone that had the capability of being that evil. Then thoughts of Micah sprang into my head. It made me question my judgment overall; the verdict was still out on Ethan.

I was sitting in a meeting with him and the rest of my team, with the warmth in me stronger than ever. I didn't have to participate in the presentation. I ended up staring at Ethan for the majority of the meeting. Every so often, he'd glance at me with a partial smile. I never pegged myself as one of those girls that had a thing for bad boys, but being around Ethan made me question it. Micah was always in trouble, even when we were kids. He had the bad boy swagger down to a 'T' and expressed it freely. Ethan was a different type of bad boy. He kept me guessing every chance he got.

Somewhere in my daydreaming, the meeting ended and people were getting ready to leave. I pushed away from my chair while grabbing my things. On my way out, I found myself staring into his dark brown eyes. Every day he would stare at me with such intensity that it made me desperate to know his thoughts. It was like I was a piece of a puzzle for him, but he wasn't sure where he could place me. He motioned for me to stay. My body was electrified with all the feelings running amok in me from staring at him during the meeting. I took a deep breath to prepare myself for another go around.

He flashed his cocky grin. His dimples spread across his face. We stared at each other for a few minutes without saying a word. He was stunning in his black Armani suit with a scorching red tie. My stomach tightened into knots as the rest of me began to tingle in all the right areas. Ethan closed the distance and settled next to me. He brought his hands out of his pockets and folded them over his chest. He grazed the side of my arm ever so slightly. Everything hummed at a higher level with just that simple touch.

"Mia, I know we spoke the other night. This is more of a formal conversation to determine how things are going for you around here," Ethan said with a wide smile.

"It's been going great. I'm very lucky to be working with such a brilliant team," I stammered.

"I figured you would fit in well with them. It's important to me that things are going well for you here," Ethan responded.

His eyes drifted to mine, showing a slow burn that hit right to the core of me. I really wanted to touch him just to satisfy the yearning within. My brain was close to leaving the building as the rest of me started to liquefy. I swore the temperature in the room had gone up at least twenty degrees in the last ten minutes. I shook my head to gather myself.

"I like this place far more than I ever thought I would," I confessed.

"Did you expect to have a hard time fitting in?"

"I had no experience coming into it so it was hard to say. It's worked out better than I could have asked for. I may end up being good at it."

Ethan rolled his eyes. "Mia, I doubt there are very many things that you aren't able to succeed at. It was your biggest selling point when I interviewed you."

"And here I thought it was my looks that got me the job," I blurted out.

Where did that come from? And why God ... why would I ever say it out loud?

Ethan chuckled. "Your confidence was definitely a selling point too."

If I wasn't blushing before, I was now. I probably gave red a completely new shade. I nodded, completely mortified. I had no clue where he saw confidence, but the sincerity he had in his voice revved up my pulse. Ethan stared at me with a look in his eyes that was becoming more intense as each day passed. It was a mixture of longing with a touch of mystery. My brain was using its last efforts not to lean into him to satisfy the deep ache within me.

"I won't keep you any longer. I foresee good things for you here," Ethan declared.

The hot and bothered feelings disappeared with the chill that ran through me. I hated lying to him. It had not been easy thus far but lying as I looked into his eyes made me feel horrible. I needed to get away from him. I had become a hot mess. My body jumped from one emotion to the next faster than I preferred. It was also glaringly obvious that my control over what came out of my mouth was a problem.

"I'm going to head back upstairs to finish out the day. I appreciate that you asked how my position was going for me. It's good to know you take a personal interest in your staff."

I was starting to believe that he didn't have the capacity to be as evil as everything else around here. He was dangerous, but not anything like Sean and Colin; he was dangerous to me because of the way I felt about him. I needed to work harder to distance myself from those desires. I gathered my binders and started to back away from the table. Ethan gave me a parting grin before I briskly left the room.

The house was dark when I got home, so my roommates were probably not back from class. I hid out in my room like a hermit. Ethan, and Harrison's offer, took up all my brain space. I thought about Ethan much more than why I was at that company.

Why would he come into my life now? I'm there to screw over his company not screw him. I want one way more than the other. That's one in a series of problems with me.

Since the beginning, I had had difficulty separating myself from the people within the company. In the past, it had never been a problem for me. It was why I was a fit for the opportunity. As Ethan stated, I kept everyone at a distance but he was becoming the exception to the rule. It pissed me off. I shouldn't be humanizing him. If Mother Nature could explain that to my body then I'd be golden, but that didn't seem like it was going to happen anytime soon. Somewhere along the line I had lost my touch, or I was lost; period.

A healthy reminder of why I ended up taking the offer was necessary. I could endure a few hours of pain to get my head straightened out. Something had to be done to shove Ethan out. I needed this undercover work to end, so getting my shit together was imperative. It would be crushing to walk in and out of that company, living a lie, for much longer.

I forced myself to start thinking about Micah. He was the only thing that made the scars within my heart open. As I let him surface, the lacerations he left inside of me bled remorselessly. The hurt increased almost as if vinegar ran through the cuts.

I thought about opening the letter that Micah left for me. I found it several weeks after he left, but had never opened it. I should open it just to get some closure. I wanted to believe that someday I'd be able to allow him into my thoughts and not have my insides shredded.

I hopped off my bed and opened my closet door. I dropped to my knees, dusted off the box containing the letter, and took a deep breath before retrieving it. I crawled back into bed, turning the envelope over in my hands. Other than Trey, it had been so long since I had seen anything that reminded me of him. After he disappeared, I shunned my memories of him. It took extra effort in our old neighborhood, but I had managed to push them into a sealed box inside of me.

Now is the best time to read this so I can get my head screwed on straight again – if that is even possible anymore. If Micah's goal was to leave me utterly fucked up when he left, he achieved it. Most days I don't know which way is up, let alone where my place is in all of it.

I ran my hand across his script as more memories filtered through my head. The pain kicked up a notch. Even though I hated him, a tiny part of me missed him because he was one of my oldest friends. He knew everything about me. I had opened up to him in every way. Apart from Bri, he had seen a side of me that I rarely shared. I never had anyone to share with at home, so it had become second nature to lock it up. He had always been there for me. When he left, it had devastated me as deeply as it did because I had never been without him.

As much as I tried not to let them surface, the good memories of Micah crept in from time to time. It had not helped the situation that those memories of him made me realize how fortunate I was to have him and Trey throughout my childhood. Micah stayed around later in the days then Trey, almost as if he knew how much I hated being alone or with Chase. It destroyed me to admit that he was a huge reason why I was able to get through the loneliness of my childhood. He gave me hope that there had to be something better out there for me. It wasn't the agony of him leaving, but the pain of losing one of my best friends.

I clutched the envelope to my chest for a few moments longer. I let the love and the hurt and the sadness consume me before tearing into it. As I opened the letter, a photo tucked inside fell out. It was a picture of the two of us taken a few weeks before he left. I remembered it like it was yesterday. We were goofing off in bed and happy as ever. He grabbed the camera saying he wanted to remember it forever. Since we were forever, he had said, he wanted to document the moment to add it to all the others we had shared. It was the typical self-posed shot, but the love between us was undeniable. My heart throbbed even more from seeing his face along with what was also running through my head. I tossed it to the side and unfolded the letter.

Mia,

If you're reading this now, then you know I'm gone. Baby, I'm so sorry. If there was any other way, I'd be right there next to you doing everything I could to take away the pain. You have to believe me when I say that this is the only choice I had. I love you so much. This is tearing me up inside.

I swear that if I could have stopped what happened I would have but these people used you against me. I thought when I became involved with them that it would be business as usual. I was wrong because it was you that they wanted all along. When the only choices were your life or getting you kicked out of school, I chose your life. I don't know why they wanted to do that to you, but I'm going to get to the bottom of it. I won't return until I know exactly what is going on. I have given them what they needed so they won't hurt you. It also buys me more time to figure everything out.

I can't take you with me to find out this information. I can't explain it all either. It needs to seem like I left you without a second thought. I've already led them to believe that was the case so I could go off on this lead. I know you have the strength in your heart to walk away from what has happened. I need you more than you need your career. You are my everything.

I'm so sorry for hurting you Mia. I'll never forgive myself. I know this doesn't make sense now, but it will. I promise I'll come back to explain it all. It hurts me more than you'll ever know to leave you. You have to remember that I love you more than anything in this world. I have to do this because I can't lose you. You are, and will always be the only person I ever love ...

I stopped reading, crumpled up the letter and tossed it aside. The pain had become intolerable. I had jumped to the conclusion that he had a hand in getting me expelled, but now there was proof of it. Tears streamed down my face against my will. My head was a mess of confusion. What was he involved with that would leave him with only a choice of keeping me alive or destroying me? What people did he get mixed up with this time? It made absolutely no sense. I should have known that somewhere along the line his involvement in the various drug circles would come back to haunt me.

The old saying is true – love is blind – or stupid – take your pick.

As I laid lost in thought, footsteps and voices echoed down the hall; Trey and Bri were home for the night. I figured they would head into his room for their nightly romp, so it surprised me when there was a light tap on my door. I sat up and wiped my eyes.

"Come in," I sniffed.

Bri opened the door and popped her head around the corner without looking at me. "Hey, I missed out on talking with you yesterday. How did you survive work after being up all night drinking with us?"

As she came into the room, she had a bright smile, which vanished when she saw my tear streaks. I tried to ease her worry by forcing a grin, but it was only a half-hearted attempt.

"What's wrong?" she questioned.

"Bri, it's fine. It's a good thing I'm this miserable."

She climbed in next to me and settled her shoulder next to mine. "Mia, there's nothing good about seeing you like this. What's going on?" she asked, bringing a hand to my cheek to wipe away a straggling tear.

I sniveled. "I'm getting a little too comfortable working there so I gave myself a reminder."

"Why are you crying? You're not making sense."

"I read Micah's letter. Well, I read part of it," I whispered.

Bri linked her arm with mine. She gave it a tight squeeze as she watched another tear cascade down. She pinched the bridge of her nose with her free hand. Her eyes skimmed over me with a look of concern.

"Mia, I wish you would've waited until I was home. You shouldn't have read it by yourself. Where is it now?" she asked.

I pointed towards my trashcan and shut my eyes. Bri untangled her arm from mine and went over to grab it. While she read the letter, I picked up the picture and started ripping it into tiny squares. I had read the first quarter of it, so the majority of it remained unknown. She muttered curses under her breath at certain parts and scrunched her eyebrows at others. At one point, her face flushed a deep red, glaring at the letter as if it would combust from the fire in her eyes. When she finished, she did the same thing I had done;

crumpled it up and tossed it towards the garbage before settling back with me on the bed.

"I'm sorry. I'm not sure how he thought telling you how much he loves you would make anything he did acceptable," Bri said heavily.

"I know, right?"

She sighed. "I can see why you stopped reading it. You didn't miss much. It was more of the same with a mysterious warning that made no sense."

"The part I read was fucked up enough, so I don't really care how it ended. Let's just hope he decides to stay away for good," I replied quietly.

Bri viewed me with concern as she tried to judge my mood.

"I'm fine. I'm not going to have a meltdown. I needed the reminder," I reassured.

"You're getting attached aren't you?" she inquired.

Bri stiffened her back as she ran her hands across her face. She tilted her head with a look in her eyes demanding the truth. I picked at my cuticles before giving her a sheepish smile.

"I like the people there and ... well ... there's this bizarre attraction to Ethan that's making everything more complicated. It's hard to keep him out of my thoughts for long," I admitted.

Bri huffed. "I've told you that you can't consider anything with him. I take it that things are still intense."

"Yeah, that's one way of putting it," I agreed.

"Why do you have to be drawn to the dangerous ones?" she griped.

"I was wondering the same thing," I answered weakly.

"I wish I could tell you that everything is going to be OK, but I can't. Shit happens. I do know that whatever does happen, you'll find a way through it. You're one of the strongest people I know," Bri said, with a firm voice, as she embraced me.

It was a good wrap-up to the evening. I'd spend the rest of the night ridding my body of the painful ache, but my head was back in the game.

"Thanks Bri. I'm glad we had a chance to talk tonight. I've missed our girl time," I said, allowing a full smile to cross my face.

She perked up and scooted to the edge of the bed, getting ready to leave. "I've missed you too Mia. I have some major catching up to do on my assignments. I know you don't mind either because your eyes are a dead giveaway that you've hit your sharing quota."

I scoffed, but she was spot-on as usual. "How are classes going this semester?"

I needed to get comfortable with talking to them about school. It barely came up in conversation. They went out of their way to refrain from studying or talking about Eckman around me. It was annoying, but I was over trying to change it. After how I had handled my expulsion, I'd probably treat me like glass too. Bri grimaced while tying her loose hair back into a messy ponytail. I knew that tick. She was gearing up for an all-nighter.

"I was a moron for skipping yesterday. It's not a wise decision this semester," Bri stated.

"Is this semester full of crappy classes?" I asked.

She gripped the back of her neck before crossing the room to linger in the doorway. "This semester sucks because I elected to get my thesis out of the way. I wasn't thinking about that when I enrolled in the sociology of criminal and juvenile law coupled with calculus and biology, so it's a heavy load."

I scrunched my nose at her intense class schedule. Woof. Bri gave me a crooked grin. "I just got a migraine from your classes. The only one I can even offer to help in is biology. The rest sound miserable."

"I'd be lying if I said they're pleasant, but I'm getting through it. My consumption of energy drinks has increased. It's the only way I can keep from falling asleep – especially in the law classes. The material bores the crap out of me. I have a test in both on Friday, so the next few days are going to suck ass. Let's do something fun this weekend as a reward," she proposed.

"What mall do you want to hit?" I inquired with a roll of the eyes.

"All of them. I need my fall wardrobe," Bri deadpanned.

After reading part of the letter and spending some quality time with Bri, I felt more balanced about everything. We had a great time shopping over the weekend. We treated ourselves to manicures and pedicures. On a spur of the moment, I decided to give my hair a drastic change. It seemed appropriate with the new clothes and freshly groomed nails. The dirty blonde hair was now platinum, with dark streaks of purple and black layered throughout it. Bri gushed that it looked fantastic.

The weekend was over in a flash. It was back to the nitty-gritty of the working week, which went by somewhat fast, with very little interaction with Ethan. It was precisely what I needed – he had managed to slither into my thoughts enough as it was. When I saw or spoke with him, it only increased his presence in my brain. I was working overtime to prevent it from happening anymore.

Feeling extremely happy it was Friday, I was twisting a piece of my hair between my fingers trying to decide if this pitch was finally complete. A course of heat ran through my entire body. I shook my head – Ethan was lurking around here somewhere. I peered over my shoulder and sure enough, there he was, staring at me unashamedly. My rational thoughts started to fall by the wayside as I soaked in every ounce of him. I took in his casual stance as his back rested against the wall with a leg kicked up.

He was breathtaking, and on display like a supermodel. His fitted jeans were hugging his body in all the right places. My eyes trailed up his sculpted chest. His white button-up shirt had a black pattern that weaved its way up the right side. I wondered what was underneath that intricate design. I had seen glimpses of tattoos that started at his wrists and stretched up to his elbows. My thoughts drifted past what his tattoos were and on to seeing his naked body. When Ethan sauntered closer to my desk, my pulse sped up as my stomach clenched tightly together.

Shit. I'm slipping. Why does he have to be so damn hot?

His eyes smoldered as he surveyed my body. I raised an eyebrow and the grin that curled at the edge of his lips transformed into a cocky smile. Unable to stop the rising heat, I flushed embarrassingly. I turned around, securing my purse to leave.

"I'm going to call it a day if that is OK," I muttered, with my eyes to the floor.

If I stared at him any longer, I'd have some serious problems. I'd fallen back on track with my purpose here. It was less difficult for me to separate it. I kept the guilt at bay and remained focused on getting more information for Harrison. Nothing new presented itself, but I was at least in the mindset that made it easier for me to be here.

I'd be back to square one if I had a conversation with Ethan. There was no way in hell I was letting that happen. It was bad enough that I had no ability to prevent the blushing when it occurred, so keeping my eyes to the ground was the best idea for me. My cheeks would not be the only body part of me on fire if I stole another peek at him.

"Yes, of course. I hope you have a great weekend." Ethan paused for a second before asking, "Anything fun planned for the evening?"

Ethan pulled his hands out of his pockets and placed his thumbs through his belt loops. His long fingers trailed down his thighs. My mouth went dry. I blinked to stop myself from mentally undressing him. I chastised myself for making the mistake of looking at him again – It was game over for me. My body ignited everywhere as I fell deeper into his eyes. I wished they'd tell me more about him, but they kept me in a trance more than anything else did.

"I hope that my evening has nothing but a large glass of wine and my amazing whirlpool for a long bath," I stammered, trying to steady my erratic heartbeat.

There goes the last bit of keeping yourself separate from this place. Great job.

His breath quickened. His reaction to what I had said cranked up the tingling in my body.

"It sounds like a nice way to end the week," Ethan said with a sexy grin.

Apparently, little to no interaction with him only strengthened my hormones and idiocy around him. I stared at his mouth without bothering to cease my intoxicating desires for him. I pondered what he'd be like in bed.

Hmm ... Ethan ... naked ... Gah, focus Mia.

"Umm ... yes, I hope it's relaxing. I'll see you Monday," I said, my voice cracking under the intensity between us

Before leaving, I took a parting glance to see he had sat down on my desk with his eyes closed. He opened them to catch me staring at him. I shook my head at my lack of self-control and made my way towards the stairs.

I got into my car and hit my head on the steering wheel. This had become my routine whenever I had intense exchanges like that with Ethan. Every effort I exerted to separate myself vanished. It intrigued me, as well as pissed me off, that this man derailed me this much.

I grabbed my purse to call Harrison to give him an update – not that I had much of one. I had been doing everything he asked by getting well-acquainted with everyone, but this company was like

Fort Knox. Obtaining any substantial information was difficult to say the least. I dialed his number to provide a recap on the week.

"Reynolds," he answered, irritated.

"Hi Harrison, it's Mia."

"Yes, Mia. How are things going?"

His voice went from agitated to charming within an instant. My distrust of him remained.

"I'm still learning the ropes while building relationships with everyone. It's going well, but they're a well-oiled machine around here so getting past the surface is tricky," I replied.

"This isn't a homework assignment with a due date. I realize that this could take a significant amount of time," he assured.

I sighed. "I know. I just wish I would have had more by now."

"It's fine Mia. Keep doing what you're doing. It's going to be more about the relationships you build. Have you spent any more time with the executives?" Harrison inquired.

I bit the inside of my cheek. I was spending more than enough time with one of them. "Ah, no ... not really," I lied.

"I know your shift ended an hour ago, so I assume that you're going above and beyond to get something for me. I look forward to your next update. Anything major to report, I want you to arrange a meeting with me rather than telling me over the phone," he said sternly.

"Umm ... OK, I will."

"Have a nice weekend Mia."

"Bye, Harrison."

CHAPTER TEN
Twenty Two

I wanted a quiet evening, but had one obstacle. I had caved in to Bri's suggestion of a roommate dinner to celebrate my birthday. I tried to say no, but she had whined for a ridiculous amount of time. She said that she had already made reservations at one of the swankiest restaurants downtown. Since it was just dinner and not a party, I agreed to it.

We were going to meet at the house before heading downtown. Pulling onto our road, I noticed their vehicles parked between the driveway and the street, but the house was dark. I parked behind Jackson's Range Rover. As I climbed the porch stairs, my anxiety grew. I prayed that Bri hadn't lied to me. I inhaled deeply before opening the front door.

"HAPPY BIRTHDAY!"

I nearly jumped out of my skin in shock. The house was full of people that I hadn't seen in months. I continued to gaze past everyone to find the four faces that were responsible for this fiasco. It was impossible through the countless red and black balloons that covered pretty much everything. Finally, I spotted Bri's face. Her eyes looked hopeful that I wasn't going to go ballistic. She dropped Trey's hand to make her way to where I stood frozen to the floor.

"Are you surprised?" she asked.

"Umm ... surprised ... overwhelmed ... I thought this was going to be a quiet evening. When did the memo change?"

"Come on Mia! It's your twenty-second birthday. You didn't really think we'd go out to dinner and that would be the end of it?" Bri whined.

"Yes, I did. In fact I was hoping for that outcome," I hissed.

Bri tugged me into the living room. "Well, too bad. Mia, there are plenty of people that want to celebrate with you. I tried to tell the guys that you wanted to have a low-key evening, but they weren't having any of it."

My jaw dropped in disbelief. "I figured you were the mastermind behind this?"

Bri shook her head, letting a smile curl at the edge of her mouth. "Nope, this was the boys. They said that you needed to be reminded of just how many people adore you."

My unease fell by the wayside. I couldn't be upset with a party. These four people were family to me. They had a long year of dealing with my bullshit, so they deserved a celebration for getting me to another one. If this was what they wanted for the evening, who was I to say no.

"Every one of those boys loves you. They'll do anything for you. I think this is their way of making up for the things they can't control, like Micah for example."

Bri bit her lip after her last comment slipped out. I shrugged, not giving it a second thought. There was truth in what she said.

"I don't deserve you guys. You're way too good to me," I admitted with a wide smile.

She rolled her eyes, securing my arm on our way over to the boys. I let out a breath of relief that I had gone with a black hi-low tank dress this morning. The guests were not in formalwear, but it was more than just casual attire. Bri turned the heads of most of the guys that we passed. She had on a dress that was cut so low it creased into her chest line. It didn't help that she drew even more eyes to that area with a diamond choker to match the dangling diamonds in her ears. The rest of her dress was sleeveless, with the same dip in the back. The part that had jaws dropping was the flare; well above the knees. Between the different cuts of the dress, her skin had little coverage. It astonished me that Trey even let her wear it. Then again, those two lived to tease each other with their bodies.

The boys had dressed for the part too. I wanted to whistle because they looked sharp. All of them had on dark-washed jeans, but it was their upper-body wear that had me beaming. Jackson styled his long locks into spikes since he was without his baseball cap. He had on a fitted button-down in midnight blue with a black tie. He rolled the sleeves to the elbows to expose his tattoos.

Shane had on a burnt orange fitted short sleeve button-up with pockets on each side. He was hot in that shirt. The tints in his brown hair that faded with the summer sun came out even more when he wore it. He kept three buttons open to reveal a white-cropped shirt underneath, which was turning the heads of quite a few girls.

Trey shocked me the most with a button-down on too. He went with a color-blocked one that was black above his pecks and gray below them. He left several of the buttons open like Shane, but was without an undershirt, which exposed the definition of his chest. His hair had grown some, so it was all over the place.

As handsome as they were on the outside, they appeared leery of what reaction I might give them. I shook my finger at each of them.

"All right, which one of your asses do I have to kick over this?"

Bri stifled a giggle as their gazes drifted to the ceiling, windows, or floor – anywhere but in my direction. I pulled everyone together for a group hug. The boys stiffened at first before returning the embrace. Stepping away, I saw wariness remained in their eyes. "I'm not going to flip out. Thank you guys."

Jackson picked me up for a huge hug. I squealed as he twirled me around before setting me down next to the shots lined up on the coffee table. Shane, Bri, and Trey joined us as we formed a circle. Jackson handed a shot of whiskey over to each of us.

With his shot held up, Jackson exclaimed, "A toast to the one of the hottest girls I know and one of my dearest friends. Happy Birthday Mia!"

Shane finished his shot and towed me in for a hug. "Happy Birthday Mia. We wanted to do something nice for you," he whispered.

I smiled shyly before turning to Trey. He dropped Bri's hand to give me a bear hug. He held me for longer than I expected before letting me go with a huge smile.

"Happy Birthday Mia. I hope you have fun tonight," he said sincerely.

I nodded as he relaxed into Bri's arms. Jackson had already filled up the shot glasses for another round. We finished them quickly. He snatched my hand after we downed our second round. He began to drag me towards some of our friends from the paper.

If the party in my stomach was any indication of my nervousness, I was in trouble. My chest constricted as anxiety swirled through me. I hadn't really been around anyone from school since I got kicked out. Seeing such a variety of familiar faces from there made me incredibly unsure of what they might say. I tightened my grip on Jackson's arm to bring him back for more shots. He whistled for the others. We did a few more rounds until my nerves calmed down.

The music from our sound system had been playing the entire time. The people that were a little tipsy before I arrived had settled into the makeshift dance floor of the living room. I clutched

Jackson's hand and headed to where our friends from the paper were dancing and drinking. My palms were sweating, so my hand slid upon his. I took a deep breath to try and remain calm.

"It'll be fine. We won't mingle long. I want to revisit the keg competition that you and Bri tend to have whenever you start drinking too much," he said, with a cocky smile.

"You're incorrigible Jackson Reid. You're always trying to start mayhem around here," I pointed out with a roll of the eyes.

He let out a hearty laugh. "Mia, I never said I was an angel. Let's go have some fun."

A song came over the speakers that made Jackson stop and pull me to his chest. He held me tight as we started to dance. He sweetly gazed at me while mouthing all the words about forgetting everything but being twenty-two. I laughed, letting him sway me back and forth as we danced. We finished dancing before heading over to talk to some of our friends from the paper. I handled it better than I expected. I suspected that my friends might have coached all the guests on what to say to me because all the conversations focused on what I was doing now. No one asked about what happened last year.

After getting reacquainted with my old friends, I went across the living room to greet another guest. I swatted Jackson for hiding him from me. I couldn't believe he invited his little brother and neglected to point him out from the very beginning. Jackson gave me an unapologetic gaze as we made our way over to him.

"Jayden! It's so good to see you. How are you?" I asked, giving him a big hug.

"Happy Birthday Mia! It's so great to see you – it's been too long. I blame this asshole," Jayden teased, poking Jackson in the ribs.

Jackson retaliated by smacking him across the head. I loved watching these two together. They had a strong love-hate relationship, but got along for the most part. They batted out a few rounds before giving me their attention.

"What's new Jayden?" I asked.

"Same shit, different day. People are always in the market to dig up something or other. I'm keeping more than busy. Of course, cutting out class would make life a hell of a lot easier," Jayden commented, glaring at Jackson.

"You're not quitting school so figure it out jackass," Jackson snapped.

"Whoa, easy tiger ... I don't think he meant them as fighting words," I chimed in.

"I've missed your humor, Mia. Jackson said things are starting to move in a better direction for you. I'm glad to hear it. If you ever need any insight on anything, don't hesitate to seek me out. You know you'll get the family and friend discount," Jayden joked with a cocky grin.

"It sounds like Jackson talks to you more than he invites you over. We might have to fix that going forward," I answered, eyeing Jackson for an explanation.

He smiled as his eyes told me to let it go. I redirected my attention back to Jayden.

"What's new twerp? Are you at least passing this semester? You have the IQ of a genius so you better have pulled your shit together. Mom and Dad will ream your ass if you fuck up another one," Jackson warned.

Jayden smirked. "I've executed a new strategy this semester that's bulletproof. I expect nothing but As by the end."

"Why are you even in school? With your talent, can't you get a job at the FBI or CIA?"

Jackson frowned at me. Jayden pretty much had his own computer hacking empire. There wasn't a person around that could catch the guy. He was without a doubt the best around at wiping any digital track. 'Ask and thou shall receive' was his slogan.

Jayden winked. "It's all about appearances Mia. I don't want to lose my street cred. Besides, no one wants to work for the government."

I laughed. "It was good seeing you Jayden. Don't be a stranger."

Jayden nodded as he eyed Jackson. They exchanged a few more brotherly jabs before Jackson whisked me away to talk to more people from the paper.

As I made the rounds socializing, the hours started to slip by and we were all tipsier. I had been dancing with Shane when it occurred to me that someone needed to stay somewhat coherent. It was necessary to avoid a real mess in the morning, or the cops showing up.

I leaned into his ear and whispered, "We need to find the others and talk about who's going to slow down. We don't want things to get out of control and piss off the neighbors."

Shane nodded and whistled to get Jackson's attention from the girl he was making out with. He reluctantly looked up. Shane beckoned him to join us. I looked around for Bri and Trey, praying they were still downstairs. I spotted them on one of the couches giving each other soft kisses while mingling with people. Jackson strolled over to us. I fell out of Shane's arms and took each of their hands to go over to the other two.

Bri raised an eyebrow as we approached. "What's up Mia?"

"We need to figure out who's going to slow down to keep an eye on things."

They agreed to the suggestion. We stared at each other with drunken eyes, not getting any closer to making a decision on who was going to sober up. Bri sat up, chewing the edge of her lip. "We're all pretty wasted at this point. Let's make this simple and just do rock, paper, scissors. Whoever loses has to stop drinking."

The rest of us nodded. I got ready with the rest of them, but they pushed me back.

Bri frowned and said, "Not you Mia. This is your party."

I took a stubborn step towards the circle. They shook their heads, not having any of it.

Jackson straightened his arm to keep me from moving forward. "Mia, the plan was to get you completely fucked up, not have you take care of the rest of us."

Shane reached for my other shoulder with a firm grip. "We're lucky you reminded us that someone needed to hold back."

I opened my mouth to protest, but Trey's hand clamped it shut. I tried to talk around his hand, but it came out as garble. Trey pulled his hand away with a drunken smile.

"Shut up Mia. It's your job to have fun tonight."

I raised my hands in defeat. They huddled together and counted down before flashing their respective choices. Jackson ended up losing. I stifled a giggle as he accused each one of them of cheating. I was about to pull him away before he went into a full-blown tantrum from Shane and Trey's teasing when two people at the door caught my eye. Since I had been seeing double on occasion, I squinted for a minute to verify who it was. Standing in the entrance of the living room was Brandon with Braden. They looked incredibly pissed off.

"Oh shit," I muttered as my face fell.

Bri caught the shift in me and glanced towards the door. "Fuck."

I led her away from the boys. "Bri, this is bad. It's obvious they know that I've been sleeping with both of them," I said, panicked.

The warm and fuzzy drunk feelings I had moments ago were starting to flee as the pressure in my head increased. Her eyes crinkled together as she looked at them.

"You were never exclusive. If they start shit, you know the boys will end it," Bri declared.

"Are you sure?" I asked worriedly.

"You know what Mia. It's time we settle the age old debate of who does this the best."

Her mouth slipped into a devilish grin as she led me towards the kegs. She whistled for Trey and Jackson and pointed to the kitchen. They saluted and continued to bicker with each other.

I giggled at them before turning to Bri with a smug smile. "Bri, I don't want to embarrass you in front of so many people."

"You think you're hot shit with your tolerance level. Why don't you put your money where your mouth is Mia?" Bri challenged.

We were almost to the kitchen when a hand came down on my shoulder. I cringed and looked over at the boys who had their eyes trained on us like tigers ready to attack. I signaled them to stand down for the time being. I slowly turned around, doing my best to keep the panic prickling through me under control.

Today would be the day that my indifference with men would come back to bite me in the ass. It's fitting for all this to go down at a packed party. It's my awesome luck working at its best.

I plastered on a fake smile and pleasantly said, "Hey, Brandon. It's good to see you again."

Brandon stared icily at me as he waited for Braden. He reached us and glared at me with the same hatred that Brandon had in his eyes.

"Braden tells me that you've been fucking him for the past several months. Is that true? I thought you were only sleeping with me this entire time?" Brandon seethed.

My eyes constricted at his vulgarity. "Yes, I was seeing Braden as well. I'm sorry if you thought we were exclusive. I thought I made it pretty clear that it was casual."

Braden looked at me with disgust and snarled, "Well, aren't you just a slut. I guess it's true what they say about the skanks from the south side."

Bri's eyes went from happily drunk to livid as she raised her hand to slap him. I stepped in to intercept her hand from hitting his face. I didn't care what either one of these assholes had to say. I used them. They were angry about it because I had no remorse. The music had stopped. Everyone was watching the drama unfold around us.

Super. This gossip is going to go real well with my expulsion. I mean, it only seems fitting that I'm also a slut on top of an academic failure. What a mess. Well, done Mia.

"I'm sorry if I hurt your feelings, but I never promised either of you anything," I reiterated.

The tension was on the rise. I pushed past them to get out of the room. My dulled senses had slowed my reaction time. My heart picked up speed when Brandon tore me away from Bri. He kept his hold on me like a vise. I struggled to get away from him as he inched us closer together before shouting towards Braden. Bri was tugging at Brandon's arms while cussing him out. The boys had seen enough and were making their way through the party guests to get to us.

"Maybe we should just fuck her like every other whore from the south side. What do you ..."

Trey's fists cut off Brandon. I wiggled away as he sunk to the floor. Bri pulled me aside as the boys surrounded them both. Blood trickled down Brandon's nose while Braden spit out pools of it. Braden scrambled away with his hands over his head as he took parting shots from Shane and Jackson. Brandon attempted to get up, but Trey stopped him with a blow to the body. His eyes were full of fury. He wasn't going to stop anytime soon. I had seen this side of him before. It scared the shit out of me. I stepped away from Bri and placed my hand on his back. His face had turned red, with his muscles bulging throughout his neck as he shook from the adrenaline. I tugged harder on his shirt for him to stop, but he kept swinging.

"Trey, that's enough!" I shouted.

"It's not enough Mia. You should never let anyone speak to you like that no matter how shitty you treated them. This asshole needs to learn some manners!" he yelled.

"Trey, please stop! He's not worth it," I pleaded.

He could easily have put Brandon in the hospital if he didn't stop soon. I looked for Shane. He'd be the only one to stop him. Shane saw the panic in my eyes and restricted Trey by locking his arms from behind. Trey tried to fight off Shane to get back to beating the shit out of Brandon, but he gripped Trey tighter. Jackson picked up Brandon and shoved him towards the front door. Bri and I stepped away from the scuffle to lean against the wall.

"Hey man, you've proved your point! You're going to scare your girl if you keep this up," Shane shouted, turning Trey to face him.

Trey snapped out of fight mode to find Bri. She stepped closer to him, assessing the blood covering his fists. Her expression transitioned from worried to tender as she placed a palm on the side of his face. His breathing started to slow as his eyes found hers.

Trey grabbed her hand and whispered, "Bri, I'm sorry. I know you hate it when I fight. I couldn't let him get away with what he said to Mia."

Bri nodded, and caressed his cheek to soothe him. His eyes drifted to me then to the ceiling. "Mia is nothing like those southy girls. Those preppy fuckers have no idea."

"Trey, I appreciate what you did but you know I don't care– "

I cut off with the sharp look he gave me. It didn't matter if I cared – he cared. Bri stood on her tiptoes to give him a gentle kiss. Her lips lingered on his for a minute before she snuggled into his side. He held her in his arms tightly as calm shifted back into his eyes.

I exhaled slowly. I glanced at the four of them and pointed towards The Cave. Before we disappeared, Jackson found the remote and cranked up the music to bring the party back to life. As we entered The Cave, I went behind the bar to grab the Patron. We had done a variety of shots throughout the night, but tequila was not one of them. After what just went down, it seemed necessary. I filled five shot glasses to the brim then slid them across the bar to waiting hands.

I raised my shot glass. "To the best friends a girl could ask for. Thank you so much for my party and everything else you do for me," I toasted.

We downed our shots. I eyed everyone and poured us another round.

Jackson raised an eyebrow. "Who's trying to cause mayhem now?"

"I've been hanging out with you too long Jackson. I'm warming up so I can kick Bri's ass in the keg stand competition that she is hell-bent on having with me," I said, shooting a wink in her direction.

Shots were exactly what we needed. After a few more rounds, we returned to the party. I lived up each moment of my birthday surrounded by a group of friends that would do anything for me.

CHAPTER ELEVEN
Last Friday Night

"Mia! Answer your fucking phone!"

I was having a real difficult time processing the words being shouted at me. I buried my head further into the cold surface beneath me, hoping that the steel rod penetrating my skull was a figment of my imagination. When that failed to work, I decided maybe rolling onto my side would help the pain in my head. As I did I found myself crashing onto the porch floor.

What the hell? Why am I outside? Have I been here all night?

I tentatively opened one eye only to have the sun blind me. My loud crash had stirred someone to my right. Before I had a chance to investigate any further, I heard my ringtone again.

"Mia! Answer your fucking phone!"

I'd answer the damn thing if I knew where it was. I hoisted myself up to a sitting position and put my head on my knees – it felt like it weighed a million pounds. There was an overly-enthusiastic construction crew thrashing into it with sledgehammers. I leaned forward and placed a hand down to stand up.

Oh shit, bad idea.

My stomach dropped to the floor. I fell to my knees and took some deep breaths to try and rake in the waves of nausea flowing through my body. After everything remained where it should, I crawled over to the porch railing to try and drag myself up. My entire body felt like it had run a marathon. I was sore everywhere. Once standing, I risked opening both of my eyes. I tried to focus, but was having difficulty just seeing straight. I stood still blinking repeatedly, trying to get the picture to focus into one solid frame rather than three that were shifting in and out.

Christ, am I still drunk?

I looked myself over to see if there were any bruises to explain how sore I was. I took comfort in the fact that one place wasn't sore. Thank God, I didn't have sex with anyone. It brought the only sense of peace to my foggy head. I heard a moan to my right – it looked like Jackson, but I wasn't sure. I stumbled my way over to the couch to peer at its occupant. It was definitely Jackson. I gripped the couch for leverage so I didn't fall on him and gave him a swift kick in the ass. He winced, presumably from the same hung-over feelings I had.

"What the fuck, Mia?" Jackson yelled, grimacing as his tone caught up with him.

"What the hell happened last night?" I shouted, cringing the second I did it.

That was an extremely bad idea. The construction crew in my head immediately switched over to chainsaws, starting to slice away parts of my brain, making each splinter count. I held my head as the sawing kicked up another notch. Jackson lifted an eyelid and then swiftly shut it and buried his head into the side of the couch.

"Shit that's bright. I don't know why we're out here," he grumbled.

My phone rang again. The repeated screams to answer it echoed through the house. I surveyed the rest of the area and gasped at the sight. People were strewn across the lawn, passed out cold, with empty red cups surrounding the entire premises. I leaned back on the railing with my fingers pressed to my head. The last thing I remembered was taking shots together in The Cave.

Why can't I remember the rest of the night?

I had gotten very drunk in the past, but had never blacked out the majority of a night. I narrowed my eyes at Jackson. It was his job to keep matters from getting out of control.

The venom in my voice was unavoidable. "Jackson, what the fuck happened last night?"

He peered over his shoulder. "What! We had a good party. It's no different from any of our other parties that we've thrown in the last few months."

Now he was starting to piss me off. Sure, we had thrown parties and had had plenty of people spend the night, but we usually managed to keep them *inside* the house rather than use them as lawn ornaments. It amazed me that the cops weren't here. The scene in front of us was one that any frat party would brag about for weeks, but here in the 'burbs – not so much.

I grabbed him by the tie and forced him to roll over and sit up. I gestured to the yard. "I'm pretty sure our parties never looked like this the following morning," I snapped.

Jackson opened his eyes to take in the surrounding scene. His eyes widened as he noticed the dozen or so people that were dead to the world on our lawn. "Shit," he mumbled, pinching the bridge of his nose.

"Well?" I asked, raising my hands.

He stared at me, totally confused. "Mia, I don't know what happened."

Before I had a chance to respond, my phone started ringing again and brought another onslaught of screams with it. Jackson gazed around, seemingly puzzled by the voices from inside.

"House meeting. Now!" I demanded.

Jackson nodded. He stood, swayed, and fell back on the couch. It reeled back some of my anger towards him.

Shit. He looks like he's still drunk too.

"I'm going to wake up the others. Please find my phone since it won't stop ringing."

Jackson waved me along. He held his stomach as he took slow breaths. I managed to get to the front door without stumbling or throwing up. I took a deep breath to brace myself for what was inside. I opened the door, not nearly prepared for the sight ahead of me. People were passed out everywhere. The entire living room had bodies on couches, the floor, and the coffee tables.

I weaved my way towards the dining room to see people passed out on the floor and table. I got to the stairs, deftly moving around the people on the landing. What I saw was more than enough, so checking The Cave or kitchen was pointless. I headed upstairs and banged on Trey's and Shane's doors. There was no movement for the first five minutes. When they finally did get up, they opened their doors with matching glares.

I motioned downstairs and flatly said, "House meeting." I looked over Trey's shoulder to see Bri burying her head underneath a pillow. "Bri, that means you too, so get your ass up."

I trotted down to the landing and shouted, "Your overnight stay is over. Everybody out!"

I didn't recognize one person that shuffled past me. As everyone cleared out, Trey, Shane, and Bri made their way downstairs. They looked just as rough as Jackson and I. Clearly, something happened last night. Everyone looked the same – hungover as shit.

I looked over to Jackson to see if he had my phone. I took it from him and shut it off without bothering to check the missed calls or voicemails. I knew someone was trying to reach me, but could only deal with one crisis at a time. All eyes were on me so I gestured to the living room so we could at least lean against something while we tried to piece together the night before. We shuffled in and collapsed onto the furniture.

"Who remembers anything about last night?" I asked.

Crickets...

We looked at each other with blank expressions and no words for several minutes.

Jackson finally stammered, "I remember a few things, but it's really blurry. I remember all of us doing shots. They got me buzzed, but I was still paying attention."

"Do you remember the last group of people you let in?"

Jackson started playing with his lip ring. "Umm ..."

My eyes narrowed. "Who was the last person you remember letting in?"

Jackson gazed around the room, looking at anything but the rest of us.

"Seriously – just tell us," I exclaimed.

"They said they knew you. They knew it was your birthday and that they were here to celebrate. They said you'd be cool with it. Plus, they had their own booze, so I didn't really see the harm," Jackson confessed.

I gulped. "Jackson, what alcohol did this group bring? Do you remember any names?" I asked uneasily.

He fidgeted with his lip ring again. "I remember hearing one of them say O'Connor."

The color left my face as I glanced at Trey. He buried his head in his hands. We knew that this had just gone from bad to really fucking bad. Shane, Bri, and Jackson watched our silent exchange.

Bri pulled Trey by his arm. "What?" she asked anxiously.

He avoided her gaze and gave me a nod to tell them.

Wonderful. I get to take the lead on this bomb-drop.

I redirected my eyes away from their inquisitive stares. They settled on the ceiling, hoping it would offer some words of encouragement. "The O'Connors are from our old neighborhood. They're bad news. We were never friends with them. We ran into them from time to time at parties, but that's about it. Their claim to fame was fucking people up at their parties." I looked at Jackson and asked, "Do you remember what they brought?"

Jackson frowned. "It was a family bucket."

I wanted to throw up, but reined it in. I glanced at Trey, who was rubbing his hands over his eyes as his face became even paler.

Jackson cleared his throat and said, "They brought in quite a few buckets. It looked like whop so I didn't question it."

I gulped with the plural mention of buckets. This was worse than I had thought.

"How would have they have even known there was a party?" I asked.

Bri's face turned red as she dropped her gaze to the floor. I stared at her with wide eyes.

"Umm ... I may have posted it on Twitter and Facebook after I got drunk," she confessed.

I put my head in my hands. We had just drank God-knows-what from the O'Connors. Today couldn't get any worse. That was when Bri's phone started ringing. She retrieved her cell from her sweatshirt pocket and gave us an apologetic look as she answered.

"Hello? Oh ... hey ... yeah, Mia's here."

Bri gestured the phone in my direction. I grabbed it with a raised eyebrow.

"Hello?"

"Why haven't you answered your phone or returned any of my messages?"

Chase was shouting so loud that I had to hold the phone away from my ear.

"What's the problem?" I asked, utterly irritated.

"I had two servers and a bartender call in sick. Can you and Bri cover today? I don't ask for your help often Mia, but I really need you today," Chase asked tersely.

All I wanted to do was crawl into a hole and die, but I couldn't say no to Chase. We never asked for favors from one another. I had to be his last resort.

"I guess. When do you need us by, and for how long?" I asked.

"I need help for the entire afternoon and part of the night. Can you be here by one?"

I glanced at the clock on the DVD player. It would be tight, but we could pull off being there within the hour. Everyone was staring at me with curious eyes.

"Yeah, we'll be there," I confirmed.

"Good. Bye."

Chase hung up. I just stared at the phone. That was the most we had spoken to each other in three years. How we managed to live together for thirteen years still boggled my mind. Every conversation throughout that time was like the one we had just had – short and detached. There was no way of knowing we were family without asking. The sad part was I had no memories of my parents. My first memories were full of fear and solitude. If Trey's mom had forgone extending a welcome to the whole neighborhood, my childhood would've been much worse. She introduced her family to me on my first day. At least that was what she told me, anyway. I struggled to recall a lot from that time in my life, which that was a separate issue in itself.

The only reason Chase tracked me down was because Bri and I had helped around the bar in high school. He probably went through his entire phonebook before he considered us. Whenever I had helped him in high school, it meant him taking a huge risk, but it never seemed to bother him. He had an attitude towards life that puzzled me. It was as if he went through his life going through the motions, not ever truly participating in it. It terrified me that living all those years with him had more than likely had an impact on my own beliefs.

I moved out from under his roof the day after I turned eighteen. It made my senior year of high school remarkable. I enjoyed every second of that year without a thought of Chase and how shitty he had made my entire childhood. He was never mean to me, but he isolated me in such a way that it seemed like there was something wrong with me. It was the negligence, coupled with the obvious dislike that made me want to be as far away from him as possible. He never displayed any love for me, but I loved him regardless of how strained our relationship was with each other.

I brought myself out of thinking about my fucked up relationship with Chase and I handed Bri's phone back to her. I had no remorse for including her in the misery that my next ten hours promised to be. In reality, I needed her to be there with me, so it was almost a blessing for Chase to request her.

"Your penance for broadcasting our party, which led to all of us not knowing what happened for the majority of the evening, has earned you a day of working at the bar."

Bri looked at me as if I couldn't be serious. I glared daggers at her to drive my point home. She shuffled out from underneath Trey and made her way to the stairs. Trey was unable to hide his shock. He knew firsthand what the relationship was like between Chase and I. I gave him a subtle headshake not to dwell on it. Bri blew past it without asking why I agreed to help him. I doubted that it would come up later. Between keeping up with customers and preventing our heads from falling off, we'd have little room to get into a heart-to-heart.

I stopped on the landing, peering back at the boys. "You guys are responsible for getting this place cleaned up. If time allows, try to find out what's in that bucket."

Trey grimaced, but nodded. Jackson and Shane remained still.

We got ready quicker than normal. Time was a luxury we no longer had, so I showered in the boy's bathroom while Bri showered in ours. We exited our rooms in faded, torn jeans and white tank tops displaying the O'Reilly's signature mark, with our hair pulled back and donning oversized sunglasses. She looked as bad as I felt, and she returned the same amused expression. I laughed and winced when it hit my head. Bri rolled her eyes as we walked downstairs. On our way to the door, Trey sat up showing concern.

"Are you sure you guys are OK to drive?"

I tilted my head to the side to give him my death stare. He knew the expression well enough not to argue with it. Bri went over to give him a kiss before meeting me at the door.

"If you need an extra bartender, give me a call," Trey offered as we walked out.

We flew down the interstate in silence. Our hangovers had us in our own personal hells. The thought of even trying to have a conversation wasn't on either of our minds. Bri kept her eyes shut with her head against the window as she massaged her temples. I wanted to do the same thing, but the car wasn't going to drive there on its own. We got to the bar shortly before one. Chase took one glance at us and shook his head. I held up a hand not even wanting to hear any of his bullshit. It took everything in my power not to flip him off and turn around.

Chase can fuck off for all I care. No 'hello' or 'how have you been', not that I'm surprised, but the least he can do is let us walk in without fucking judging us.

His bar was pretty basic. After walking through the front door, there were booths that lined the walls, with tables scattered throughout the rest of the area. There were sections that Chase had arranged for pool and darts. The jukebox was near the bar, along with a popcorn machine. The bar was circular and by the back wall with a small path around it, and a walkway through the center to make it easy to get around. The register was in the middle facing towards the cut-out window on the right side of the wall that allowed you to see into the kitchen.

There was a door in the middle that led to the kitchen, which was to the right and a supply room was on the left. Beyond that area, there was the back door that dumped you into an alleyway, where I usually parked. Chase's truck was usually back there as well, since he had turned the second level of the building into his apartment.

We grabbed two aprons from the supply room then propped ourselves behind the bar to wait for people to start coming in for their afternoon fix. By happy-hour, there was very little room to move around with the amount of people that came in for the drink specials. I cringed at the thought, and prayed a regime of water and Excedrin would be enough to keep me going. I glanced at Bri – she had her head in hands. I grabbed two glasses and filled them with water. I squeezed her shoulder before placing the glass in front of her with some tablets.

"Take these. It's not going to make it go away completely, but it should help."

"How do you know?" Bri asked, pulling her arms from her head.

"I took some before hopping in the shower. It's starting to work. Don't get me wrong. There is still a sledgehammer pounding through my skull, it's just less intense."

Bri shrugged as she popped them in her mouth and took down half of her water. "A bar is the last place anyone should be when they're this hungover. I'd rather walk through the fires of hell with gasoline all over me than be anywhere near alcohol," she griped.

I gave her an empathetic nod. "Thanks for doing this Bri. I really do appreciate it."

She smirked. "It was a bitchy move to rope me into this but don't worry about it."

There wasn't any more time for chitchat. More customers started coming in and we were busy taking orders and pouring drinks. The first whiff of hard liquor made my stomach feel like it had ate itself then up-chucked it all in one motion. I was lucky my gag reflex was solid. I looked over at Bri on the other end of the bar as she mixed her first drink. Her naturally tan skin was green. We caught each other's miserable eyes. Today was going to be a very long, painful day.

CHAPTER TWELVE
Trouble

We had been at it for two hours before catching a lull in the customers coming in. I took advantage of it by washing glasses behind the bar. Bri was verifying that everything was in stock for the night crowd. She was inspecting our supply of Jack Daniels at the other end of the bar when she gasped loudly. I glanced over my shoulder to see what the big deal was. Bri was stumbling her way back towards me with her hands to her eyes and rubbing them as if to clear her vision. I couldn't figure out why, so I went back to the dirty bar glasses.

"Sweet Baby Jesus! God's gift to women just walked in," Bri said hoarsely.

I groaned. "I've known Trey my entire life. Do you really have to refer to him like that?"

Bri turned me to face the front door. I tossed my rag on the bar and looked around. "I wasn't talking about Trey. I was talking about that fine specimen of a man," she whispered.

My breath caught as my eyes absorbed Ethan. He was in torn jeans and a white button-up shirt with the sleeves rolled up to show off his tattoos. My pulse quickened when he gave me a crooked smile. He motioned to an area of tables to the right of the bar; silently asking if anywhere was OK to sit. I nodded and indicated I'd be over in five to take his order.

His eyes lingered on me before he settled at a table. The fire that typically burned inside of me whenever he was around was on the move. I swallowed hard with the realization that this really was about to happen. This afternoon was about to wreak even more havoc for me than our times together at the office. I had gotten lost in his looks, and my inability to fight it today meant that I failed to remember Bri was watching us. She arched a brow. When I remained silent, she forced me to face her.

"That's Ethan," I said, feigning indifference.

Bri glanced at him and then back at me with cartoon-character-like speed. "That's Ethan? As in the Ethan you work for now, Ethan?" she asked.

I nodded while lightly chuckling. I could tell Bri wasn't as amused by the hardness in her eyes.

"What you said before was the same thing I thought when I saw him for the first time."

She giggled. "Who wouldn't react that way around someone as gorgeous as him? I've never seen anyone that beautiful. It's making me reconsider polygamy and open relationships."

"I can't believe you said that out loud."

Her lips curled into a twisted grin. "I can't help it. He's fine with a capital 'F'. It wouldn't matter if I made a pass at him. He seems to have eyes for only one person in here."

I looked around to see who else was here. When I had looked before, there was no one under the age of fifty. There had to be someone new in here for her to make that comment. A small pit formed in my stomach, wondering who might have caught his eye.

Bri rolled her eyes as she playfully knocked at my head. "I'm talking about you, you idiot. He hasn't stopped staring at you since he figured out that it was you behind the bar."

"Whatever," I retorted, throwing my dishrag at her.

"The looks you two were exchanging are enough to make me want to put the fire department on standby. You better go over and take his order before the bar spontaneously combusts," she remarked.

I grabbed my order pad and made my way over to his table.

"Hey Ethan, what brings you down here today?" I asked.

I wanted to slap my forehead at my own stupidity. Until now, my face had remained crimson-free, but suddenly I flushed scarlet. His lips twitched at the corners to form a grin that flashed his gorgeous dimples.

"Hello Mia. I was putting in a few hours at the office. I stopped in to get something to eat before heading home." He raised an eyebrow at the note pad in my hand. "I'm surprised to see you here. I wasn't aware you had another job."

He kept his eyes on me with their usual intensity. My heart raced ahead while other parts of my body joined the sensation party that it seemed to throw whenever I was this close to him. His eyes had already given my body a once over. After spending far too much time on my cleavage, he settled on my lips. He brought his tongue out to graze his bottom lip. I started to come apart watching his tongue gently caress his lip as if he was trying to tease me.

"Oh, this isn't another job. This is my uncle's bar. He's short-staffed, so I'm here to help. Umm ... the Juicy Lucy is the best thing on the menu. It's what I would recommend if you want to make your virgin trip here an unforgettable experience."

I did not just say that out loud. Why, God? Someone please shoot me now.

Ethan chuckled, and who could blame him. Officially embarrassed, I looked away from his face to notice he had folded his menu up. His eyes danced with amusement across his face.

"It's already unforgettable. I'll go with the Juicy Lucy and a beer."

Still mortified, I jotted down his order without looking at him. Irritation flooded through me as he continued to laugh at my expense. "What are you laughing at?"

Ethan stopped chuckling and crinkled his brow, apparently intrigued by my outburst. "It's different seeing you away from work, or listening to you for that matter. I was laughing because ... well, you're definitely straightforward with your thoughts," he answered.

I rolled my eyes. "You look as different out of a suit as I'm sure I do out of a skirt."

Ohmigod! I said that out loud too. What's wrong with me?

I tried to improvise by motioning to his tattoos. Ethan bit his lip to hold back laughing any harder. His gaze ran up and down my body with no shame. He had me tingling everywhere. I wished it were just the two of us in here, with zero chance of being interrupted when we tore each other's clothes off.

"You look different in jeans and a tank top. Younger but more relaxed." Ethan paused, and gestured to his tattoos. "These are a happy addiction. Do you have any?"

His eyes penetrated mine with thoughtfulness behind them. I needed to get away from him and his sexy ... his sexy ... well – sexy everything. Every part of me was on carnal overdrive, with the only goal in mind being hot and sweaty sex. It was probably because my body was struggling in general. Tossing Ethan into the equation was a bit more than I could handle. The construction crew in my skull reminded me of their presence as my head started to pound again.

I ignored his question and asked, "Uh, what kind of beer did you want with your burger?"

"Miller Lite on tap if you got it."

"We do. I ... uh ... I should get your order in," I stuttered.

"Sounds good, I'll be here," Ethan replied, waving a hand in the air around him.

I walked to the kitchen window to get his order to Chase. Bri's eyes bored into me every step of the way. After his order was in, she ushered me to the other end of the bar. Bri took us as far away from Ethan as she could. My head pounded even more while the rest of my body burned to be next to him a little longer.

"Mia, you are *so* in trouble," she commented, notably concerned by her tone.

"I took his order and made small talk. That's all."

I tried to sound nonchalant but failed miserably. I massaged my temples to subdue the pain, which was only increasing with the situation at hand.

"Seriously, don't lie to me," Bri scolded.

I opened my mouth to defend myself, but her annoyed expression cut me off.

"If there weren't people in here, you'd be across the table screaming each other's names."

I shut my eyes from her critical gaze. She was not helping with the sledgehammers beating down in my head. Bri forced my eyes open before fidgeting with her necklace. She glanced at Ethan and then over to me, muttering under her breath.

"You're imagining things. Is there an attraction there? Yes. It's harmless."

Her lips became a thin line as her fingers drummed across the bar. "God Mia, please tell me you're not that dense. Actually, I know you're not, so just stop. The looks you were exchanging could be the sole cause of global warming. I think Antarctica just slipped into the ocean."

I scoffed. "You're talking crazy Bri."

She looked at me, not buying a lick of what I was saying. Bri appeared beyond irritated, judging by the crease in her forehead. She massaged the area with her fingers and opened and closed her mouth several times before continuing her rant. "Am I? Are you two like this at his office? It's blatantly obvious you want to screw each other. I can only imagine what you're like around him for eight hours a day."

"I don't see him that much at the office," I disputed.

I paused to verify that our tables were good, with no new customers to serve. My eyes lingered over Ethan's area before going back to Bri.

"I still think you're in trouble. I wanted to fan myself while watching you two. The sexual tension spoke volumes. And don't even get me started on the silent talking you do when you ogle each other," she persisted.

I dismissively rolled my shoulders, but Bri was resolute in her opinion. She brought my face into her hands to force me to see the seriousness deep within her green eyes. "Mia, I know you have a lot riding on being there. He literally is the last person that you can even think about getting naked with right now," Bri pointed out.

Before I had a chance to respond, Chase hollered from the kitchen that my order was ready. I shuffled away from her to grab a glass and set it under the Miller Lite tap. With his order in hand, I grabbed his beer and headed over to his table. I took a deep breath to gather myself before attempting round two with Ethan.

I strung out my approach so I could appreciate him from afar. He had a patch of exposed skin that was visible from the few buttons he had left open. I caught a glimpse of a tattoo but nothing definitive. My eyes trailed across the tattoo to his muscular arms then down his torso. I was beyond interested to know whether it was a six-pack or eight-pack underneath that shirt. Every part of him had definition so my money was on an eight-pack. Everything south of me clenched tightly, wanting to satisfy the ache he created. I gave my head a quick shake to get myself back into a state of mind that would allow me to articulate a simple sentence. With this hangover, it took greater effort than usual.

"Sorry about the wait on your beer."

Ethan set his phone down and gazed at me with a dimpled grin. "It's no trouble at all. I could tell you had stuff to deal with at the bar." He motioned to where Bri was watching us. He raised an eyebrow, displaying his curiosity as she stared at us unashamed.

"Umm ... yea ... something like that. Enjoy your food," I responded, fiddling with my apron.

Ethan tilted his head as a softness entered his eyes. "Mia, this is a little forward but I was wondering if you wanted to join me. I enjoyed talking with you the other night."

My heart surged from his invitation. Every part of me longed to sit with Ethan all afternoon. I closed my eyes to push those feelings away. After my pulse had slowed down, I opened my eyes to answer him. He looked at me with hope spread across his face.

"It's a nice thought but I really can't."

My voice had more sadness to it than I was expecting. I saw the disappointment in his eyes. I twinge ran through my chest at his expression. Ethan picked up his beer and took a long drink.

"It's not that I don't want to or anything. We're already short-staffed and to be quite honest I'm not ready to attempt food yet," I admitted.

"I take it you had a good time last night?" he asked.

My face flushed as I recalled last night, this morning, and what were now the lost hours of my twenty-second birthday. "It was a great night. I'm certainly feeling it today."

Ethan raised an eyebrow. "Any special occasion, or was it another typical college party?"

"Actually, it was my birthday yesterday and my friends wanted to celebrate it," I snapped.

Christ, he pushes my buttons. I can feel the rainbow of emotions around him in a matter of minutes. I don't like it.

"I was wondering why you didn't say anything yesterday," he

said, grabbing his burger.

"How did you know it was my birthday?" I asked, picking at my cuticles.

"Background checks ... they give us all sorts of fun details like that when we run them."

Ethan took a bite of his burger. His face spread into a satisfied grin. I wished it would erase the idiotic feelings soaring through me. I'd stammered out some of the stupidest questions to the guy, but the latter was another one to add to the list.

"I'll let you enjoy your food while it's still hot," I mumbled.

"I hope you had a wonderful birthday," Ethan said sincerely before sipping on his beer.

"Thanks. I'll ... ah ... check in on you later."

I returned to the bar with Ethan at the forefront of my mind. Bri eyed me as I busied myself with washing the glasses again. She handed a drink over to the gentleman in front of her and took his money. As she walked past me to get to the register she made no effort to contain her growing frustration.

"Trouble," she muttered.

I checked on Ethan a few more times while he ate his food. I held back from lingering and kept our conversations brief. There was no need to add any more fuel to the fire in Bri's thoughts. Once he settled the tab, he got up to head out. Before exiting, he turned around with a wicked grin.

"Thanks for lunch Mia. You were right. The Juicy Lucy was delicious. It was an unforgettable virgin experience!" Ethan shouted.

Everyone in the bar started laughing. It utterly mortified me. Ethan knew it as he walked out. Bri thought his entire departure was hilarious and took no shame dropping to her knees in laughter. She remained on the ground giggling hysterically until tears dripped from her eyes. I shot her a glare before going over to his table to clean it up.

If I had thought that the day couldn't get any worse, I was wrong. The night crowd rolled in. They were a more rambunctious group than I had remembered. A handful of patrons lingered around, but Chase told us it was fine to take off. We were preparing ourselves to head out for the night when a fight broke out at the front of the bar. I glimpsed upfront only to regret ever acknowledging that anything was wrong.

Great. The Fitzpatricks. This is going to get ugly.

A younger group had come in earlier and took up residency in the Fitzpatrick's booth. It was an unspoken understanding between everyone in this area. When they walked in and their booth had patrons in it, the expectation was that whoever occupied it moved immediately. Here in lied the problem this evening – the group occupying it tonight refused to move. I knew right off the bat that they weren't from around here. They were definitely from one of the northern suburbs. The Fitzpatricks didn't waste any time in letting them know exactly where they were and whom they were dealing with.

As the fighting intensified, knives suddenly came out. I glanced over my shoulder to look for Chase, but he remained in the kitchen. These kids weren't backing down. I wasn't sure if it was the liquid courage or their sheer stupidity, but they were getting right back in the Fitzpatricks' faces. That was when the eldest Fitzpatrick had obviously had enough. He pulled out his gun and fired a shot across the bar at an empty table with beer bottles cluttering it. The sound echoed off the walls as screams filled the bar. My heart thumped in my chest as the lump in my throat restricted me from swallowing. I had to keep it together for Bri. I pushed her around the bar, into the walkway, and out of sight.

"Mia, what the hell is going on?" she asked.

I brought a finger to my mouth indicating to keep quiet. I motioned for her to duck down with me. She slumped to the floor with terrified eyes. I squeezed her hand with everything I had. She opened her mouth to say something but I put my hand over it. We heard chairs thrown and threats shouted while the rest of the patrons scrambled for the door. The scuffling of men grew louder by the minute, with more shots being fired. I kept looking for Chase, but he hadn't come out to stop it. He never seemed to care when shit like this went down in the bar. He let it play out, which baffled me. Bri started squirming next to me. I dug my nails in her hand to get her to stay still.

"Be quiet Bri. Don't say a word," I warned.

She looked at me wide-eyed and terrified. I didn't blame her since this had never happened when she helped out in the past. This was nothing new to me since I had once lived above it. One of the Fitzpatricks fired a shot to the front of the bar. It took out one of the bottles above us. Bri started shaking uncontrollably, tears streaming down her face. I stopped breathing and glanced behind me to see if it was enough to pull Chase away. He didn't have tolerance if the violence affected his liquor supply. He emerged in the kitchen window, clearly pissed.

I stood up to see if he was going to do anything. He looked at me signaling not to make a move yet. The Fitzpatricks had scared off the kids that were dumb enough to taunt them. They were the only people left in the bar. They looked at me with slick grins. Bri started to rise, but I shoved her down immediately. Her eyes continued to water. I ignored it, keeping my focus up front. They strode to the bar and gestured for a drink. I glanced at Chase to see what he wanted me to do. He motioned to serve them. I walked around the bar and grabbed a handful of glasses to fill them up with Guinness.

He's such a fucking asshole. Why does he let shit like this happen without a care?

I took a deep breath to push every ounce of my fear away. I was able to handle this. I knew that much from years of experience. The four of them smirked when I slid their full glasses of beer in front of them.

"Good to see you again Mia. It's been too long," the eldest commented.

He typically did the talking for the rest of them. The other three gave a nod, with one of them licking his lips. Acid crept up my throat. I fought the urge to throw up.

"It has been, but so is life. You get busy, you know," I said coolly.

"It does get busy, especially in our line of work," he said with a villainous grin. He looked towards the empty kitchen window and hollered, "Sorry for the mess Chase. We'll take care of the damages. Those preppy motherfuckers needed a lesson on their whereabouts."

Chase appeared in the window with a tight smile. "No worries. If you guys don't mind finishing your beers, I'm going to close up."

The Fitzpatricks raised their arms, feigning disappointment, but didn't argue with Chase. They downed the rest of their beers and tossed a few twenties on the bar. The elder Fitzpatrick paused before walking out the door. I held my breath, I just wanted them to leave already. During that entire exchange, I had refrained from looking at Bri because I didn't want them to acknowledge she was here. They seemed to have missed that much when they started their brawl.

"Don't be a stranger anymore Mia. We know you aren't in school so you should pay the old neighborhood more visits," he said on his way out the door.

I gulped down the rising acid in my windpipe. As they left, I wrung my hands out to stop the inadvertent shaking that had started at some point. I rounded the bar to get Bri. She had curled her knees up with her chin on her legs as tears streamed down her face. I crouched down and wiped the tears from her eyes.

"Let's go. It's over now."

She looked at me with raw eyes, completely terrified. I sat down next to her and wrapped my arm around her shoulder. "I'm so sorry Bri. I know you're scared, but it'll be OK. Let's just go home," I said, coaxing her to get up with me.

"How are you so OK right now?" she asked, rising to her feet.

She gazed at me, taking deep breaths. Once her breathing had evened, her face flared with anger. I tossed my apron underneath the bar, picked up my purse, and grabbed my car keys. Bri met me at the door where she discarded her apron and grabbed her purse. We made our way through the back and over to my car.

"This isn't the first time this has happened, is it?" she snapped after a few minutes.

"No, it's not. It's life down here. You get used to it. The gunshots are nothing new."

As we approached my car, Bri yanked at my arm to get me to stop. I turned to see the frustration emanating from her.

"It's one thing when you hear them outside in the distance. It's an entirely different matter when they're fired right above you. These are the types of people you're willingly involving yourself with now. Are you insane?"

I removed her hand from my arm and unlocked my car. She got in on her side in a huff. "I'm not crazy. The two things are totally different," I contested.

Bri banged her hand against the window. "They aren't different. It's the same. It's already dangerous, and now you have a guy mixed up in all of it. This was a bad idea to begin with, but now its just trouble."

I didn't argue with her. She had had more than enough tonight. Bri glared at me for an answer, but I sealed my lips and started the car. My body was close to falling over as it worked to find some calm. I was beginning to see the numbness in a new light, because at least that was easier to deal with than the rollercoaster of emotions I had gone through today. It was exhausting jumping from one extreme to the next.

CHAPTER THIRTEEN
No Time To Rewind

After being around Ethan outside of work, I hated admitting Bri was right, but she was. He was trouble for me. It was becoming a bigger problem every day. No matter how much I told myself I had to stay away from him, there wasn't a way around it. I knew almost anyone would evaluate this situation and point out the obvious – quit. I saw Bri bite her tongue daily on that one. Call it stubbornness, call it stupidity – call it whatever the hell you want, but that wasn't an option for me.

I kept giving myself that mental pep talk while lounging around early Monday morning. Our Indian summer was starting to slip away, with only a few more real warm days left. Since the temperature had dropped lower than expected, I had bundled up in sweats and a hoodie. The chill ran throughout the house. I was up early, but that was nothing new. I figured a cup of coffee before getting ready for work would be a good start to the day. If time allowed, I'd go for a run to extinguish the extra energy. It would help push Ethan out of my head. I hopped along the icy floor with my phone. I turned to go down the set of stairs leading to the kitchen but stopped dead in my tracks.

Micah.

It had been almost a year but there he was in the flesh. He was in his faded jeans that I used to love on him. He had a V-neck T-shirt on that clung to his muscles. His olive skin appeared to be darker than it was the last time I saw him. His sandy blonde hair was longer and under a backwards baseball cap. His chiseled face had stubble giving him that five o'clock shadow appearance. I refrained from looking into his midnight blue eyes. Micah seemed the same in many ways, but so very different in others. I began to crumble as the inner pain spread through me.

I moved closer to the wall to keep from falling over as my hand flew to my mouth to prevent me from screaming or crying. My heart took off along with my head as it spun like a top; my feelings beginning to pour out of me. My poor brain was already on empty – now, it had to process a whirlwind of emotions. I desperately tried to catalogue each one as they passed through my head and heart in a vain attempt to pick one and settle on it – shock, anger, sadness, loneliness, hatred, anguish, love, and finally – rage.

I stood there staring at him for what felt like hours. Regaining my composure, I readjusted my direction and flew past him. I glanced over to him and motioned to the front door. It took a huge amount of effort not to look at him too closely. The last thing I needed was to look into his eyes and feel even more. Micah held up his hands, asking for just five minutes.

"Get out!" I seethed.

"Mia, we have to talk. You have to hear me out," he pleaded.

Is he serious? He can't be. After all this time, he thinks a simple chat is going to make any difference to me whatsoever?

I let out a long, deep breath. Once I was slightly calmer, I pointed to the door again. He remained on the couch shaking his head. "Micah, so help me God, I'll grab you by the balls and drag you out of here if you don't leave right now," I snarled.

The fragile hold I had on myself was slipping away by the second. My veins were on fire as the blood boiled through them.

"No, we need to talk. There are things you need to know," Micah reasoned, sternly.

I stared at the ceiling and prayed for some divine intervention, or else I knew it was going to end in some serious bodily damage. I was currently in a state of mind that only saw violence as a means of resolution. God didn't disappoint. An epiphany washed over me. If I could just get to my car, I could be rid of him. My keys and shoes were upstairs but that I could work around. I had shoes in my car and could hot-wire the damn thing to get the hell out of here.

"Fine, but you're not welcome in my home. If you want to talk to me, you're going to do it on the porch," I said, narrowing my eyes.

Micah stared at me, trying to discern if I was serious. I raised my eyebrows and tossed my hands to the side.

"I just want you to take five minutes to hear me out," he reiterated, walking outside.

With his back to me, I pulled the front door shut and sprinted towards my car. I reached it but heard him approach. I quickly pulled my door open, but he slammed it shut. I whipped around, making the mistake of looking him square in the eyes.

As we stared at each other, more emotion coursed through me. A degree of happiness surfaced as Micah looked into my eyes and saw how much heartbreak he had caused me. He could see the hatred that now replaced any love I ever had for him. I saw the deep blue that I had loved, but I saw pain and heartbreak in his eyes that matched my own.

Fuck! I don't want to see that.

Frustrated beyond reason, I threw my hands in the air and hastily moved out of his reach. The wet dew of the grass, coupled with the cold breeze, had me shaking. I reached the front of my car and pulled up my hood before clutching my arms around myself for warmth. Micah took a cautious step towards me, but I shook my head. He stopped and braced his hands around his neck. He squinted at me with a longing in his eyes.

"Mia, I just want to talk to you. Did you read my letter? I came here to explain things to you," he pleaded.

"Explain! Explain what, Micah?" I shouted.

He attempted another step to close the gap, but I held up my hands. He hesitated at first, but then stepped back with his arms crossed. His eyes met mine as he tried to find some access to my tender side. My eyes darted to the ground in response.

"I don't think there are enough words in the English language that could help you explain anything that I'm going to be able understand about last year. I read your letter but stopped halfway through because it made me physically sick to continue reading how much you *apparently* love me."

Micah started to open his mouth, but I silenced him with a finger. "It's beyond too late for your side of the story. You *left* me. You just took off that night not to be seen or heard from in nearly a year," I yelled as the first tears broke free.

The last thing I wanted to do was cry. His eyes saddened. He tried moving again.

"No, don't you fucking come near me!" I screamed.

I held myself even tighter as my shaking amplified with the rising levels of anger charging through me. Micah flinched. His eyes glistened as he watched me.

"You have done enough damage to me. I really want you to go now. I don't want to hear anything you have to say because it's never going to make a difference to me!"

"I still love you, Mia. I never stopped loving you," Micah said quietly.

Love me. Is he serious? I just might go insane if he tells me he loves

141

me again.

I scoffed. "You don't love me. Quite frankly, I'm not sure you ever did."

"You know I did. I'll always love you," he insisted.

He's trying to make me go crazy. It's the only explanation.

Micah started to move. It forced me to take steps away from him. I was practically in the neighbor's yard at this point. His face fell as I continued to keep a distance.

"If that is what you call love, then I want no part of it," I cried.

Micah stared at me, having the audacity to seem surprised. My face flushed as my temper hit its boiling point.

"What we had wasn't love. You don't abandon people that you love. You certainly don't destroy people that you love. And you've accomplished both with me!" I yelled.

Micah gritted his teeth as his temper rose. "If you'd just let me explain instead of cutting me off or running away every five seconds."

"YOU BROKE MY FUCKING HEART AND DESTROYED ME ALL IN ONE NIGHT. WHO DOES THAT? I MEAN, IT WASN'T ENOUGH THAT YOU BROKE MY HEART BUT YOU HAD TO DESTROY MY FUTURE. DESTROY MY LIFE! WHO DOES *THAT*? THEN TO TOP IT ALL OFF YOU LEFT WITH NO EXPLANATION WHATSOEVER. YOU LEFT ME WITH NOTHING!"

Huh. So this is what insanity feels like.

Tears started streaming down my face. I started to shake even more. I broke my gaze from him to stare at the ground. I took a deep breath to calm down. After a moment, I refocused my eyes, surprised to see him suddenly enraged.

Seriously! He's angry with me for pointing out the obvious. You've got to be kidding me!

"I've moved on. It's over between us. I don't want you around here or me."

His face became hard, his eyes, resolute. "You can't make me stay away. I have friends that live here too."

"Yes, I can. If you think for a second that anyone here is going to let you come around me, then you're sorely mistaken. A lot has changed. The people you think are your friends want nothing to do with you," I retorted, rolling my eyes.

Micah's mouth slipped into a smug smirk. "Whatever. You're being over-dramatic as usual. Some things never change," he hollered.

Motherfucker! Over-dramatic? I'll give him over-dramatic.

I heard movement in the house. I paused to look over my shoulder to see Bri and Trey standing on the porch. I forgot Trey's room was right above where I had just been screaming at the top of my lungs. I glanced around to ensure that a bigger audience wasn't behind me. The last thing I needed was to have the neighbors watching and wondering why I was carrying on like a crazy person.

I gazed over at Bri. It surprised me. Her face was full of rage. It brought a new meaning behind the phrase 'if looks could kill'. I glanced at Trey. He stunned me too. Trey had his fists curled with hardness in his eyes. I gave Micah my attention again. He stood cockily, goading me into fighting with him some more.

"Leave, or I'll go get someone to make you leave since you can't take a hint," I snapped.

"No, I think I'll stick around and catch up with people," he said icily.

That was all it took for Bri to become unhinged. She ran across the yard and went at him, swinging her arms repeatedly on his chest. Micah didn't move an inch.

"You fucking bastard. Why can't you just leave? Haven't you done enough to her? Just fucking leave already!" she screamed.

Trey was on her heels to drag her away. He let her get a few good swings in but then started to pull her arms behind her. Trey tugged her into him and kissed her head to cool her down. He looked over at me and then down again at Bri. I knew my face held nothing but defeat. I was on empty, and about to lose it if I had to endure Micah any longer. Bri shook with fury, so it was easy to determine where her thoughts lay. Trey turned to Micah.

"You need to go. You're not welcome here," Trey said quietly.

Micah's jaw dropped as he stared at Trey in disbelief. Those two had been best friends since they were able to walk. His reaction didn't surprise me. I prayed that he listened to Trey and got in his car before this did come to any more blows.

"We were boys ... you and me ... and you're just going to toss me out to stand on the same side of the girl you're fucking," Micah spouted off.

Shit. He knows better than to antagonize Trey. Fucking idiot.

Trey swiftly moved Bri to the side and swung at Micah all in one maneuver. Micah was prepared for the first blow and blocked it, but Trey was the bigger, more experienced fighter between the two of them. He took several more swings. Micah was on his back within seconds. Trey got a few more blows to his head and sides before letting up. He pulled Micah off the ground and shoved him towards his Mustang.

"That's my girlfriend, you asshole. If you had stuck around, you'd know that. You never fucking deserved Mia and what you did to her is unforgivable – to all of us. Now, for the last time, get the fuck out of here!" Trey bellowed.

Micah started spitting out the blood that had pooled in his mouth. He glanced at me before opening his door. The fire in his eyes made me gaze away. I knew that look. He'd be as relentless with this as he had been with every other thing I had watched him pursue over the years.

"This isn't over Mia. I'll find a way to make you hear me out," he assured.

I flipped him the bird as he started his car. He tore out into the street, leaving a cloud of dust behind him. I walked past Bri and Trey to take a seat on the front steps. My arms wrapped around my knees as my eyes closed. I was physically and mentally exhausted. As Trey walked up the stairs, he placed a hand on my shoulder and gave it a squeeze before going into the house. Bri shuffled down next to me and leaned her head against my shoulder.

"Are you OK?" she inquired.

I lifted my head and wiped away my lingering tears. I turned towards Bri and saw the same concern in her eyes that was there the day after Micah had disappeared on us.

"I'd be lying if I said I was fine, but the truth is that I'll live. It sucked that he showed up out of the blue, but I'm happy with the outcome," I whispered.

"You are?" she asked, shocked.

"Yeah, I am. I stood my ground. I got him to leave ... well, Trey did, anyway," I admitted.

"Umm ..." she murmured as her eyes skirted to the ground.

"Spill it Bri. You have your 'I want to ask but I don't want to because I think she'll bite my head off' face on."

She shifted her focus from the ground back to me. "Are you ever going to hear him out? I mean ... don't you think it might help ease the pain? It's clear you're still in an unbearable amount of it. I'm a little angry at myself for not seeing how much until today."

Bri did her best to prevent the sadness on her face, but it was there anyway. Her eyes glistened as she held back her tears. I knew where her thoughts were immediately. The sorrow in her voice made my guilt deepen. Micah had caused more damage to my world than he could've possibly imagined last year. What happened the night he left was across her face and the grief there was undeniable. I was barely able to look at her. It started to blend in with every other raw emotion in me. She had a horrible memory of me because of Micah's actions. She saw a side of me that I could never erase from her mind.

I knew she never thought less of me, but it was hard to have that between us. The entire ordeal brought us closer, but it was at a steep price. She needed me to be honest with her about everything I bottled up. That much was clear as she nervously bit her manicured nails.

"Bri, every day I wake up, it still hurts. There are days when it hurts more than the others, but I'm learning to live with it. I think that's part of the healing process. I had an outburst today, but I didn't break into a million pieces. I'm not breaking anymore. That's what matters the most to me."

The tears she had been holding back started to stream down her cheeks. I took her chin and shook my head. She sniffed and forced a small smile while wiping her face.

"If I let Micah back into my head, he'll make me second-guess everything. If he really is back for good, I'll get that closure with him, but it was never going to happen when we first saw each other again."

Bri stared blankly then seemed to understand. After a few minutes, I stood up to head into the house. I looked at her as she stared aimlessly across the yard.

"How much of the show did you catch?" I asked.

My lips curled into a silly grin as I gestured out to where we were standing on the lawn. She burst out laughing and followed me into the house.

"We caught almost all of it after you ran out the door. We could tell he wasn't going to leave. We knew you were hitting your breaking point, especially when you started screaming at the top of your lungs," Bri replied as we walked through the hallway and into the kitchen.

I stopped at the fridge to dig some stuff out so we could make some breakfast. Bri grabbed the toaster and tossed some bread in. I handed her the eggs and started placing bacon in a pan. The sizzle of the eggs and bacon brought some much-needed noise to our very quiet presence. I nudged her shoulder, dying to know about one thing.

"So, you're his girlfriend now?" I commented, while moving the bacon around in the pan.

Bri rolled her eyes as a soft smile spread across her face. "It's the first time he's ever called me that. He did it in a fit of rage. I'm not sure if it counts."

Bri tried to be nonchalant, but it was clear that she was beyond happy to hear him finally say it.

"It counts. If you think for a minute that he hit Micah to get him to leave me alone, you're dead wrong. Trey punched Micah because he disrespected you," I reassured.

She fished some plates out of the cabinets near her head. I laughed at her unbelieving expression. "How can you be so sure?" she asked.

"It's kind of like at my surprise party. Those assholes disrespected me. I didn't care, but Trey handles situations like that differently. He doesn't do well with anyone insulting someone he cares about. It takes a lot for him to lose his temper but disrespecting his loved ones is like his anger trigger zone. He'll flip out every time," I explained.

Bri stood in a daze before flipping the eggs. Her eyes filled with happiness when it sunk in that he loved her. I shut off the burner and tossed the bacon on a plate. She did the same with the eggs. We grabbed our breakfast and set it on the island with a pitcher of orange juice.

"It was kind of sweet to watch, and a refreshing change of pace from the train wreck I was starring in," I remarked.

"I think I'll savor the moment before I bring it up to him," Bri concluded.

After we had dished up our plates, I stared at my food for a few minutes before grabbing my fork. My extra time before work had vanished. I needed to start hustling. I wasn't sure how long Bri had been watching me, but she cleared her throat to get my attention.

Might as well just let her get whatever she needs to out. It's not like this morning could get any worse.

"What is it Bri?" I asked, rotating to face her.

"Mia, why didn't you want him to touch you?" she inquired, playing with her food.

I stared at the island. Bri was watching me, her expression thoughtful yet curious. I cracked my knuckles and focused on her. "I didn't want him to touch me because his touch has always set my body off in one direction or another. I was rarely loved as a child. When I started feeling something with him, it was more intense than what most people probably experience. You have to understand that Chase *never* hugged me. I got hugs from Micah's mom and Trey's mom, but it was different."

Her eyes saddened. Bri knew our lives were diverse, but I had never shared this part of that difference. I took a deep breath to continue with the unpleasant admission.

"As we got older, Micah would brush against me and an instant calm rushed over my body. As time went on, the calming effect made me feel safe. I'd never really had that until him."

Her expression fell even further. I looked away for a moment before continuing. "When Micah and I started dating, I experienced what it was like to be loved. As that all happened, the effect that his touch had on me changed. When I fell in love with him, his touch would ignite my body," I confessed.

Bri had given up eating. She was holding her head as she listened intently, like I was telling her a bedtime story. I smiled and said, "I didn't want to him to touch me because I don't want to know if that feeling is still there. He hurt me so badly that I can't take the chance of feeling anything safe, or burning inside me for him. I need that tie to be severed. Does that make sense?"

"It does. I knew how in love you were with him, but I didn't know his touch affected you that much," Bri admitted.

In the back of my mind, I wondered what giving into Ethan would do to me. It would probably wipe away any effect Micah had over me.

I curse the stupid universe for taunting me with that man.

She picked up her fork to take a bite, but stopped to turn towards me, with another question lingering in her eyes. I rolled mine but decided to let her get out whatever she was mulling over. "Bri, I'm going to be late. What now?" I whined.

She placed her fork on her plate and tapped her fingers along the island. "I'm sorry Mia, but I have to ask because I've been around you and Ethan firsthand. I can see what his presence does to you. You're very dismissive about it, but I can tell there's something very intense between the two of you. I'm not sure if it's lust or if you really are that connected to one another. If Micah's touch did that to you, what's going to happen when Ethan crosses that threshold?"

I blushed fiercely. Our mind-meld moments were nice, but at the moment, it was a nuisance. "What Ethan does to me without touching me, I still haven't figured out. It's much stronger than anything I had with Micah. I try my best to avoid any physical contact with him. I won't quit, but I'll admit that it's become difficult to resist. My plan is to keep my distance from him."

Bri arched an eyebrow and let out a heavy sigh. "You were right that first day Mia. The universe has a fucked up sense of humor to bring someone like Ethan into your life. Please try not to do anything stupid with him. Something tells me that only more heartbreak will lie ahead if anything happens there."

I can't argue with her there. Giving into Ethan might as well be my own self-destruct button. The problem is that my will to prevent myself from hitting it is growing weaker as each day passes, and that scares the shit out of me.

CHAPTER FOURTEEN
Wreaking Havoc

I broke every speed limit just to get to work on time, embarrassing myself as my wheels squealed to a halt in the parking lot. Several people stopped to stare. Grabbing my stuff, I ran in and out of people taking their sweet-ass time. I slid into my desk with a minute to spare. I did my best to remain focused on the tasks assigned to me. As hard as I tried, my disastrous start to the day had affected my mood anyway. I was short-tempered and flighty for most of the morning. On more than one occasion, Connor snapped his fingers at me to get me to pay attention. After a few mortifying rounds of that happening, I was able to focus on the campaign we would be proposing soon.

When Connor dismissed everyone for lunch, I went to the cafeteria to buy something to eat at my desk. I kept my ears open for anything that might help Harrison so this charade could end, but it was a half-hearted attempt. On my way out of the cafeteria, a flash of fire spread through me – Ethan was staring at me as he leaned against the wall in the hallway. As I got closer, the draw to him grew stronger. The inexplicable vibe between us was the last thing I needed to deal with today. I was already hanging on by a thread. I gave him a thin smile and continued towards the elevators to get upstairs. Ethan fell in stride with me. I sighed. He was eager to question me. It was all over his face.

"Mia, a minute," he commanded, stopping short of the elevators.

"Yes, Ethan," I answered with my temper slipping into my tone.

He bristled. "I ran into Connor. He mentioned it had been a long morning and that there might be something bothering you."

"I'm fine."

Ethan crossed his arms, clearly not buying my dismissal. I wanted to roll my eyes but refrained.

"Why is your manager worried that you might become a liability?"

"I had a bad morning. I can assure you that it won't happen again," I snapped.

Sheesh. I need to lock it up.

Ethan narrowed his eyes, not caring for that tone either. We stared at each other for several minutes. My chest compressed. I wasn't sure if it was the weight of the morning or the mystery in his eyes that pulled at me to lean into him.

"I was just asking," he pointed out.

"I'm sorry. I have no intentions of becoming a liability," I replied, feeling defeated.

"So you're not going to share what's bothering you?" Ethan pressed.

"Do I have to?" I asked with a heavy sigh.

"No, you don't have to. I was hoping you would, but your personal life is your business. It only becomes my business when you fall short around here. You've assured me that it won't happen again, so I'll let it go ... for now."

"I'm going to head back upstairs to get some work done."

"By all means, don't let me stop you."

Ethan was beyond angry with me. It stretched across every part of his face. My stomach became unsettled. I shook my arms to rid the tingling that had increased every minute of that brief interaction. I hit the stairwell begging my mind to purge him from my system with every step. It wasn't doing a very good job because my heart sank with the knowledge that I pissed off Ethan. I shoved that all to the side and opened the door to the third floor to get back to work.

Throughout the second half of the day, I did my best to wipe away my behavior from the morning. Connor and the team sensed the shift. We made significant advancements on our upcoming proposal. As we wrapped for the day, I gathered my things to head back to my desk. When I came around the corner, I saw Ethan in my chair with his legs on my desk as he took in the floor. I groaned in exasperation.

Fuck. What now?

I strode to my desk and deposited the binders in my hands. He was more than cocky in his demeanor. For once, my body steadied itself with the rage that had been lingering in my system since this morning.

"Ethan," I said, faking a smile.

"Mia," he replied, swinging his legs down.

"Did you need something before I head home for the day?"

"Nope, I happened to be up here to hear a proposal from another team. Your desk allows me to have a good view of the entire floor. I like to make sure that my employees are doing what they're being paid to do," Ethan emphasized.

The acidic tone he used sent shivers up my spine. He was here to remind me that my outburst with him earlier was far from acceptable. This was his way of warning me not to let it happen again. I had no words in response, so we sat in an awkward silence. Ethan cleared his throat to get me to look at him. His eyes had an edge to them. The pit in my stomach surfaced while the rest of my body chilled and my ire with him started to fade.

"I assume you had a better afternoon?"

His condescending expression was enough to re-fire my anger. This was a bad day for the record books. My body refused to stick with one emotion. Half of me wanted to lash out at him. The other half was ready to give in to my heady yearning.

"Yes, it was much better."

"Good. I think I've seen enough of this floor. I'll let you finish up your day."

Before leaving, Ethan gazed at me with a smug grin. I looked away. I didn't need anything else to fuck with my head.

When I got home, I avoided everyone by heading straight for my room. Not one of them tried to stop me either. I lay down with no intentions of sleeping, but it happened anyway. I woke up in the middle of the night and shimmied out of bed to turn on the lamp. Light flooded the room. I rummaged around in my laundry basket for a pair of clean pajamas.

After changing clothes, I grabbed my purse to find my phone to set an alarm. After my attitude with Ethan, he'd be paying extra attention to me. Cutting it close for a second day in a row wasn't an option. While setting my alarm, I noticed some new text messages. I gasped because there were ten of them from an unknown number. Curious, I opened the first one.

Mia you can push me away all you like, but you know we need to talk!

I groaned. If my brain hadn't still been waking up, I would've been able to put together that the messages were from Micah.

I can't believe you wouldn't even give me a chance to explain. You say you don't owe me that, but you do. I'll always be a part of

your life.

I shoved the crap on my desk to the side and situated myself on it. I rested my head against the wall to finish reading the rest of his messages.

You have no idea what this has done to me Mia. It's killed me to be away from you, my friends, and my family, but I left for you.

I squeezed my knees as anger flowed through me, and carried on to the next one.

I had no choice but to leave to find out more. Do you really believe I wanted to destroy you? I think you know me better than that. Please let me explain!

It blew my mind that he was continuing to beg for a chance to explain things to me.

Fuck! Just answer one of these texts. I refuse to walk away from you. There are things you need to know for your own good. Stop being so damn stubborn and talk to me. You're hatred is blinding you. You'll regret not hearing me out. Mark my words Mia.

I took a deep breath. I'd have to deal with him eventually, but it had to be on my terms, not his. This morning had sucked with him showing up out of nowhere.

You think this has been easy for me? You think I wanted to leave? I can't believe you're so quick to believe that I'd destroy you with no reason. If you had any idea – Fuck! I won't do this by text. You have to let me talk to you!

He sure had a pair of brass balls to act like I was out of line for shutting him down. My anger kicked up another notch. It grew with each message, but it was refreshing after keeping it at bay for most of the day.

I can't believe you acted like I never loved you. I've loved you since I was a little boy. I'll never stop loving you. You're the love

of my life. I didn't expect you to be OK with what happened, but fuck, you hurt me too by doing what you did this morning. It keeps getting worse. I can't go anywhere without someone telling me about all the guys you've slept with since I left. I didn't expect you to wait for me, but shit, you could at least talk to me.

He sure was verbose, I thought, as I read through the messages. I shook my head at the nerve he had with each new text. Maybe he was the insane one. If he thought I'd sit around and wait for him to show up with an explanation, he was off his rocker. It took months for me to start functioning somewhat normally. Once there, I had never planned to be celibate.

Are you doing this to get even? I can't figure it out. I've always protected you. I relied on you remembering that when I made the most difficult decision of my life, but fuck, both choices were shitty. Even with the choice I went with, I lost you. You don't think that broke my heart? You're acting like your heart was the only one that shattered, but mine did too. You got our friends to get through that. I fucking had no one and I came back to no one. I lost my life because I chose you. Now, you won't even hear me out.

He had elected to leave, so it flabbergasted me that he tossed *that* in my face. If he would've stuck around to explain himself, there was a possibility that neither one of our hearts would've broken, but he chose to leave me. How he ever thought he could return without matters being different was beyond me.

You didn't even give me the chance to tell you that I'm sorry. I know I fucked up your life. I'll never forgive myself for it either. I need to talk to you. My mom refused to give me your new number. That's why I showed up. After our blowout, I had to beg her to give it to me. My family never stopped caring for you and you pushed them away. My mom has always treated you like her own. She's still looking out for you. She begged me to come home

and explain myself right away, but I had to go and you need to know why. I need to explain. I'm begging Mia. Please!

My chest started to spasm with the mention of his mom. I refused to answer a single phone call from her. The anger receded a bit, as a painful ache spread everywhere. He not only messed up my life – he left me fucked up. I barely recognized myself. He did a fine job at pointing out one of the many reasons why. His mom cared for me just as much as Trey's mom, and I shut her out. I treated people horribly. The worst part was that I stopped caring when I did it. A tear started to form at the corner of my eye. This was precisely why I wanted Micah to leave me alone. He created the person I had become. I had no clue how to fix myself. I wiped away the tear and opened the final text.

I know you still love me. You don't just stop loving someone. I'm still in your heart. I know it. You can tell me what we had was never love but you're lying to yourself. You've loved me since we were kids. I'm a part of you. I know I'm still in your head. You proved that this morning. Please let me talk to you!

He was in my head, but not in a good way. I blocked his number and set my phone on my desk. The anger and the ache fought with each other as I crawled into bed. I wouldn't let him destroy me any further. I had to get my shit together. I dug for the indifference and pushed it to the surface.

The rest of the week at work went much better. Connor and Ethan paid extra-close attention to me, but I had been nothing less than perfect since Monday morning. I focused more on getting information for Harrison. I sat with a new group of people over lunches to get any further insight on what went on there. Most of the chatter at lunch or around the water cooler was the typical office gossip. I continued to wait for the day to come that something deeper than 'who slept with whom' was the topic of discussion. There had to be a day that would have everyone in a tizzy over something work-related. It had to happen occasionally. People couldn't be that shallow all the time. I spoke with Harrison on my ride home, but there wasn't much to report. He reassured me to keep being patient with matters. He never seemed upset when I didn't have anything to report. That was unsettling for me.

The rest of the week at home sucked all-round. There was tension in the house due to Micah. Everyone had an opinion on what I should do about his return. By the end of the week, I avoided them all together. I missed my friends but being the catalyst for an argument every time I walked into the room had worn me down. When I got home Friday night, the driveway was empty. They were more than likely barhopping. On my way into the house, I kicked off my heels before going into the living room. I tossed my phone on the coffee table and headed for my room to change into comfy clothes.

In a pair of jogging pants and a hoodie, I went down to grab some popcorn for a quiet movie night. While it popped, I surveyed the kitchen. It was surprisingly clean. A benefit of not having a party this week was a semi-clean house. I reached above the stove to find a large bowl. Before leaving the kitchen, I checked the kitchen door leading outside. The lock was in place, so I grabbed my bowl of popcorn and shut the lights off. I frowned on my way into The Cave. It was odd being in here without the boys. They were practically part of the décor.

I set the popcorn on the end table next to the recliner. I intended on making that spot my home for the evening. I walked over to the shelves that contained our massive DVD collection to locate Magic Mike. I needed some hot bodies after this week. I turned on the flat-screen before putting the movie into the DVD player. I got cozy in the chair as the credits began to roll.

I was close to halfway into the movie when I heard what sounded like pounding coming from the front of the house. I dismissed it as the wind outside. It was windy with a significant thunderstorm forecasted for later this evening. On command, the wind howled loudly. The pit in my stomach subsided. I figured it was the branches hitting the side of the house. I redirected my attention to the hot men on the screen.

After about five minutes, I heard the pounding again. My heart started to race as I listened. It still sounded like the branches of the trees scratching the house. To help ease my nerves, I went to retrieve my phone from the living room. I glanced out the windows but didn't see much since it was so dark. As I turned to head back to The Cave, I heard a floorboard creak. I shrugged it off since my senses were on overdrive, along with my imagination.

I was almost back to The Cave when the pounding picked up again. It was coming from the front door. I returned to the front of the house to investigate. As I got to the living room, the front door swung open to reveal Micah, who was beyond angry. Before I could get out of sight, he saw me. I ran as fast as I could for the stairs. Every room up there had a lock. It would buy me time to reach someone. My heart and nerves were in competition with each other as to which could rise faster. The panic increased with each step. I took the stairs two at a time and reached the landing of the upstairs hallway. Micah was half a second behind me and terror filled me as I struggled with Trey's door handle.

"Come on damn it," I cried, slamming my hands against it.

Just as I got the door open, Micah tugged me back by my ponytail. I screamed as he secured both of my arms and forced me up against the wall. His grip was so tight that I was afraid he'd break one of them. His breaths were long and heavy, with rage covering his face. I tried to pull my knees up to free myself, but he pinned my bottom half with his leg.

"I told you I'd make you listen. You shouldn't have pushed me this far," he seethed.

This wasn't Micah. He had a temper, and could be irrational, but he was never like this with me. The only time I remembered him being like this was when he was using drugs. I glanced at his eyes to confirm my suspicions. His pupils were like saucers for how dilated they appeared. He was on cocaine. That meant I was in more trouble than just having a pissed off ex in the house.

"Micah please let me go. I promise I'll listen to what you have to say," I whimpered, trying to reason with any part of him that wasn't higher than a kite.

He tried to focus his eyes. I squirmed, but that made him squeeze tighter. I cried out as he started cutting off my circulation. The terror in my stomach ran icily through me. "Micah, you're hurting me. If you love me like you say you do, then you wouldn't hurt me this way. Please let me go," I pleaded.

He loosened his grip but kept me secured to the wall. He cocked his head to the side as a pompous grin formed at corners of his mouth. He licked his lips as if he was about to kiss me. I turned away, but he grabbed my chin. With a firm grasp, he lowered his mouth to mine. Before our lips touched, Trey ripped him away. I slid to the ground, shaking uncontrollably. Trey threw Micah up against the opposite wall, swung his arm back, and went in for a blow to the head. The crack of Micah's jaw echoed through the hall.

"You fucking asshole. Once this week wasn't enough, you had to come back for another round? When are you going to learn Micah?" Trey bellowed, delivering another crushing blow to Micah's side.

Trey kept swinging at Micah like he was a punching bag. The crack of Micah's ribs brought me out of my state of shock. He would kill Micah if I didn't stop him.

"Trey, stop!" I cried.

Micah clutched his head and passed out. Trey glanced at me in confusion.

"Are you serious Mia? I come home to see you pinned against the wall and you want me to stop kicking his ass for doing that to you!"

He raised his arm again to swing at Micah, but I tugged on his arm to stop him. He pulled away to look at me. The fear, the panic, the pain, the hatred, the disgust, the sadness, the love – it all ran through me like a freight train. I walked into Trey's chest and wrapped my arms around him to remain upright. I glanced at him with tears in my eyes.

"Trey, it's not the Micah we know. He's using again," I whispered.

He stood frozen for a moment, then pulled me closer and draped his arms around me. Trey let me get out the sobs that had built in my chest. When I'd calmed down some, he let go. We stared at Micah, who was out cold on the floor.

"How do you know he's using again?" Trey asked.

I sniffed. "He broke in here in a rage. He was forceful with me. But mostly, it was his eyes. I remember what he was like before. It hit me after I got close enough to see his eyes."

"We should call the cops Mia. What he did tonight is enough to get a restraining order."

"If I truly want to go down that road, I'll file one. I just want to get him out of here. You should call his mom and let her know he's using again. He doesn't have us to help him so someone that cares about him should know."

"Why do you care what happens to him?" Trey questioned, exasperated.

"I don't, but I'm not going to ignore something like this either. Could you live with yourself if he ended up dying because he was using again?" I countered, exhausted.

"Of course not but I'm surprised you give a damn."

Trey stared at me in utter shock. I looked away from the scrutiny behind his eyes.

"I may hate him, but I have to help him. I know how bad it'll get if he keeps using. I'm angry, not inhumane," I admitted.

It confused me as much as Trey, but everything inside of me worried about Micah. I had walked that path with him once already. He almost died because he had no control over it. It nearly destroyed him, his family, and us. I'd never forgive myself if my own hatred led to his death. I refused to let him have that over me, so taking the high road seemed like the best option.

Trey crouched down to slap Micah awake. The blows to the head had seemed to knock some sense into him. He got up with more focus in his eyes, so he had to be coming down. Micah glanced at me, then at Trey before his eyes drifted to the wall behind me. He looked at me as shame filled his features. I looked away from the apology that he begged to give from the sorrow in his eyes. Trey shoved him down the stairs and out the front door. I slumped to the floor and pulled my knees up to my chest. I shuddered at the thought of what Micah could've done to me. I longed for the good old days when things weren't so life and death. My life at work was dangerous. Now, my life at home stood a chance to match it. Trey came back upstairs and slid down next to me.

"I'm glad you came home," I whispered.

"Me too," Trey breathed, giving my hand a gentle squeeze.

We may have our differences on almost everything, but we shared a bond that was different from any of our other friendships. It was a bond built in our childhood that would be there forever. We sat in silence for a few more minutes before Trey got up and pulled me with him. He hugged me then went to his bedroom. I did the same thing, wanting nothing more than to end this night.

CHAPTER FIFTEEN
Playing With Fire

The weekend passed without any further incidents. Trey and I buried what happened on Friday. Neither one of us wanted to relive that ugliness so we kept it between the two of us. I was happy to know that Micah's touch had no effect on me. However, Friday night might not have been the best time to make a final call on that. I doubted anyone would've felt anything under those circumstances.

I settled into the office early Monday morning. It was a strange day with no meetings, so it dragged. I had accomplished all of my work before ten, leaving me feeling that it may be the longest day ever. I was staring at the same email for a long time, but my mind was focusing more on pushing Micah out of my head. When Ethan's voice rang in my ears, I almost fell out of my seat.

"I guess that pencil just had it coming."

I glanced up to see Ethan standing a few feet from my desk. My heart rate sped up as my cheeks turned crimson. I really needed to get a hold of my physical reactions around him. It was embarrassing. He sauntered over to me with his hands in his pockets.

"Huh?" I stammered.

Ethan flashed his dimples as he pointed to my hand. "The pencil. You just snapped it in half."

I looked at my hand. The pencil was indeed in two pieces.

"I'm going to go out on a limb here and say something is bothering you again."

Shit. I really am off.

Usually, I sensed his presence. If I ever figured out how to turn that switch off, I'd be eternally grateful. Ethan cocked an eyebrow as he took a seat at the edge of my desk.

"I'm fine. I was ... umm ... reading this correspondence," I stuttered.

Ethan rolled his eyes. "The email you've been sitting on for the last twenty minutes is an advertisement for paper. Do you want to try again?"

He was using that tone that bordered between sexy and intimidating. I shook my head in confusion. Last week Ethan grilled me and got pissed at my attitude. Now, he was the picture of concern. My mind started racing in time with my heart as I tried to figure out the mystery behind him. He kept a curious eye on me as I continued to fidget under his hypnotic presence.

"Ethan, you've known me for a very short time. How could you possibly know that something is bothering me?" I questioned, batting my eyelashes like a damn schoolgirl.

Yeah, I'm embarrassed at my actions, but desperate times call for desperate measures.

"I know when something is bothering you. Your eyes become deeper. You pull your eyebrows in when it's something that's upsetting you. It was all over your face when I walked in. I was wondering where your next thought was going to go. You answered it by snapping your pencil. I spoke up so that the stapler didn't also see an untimely end," Ethan replied, flaunting those damn dimples again.

His observations made my heart thump even harder. It was troubling on so many levels that he could read me as well as he just did.

"I apologize for my wandering mind. Is there anything I can do for you?"

"I have something very pressing to take care of now," he stated with a twinkle in his eye.

Given his proximity, along with the sparkle behind his eyes, my lower half became damp as my breathing picked up. My body did the speaking in terms of my sexed-up feelings for him. "What do you need to take care of?"

"It's clear that you have a lot on your mind. Let's go take care of it before it gets out of hand. We have a big proposal coming up. The last thing we need is a team member off in la la land during it," he said, still clearly amused by me.

"I can't leave work. Connor will flip out if I just leave, not to mention what anyone else would think. Besides, I'm not going to tell you what's on my mind. It's not part of my job description to share my every thought with you," I snapped.

Good grief Mia! Stop lashing out at him! He's going to can your ass if you keep it up.

Ethan leaned closer and narrowed his eyes. The glimmer behind them vanished. "I'll take care of them. I'm offering you an out for today. You seem to need a distraction."

I gulped. "What kind of distraction?"

My mind was begging me to retreat while my body pressed forward, not giving a damn about why this was a bad idea.

Seriously, what is wrong with me?

His eyes softened as he asked, "Do you trust me?"

My words abandoned me, so I nodded. I did trust parts of him. He cocked his head to the side to determine if I was telling the truth. After a few minutes of unabashed staring, I gave him a subtle grin.

Ethan shook his head before a tender smile appeared on his face.

"I'm going to take you somewhere that will help ease whatever is bothering you."

I nodded again. It exhausted me to continue fighting the feelings I had around him.

"Let me go talk to Connor. I'll let him know that I'm taking you out on assignment. Wrap up whatever you need to finish and meet me in the parking lot in twenty minutes."

As hard as Ethan was trying to be casual, his face gave him away. It thrilled him that I had agreed to leave with him. I closed down my computer and tried to be invisible when leaving the floor. While I waited outside for Ethan, my thoughts drifted to my unexplainable attraction to him.

My raging hormones were throwing a dance party at the idea of being with him away from work. My brain kept screaming I was insane. It demanded me to back out of this adventure right now. I rationalized that this would be my chance to show him my true colors. I hoped my bitchiness would come out to play, he'd grow tired of me, and our intense vibe would fade away.

It was out of character for me to blow off my responsibilities. Frankly, I didn't have the heart to care. The best part about skipping out of work and spending the day with Ethan was that I had an escape from Micah, Harrison, and my life overall. It was like the land of make-believe that we all loved as children. This was my chance at having a day where my problems ceased to exist while I spent time with a person I couldn't have in real life.

I was beginning to wonder what was taking Ethan so long when a glamorous car stopped next to me. His face appeared after he rolled down window. There would be no way to know it was Ethan if he had left it up. The tinted windows were so dark that they were almost black. My jaw dropped at the sight. His car was like the king of all BMWs. Ethan slid down his shades while laughing at me. He leaned out the window with a cocky smile.

"Do you plan on getting in or would you rather keep your mouth open until you're standing in your own puddle of drool?"

I rolled my eyes. "If I didn't work for you, I'd have a colorful comeback. Since I do, I'll keep my filter on."

This car just screamed ... well it screamed hot, sexy and dangerous – and right now I wanted to sign up for all three. Once I was inside, Ethan headed towards the interstate. This car was amazing, but watching him drive shot all sorts of hot feelings through me. I should've known the sexual tension between us would amplify. It was freaking palpable now.

"You don't have to keep your filter on with me," Ethan remarked.

I glanced over as his smile went from charming to downright sexy. He was hot in this car. I couldn't ignore my erratic pulse or the scorching burn between my legs. It was like the guy had a how-to book for my body, but refused to share just how well he knew how to press all my buttons.

God, help me. I agreed to spend the whole afternoon with him.

I smirked. "When I don't have a filter on, shit just tends to fly out of my mouth, so consider yourself warned."

Ethan chuckled. "I'm looking forward to it."

I glanced out the window to figure out where we were going. The silhouettes of the suburbs I saw as we flew down the interstate were not helpful in making that determination. "Where are we going?"

He took his eyes off the road and turned towards me while tapping his nose.

"Seriously, you aren't going to tell me? Isn't this like kidnapping?" I whined.

Ethan casually lowered his shades with mischievousness in his exposed eyes. "It's not kidnapping when you accept an invitation to spend an afternoon with someone. It's kind of like that saying: 'you can't rape the willing.'"

I gasped in shock.

What the hell does that mean?

Ethan howled with laughter. Butterflies flew across my stomach while the rest of me grew even more aroused. Ethan took off his shades and secured them in the visor above him. "You should see your face right now. It's priceless. Don't take what I said out of context. All I'm trying to say is that you accepted this invitation. You didn't seem too interested in what it meant when you got in the car so I think I'll keep it a secret."

I let out an agitated sigh. It increased the pleasure in his eyes.

"I'm going to enjoy watching your reaction when we get there," Ethan added.

"Glad I entertain you. I knew I served a purpose at the office," I said wryly.

His head snapped in my direction with less amusement than seconds ago. "Oh, you do much more than entertain us. You're doing very well with the work assigned to you. It leads me to my next question. Do you enjoy working for us?"

"I really do like working there. Everyone is great," I replied quickly.

"So it isn't your job that is causing you to be so ... withdrawn?"

I gazed out of the window as the pain in my chest started to grow. "Can we not talk about it? I'm very sorry I've been so transparent."

I turned my head to him hoping he understood. There was concern in his eyes as he watched me. An awkward silence descended over the car. I started to think of something to say that would drive this conversation back to him. "How have you been able to become as successful as you are at your age? It's quite impressive," I said quietly.

Ethan drummed his fingers along the steering wheel. His body stiffened. It was clear that this particular subject was touchy for him. "I'm sure you have your speculations seeing as it's a family business. Everyone usually does. I started shortly after turning sixteen and worked my way up. I graduated from college with a Bachelor's degree in business and earned a Masters in marketing. I went to school while working for my father's company. "

My jaw fell. I quickly snapped it shut. "How the hell is that even possible?"

Shit. Not what I wanted to verbalize.

Ethan loosened up a little with my candor. "I'm guessing this is you without your filter. I like it. Anything is possible if you put your mind to it."

"I didn't mean it's impossible. It's remarkable. I'm sure it came at plenty of self-sacrifice. I don't think I could've measured up to that level of excellence," I admitted.

His happiness faded. His eyes became distant. He focused on the road. "I guess you could say it's like that old saying. Work hard – play hard. From the looks of it, you know how to do both. You seem like a person who has a full social calendar. It's also clear that you have a disciplined work ethic."

Before he could jump on anything else, I went to turn on the radio but stopped due to the complexity of his dashboard. I was looking at so many buttons that touching the wrong one might just result in ejecting me from the vehicle. I must have been staring for a while because Ethan had to clear his throat to get my attention. I gazed over to find his lips curled into a smug smirk.

Damn him and that smirk.

"What?" I asked petulantly.

"Do you need help to turn on the radio? I'm assuming that's what has your mind in overdrive. That poor hamster running up there must be ready to collapse with how hard you're thinking right now," Ethan teased.

Even when he was making me the butt of his jokes, he was sexy. I tried to contain the giggle fighting to the surface, but it slipped out. He grinned even wider.

"Yes, I'm trying to turn on the radio. Yes, I'm confused because there's more buttons and gadgets in here than the fricken space shuttle. And yes, my hamster has become over-worked. His name is Larry and he's used to his eight-to-five schedule. He thought he was getting the afternoon off too. Now, I've just put him into overdrive," I retorted.

Ethan howled with laughter. "I love it. Finally, a woman who knows how to take a joke, poke fun at herself, and throw out a few zingers of her own. I must say, without your filter, you are a different person."

"You have no idea," I replied, rolling my eyes. "Can you turn on the radio now?"

"What would you like to listen to?"

"Whatever, I'm not picky."

Ethan grunted. "That narrows it down."

I shrugged. "Seriously, it makes no difference to me. I love all types of music."

He raised an eyebrow as his fingers flew across the dash. Seconds later an indie song I loved surrounded us. He didn't seem the type of guy for this genre. It had me in awe.

Ah hell. This man isn't a type. He's an enigma to every woman on the planet.

"Are you shocked that someone like me would listen to this music?"

"Yes, I'm a little surprised," I confessed, smiling shyly.

Ethan winked. "Good, I'd hate for you to figure me out and get bored."

I was seriously in trouble. That wink lit my core on fire. I noticed we were getting off the interstate. I loved the area that he took us to because it wasn't as uppity as the rest of the city. Along the shore, there were the usual ma and pa shops. They travelled along the pier for miles and ended with a tiny amusement park.

"We're obviously doing something near the water if we're heading this way. Care to elaborate now that we're getting closer?" I inquired, gesturing towards the pier.

The bastard had the audacity to tap his nose again. I huffed and gazed out the window. "Why are your windows so tinted? It's like the president or a drug dealer should be in here. I mean they're almost black. How do you even see?"

"Wow. I don't think you could come up with two more opposite ends of the spectrum. Let's just say that I like my privacy. If people can't see inside, then they're only left to wonder."

Ethan turned towards a hotel near the beginning of the pier. My body was ready for anything that would happen in a hotel room with him but my mind still had a fraction of control over me. It screamed I shouldn't be with him at all.

"You must lose whenever you play cards because your face exposes what you're thinking every time," Ethan teased with a charming grin.

"What do you mean?"

"It's not what you think Mia. I'm pulling into the hotel to valet my car."

Humiliated at my assumptions, I looked away. As we pulled up, the valet approached to take the car. Ethan got out to have a word with him. I fumbled with my bags and didn't pay attention to what they were discussing. It startled me when he opened the door for me. I grabbed my purse, but he shook his head, indicating to leave it.

When hopping out of the car, I took his waiting hand. It turned out to be a *very* bad slip on my part. I lost my breath. Fireworks exploded inside me. My entire body ignited as the sparks ran through every fiber of me. From my head to my toes, I was on fire. Avoiding any contact with him so far had resulted in his touch intensifying every reaction my body had to him.

Just great.

Ethan held my hand snugly as he escorted me out of the car. Still dazzled by the softness of his hand, I barely caught the passionate look in his eyes. I saw a lot in his deep brown eyes but never that look. He felt this too.

Shit.

Once standing, I wiggled my hand free. Ethan looked puzzled for a minute but dropped my hand and motioned to the direction we were off to next. This was a bad idea. I was stupid for even being here with him, but it was too late to turn back now. I had to figure out a way to keep distance between us. Allowing him to touch me again would be flirting with more trouble than I could handle without screwing up.

We walked along the pier in silence. The only sound we heard was the light breeze that brought in the waves as they lightly crashed against the pier. It truly was beautiful down here. The lake went on for miles until you couldn't see anything but the water. The majestic shades of blue made you wonder what was out there to explore. Eager to break the silence, I looked over to Ethan, who was deep in thought.

"Do you come down here often?" I asked softly.

His lips settled into a firm line. He took a deep breath with profoundness in his eyes. "When I need a break from life, I come here. It's a great way to heal an aching spirit."

Whoa. That's deeper than I was expecting from him.

"I can see how this place would make you feel that way. Where are we going next?"

His seriousness faded as a warm smile spread across his face. He pointed to a shop behind him. It was a rental place for speedboats and lake gear. My jaw dropped at what he was proposing for today.

Ethan chuckled. "You're facial expressions are priceless. This is why I didn't tell you when you asked. I figured I'd get one hell of a reaction."

"Seriously, it's going to be freezing on the lake," I whined.

"Yes, we're going out there. You'll be fine. We'll get plenty of gear that will warm you right up," he insisted.

"And what, pray tell, are we going to do out there with a speedboat and this warm gear you speak of?" I questioned suspiciously.

"Wakeboard of course," he answered straightaway.

"Wakeboard!" I squeaked.

Ethan beamed. "Yes. Have you tried it before?"

"No. Something tells me that I'm just going to make an ass out of myself if I try it."

"You're going to learn today. It's the best kind of therapy for a troubled mind and soul."

My heart skipped a beat with his sincerity. As he gazed at me, a shy smile crossed my face. "How so?"

"You don't have much room to think about anything other than the water, the boat, the waves, the board, and not falling on your ass."

"I've never done this before. I'm going to fall on my ass anyway," I muttered.

"I'm going to teach you. There isn't one person I've taught that falls on their ass. Consider yourself lucky to be in the company of someone that will keep that from happening to you," he retorted, arching an eyebrow.

"Lucky – I was thinking more like crazy," I mumbled under my breath.

Ethan winked. "I'm a little of that too."

The desire across his face played into the overly amped-up

feelings coursing through me. Jumping in the water would be equivalent to taking ten cold showers. It was precisely what I needed to get everything inside of me back in check again.

"If I make an ass out of myself, you can't laugh at me," I demanded.

Ethan held up his hands innocently. I raised an eyebrow to get an agreement to that request.

"I won't laugh at you. I'm sure you'll do just fine. Can we go in now or do you want to continue to debate it some more?" he asked sarcastically.

I nodded, but didn't move. "I don't have my purse with me."

"I already took care of everything. You don't need any money," Ethan said dismissively.

I gazed into his eyes. It reminded me of the first day I saw him. His eyes had a way of sucking you in for whatever he wanted. Right now, they begged me to let the money go and enjoy the day with him. My insides twisted and turned with conflict. He really seemed to want to help me. Against my better judgment, I walked into the store.

CHAPTER SIXTEEN
Blurring the Lines

Ethan grinned so wide that his dimples were again on full display. I had to admit that it was nice to be the reason behind that smile. We strolled up to the counter where he greeted the clerk with a fist bump hello.

"Ethan, my friend, it's good to see you again. I have everything you requested. The wetsuits are in the back, but I left the swimsuits up to you." He paused, eyeing me. "I've found out the hard way that most women like to select that particular item themselves."

Ethan laughed as I walked away from them to find a suit. Passing racks of endless bikinis, it was clear I wasn't going to find anything modest.

"This just keeps getting better and better," I muttered.

It's your own damn fault for agreeing to something as stupid as this outing!

Shut up! I was well aware of what I had got myself into at this point. I was ready to crawl into my brain and kick the shit out of my subconscious. I shrugged off that urge and focused on picking a suit. I stopped to thumb through the bikinis. I went with one that was simple. It was sky blue with faded white stripes. I looked down to check the price tag.

"Holy shit! A person can buy an entire outfit for this amount."

"You're right but this is a pro shop. Everything is top of the line," Ethan whispered.

He scared the crap out of me. My heart was racing as I looked at his board shorts. He had a pair of black trunks with red lines racing down the sides. Ethan scanned the suit I picked out and ran his tongue across his bottom lip. My mouth parched as I watched his tongue run back and forth.

"Nice choice. Are you ready?"

I swallowed back the lump in my throat and nodded. We walked to the back of the store. The back wall had stalls to try on items. The walls off to each side contained full-length mirrors. Ethan strutted over to a stall to change into his trunks. I went with a stall a few down from his and slipped off my heels, skirt, and blouse. I changed into my bikini and prayed I'd be able to contain my bodily reactions just this once.

When I opened the stall to grab a wetsuit, I caught a glimpse of Ethan in the mirror. The sight of him instantly had me wet in all the right places. He had the most defined abs I'd ever seen on a man. His arms had such definition that you could see veins popping out, but not in a bad way. Tattoos covered almost every inch of his body. There were a few bare patches here and there but not many. I had been curious before, but now they were on full display and they were sexy as hell. His back had the same definition as his front. His trunks hung off his hips in such a way that I bit my bottom lip to keep from moaning. My vision sank to his legs only to find that his calves were as toned as his arms. His body more than complimented his gorgeous face. I squeezed my thighs together. I've never wanted to have sex so badly in my life.

I didn't realize that Ethan was staring at me too. He was also using the mirror to do it. In my daze, I had walked out from my stall. My heart fluttered at the scorching look Ethan was giving me as he ran his eyes up and down my body. I wasn't sure if it was the embarrassment or how incredibly turned on I was, but warmth surfaced throughout me. I broke our heated connection and stumbled towards the wetsuits. I grabbed the one that was noticeably smaller and went back to change into it with a small smile on my face. I survived seeing him with next-to-nothing on without making an idiot of myself. When I left the stall, Ethan was leaning against the door.

"What's that stuff for?" I asked, pointing to the items in his hands.

Ethan beamed. "I recall a lot of whining about how cold it was going to be so I grabbed you a hoodie. The bag is for the clothes you had on."

I gave him an exaggerated roll of the eyes and took the items. I went to grab my clothes and tossed them in the bag. Ethan headed towards the wakeboards. I pulled on the pink hoodie and met him by the boards. He'd already picked them out. His buddy was waiting to fit the boots on what had to be my board.

Ethan disappeared for a few minutes. I was happy his friend wasn't the least bit interested in keeping up conversation with me. I was far too busy trying to cool down my body. I was almost back to a respectable temperature when Ethan returned with sandals for us. He had selected a pair for me that matched the hoodie. I nodded in approval.

He leaned against the front counter without breaking eye contact with me. His deep brown eyes entranced me and killed every effort I had made to calm my body. Everything south of me clenched in anticipation of what came next with him. I started to fidget. His buddy had to remind me to stay still. It was enough for Ethan to redirect his attention to checking out some boards, but I caught him stealing glances in my direction.

After my board was ready, we lingered in the shop while his friend went out to the boat with the boards and life jackets. Ethan sure seemed like he got the royal treatment. Maybe it was just here but I suspected it was like this wherever he went. After his buddy returned, Ethan met him at the counter to get the keys. I distracted myself with some of the cute clothes on the racks.

"We can stay here and shop, but it's not as exciting as what's out on the water," he whispered seductively in my ear.

His warm breath trickled along my neck. Waves of desire soared through me. I hoped he didn't hear the heavy beats of my heart. I hastily marched past him towards the door outside. He caught me a few feet outside the door. Needing to cool down, I playfully grabbed for the boat keys. I wasn't fast enough because he deflected the attempt by grabbing my wrist. My breath wavered. I wrestled my wrist free from his grip. Ethan smirked and let go as he slid the keys into his pocket.

"Mia, I've seen you drive a car. If I let you drive the boat, you'll have it flipped before we make it twenty feet," he joked.

"Are you implying I'm a bad driver?"

It was another item to add to the never-ending list of observations he'd made about me. Maybe I didn't sense his presence as much as I thought I did. Ethan seemed to know more about me than I'd ever consciously shown him.

"I'm not implying anything. I'm giving you facts. You drive like a bat out of hell. Animals even seem to know it. They have the sense of mind to stay the hell out of the way when they hear your approach. It must be some special signal they have because I've never seen squirrels scurry out of a parking lot faster than when you're driving up," Ethan teased.

I bristled. "I'm not that bad of a driver."

"Yes, you really are. I'm not trying to hurt your feelings. I'm just saying," he defended.

"Whatever. Maybe I'm just practicing for my NASCAR tryout," I argued.

Ethan snickered. "Yeah, sure you are."

He stopped at a section of the pier that had dozens of parked boats below us. Ethan trotted down the few stairs that separated the pier from a lower landing that the boats were tied to. I followed him to the fifth boat from the stairs. A grin spread across his face as he tossed his bag into the boat. Ethan held out his other hand to take mine. I passed my bag over while muttering under my breath at his inability to let go of my driving skills.

"Get in the boat already so we can get out there and have some real fun. It will wipe that pout right off your face," he said, jumping from the dock into the boat.

"I'm not pouting."

"I guess that downward curl is all natural. Are we going to do this or what?" he asked impatiently.

Ethan extended a hand to help me into the boat. I sucked in a deep breath before taking it. The soft and smooth sensation of his skin sent my heart rate through the roof. The sparks from earlier were stronger. Tingles spread throughout my body. I let my hand linger in his to savor his touch. Earlier I had been too busy mentally freaking out about why I shouldn't let moments like this happen. I almost missed the fact that holding his hand felt very comfortable – like it belonged there.

I held on tightly and jumped aboard. I looked at his waiting eyes that swam with a yearning for more. I straightened myself and settled into the passenger seat. Ethan relocated the boards and life jackets to the back of the boat. I rested my chin on my seat. I broke my gaze from staring at his fine backside long enough to notice that some other stuff was in the boat. When he turned around, Ethan caught the puzzled expression on my face.

"What?"

"Is that a cooler?" I asked, pointing to the box next to the piles of towels and blankets.

"Yes. When you're on the water, you need to do it right. That means bringing refreshments and snacks with you. The blankets are to keep warm. I seem to remember someone throwing a hissy fit over how cold it'd be," he replied.

I gave him a roll of the eye and tossed his words at him. "Are we going to do this or what?"

His lips slid into a cocky grin as he made his way over to the driver's seat. "You better hang on smart-ass. It's like I told you earlier. I work hard and I play hard."

My eyes grew to saucers. Once we were clear from any other boats, Ethan let it rip. He shifted to a gear that sent us soaring. For all the luxuries this boat had, it lacked 'Oh Shit' handles for a person to grab when you were about to fly right out. We zipped across the water so fast that at one point, I was sure we caught air. I clutched my seat and the side of the boat. I turned to give Ethan my death stare. He didn't even flinch at the anger seeping from my eyes. He roared with laughter. If remaining in the boat hadn't been my number one priority, I'd have reached over and smacked him.

After testing my patience a little more, he heeded the warning and slowed down. The slower speed allowed me to soak in my surroundings on the lake. The water splashed up and waves of mist sprayed my face. I smiled, taking in the fresh smell of the lake as it mixed with the breeze. My eyes drifted to the sky, where the sun was settling above us. By its location, it appeared close to noon. The sky was bright blue without a cloud in sight. I peeked over at Ethan to catch him staring at me for once. He seemed so relaxed – he was almost giddy.

Ethan decelerated near a secluded spot. It was far enough into the water that it separated us from any other passing boat but close enough that the shoreline remained visible. I squinted back to the pier. It was a breathtaking sight at this distance. The city had become a tiny outline behind it. I was looking at two different worlds – the surreal, calm world here on the water and the real world back on shore – with all the chaos, problems, and responsibilities. I looked at Ethan and smiled shyly while waving my hand to our surroundings. "I get why you like it out here so much. It's amazing."

Ethan grinned as he cut the engine. "I thought you might like it, which is why I wanted to show you my spot. Everything out here is peaceful and just out of reach from the real world. It makes me forget everything and just live. After all, isn't that what life is all about?"

I nodded. I had seen quite a few sides of him but not this one. It made my heart flutter for an entirely different reason than his looks. I tried to shove my mix of emotions aside, but it was a half-hearted attempt on my part. I liked everything about him. There was so much more to him than what was on the surface. He was kind, funny, smart, and unquestionably a deep person. He was the kind of guy that every girl dreamt about having in her life. Granted, I was treating today as a day of make-believe. Painting him into the picture of Prince Charming wasn't helping me retain my last shred of control to keep from crossing any lines. It was time to jump in the water because my urge to cross that line was growing stronger by the minute.

"If I horribly suck at this, you can't bring it up again – like, ever," I muttered.

Ethan chuckled, but agreed. He went to the back of the boat to grab my board. Watching him, a fact hit me that hadn't when I got into the boat. I cleared my throat to get his attention. He glanced over to see my smug smirk. Ethan gave me a crooked grin.

If you weren't so busy frothing at the mouth in the pro shop, you would've put that together earlier. Would you get it together already?

Fuck off! The inside of my head was a mess. I shook away the voice in my head and focused on enjoying my break from reality.

Ethan was waiting for me to elaborate. "I see two boards in your hand, which means I get to drive the boat after all," I commented.

"Is that the reason behind your smart-ass grin?"

"Yes it is."

Ethan shook his head. "Let's take one thing at a time. First thing is to teach you how to board. If you're successful at boarding, we'll move on to teaching you how to drive the boat."

"I can manage a throttle and wheel," I retorted.

He cocked an eyebrow. "Are you ready to fall in love with wakeboarding?"

I shrugged. "I don't love things easily. Let's shoot for me liking it."

"I can help you get your board on in here or you can strap yourself in out on the water. I'll admit that you want to be in the water when strap yourself into the board."

"You just want to laugh your ass off when I get in the freezing cold water," I sneered.

"It's one perk to that option, but that's not the reason. When you're in the water, it's easier to slide on the board," Ethan stated.

"Fine, I might as well go for the easier route."

"I'll get in with you, show you how to secure the board, and cover the basics of boarding with you," Ethan said, tossing me a lifejacket.

I slipped off the hoodie and replaced it with the lifejacket. I stopped to gaze at the water below. Before I had time to prevent it, Ethan shoved me into the lake. I got soaked from head to toe. I regained my bearings and saw him curled over laughing hysterically. If looks could kill, he'd have been dead. He stood up after he took in my expression and bit his bottom lip to keep from laughing any more. Ethan put on his lifejacket and took the end of the rope as he hopped on the back of the boat. He jumped in feet first. It allowed him to keep his head above water. I scowled and pulled the hair tie from my wrist to twist my hair into a ponytail.

Ethan swam out and started to tread water next to me. He smiled sexily as I tied my hair back. He placed the board horizontal with the back of the boots hitting the top of the water in front of me. While I was busy with the boots, his hand approached my face. I turned as he grabbed a piece of loose hair and tenderly tucked it behind my ear. Ethan slid his hand down my cheek before putting it back in the water. My face tingled and my heart double-timed as I stared at him. The intensity in his eyes had my body heating up again.

Heating up in freezing cold water. How that's possible is beyond me.

"So teach. How do I do this? The board is on. I'm leaning back feeling a little like an idiot and you aren't giving me any pointers on what comes next," I remarked.

Ethan smiled and explained what I needed to do. He covered the technique to bring myself up and stay up then moved on to going from side to side successfully. The last thing he went over was the hand signals for the speed of the boat. When I had it all down, I grabbed the rope. He swam back to the boat. Before he hopped in, he turned back to me.

"Mia, whatever you do, don't try to jump the wake. If you get a feel for this, you're going to want to, but don't do it," he commanded.

I rolled my eyes as anxiety prickled across the rest of me. I wasn't entirely sure about this whole idea. He climbed into the boat and made his way to the driver's seat. As the engine roared to life, I went from somewhat to a-hell-of-a-lot nervous. He pulled out slowly before picking up enough speed to extract tension in the rope. As the tension grew, I knew it was now or never. I closed my eyes to remember everything he told me as the water rushed around me. I opened my eyes and leaned back. I kept the board horizontal until just enough resistance was there for me to swing it forward. My feet took over steering it in front of me. I was upright on the board flying across the water.

Holy shit, this is amazing.

The adrenaline rush was awesome. I put up my right hand to let him know that the speed was good. After going for a while on one side, I leisurely made my way over to the other. Another rush of adrenaline ran through me after making it to the other side without falling. I went back and forth for a while, enjoying every second of it. It was perfect, because I didn't have a care in the world. I had no idea how long I was out there, but my arms started to become weaker so I released the rope and sank into the water. While waiting for Ethan, I slipped the board off to use it as a buoy.

Ethan slowed down next to me with a huge grin on his face. It shot another round of heat through me. I smiled and swam towards the boat. Once close enough, I glided the board across the water to him. He set it in the boat before extending his hand to help me up. Unaware of how drained my body actually was, I tripped over the back and fell into his chest. Ethan steadied me by gently grabbing my arms. My heart sped up as he held me. I should have been cold with the breeze lightly blowing across my face, but I was ablaze with my desire for him. His breath faltered as he held me tightly. His eyes contained the same amount of passion that was flooding through my body. I wiggled out of his grasp before things went further between us.

"So what did you think?" Ethan asked hoarsely.

"That was fucking awesome!" I exclaimed.

"I figured you'd like it. Why did you drop the rope?"

"I got tired. I wanted to end the ride gracefully rather than falling on my ass," I said, grabbing a towel and blanket from the floor on my way to the front. I turned to Ethan with a devilish grin. "Besides, I want to drive this boat."

"You're way too eager. I'm not sure I should let you. Your eyes are dancing just at the prospect of it," he said, shaking his head.

"Oh, come on Ethan, you know you're dying to board too. Just show me how to drive. I promise I won't kill you by flipping it," I whined.

He motioned for me to take the driver's seat. I scrambled over to it. Ethan approached from behind, causing my breath to hitch as he settled next to my shoulder. He went over how to drive the boat in detail. I nodded with each instruction, but he still wasn't satisfied. We did a few test runs, which proved to be nearly disastrous for my focus. He slid his hand over mine to help me adjust the speeds until I got the hang of it. It was becoming easier to have him touch me, but the bad thing was that it made me want so much more than subtle brushes. I started to crave his hands all over me to satisfy the ache deep within me.

Once he felt comfortable that I had it down, we stopped so he could hop in the water. I ended up being able to drive the boat with no issues. While Ethan boarded, I appreciated the water as it sent waves off to the waiting shore. My mind was as clear as the cloudless sky above me. Occasionally, I stole a quick peek over my shoulder to watch Ethan. He had a grin on his face throughout his ride. It would grow wider after he landed one of the many tricks he had been doing. He was amazing out there. My face spread into a wide smile. It made me happy to see him so young and free. We spent the rest of the afternoon boarding and enjoyed the serenity of being on the water.

Our stomachs got the better of us, so we stopped to eat. We sat across from each other eating hoagies while sipping on sodas. In no hurry to get back to shore, we stayed out on the water. We talked about everything from our interests and hobbies to the types of movies, music and books we preferred. Somehow, we managed to avoid anything too personal. The sun had begun its descent and its sharp brightness had faded away to a smoldering blaze of red and pink.

"We should get going before it gets too dark," I whispered.

Ethan sighed, but nodded. We packed up and took our seats to return to shore. Ethan took us across the water at a much slower pace than he did when we came out here. It was a silent ride back. He avoided looking at me. I did the same. A deep-rooted pain slashed through me that we had to return to the real world. It sure had been a fun day in the land of make-believe. He was the best distraction. I shook my head. He was so much more than that today. Ethan was amazing. The one man that sparked something in me that I thought was all but dead and I couldn't be with him.

Life really is a bitch sometimes.

Once on dry land, we returned to the shop to change. His buddy took the boat key from Ethan and directed us to the back of the store where we could steal a quick shower. I stood by my thoughts earlier. Ethan got the royal treatment. After showering, we were in our clothes and ready to return to reality. I went to return my board, but Ethan grabbed it.

"This isn't a rental. It's yours."

I sighed. "Ethan, this is too much. I need to pay for it."

"Mia, you're not paying me anything so just drop it," he said defiantly.

"What am I supposed to say when people ask me about my absence today? Because today was a hooky day that even Ferris Bueller would be proud of," I snapped.

Ethan tried not to laugh at me by biting his lip. My anger paled as I watched his teeth travel along his lip line. I fought the urge to close the distance and kiss him. He wasn't very successful because he started chuckling. It halted my wayward urge.

"You really do have a mouth on you," he pointed out.

I smirked on my way out of the store. Ethan carried my board and bag of newly-acquired items. We walked along the pier in silence. Before long, we were at his car and on our way back to the office. The ever-present sexual tension was still there, but there was melancholy too. The music playing on the radio matched the mood.

"Ethan?"

He acknowledged with a slight nod of his head but never took his eyes off the road.

"I need to know why you did this for me. I'm sure you don't do these things with many people. I can tell how personal it is to you."

He took his eyes off the road to focus on me. The desire behind them shot right through me. "You seemed like you needed a break – a chance to heal whatever has been bothering you. It's been a look in your eyes that I'm familiar with, so I took you to the place that helps me. I can tell from being with you today that it had the same effect on you that it does on me."

My heart swelled at his response. My hand drifted from my lap over to his hand. This was the first time I initiated the contact between us. When our hands touched, it startled him. Ethan sucked in a quick breath. My body exploded at his reaction. After having a day of me squirming out of his embrace, Ethan secured his hand tightly to mine by lacing our fingers together. I relished every single second of it.

How can something that feels so incredibly right be so wrong?

We rolled up to my car in the empty parking lot. I started to drop my hand from his but he tightened his grip to pull me toward him. By the passion in his eyes, he was going to kiss me. I wanted that moment with him more than my next breath. His face was within inches of mine. The cool wintergreen of his breath wafted across me. My heart started to beat in time with the butterflies going berserk in my stomach. I started to lean into him when my eyes caught the company logo. I halted my forward movement and closed my eyes for a second.

Mia! You can't do this! You can't be with him! Don't even think about it!

My very last ounce of sense beat down every wanton part of me. It squashed the butterflies. My heart slowed down, but that had more to do with agony of having to push him away from me. I opened my eyes and inhaled a deep breath of air.

"Ethan, I'm so grateful for what you did for me today. We can't cross any more lines. My life is complicated enough without something like this happening," I pleaded.

The pained expression in his eyes ripped me apart. He held my hand for a few more minutes and then let out a heavy sigh before releasing it. I gathered my things and got out. He rolled down the window and asked, "What about your board?"

"Why don't you hang on to it for me? It'll give me a reason to bug you to take me out there again," I suggested with a half-hearted smile.

Christ, what is wrong with me? I just said I don't want to complicate things any further and then throw out a line asking for another outing like today. I need help.

I turned away from him to find my keys. I unlocked the door with an eagerness to leave before I said or did anything else idiotic. With my stuff secured behind me, I straightened in my seat to close my door when his hands stopped it. Ethan opened the door and leaned towards me as his eyes scorched mine. My brain stopped working with that look. I didn't realize that he had pulled me out of my car and pressed me up against it. He gripped my neck with his other hand before delicately placing his lips over mine. Ethan ran his lips across every part of my mouth before deepening the kiss.

My lips ignited the second his were around them. It was raw and passionate at first but he pulled back to appreciate every aspect of them. He brought my bottom lip down ever so slightly. Ethan caressed it with his tongue before doing the same thing to my top lip. I gave him full access to lick and stroke the rest of my mouth. My body had been yearning for him for so long that I threw myself into the kiss as much he had when he initiated it. My hands found their way into his hair as our lips savored every inch of each other. He pulled me so close that I felt his heart beating just as fast as mine as we continued to get lost in each other's mouths.

I had no idea if it was seconds or minutes that we spent exploring each other's lips and bodies. My body burned with desire as he ran his hands down my back before settling in the lower part of it. His lips gently kissed the lines of my jaw. A small moan escaped as he continued kissing along my throat. Each lick of the tongue from him was hungrier for more. My hands slid down his sides to find his hips. My body went from burning to aching for him.

I tried to get my brain to start working again. I didn't have much longer before giving him every part of me. With my eyes closed, I released my grip on his hips. His lips stopped moving when I tilted my head to the side. I opened my eyes to face the disappointment that I knew would be in his. I placed one last tender kiss on his bottom lip before whispering I had to go. Ethan nodded and let me get back in my car. His parting gaze smoldered every part of me.

As I pulled out of the parking lot, tears started to stem in my eyes. From the moment I met Ethan, he had awakened feelings inside of me I'd never experienced and couldn't explain. I was more alive than any other moment in my life because of him. My hands banged against the steering wheel as the first tears fell. I never anticipated I'd start falling for him and that was exactly what happened today. I thought it was lust, but it was so much more. He made me forget about all the problems life threw at us. It wasn't his appearance that brought my heart out of its slumber. It was simply Ethan. The part that hurt my heart the most was that he wanted me, too. We wanted each other, but it wasn't part of the plan. With that thought, the tears began to flow freely. If I gave into a relationship with him, I'd be in way over my head without a chance of coming out of this deal unscathed.

CHAPTER SEVENTEEN
Tick, Tick

My drive home was fast, due mostly to the state I was in, and the continuous tears. They streamed in time with a thousand different emotions coursing through my exhausted body. Parking in our driveway, I hoped everyone was either out or in their rooms.

If only I could be so lucky.

As I made my way through the front door, I saw Bri and Trey on the couch watching a movie. She lifted her head off Trey's chest and gave me a bright smile.

"Hey, Miii– ," Bri broke off after seeing my flustered face.

I gave her a forced smile on my way upstairs. I reached the landing and kept a quick pace on my way to my bedroom. I tossed my stuff onto the floor before flopping onto the bed. I brought my arm over my face and closed my eyes. Minutes later, Bri tapped on my doorframe.

"Mia," she said softly. She entered my room and sat at the end of my desk after turning on the light. "Mia, what's wrong?" she asked.

I kept my face out of her line of view. I knew she would be disappointed as soon as I told her.

Hell, I'm *disappointed in me. What the hell am I doing?*

"I really fucked up today," I breathed.

Bri leapt off the desk and settled on the pillow next to me. She brought my arm down and held my hand tightly. Tears started to build in my eyes again. Bri was on her side waiting for me to answer. The unwavering concern in her eyes reminded me how very lucky I was to have her as a best friend. I was glad that she was my person, and that I could go to her with anything without fear of losing her in my life. I loosened the grip she had on my hand. In a minute, she'd have her nails embedded into my palms.

"Well, you know how attracted I am to Ethan, right?"

"Oh Mia, please tell me you didn't sleep with him," Bri snapped.

I caught her out of the corner of my eye. She narrowed her eyes, insisting for either a denial or confirmation. I blinked as a deep breath passed through me.

"No, I didn't sleep with him, but I may as well have. He kissed me and I kissed him back."

"Wait – *what?* Why would let him kiss you? How is that even possible when you're at work? I thought you were staying away from him!" Bri shrieked.

I bit the insides of my cheeks at her growing irritation with me. "Well, that's the thing. I spent the entire day with him out of the office."

Bri sat up in a rush, shooting me a glare. "Mia! Why would you agree to a day alone with him when you damn well know you have a hard enough time being in public with him? I swear sometimes I'm talking to a brick wall when I talk to you. Have you heard anything I've warned you about when it comes to him? Why would you do that to yourself? And *why* would you let him kiss you!" she yelled, not trying to contain her volume in the least.

"My brain screamed 'stop', but it wasn't doing the talking for me. I didn't let him kiss me. I sidestepped his first attempt. The second attempt took me by surprise because I didn't see it coming. Once his lips touched mine, I couldn't have stopped it even if I wanted to," I confessed.

I peeked over to determine where she stood on the anger-o-meter. The harshness behind her glare wavered as she took a drawn-out breath.

"Start from the beginning and tell me how the hell this all happened," Bri grumbled.

My eyes went back to the ceiling. I spent the next half-hour recapping my day with Ethan. I thought about our various conversations, the desire in his eyes, his touch, his laugh, and the tenderness of his lips on mine. My body warmed with the desire he brought out in me. As I explained my day with Ethan, I glanced over to gauge Bri's reactions. The annoyance across her face lifted, as she became more reflective with each detail I gave her.

"What am I going to do?" I asked unevenly.

I began to twist my hands together. I sighed at the thought of the clusterfuck my life had become in the last twelve hours – of my own doing, too. Bri sat quietly for a while, and kept her focus towards the window. The wind had picked up, with a storm on the way.

"Mia, for as long as I've known you, it's always been about logic and reason with you. I don't think you've made very many decisions where you just followed what your heart wants for you, regardless of what reason had to say."

Bri stopped my anxious hands as her lips slipped into a content smile. "This thing with Ethan is different for you. I've seen it with my own eyes. Your heart has taken over and is agreeing to things you normally wouldn't agree to if you dwelled on it."

I gaped at her. She laughed and snapped my jaw shut. This was why I loved Bri. She had a way of seeing more in you than you could ever see in yourself. With Ethan, it was my body and its unexplainable pull towards him that dictated my actions. My heart had become just as drawn to him as my body, and that made everything even more complicated. A single tear slid down my cheek. She reached over to wipe it away and gave my cheek a gentle squeeze.

"Bri, this isn't just what am I going to do about Ethan. What am I going to do all together? This is such a fucking mess," I whispered. My bottom lip quivered as I fought back the tears.

"Mia, what you're going to have to ask yourself is what you're willing to live without. You can't have what Harrison offered you *and* Ethan. You're going to have to figure out which choice doesn't leave you with any regret," she replied, letting her head fall to my shoulder.

I rested my head against hers. "As strongly as I feel for Ethan, I don't fully trust him. It's impossible, knowing what I do about his company. I don't have any idea where he fits in all of it. There is a part of me that wants to find that out. I'm not ready to decide."

Bri chuckled. "I'm glad to hear, that despite how intense he makes you feel, that you do question him. In the end, you're going to have to make a choice."

She pulled her head back with concern in her eyes. "With how things are progressing, I urge you to make that choice sooner rather than later. Lord knows what it's going to do to you when you do end up sleeping with him," she murmured.

I scoffed. Bri cocked an eyebrow with a sharp glare that silenced me.

"You'll end up sleeping with him. I can see that already. You're just going to have to figure out which one breaks your heart the least. I can't help you with this choice, but I'll always be here to listen with a shoulder to cry on when you need it."

"I do have some self-control you know," I said, poking her in the side.

"Mia, please, I've seen the two of you together. It's only a matter of time," she teased, tossing a pillow towards me.

My face spread into a sheepish grin and she laughed. I groaned loudly into the pillow. Man, when I wanted a mess, I sure didn't go for a small one. I went for an all-out catastrophe. Her giggles subsided. The room had become silent. I looked over to see that the humor had disappeared from her face. Bri was uneasy about something.

"I know you don't want to hear this but I'm going to say it anyway. You need to talk to Micah. He obviously has something to tell you. Shutting him out isn't helping you. You've been really off and it's because of him. You should talk to him and get some closure."

I broke away from her anxious gaze. She fiddled with the rings on her fingers. I inhaled deeply and hugged the pillow to my chest. "Bri, there's something I have to tell you about last Friday."

She sat up in a worried frenzy. "What are you talking about Mia? I thought you hung out at home while we were at the bar."

"I was at home. What I didn't tell you is that Micah broke in."

Bri gasped. "What happened?"

I tossed the pillow aside. The entire night had been stuck on replay in my head throughout the weekend. I trembled every time I relived the point of the night that had left me scared to death of him. "He was higher than a kite on coke, which is why he probably broke in. I tried to get away from him, but he ended up grabbing me before I could safely lock myself in a room. It got physical. Before anything terrible happened, Trey stopped him," I confessed.

"Why didn't either of you call the cops?" Bri asked, nearly shouting.

"Trey wanted to but I wouldn't let him."

Bri huffed and tossed her hands in the air. I narrowed my eyes to cool her down.

"I may hate him but I'd never be OK with not doing the right thing, which is making sure he gets help. He's hanging on by a thread. If I called the cops or got a restraining order, it would push him even farther over the edge," I reasoned.

Bri groaned. "Mia, why do you care about what happens to him?"

I exhaled at what was starting to become a popular question. "I don't care. I'm angry, but I'm not heartless. If you were in my shoes, would you nail him to the wall with vengeance or would try to take the high road by helping him from a distance?"

"Mia, you're confusing the hell out of me. He shattered you; left you ... well for lack of a better phrase ... completely fucked up, for a very long time. If you're willing to go out of your way to help him with getting clean, then why aren't you willing to hear him out?" Bri snapped.

"His return completely blindsided me. I need the closure, and so does he, but I'm not quite ready yet. I need some time before I'm around him again. If he hadn't broken in here last Friday, I probably would've talked to him by now."

Bri glared. "I'll say it again Mia, the *sooner* – the *better*. How many walking time-bombs do you need in your life?"

"I never said my life was boring," I replied with a guilty smirk. Bri scowled. I gave her shoulder a nudge to get her to loosen up. "After spending the day with Ethan, I know whatever Micah has to say isn't going to hurt me. It's not like he's a thought of the past. I just know that there's so much more out there to experience than what I had with him. Ethan evokes feelings in me that I never knew were possible," I admitted.

The smile that had crept over my face stood no chance of containment. Her resolve wavered as a small grin replaced her irritation. "I do give Ethan props for bringing back your real smile. I've missed seeing happiness in your eyes. I'm glad he brought that back today, even if it complicated your life a little."

I raised an eyebrow.

Bri chuckled. "OK: complicated your life a lot. But I think it was worth it. Look at what you've been able to figure out from it."

I spent most of the night thinking about Ethan, and decided to act as if yesterday had never happened. I hoped that he would maintain the professionalism between us. If he did, I stood a chance of not having to deal with it. The problem was that it relied on keeping some distance between us. It was going to make my investigation for Harrison even more difficult.

I sat in the parking lot the next morning, giving myself a mental pep talk for the day. It mainly revolved around one phrase: avoid Ethan. My stomach was in a ball of knots on my way into the building. Its glass façade worked to my advantage as I gazed around to see if Ethan was lurking around upfront. He was nowhere in sight so I picked up my pace to get to my floor without running into him. After swiping my access card, I hustled over to the stairs.

I was so busy trying to verify his whereabouts that I wasn't paying attention to anything else and ran into someone about to exit the stairwell. A set of strong hands gripped my arms to keep me from tripping. My body burned with desire, then dread. Of course – I'd run into Ethan. He steadied me while chuckling at my entrance. Once stable, I pulled away from him, but stealing a quick glance to determine where his head was at this morning. Ethan gazed into my eyes with more longing for me than he'd ever shown.

Shit. Those eyes scream 'there's no way in hell he's letting go of last night'. Fuck.

I gave him a tight smile on my way towards the stairs. "I'm sorry for nearly running you over. I'm running behind this morning. I should be a little more mindful of who's on the other side of doors before I run through them."

Ethan squinted and rolled up the cuff of his bright red dress shirt. It went well with the plated slacks that, of course, fitted his body in all the right ways. My mind drifted back to how well his trunks had hung on him yesterday. It then slipped over to the carved definition of his body and the firmness of his legs and arms. Eventually, it fell to how amazing his hands were on me, and the taste of his lips. My body was hot and wet and I was ready to throw myself at him in the stairwell without regard.

MIA! GET A HOLD OF YOURSELF! FOCUS!

I jerked my thoughts back to reality. He peeked at his watch to confirm the time. When Ethan gave me his attention again, his amusement with me was all over his face.

"It's fine Mia. It's obvious you were running from something this morning, but I'm guessing it has nothing to do with being late for work," he goaded.

I glared at him. I was happy that he had pushed my buttons with that tone because it chilled all my tingles and fired up my temper. He cocked an eyebrow, clearly baiting me.

Two can play this game.

"Ethan, I don't know what conclusion you're drawing up in your head but I'm running late. I told Connor I'd be here five minutes ago," I bit back.

Before I reached the stairs, Ethan closed the gap between us. He left no room between us and we stood chest-to-chest, equally determined to get our own way. My heart tripled in pace. I held on to my lingering frustration and motioned for him to move.

He leaned into my neck and seductively whispered into my ear. "I know what you're doing Mia. It's admirable you can make it seem like nothing ever happened between us. For the time being, I'm willing to play this game, but you won't win. Keep that in mind the next time you need to come up with an explanation to avoid me."

I trembled at the way his breath trickled across my skin. My hairs were standing on end. It took everything in my power to walk past him, acting like what he said meant nothing whatsoever to me, when on the inside, I was a bloody mess. He wasn't going to back down. I wasn't sure if it turned me on or tormented me.

Throughout the week, Ethan went out of his way to make my life at work a living hell. He made torturing me his new pet project. He managed to find time within each day to corner me and remind me of my inexplicable attraction to him.

Like I could forget. Bastard.

I had wished that he was unaware of what he did to me whenever he was near. Ethan proved to me that he was *very* aware. He used it to his advantage every chance he got. And the asshole was slick about it. He always found moments where we were alone. It made no difference where I was within that building because he was there. He was fricken everywhere *all the time*. I'd even had to give up my addiction to caffeine. It made me somewhat of a bitch between the hours of eight and five. The poor guys on my team started tiptoeing around me. They were always unsure of what version of me they were going to get if they said the wrong thing.

Ethan snuck up on me whenever he had a chance and hovered until my body crumbled to his advances. I wanted the last word every time we were around each other, but I was never able to articulate a coherent sentence. He'd whisper sweet nothings into my ear or subtly touch me so that my body drifted to a different dimension. It left me with an inability to speak every time. After every heated run-in, he left with the same smug-ass smile.

I knew giving into my feelings for him was more trouble than I could handle. Unfortunately, I was approaching a point where I questioned if it was physically possible to avoid it. We no longer had personal boundaries whenever we were alone. He had become more creative as the days progressed. He had trailed his hands along almost every inch of me. He never made a move to kiss me, but that was the least of my concerns. Each time after his hands had grazed me, it took me hours to calm down from him turning me on with no release. I spent the majority of my days trying to avoid any contact with him. It interfered with trying to find out more for Harrison. This offer was always a risk for me, but I had never factored anything like Ethan into it. I knew what I was doing was questionable to most people, but now it was downright insane. To say I'd become a mess after we kissed was a *major* understatement.

By the time Friday arrived I was more than happy for the weekend. It made me proud of myself that I had made it that far. The only thing holding me back from giving into him was my sheer stubbornness. I also knew Ethan underestimated that quality within me. I caught the annoyance in his eyes after he'd whisper nonsense into my ear that didn't crumble my will to deny him.

Ethan had a meeting with my team that afternoon to determine our progress on an upcoming marketing pitch. He was more agitated than usual. He cut people off and pressed for us to get through our respective points quicker. Our presentation was flawless so I couldn't help the smug smile that I directed towards him. He had been watching me on and off during the meeting, but kept an edge in his eyes that masked his thoughts.

The only reason I caught his irritation was because of his unconscious fidgeting. I had no guilt about being a catty bitch towards him. The bastard had earned it after what he put me through all week. When the meeting finished, we rose to head back to our floor. Ethan pulled Connor aside and was talking to him in a stern voice. Connor glanced at me and nodded his head. It made me want to get the hell out of there before anything else happened. I was almost out of the door with my weekend just within reach.

"Mia, hang on a minute," Connor said.

Fuck! So close.

Connor waited for everyone else to exit the room. It sucked up one way and down the other. The extra time fueled my frustration with Ethan. I went to the opposite end of where he was standing, with the conference table between us. Connor stood in the middle with a cautious eye on Ethan and me. We were in a standoff to see who could incinerate each other first with our glares. Connor cleared his throat. We turned to give him our attention. I focused on Connor with a fake smile.

"Ethan has requested your assistance on a deal he's trying to close soon. You're going to work with him until he secures the account," Connor instructed.

You've got to be kidding me!

"Sure. If that's what Mr. Fitzgerald needs, I'll be happy to help him," I replied sweetly.

I wanted to wipe away any ecstatic feeling that Ethan had right now. I really wanted to lash out at his arrogant ass. Connor nodded on his way out of the conference room. He paused at the door. It was obvious that our behavior and this request confused him. Once he left, I turned to Ethan and shot him my death stare. He stood statuesque, with his hands in his pockets. The look in his eyes was beyond egotistical. He had made a power play against me. I slammed the binders in my hands onto the table.

"What the fuck Ethan?"

"Watch your language Mia. I'm still your boss," he snapped.

My blood boiled with rage, incinerating every part of me. I took a step back and threw my balled fists into the air. He was seriously trying to play the boss card. I grasped my neck in defeat. "Fine, as my boss, can you please explain to me what deal needs my assistance? I don't see how I'm the best candidate for it considering I've been here the least amount of time."

His eyes were like daggers as he stared at me. This was a first for us. There was no sexual tension in the air. It had evaporated from the heat of the anger blistering through us. I brought my hands down to my hips. His face flushed as he slammed his palms down on the table. "Don't be a smart-ass. I'm tired of playing games with you," Ethan shot back.

"Unbelievable. Do you realize how ridiculous this has become? If your efforts haven't worked thus far, they aren't going to. I've made that obvious," I said bitterly.

Ethan rushed around the table and stood as close to me as possible without touching me. The anger was still very much present in his features, but I didn't care. I angled my head towards his without showing an ounce of weakness. My fury dominated every facet of me. He leaned in even closer to bring his nose within inches of mine. A gasp from within me slipped out against my will. He was so close that the heat emanated from him. The vein in his forehead throbbed and the ire in his eyes was undeniable.

"You've never been clear about why you won't move forward with me. I know you want me and I want you. It has been glaringly obvious since day one," Ethan bit back.

His warm breath spread across my face. My anger began to fade as a tingling sensation swept through every part of me. I hated doing it but stepping away from him was necessary. The fiery rage coursing through me was slowly morphing into a whole different kind of burn.

"If you remember from my interview, I got expelled from school. Around the same time, I got out of a long-term relationship. I'm still in the process of getting my life back on track. The last thing I need right now is a relationship, especially one with you."

Ethan groaned and tossed his hands in the air. "I don't understand what that has to do with taking a chance on something you want. Don't for a second tell me that you don't want this with me."

If he doesn't drop it soon, I'm going to end up shouting at him at the top of my lungs or punching him in the face. At the moment, I'm leaning towards the latter.

"I can't do this with you. I need to get back to my desk to finish the day," I said icily.

I took another step back, willing the anger to stay strong. He had pissed me off but my body was struggling to remember. Ethan inched forward with every step I took backwards, until I backed right into the shelves lining the wall. I braced myself against them. He placed his hands next to mine. He towered over me and kept his body within inches of me. It left me with no room to move away. The problem was that our current situation was flipping my 'on' switch. His behavior this week had made me more than horny. This particular position sent all sorts of naughty desires through me as my body overheated with its need for him. My heartbeat skyrocketed and my breathing was raspy at best.

Son of a bitch! Stupid betraying body!

His eyes remained glued to me, but the rage started to subside as cockiness took over. Ethan trapped me there for what seemed like an eternity, absorbing every loud beat of my heart. Before he pulled away, he leaned in one last time.

"Go finish your day. Monday, you're *mine*."

Ethan strode backwards to the door, never taking his eyes off me. He stood at the door for a moment before giving me a parting glance. I inhaled deeply several times after he left. I was very thankful that I was bracing myself with the shelves because my knees were about to give out on me. The reality sank in that it was only a matter of time before I did something stupid around him again. Even when I was furious, my body remained drawn to him.

CHAPTER EIGHTEEN
Boom

By the time I got home that evening, my anger was back in full force. On my way in, I tossed my heels to the ground. A huge thud echoed around the room as they crashed and skidded across the floor. The chuckling from the hallway startled me. I looked up to see Bri on her way out of the kitchen.

"Ethan?" she asked nonchalantly.

"Yes," I fumed.

I threw my purse towards the wall with the same force, stormed into the living room, and flopped into the recliner. My hands flew to my head to massage the tension. Bri sat on the couch next to me. She tried to stifle her laughter but gave it minimal effort.

"Are you going to tell me what has you so wound up, or do you want me to let my imagination wander? You know all the dirty little scenarios I can come up with on my own."

I glared at her. She held up her hands innocently.

"He did the unthinkable today."

"And what would that be?"

"He pulled me off my team to work with him."

Bri sealed her lips to keep a smile from spreading across her face but failed miserably. It made me even more irritable. "It's not funny Bri. This last week has been torture. I can't imagine what Ethan has planned for me when we're alone with each other the entire day," I snapped.

"It is kind of funny Mia. What did you expect?" Bri questioned.

"Oh, I don't know. I thought deflecting all his attempts and going out of my way to avoid him would send a strong message," I vented.

She scoffed. "Seriously; you thought acting like it didn't happen would be enough to deter him? He's a powerful guy who wants you. You shouldn't be surprised that he did what he did today. He has the upper hand in this game."

"I held my own against his advances all week. Why can't he just let it go already?"

"He made it clear to you that he wasn't going to give up. It was only a matter of time before he used his authority over you," she countered.

"Bri, you're not helping. What the hell am I going to do now?" I pleaded.

"I don't know. All I can say is that next week is going to be one for the books," she mused, with a hint of a smile.

"Stop acting like you aren't amused by this entire situation," I sniped.

Her head shot up as fury flashed through her eyes. I flinched and sank further into the chair. "Mia, you got yourself into this. I don't know what more you want me to say. If I thought you listened to me at all, I'd be less amused. I warned you about him, just as I warned you that taking the job was a bad idea," Bri snapped.

"I'm sorry. You're right. I'll figure it out."

I didn't question myself often because of my stubbornness, but I was seriously questioning my choices now. Thinking about it made me very exhausted. I was always hiding something from someone. It was wearing me down just as much as Ethan. Bri sighed and got up from the couch. She pulled me up and dragged me towards the stairs.

"I know what will take your mind off things for the night."

I was fine with having no thoughts for a while. As we climbed the stairs, I couldn't overlook how quiet it was around here. "Where are the guys?"

Bri almost missed her footing. She was ahead of me, but her back tensed as she balled her fists. Her behavior confused the hell out of me. Bri regained her footing on the landing upstairs. "They stayed on campus to catch some game. Trey was going on and on about it, but I zoned him out after a while. He said they planned to stop at the bar, but he expected to be home at a decent hour."

"Good luck, with Jackson in that trio," I remarked.

"Yeah, that's what I thought too," Bri admitted.

When we passed Trey's room, I noticed her uneasiness as she glanced at his closed door. I'd been a crappy best friend to her by not paying better attention. Something was on her mind and Trey's absence tonight bothered her.

"Hey – talk to me. What's going on?" I asked, grabbing her arm to stop.

She leaned against the wall. I rested against the opposite one.

"We've been off lately. I mean we're together, but there's this space there. I'm not sure what it is, but I don't like it," Bri said as her eyes drifted to the floor.

"Are you two having problems because of me?" I asked softly.

"It's not because of you. It's new for us – for him. I don't think he knows how to handle having a label on our relationship. It's just not a good time for him to be having doubts."

Bri paused as a sadness washed over her. I watched her carefully. "I don't want to talk about it Mia. Yes, there's tension with everything that has been happening around here that you've been a part of, but it's not the root of the issue with us. I just want to go out tonight and forget about everything as much as you do," she pleaded.

The desperation behind her eyes begged me to drop it. Whatever was going on between them was hurting her. My guilt climbed for not noticing something was wrong sooner. "What did you have in mind?" I asked, raising an eyebrow.

Bri perked up. "If the boys want to have a boy's night, then we should have a girl's night. Go get on one of your clubbing outfits and meet me in the bathroom."

The way she was looking at me made me wonder what else she had up her sleeve. She needed a break as much as I did. We carried on to our rooms to find our clothes for the evening. I decided to go with a short, black mini-skirt with a low-cut, studded tank top in deep purple. Both revealed more skin than was acceptable for a public place, but I didn't care. I found a pair of matching heels with my short, black jacket to complete the ensemble. When I strutted into the bathroom, Bri let out a long whistle.

"Mia, you look hot. Nice choice," she squealed in delight.

She looked fantastic, but that was no shock. Bri was a fashionista, after all. She had selected a very simple, but very eye-catching dress with an open-back, in bright red. It gave you little to wonder, as it clung to her tightly. Her hair was up. She had switched her earrings to ones that dangled with several long silver necklaces entwined together. Bri had already done her makeup and was waiting for me. I gave her the signal for perfection.

"You should talk, Sass. This is going to be a fun night."

"That's the plan girly," she agreed, shoving me playfully towards the vanity.

We decided to forego any clubs on campus. We went to Skye

because it was the hottest one downtown. It had been a while since either one of us had been to this part of town to party. It was pricey so staying closer to home usually won every time. If you drank too much downtown, the cab fare back to the 'burbs was astronomical.

Skye was phenomenal. There were two stories, so you could dance your ass off on the huge dance floor on the first level or, for seclusion from the crowd, you could chill upstairs. A glass staircase took you up to the second level, where tables and booths were scattered throughout the floor. The view allowed you to see the entire ground floor. The walls of each side, whether you were upstairs or downstairs, had a long bar to place your drink order. Tucked away in the back was a DJ booth. Every several feet were pillars to keep the dance floor separate from the bars. Both floors had lighting on the surface in vibrant shades of red, blue, purple and yellow. The light spread from the floors to the ceiling. It was a fine mix of sophistication, but not so stuffy that you found yourself bored.

We had been there a little under an hour and spent plenty of time on the dance floor shaking our asses. We were at the bar to get some well-earned refreshment. Since we were downtown without the guys, I tried to make a conscious effort not to drink too much. I ordered a Miller Lite. Bri huffed before she shouted her order. "Vodka tonic. Make it a double. And bring two tequila shooters."

"Really, Bri? Shooters?"

She scowled with a hand wave to the throat. Her stink eye kept me from pressing her on it. "We're out to have fun. You said you were up for anything. I need this and so do you."

"I just don't want either of us to get so drunk that we do something stupid tonight, like go home with a random. Lord knows I've hit the stupid quota for both of us. I want to have fun, so promise me you'll let me know when you've hit your limit," I requested.

Bri gave me an exaggerated roll of the eyes. I arched an eyebrow.

"I'll be sure to tell you when I'm ready to pass out or have sex with a stranger."

The bartender that took our order was back with our drinks and shots.

"To not passing out or having sex with randoms," I kidded, toasting her shot glass.

Bri laughed before tossing hers back. She ordered two more, not easing my concern in the least. I gave up on figuring her out. Bri engaged in casual flirting with the bartender as she placed our order. I turned around to watch the people in the club.

"Second round," she said, sliding my shot to me.

"Thanks," I accepted, downing it quickly.

She glanced over every so often as she swirled her drink. I downed the rest of my beer and set the empty bottle on the bar.

"See anything you like out there? You haven't danced with anyone since we got here. It's been awhile since I've seen someone shuffle out of your bedroom," Bri pointed out.

"You haven't danced with anyone either. Regardless of whether you're in a relationship, it's never stopped you before," I countered.

She grabbed my hand and shuffled us towards the dance floor. Arguing with her wasn't an option. I followed without a word. We were in the center of the floor with a dozen male suitors hot on our tails. Bri dropped my hand to turn into one of the hot bodies next to her. A soft hand came down on my shoulder. I looked behind me to find its owner and smiled at the handsome stranger. His eyes were full of hope as he gestured for a dance. I nodded and fell in beat with his tall, lean frame.

The songs that the DJ played were off the hook. I danced indecently with hot-and-mysterious for several songs before stopping to find Bri. She was with a circle of guys with a wide smile on her face. She was having a real good time, and that had been the plan. I caught her eye and tilted a hand to my mouth. Her smile grew even wider as she separated herself from the guy behind her to follow me. When we reached the bar, I placed the same drink order as earlier.

"I'm glad you've given up on being so responsible," Bri remarked.

Her mood was far more upbeat than it had been all night. Her smile grew when our drinks and shots appeared. I laughed with the cheeriness in her voice. If this was what she needed to let loose, who was I to get in her way or not support it.

I raised my shot glass to hers and said, "To being in our twenties ... the only time you really get away with being young and stupid."

"To being young and stupid," Bri toasted.

She rolled the shot glass across her lips before tilting her head back to take it down in one gulp. After we finished the round, the warm and fuzzy effects of the alcohol were starting to surface. It was going to make this time around on the dance floor even more interesting. We headed out there and found a new group of guys to dance with. We switched partners as the songs changed. As the current song came to a stop, the guy I had been dancing with excused himself to the bar. It was a damn fine idea. I walked over to get Bri. As we approached the bar, I caught the attention of the cute bartender that had been taking our order all night.

"The usual?" he shouted.

I smiled and nodded. In a matter of minutes, our drinks appeared. We grabbed them with enthusiasm. I took down the shots back-to-back before diving into my beer. Bri was way ahead of me with both shots gone and her mixed drink almost finished. It wasn't a good sign. "Bri, maybe we should call the guys to meet up with us," I suggested.

"We don't need to because they're already here," she said, surprised, pointing to the second floor.

I looked up to see them sitting at a booth near the edge of the railing with several girls. Jackson's hands and lips were all over a busty blonde. Shane was talking with a pretty brunette next to him. Trey wasn't acknowledging the blonde seated near him. He was far too busy staring at us with a fury in his eyes that wilted my insides.

He's hit wrath mode. This does not mean good things for Bri, or for me. Shit.

"Did you call them?" I asked.

I finished the rest of my beer to ease my nerves. I looked at Bri and her good mood had vanished. She was freaking out about Trey too. He made an extra effort to stare her down. She turned around to avoid the scrutiny.

"No. What the hell are they doing here?" Bri muttered under her breath.

"I don't know but we should go up there now."

"I don't want to fight with Trey. He's pissed and fighting with him in a packed club isn't on my to-do list for tonight."

"Bri, it's going to piss him off even more if we stay down here acting like he isn't here."

She reluctantly agreed. We finished our drinks before heading to their table. I hoped a peace offering of drinks would cool down Trey. I ordered up their favorite drinks, along with another round for Bri and I, and shots for all of us. The bartender took down our order and confirmed the bar upstairs would deliver the drinks to the boy's table.

As we climbed the stairs, I couldn't hold back the smile on my face. The boys looked smoking hot tonight. Jackson's hair was all over, with strands brushing along his eye line. He was in a pair of darkly washed jeans with faded portions running down the front of each leg. A dark blue V-neck shirt was barely visible due to the tight, black, biker jacket he had on to round off the outfit.

Shane had kept his hair finely combed. He was in jeans as well, but they were more denim than the pair Jackson had on. He had selected a black and metallic button-down color-blocked shirt with the sleeves rolled at the sides. The black sprang from the spots on his shoulders and the pockets on each side of the shirt.

Trey had gone with black jeans and a white T-shirt with graphics in black in the center of it. He finished it off with black, zip-up leather jacket that was tight around his arms. His hair was all over the place, but that had more to do with him running his hands through it every few seconds.

Once we were at the table, Jackson pulled out his tongue from the girl on his lap. His mouth turned into a wide grin. Shane perked up with a crooked smile. The girls with them scowled at us.

"I'll be damned if it isn't two of the hottest girls in the club – and they're at my table. I must have been a real good boy today," he joked, shooting me a wink.

"Hey boys, funny running into you here," I greeted.

"Yeah, it's *real* funny. It sure looks like you're enjoying yourself," Trey snapped. He stared at Bri with such rage that we all felt sorry for her.

"Whoa, easy ... we're out for a girl's night," I defended.

Trey stormed past Bri towards a hallway that led to the bathrooms. She looked at the ground for a minute before following him. Her shoulders sagged as she walked away. Trey appeared to be on a mission to make her feel like shit for being here. I watched her for another minute before looking away. Jackson and Shane dismissed their girls. I slid in next to Jackson before glancing towards Bri and Trey. They were in a heated argument. Trey's face flushed as he kept his hands in tight fists. Bri's temper was flaring too. She raised her hands towards him on several occasions as she fought back tears. Whatever they were discussing wasn't pleasant. I shook my head, disappointed that her evening was going in that direction. I turned to the guys and nodded towards Bri and Trey. They shook their heads with no explanation. Our drinks arrived. I grabbed my beer and took it down in two gulps. I set down the empty bottle before picking up a shot.

"Seriously, what are you doing downtown?" I questioned.

"Idiot over there thought he'd have a better chance finding some ass downtown. He came to the realization tonight that he has more or less slept with the entire female population on campus. He had to widen the pool to increase his chances of getting laid," Shane said indifferently.

I snorted. "Well, it was only a matter of time."

"Both of you two can fuck off," Jackson snapped.

Shane and I laughed even harder at the perturbed look on his face.

"So ... uh ... how long have you guys been here?"

"Not too long. We saw you dancing and were about to join you when those chicks sat down. I'm going to go get us some more drinks," Shane declared.

He rose from the table and headed to the bar. I looked over to the hallway for Bri and Trey, but it was empty.

"They probably went into the bathroom for a quickie," Jackson said with a devious grin.

"Christ, you can be an ass sometimes."

Jackson smirked. "I'm just saying. She's going to have to do something to calm him down. Trey was livid watching you two dancing out there."

I ran my hands over my face. The whole ordeal had me more than confused. "I've danced a lot sluttier and so has she. I don't understand why he's that pissed off. It's not like she was making out with someone in front of him," I rebutted.

Shane returned with a plate of shots and drinks. I downed the first shot and took a quick sip of beer before slamming another shot. Jackson arched an eyebrow as I set down the empty shot glass.

"I'm a little more at ease with two of my best boys," I admitted with a shrug.

Shane gave me a huge grin as he finished his shots. Jackson chuckled before taking down his. By the time we had finished the second round of drinks, Bri and Trey were on their way back to the table. They had very satisfied smiles on their faces. I shook my head as Jackson burst out laughing. I smacked him. He laughed even harder.

"I only tell it like it is Mia. They fuck like bunnies. Throw in a little alcohol and jealousy and what did you think was going to happen when they left this table together?"

They slid into the booth next to the rest of us. I raised an eyebrow at Bri.

"You said I only had to tell you if it was a random stranger," she said with a smirk.

I rolled my eyes. They picked up their waiting drinks and snuggled into each other. They were becoming nauseating. I grabbed Jackson's hand and started to slide out of the booth. "The music is tight. Let's go dance. With you, I don't have to worry about being groped."

"I'm just a piece of meat that you use when you see fit," Jackson joked.

"Oh, shut up and dance with me," I requested.

He shook his head to rid his eyes of the hair covering them. Shane got up to join us too. I suspected he wanted no part in being the third wheel with Trey and Bri. They had already become shameless as they stuck their tongues down each other's throats.

Jackson grinned. "Fine, but you better make me look amazingly sexy."

"I'll do my best," I promised.

Once downstairs, Shane veered off after a blonde. Jackson and I hit the dance floor, falling into the rhythmic beat of the music. Dancing with him was easy and not just because I didn't have to worry about him taking advantage of me. He had moves that made dancing with him fun. The music transitioned to a slower song. I clasped my hands on his shoulders. Jackson pulled me closer as we swayed to the slow beat.

"Have you found anyone you're going to chase tonight?"

Jackson gave me a thoughtful look before gazing around the dance floor. "There are plenty of girls in here. I'll find someone to go home with by closing time. Right now, I'm having fun dancing with my best girl."

I tilted my head back. "Best girl?"

Jackson beamed. "Yes, my best girl. You're my best friend Mia. You wanted to dance so I'm out here dancing with you."

A small smile crossed my lips. Jackson considered me his best friend. I rested my head on his chest. It was a nice reminder that I really did have people that cared about me, regardless of how shitty I treated them at times. I held on to that thought until the song ended. "I'm going to go find Bri. This is a girl's night after all."

Jackson slid his arms down my sides with a wide smile before he took off into the dance floor. I couldn't help but laugh watching him go after his next conquest. When I was on my way back upstairs, I froze from the hand that slipped over my waist. It had my stomach scorching underneath its hold. Only one person could do that to me.

CHAPTER NINETEEN
Right Kind of Wrong

I slowly turned to face Ethan. He was drop dead gorgeous. He had on a pair of snug dark indigo jeans that had parts faded throughout them. His chest rose as he stared at me with a fierce hunger in his eyes. I saw the lines of his abs through his fitted button-down steel shirt. He had left several of the top buttons undone, so parts of his tattoos popped out. The look in his eyes sparked every nerve-ending in my body. I'd always known being around him with alcohol in my system would be a bad scenario. I never imagined it would make feel like I was on fire. He was looking at me with a combination of heady desire and inexplicable irritation.

"What the hell are you doing here? Are you stalking me now?" I snapped.

I attempted to remove his hand, but the effort behind it was marginal. Everything within me relished his hands all over me. My knees became weak with the heavy want coursing between my legs. My upper body constricted with my wayward needs. Ethan tightened his grip as he whirled me around so that my back was on his front. The music shifted to a slow, deliberate song that was fitting for my predicament. I cursed Usher underneath my breath for coming out with this song. Ethan had buried me into his body. It was impossible not to notice his hardness. He ran his hands down the front of my thighs until he hit bare skin.

"It's hard to stalk someone when they're in the club that you own," he shot back.

"You own this place?" I stammered.

"I have a vested interest, so I come in on occasion. You can imagine my surprise when I discovered you were here," he remarked.

My concentration was dwindling with every stroke he made upon my body. Ethan continued running his hands up and down my thighs, causing my heart to beat out of my chest. I bit my lip to keep from moaning from the pleasure when his fingers lingered towards the inside. My hands took on a mind of their own as they slid down his waist and thighs. His breaths trickled across my neck. It heightened the erotic dance south of me. I was in the danger zone with him. I fought to find my rational side to avoid undressing for him right then and there. My mind grasped at the few functioning brain cells to keep him talking. It was my last line of defense to keep him from kissing me.

"Why are you so upset?"

"I'm angry because you keep denying me when it's clear you want me. To top it off, you come to my club and dance with countless men right in front of me," Ethan growled.

He ran his nose down my neck before licking away a bead of sweat. I gasped. The hand that he had moved to my waist slipped underneath my top. He caressed my belly before running his fingers further down, making every ounce of me come to a dull ache. Against my will, my body moved in ways to encourage him to travel further south to take full advantage of me. Ethan's hands settled along my waistline, lazily trailing his fingers along it. My mind screamed one last time that this was not an option for me. In a last-ditch attempt, I paused his hands so he wouldn't go any further. Ethan whipped me around to face him. The passion in his eyes was unmistakable.

"I'm trying to do the right thing," I moaned.

His hands drifted underneath my shirt and up my sides on their way north this time. As he progressed along my rib cage to the lower line of my bra, he moved us off the dance floor. Ethan pushed me up against a pillar at the far end of it. He brought his body right into mine. He tossed in an occasional thrust of the hips as he pinned me, just to remind me how very well he knew my body. Ethan cupped my breast with tender strokes of his hand before pressing his lips on a spot underneath my ear lobe. It was enough to melt every part of me. I was throbbing all over for him.

"You want me. I want you. I don't care what's right or wrong," Ethan hissed.

I tilted my neck as he trailed deep kisses down my collarbone and exposed shoulder. I wanted him so much that it was close to making me burst. I moaned even louder when his teeth grazed the crook of my shoulder. He sucked along my neck with eagerness, making no effort to hold back his want for me. I slanted my head to bring my lips vigorously down on his. My tongue drifted across the top of his mouth before his tongue met mine where they danced to the beat with the music around us. My hands moved down to his hips as he pumped against me. I slid them even further down to his ass. Ethan responded by grinding harder and grabbing one of my legs to raise it around his hip.

Our bodies melded together in an erotic dance as our mouths devoured each other. I lost myself in the music, in his lips, in his body, in his hands, and in the desires he brought out in me. His hands ran up and down my body while his lips and hips brought me to the point of no return – I ached for him. I couldn't lie to myself any longer, and I was over trying to pretend. My lips lingered on his until I had his gaze locked with mine.

"I want you, but not here," I panted.

"Are you fucking serious? What game are you playing now?" Ethan bellowed.

He moved his lips down to my neck. I groaned as he sucked hard along my collarbone and shoulder. My body was beyond sensitive when I pulled away.

"I'm not playing a game. I'm not having sex with you for the first time in a public place. Don't you have any respect for me?"

Ethan stepped back as he processed my point. I took a minute to catch my breath. My heart thumped with the song playing while the rest of me clenched together in its need for him. "I have to tell my friends I'm leaving with you," I breathed heavily.

"Fine, I'm coming with you," he said, running his lips softly across mine.

I exhaled shakily at his gentleness but refrained from letting it go any further. We'd be right back to where we were five minutes ago and it wasn't any closer to where I wanted to be with him. I lowered my hand to his and laced our fingers together. We made our way through the dance floor and hit the stairs at a fast pace. We approached the table to find Bri and Trey absorbed in each other's lips. It was torture watching them play out what I wanted to be doing.

"Ah, guys – I'm going to head out for the night," I said quickly.

Bri swayed back from Trey. She let out a frustrated huff before sliding to the edge of the booth. She looked at our entwined hands and shook her head in disapproval.

"Mia, a quick minute?" she requested, pointing to the bathrooms.

If I had a dollar for every time I heard a variation of that phrase.

I nodded and began untangling my fingers. As Ethan let go of my hand, his face fell with uncertainty. I brought my lips to his for a soft kiss. I let my eyes linger on his, fantasizing about every ounce of passion waiting for us tonight. He kept his forehead pressed on mine. His desire radiated from every part of his body. Bri yanked me away from his thrall and marched us towards the hallway. She pushed the bathroom door open with force.

"What are you doing?"

"I'm leaving with Ethan."

I gazed at her with a nonchalant attitude. It was obvious what was about to happen, so why she asked was beyond me. Bri shook her head in frustration as her eyes flew to the ceiling. She muttered a few choice words before giving me her attention again. I stared at her, unaffected by her ever-changing mood swings this evening.

"Are you sure you're ready for what you're about to do?"

"What do you mean? I'm not the one that's already had sex tonight."

"Oh, don't fucking go there. We were watching you two. You practically had sex with him on the dance floor. We're talking semantics at this point. What the hell are you doing?" Bri shrieked.

My face flushed from her boldness. She arched an eyebrow to goad me even more.

"I can't deny it anymore. I've wanted him from the second I met him. Maybe if I get it out of the way it'll make everything else clear," I shot back.

She huffed. "You're an idiot."

"I didn't come in here for your approval, Bri."

"Remember, I warned you."

"If memory serves, you told me I was going to end up sleeping with him. Now it's about to happen and you're acting like you never mentioned it at all," I retorted.

We glared at each other, while remaining resolute in our arguments. Bri took a deep breath to maintain her temper. I did the same, to keep from shouting at her if this went on for much longer.

"Mia, just because I said it doesn't mean that I wanted it to happen. I was hoping you heard everything else we discussed and got yourself out of that company. If you had listened to me from day one, we wouldn't be standing in here having this conversation. Here's a final piece of advice. You might want to keep him from marking you," Bri snapped, gesturing to my shoulder.

I gasped at the deep purple marks lining my collarbone and shoulder. I hadn't had a hickey since high school.

How did I miss him doing this to me?

"Bri, you've been telling me all along that I need to make a choice. That's what I'm doing tonight. I'm following my heart. It's telling me I want this with him. I can't handle trying to contain everything that happens inside of me whenever he's around any longer. I'm going to explode soon, and it's not going to be pretty if I do."

She sighed. "I want you to be happy, but I need to ask something of you in exchange."

I raised my hands to the sides in a dramatic fashion. "What do you want from me?"

"I want you to make a *real* choice. If you're going to have a relationship with Ethan, you aren't going to be able to work with him and dig around for damaging information on his company. It'll destroy you. Harrison's offer dictates that you find out as much as possible so that he can print his piece. You can't have both. I want you to pick one and let go of the other within the next week," Bri demanded, with a hard look in her eyes.

My hormones had stopped me from being in a negotiating mood a while ago. I nodded and opened the door. She followed me, with her hands to her hips.

"I mean it Mia. You need to pursue a relationship with Ethan or continue with what you signed up for with Harrison. Either way, I want you to pick one and be done with it."

"I will make a choice," I promised.

Leaving the hallway and Bri behind me, I weaved my way back to the table to grab Ethan. The need for him grew stronger by the minute. On my approach to the booth, I sensed a bit of tension between Trey and Ethan. Each man had their arms across their chests as they stared at each other in a heated standoff. I pressed in close to Ethan and ran my fingers down his rigid arm until he loosened his stance. I took his hand once it was free and rose to my tiptoes.

"Let's go," I whispered heatedly.

His breaths increased as my lips lingered at his earlobe. Ethan broke his focus from Trey to look at me. The burn behind his eyes matched the want that had settled into one, large knot within me. I tugged at his hand, urging him to follow. He obliged, as Bri slid into the table next Trey. She noticed the tension too and let out a gush of air.

"Mia, what are you going to do about your car?" Bri questioned.

"I'll make sure she gets it," Ethan answered.

It was a challenge to get to the exit. Every few steps had us in a heated embrace. We paused several times to run our mouths across each other's, while our hands journeyed lower with more brashness each time. After we made it through the club doors, we staggered at a pace that matched the erratic beats of my heart. His mouth licked along my neck as my lips sucked along his throat before wandering to his shoulder. We made our way through the parking lot and took advantage of steady surfaces when our bodies hit them.

I wrapped my arms around his neck as my fingers glided into his messy hair. Ethan started to kiss me with such a want that my fingers pulled his hair with so much force that he hissed loudly and yanked his mouth away from mine. I softly ran my lips across his in apology. Ethan deepened the kiss as we started walking again. My hands went down his abdomen and underneath his shirt where they appreciated every carved line on his body.

Everything south of me was on fire with how much I needed

him inside of me. I brought my hands to the buttons of his shirt and started unbuttoning each one. Ethan had his hands along my waistline where he played with button on my skirt. He changed directions and coasted his hands up my stomach where he tugged at the straps of my bra.

Ethan pressed me against what I assumed was his car. He moved away but kept his scorching eyes on me. He rested his forehead against mine as his hand tucked an errant piece of hair behind my ear. My heart started to melt at how gentle he had become with me. He switched gears physically the same way he did mentally. It made it difficult for me to keep up. His heated pants had me drowning in need for him. He brought his lips to my earlobe and gave it a soft bite.

"Do you have any idea how beautiful you are to me?"

Unable to speak, I shook my head. I let out a low moan as he continued nibbling at my ear. His lips licked down my neck before settling into the crook of my shoulder. I grabbed his jaw to bring his mouth back to mine. I trailed my fingers along his waistline before digging into his pockets. As sweet as he was being, I needed so much more. It didn't help that need one bit when my fingers grazed along his hard length as I tried to locate his keys.

Ethan laughed against my lips. He brought his hand down to his pocket to fetch out his keys and my hand. He picked me up as he unlocked the door. He pulled me inside with him and closed the door. I remained on top of him as he settled into his seat. My lips went to his neck, making their way down to his exposed chest. I tore his shirt down to his elbows where he finished the job for me. He tossed his shirt behind us before gently removing my top.

I groaned as his lips went from one side of my collarbone to the other before he dropped them to my breasts. After he shoved the straps of my bra aside, his tongue caressed each nipple until they stood on end. It intensified my want for him. Every shred of my sanity went out the window as I worked to satisfy my need for Ethan. I tilted my head back and drove my hips into him with force. My clear-cut implication of what I wanted from him brought his lips back to mine. Ethan kissed me as if he was satisfying his own cravings for me. I rocked into him again with no shame. He groaned with pleasure. His hips met mine with every push I exerted.

"Mia, you said you don't want our first time to be in public, but you're making it shockingly difficult right now," Ethan moaned.

I drove my hips into him with even more force. I didn't give a damn that we were in public. The hot pool of desire between my legs wasn't getting the satisfaction it needed with our remaining clothes in the way. My fingers fumbled with his fly to open it. Ethan separated our lips and grabbed my hands to stop me. He stared at me with reckless desire, but there was a faint amount of uncertainty in his eyes.

"Are you sure you want this now?"

"Yes, I can't handle it any longer Ethan. I need you," I begged.

He slammed his lips back to me, his mouth capturing every part of mine. His tongue slithered at an erotic pace. Ethan lifted my legs and slid down my panties in one swift movement. He readjusted his jeans to free himself just as fast and lowered me on to him. I almost fell apart with how amazing it was having him inside me. Ethan moved at a slow pace to allow my body to accept his considerable length. Impatient for more, I drove harder, needing him deeper. He met each of my thrusts with vigor. My body erupted with sensation. As I rocked into him each time, the tingling throughout my body amplified even more.

"Fuck ..." Ethan hissed.

His hands travelled up my back before tightening on my shoulders and bringing me into him even further. My body expanded as we carried along at an impassioned pace. It made everything inside my body burn for more. My hips obliged by pushing deeper. His head fell to the seat as he gripped me even tighter. He leaned forward to torture my breasts with his lips.

"I've wanted you for so long. Fuck ... it's like you were made for me ..." he muttered.

We pressed closer together, our bodies sliding against each other. He decided to change the pace to one that was far more relentless than what we went at so far. Ethan began to pound even rougher. He was as far within me as he could go. It had every part of me clenching around him.

"God ... Yes ..." I screamed.

His lips sucked along my breasts so hard that I dropped my head to his shoulder. I bit down as the fire inside me grew to an inferno. We started to rock into each other with more force. I couldn't get enough of him or the mind-blowing sensations taking over my body. His mouth went from my breasts to my earlobe. His lips caressed every spot that they touched on my skin. My breathing matched the pants that Ethan exuded in between each stroke of the tongue.

"You wanted this now but I want so much more from you tonight. Let's finish this so we can get to that part of our evening," Ethan groaned loudly.

"I need it to be faster if you want to move this along," I hollered without a care.

Ethan did exactly as I asked. His hands moved down to my hips as he continued to drive into me. I squeezed around him as the blaze within my core exploded throughout my entire body. I screamed, riding out the pleasure with him. My fingers tangled in his hair and jerked hard as he released into me. I rested my forehead against his as we came down from our intense ecstasy. His car filled with the symphony of our ragged breaths, matching the rapid beats of our hearts. Ethan was still somewhat hard, making me start to tingle all over again. Unconsciously, I clenched against the hardness. He shifted me further down his lap.

"I think one brazen act this evening is enough, don't you?" Ethan asked.

I can't believe I begged him to have sex with me in the parking lot of a packed club. And I was loud – really loud!

"Umm ... yes, I think one is more than enough," I whispered.

My cheeks flushed even hotter than the rest of my body as I looked at him. Ethan pulled out of me with ease. He wrapped his arms around my waist as his nose grazed along mine. His tongue outlined my lips and a small moan escaped from me. He was turning me on all over again.

"I take it you don't do that often."

"Try never."

Ethan ran a trail of kisses along my jaw. I snuggled into him as my fingers trailed up his detailed chest. The urge to get lost in him again grew with each stroke. From the wetness that was slicked on the inside of my thighs, my body was without a doubt ready. Though he was no longer in me, it was evident that he was just as eager for more. It became more apparent with each touch I gave him. If we kept up this slow, sensual torture on each other, we'd be gearing up for round two. I took in his heated breaths before releasing his grip from my waist.

He stared at me for a moment then retrieved his shirt. I shuffled off his lap and over to the passenger seat. I grabbed my top and slid it on as he retrieved his from the backseat. A small smile crept upon my lips as I watched him zip up his jeans and button up his shirt. It was a shame the shirt needed to go back on at all. I giggled as my eyes went past him to the darkness of his windows. I was sure that the moans and the movement of the car gave plenty away but at least no one could see who was in it.

"What?" Ethan asked.

"I understand your answer about the windows a little better," I said, motioning to the tint.

Ethan flashed a devilish grin. "I've never had sex in this car. It never crossed my mind, not even with you, but then you started begging."

"Hardy har har. Can we go now?" I asked with a roll of the eyes.

Ethan grabbed my face and swept his lips across my mouth. His tongue touched mine before he broke off the kiss. I tried to resume it, but he stopped me by placing a finger between them. "I have so much more planned for you, so buckle up and prepare yourself. Your life is about to be changed in ways you never thought imaginable."

I sat back in shock and grabbed the seat belt in response to his command. I continued to gape at him as he peeled out of the parking lot. He weaved in and out of traffic towards the part of the waterline that brushed into the city. I rested my head against the window. I needed a minute to process things. Everything about him was so incredibly right.

Ethan pulled into a high-end apartment complex. He rolled his window down to swipe an access card that opened the garage. After he parked his car, Ethan ran his fingers up my arm. They left a trail of heat on every spot. He placed his hand on my cheek so I'd look at him. I smiled shyly as he sat sideways, staring at me with such passion in his eyes that my insides became molten lava. He gently released my face and opened the door. We made our way to the elevators without a word. Once inside, he hit the button for the top floor.

As we went up, Ethan shuffled us until my back hit the wall of the elevator. He brought my hands above my head as his elbows settled outside of my pinned arms. He lowered his face within inches of mine. I stood, bewitched, under the spell he had over me. He placed soft kisses across my upper and lower lips before he pulled away. I tried to move closer, but it was difficult since he immobilized me. I burned from every angle to be near him.

"Patience," Ethan whispered.

I huffed. "If you want patience, stop teasing me."

"It sucks to be teased, doesn't it?"

His lips went to my earlobe, where he nibbled his way back to my mouth for a brisk kiss. I looked anxiously over his shoulder to see if we were near his floor. I wanted to rip off his shirt for the second time tonight. He dropped my hands and moved to the opposite side of the elevator. I gasped at the sudden loss of his body. He laughed. I moved to close the distance, but he held up a hand for me to stop.

"Are you trying to make me blow up? Why did you do that only to put on the brakes?"

"Now you understand what you did to me when you broke off our first kiss."

I glared at him. "Is this some sort of lesson?"

"Maybe," he said with a mischievous grin.

I silently mouthed the colorful thoughts running through my head.

"You drive me insane when you allow yourself to be so damn flippant," he growled.

"You seem to bring out every feeling in me before I have a chance to run it through the part of my brain that controls my rational side. Most of the time, I'm happy if I can filter anything when I'm around you," I admitted.

He sighed. "I like that you lose control around me. It's the only time I get a piece of the real person behind the wall that you have up around the rest of the world."

Ethan left me stunned as he got out of the elevator. I stumbled out and followed him on his way down a long hall. He walked for a minute before turning around to face me. I froze, waiting for his next move. He marched back to me. His lips met mine with force. His tenderness disappeared as he pressed against me with urgency. We stood there in the middle of the hallway exploring each other's mouths before he stopped again. The starting and stopping was driving me nuts. He stepped away, with grief across his face.

"Please don't shut me out anymore," Ethan whispered in anguish.

"I won't," I said with wide eyes.

His tone sliced through every part of me. The pain in his eyes showed how much I had hurt him by pushing him away this last week. It simmered some of my wayward desires.

"I'm going to hold you to that Mia."

He took my hand on our way to the apartment at the end. He let us in his place, not bothering with the lights or a tour. We hurried along to what I assumed was the bedroom. He stopped before opening the door. He ran his fingers along my arms at a deliberate pace. It sparked my insides as he traced a trail to my lower back where he rested his hands. I melded my body into his. His fingers drifted across my backside as his thumbs sketched small circles. It sent the burn inside me further south at a rocketing pace.

He kissed me with resolve as he opened the door to his bedroom. The only light came from the full moon illuminating the sky. It flooded the room through the exposed window. As we shuffled along, lost in each other's mouths, his hands ran underneath my top until it was off. My hands worked with the buttons on his shirt. I discarded it from his body with more gentleness than earlier. Everything was moving in slow motion. I was able to appreciate every defined part of his chest and arms. He let out a soft moan when I traced my fingers along his waistline. I let them drift underneath his boxers.

He picked me up and lowered me on the bed. He hovered over me as his lips trailed down my chest to my bra where he gently sucked before discarding it, reigniting the inferno from earlier. I purred in anticipation of having him back inside me. My hands went to his chest. My fingers outlined his tattoos with reverence. He ran his lips down my stomach, stopping at my belly button where he swirled his tongue before continuing further south. He removed my skirt and paused for a moment to look at me.

The unmistakable passion in his eyes as they ran across my body made every part of me blaze. I unbuttoned his fly and brought his jeans down. He reached a hand around to pull them off. My eyes sprang open as I took in his very long, hard length. I had no idea how big he actually was until now. That wasn't what surprised me the most. He had a piercing down there.

How the hell did I miss that earlier!

Ethan dropped his head as soft chuckles escaped. I'd given him yet another occasion where he got a priceless reaction out of me. I shoved at his shoulders, not particularly happy that he was laughing at me.

"I guess I don't need to ask if you've ever been with someone that has this particular piercing?" he teased.

I blinked and shook my head. His humor vanished as he swept his lips down my throat. His fingers did a similar motion further south. I arched my back and screamed at the dual sensation. He continued rubbing his thumb along my hot spot as his fingers eased in and out. I wanted to do the same thing with my hands, but I wasn't exactly sure what would be pleasurable for him with a piercing there. Ethan didn't seem to care as he carried on at a relentless pace. Every fiber of my body electrified at his touch. My lips found his shoulder where I pressed tender kisses as my hands ran up his chest. I grasped his neck as my mouth sucked along his throat in the same fashion that his lips coasted along mine. We had each other breathless with the intensity of every kiss. Ethan tilted his head away as his eyes conveyed the hunger he wanted to satisfy.

"Are you ready Mia?"

I bit my lip and nodded. I was more nervous than earlier, but I didn't want him to see it. I let out a shaky breath as he slowly entered. My worries vanished as I absorbed the immense pleasure of having him back inside me. I had no idea if it was his length or the piercing, but sex with him was unbelievable. The sensations within my core blasted throughout me again. He moved at a slow pace that made my body crave for more.

"Fuck. This feels amazing. You're incredible," Ethan moaned loudly.

He inched his way deeper. I rolled my hips with each thrust he gave me. It was much different going at an unhurried pace compared to the fast momentum from earlier. He eased until every part of him had consumed me. He pulled back before thrusting forward again.

"Yes ... Ethan ... Yes!" I cried out.

Our bodies rode together with effortlessness. It was so damn hot that I couldn't control anything within me, let alone what flew out of my mouth. My hips kept up with his steady rhythm. He secured his hands with mine and brought them above my head as his lips met mine. He tenderly kissed my top lip before doing the same to the bottom. We continued, with no rush to finish anytime soon. The only thing filling the room was our heated breaths and moans. Beads of sweat formed on various parts of our bodies as we rocked together.

I had no idea if it was minutes or hours, but my body reached its point of release. I clenched around Ethan as he picked up his pace. He groaned as he drove into me harder than he had earlier in the evening. I screamed at the roughness as he continued at a faster pace. As he grew closer to his climax, he started to tremor. I took in his deep brown irises that had so much passion behind them. It made everything in me peak at an even higher level. He continued to shudder as I trembled, my insides squeezing against him. I climaxed hard around him. He followed me with a loud moan. Ethan sprawled across my chest, showing no signs of movement, as I tried to catch my breath. My heart surged as I heard his heart beat rapidly. He released our hands and brought them down to our sides. He kept his fingers wrapped with mine before turning my hand over to press a gentle kiss on the outside of it. Our pants began to fade as our bodies came down from the power of our lovemaking.

Everything about this time was nothing short of perfect. It made me kind of hate him. I was never going to be able to be with another guy after being with him. I thought when he kissed me that he had ruined me, but right now effectively did it. There was no way I was going to bounce back from this moment with him. I'd never be able to rid this level of euphoria from my memories. Every part of my body had succumbed to him tonight. He had infiltrated the wall within my heart. He had pressed upon it until it had cracked at his advances. In his pursuit for me surrender to him, he stole a piece of me. It aggravated me as much as it exhilarated me because I didn't share that side of me anymore.

I became very tired pondering what just happened between us. It was so much more than sex. Ethan slid out and brought me into his arms before crawling to the head of the bed. He laid me down on the pillow and kissed the tip of my nose before he fell next to me. My mind quieted itself as he breathed slowly; each one bringing such comfort to me. They were a repetitious plea, telling me that I belonged with him. He wrapped his arms around me and I rested my head against his chest. I fell asleep listening to the steady beat of his heart.

CHAPTER TWENTY
Blown Away

I slept for what might have been a few hours before discovering something else about Ethan. He enjoyed having sex just as much as I did, so we didn't sleep for very long. We went several more times until the wee hours of the morning before exhaustion made it impossible for another round. It was without a doubt the best sex of my life, and it got better each time.

My eyes fluttered open at the brush of his hands. My brain struggled to determine the time of day. The sun was bright as it poured into the room. I needed to get a better grip on not letting him take over my every thought. I was lying on my stomach. Ethan was at my side with his fingers trailing along my back. After a while, he settled on a spot between my neckline and shoulders. He swept my hair to the side before tracing a diamond pattern. My body drank in the delightful sensations he brought with each stroke. He removed his fingers and replaced them with his lips. Ethan placed a tender kiss on each tattoo. A moan slipped from me as his lips went up my neck. I rolled over to bring his mouth to mine. Our lips met with passion. He lingered at my bottom lip before he pulled away to look into my eyes. His fingers ran through my hair with tenderness.

"When I asked if you had any tattoos, you ignored me. I assume there's a reason you avoided discussing it with me."

I sighed. "The four that you see on my back are all that I have."

I had hoped that would be the end of it, but his eyes persisted, asking for more. It irked me that he had been able to sense a story behind them. He stared at me in a way that begged for me to allow him in even further. I couldn't deny the thoughtful look in his eyes. It tugged at my heartstrings. His hands cupped my cheeks as he encouraged me to share more with him.

"I got them a while ago."

I rolled onto my stomach. I didn't want to look at him when the rest of the story came out.

"Will you tell me what these mean?"

His fingers made their way back to my tattoos. I savored his soft touch. He was so damn sweet sometimes that it was impossible not to give in to him.

"They're a reminder."

"What are they are reminder of?"

"As hopeless as life can seem, it's never a reason to give up."

"What do they mean?"

"They're Chinese symbols. The top one is the symbol for dream. The one to the right is the symbol for live. The one to the left is the symbol for love. The last symbol completing the diamond is the symbol for laugh. They're my reminder to never give up."

"What happened that meant you needed a permanent reminder?"

My eyes started to water. I started to shake as the memories of that night flooded through me. Even swaddled in the comfort of his arms, the pain spread to the surface in surges. Ethan rolled me over so that I was facing him. He brought his thumb up to wipe away a tear that was starting to fall. I buried myself into his chest as he closed his arms around me.

"Talk to me," he whispered.

"It has to do with my expulsion from school. The reason I got kicked out was because my ex-boyfriend framed me. He set it up to make it seem like I wrote an article that would damage the reputation of the school and the board members. He said he had no choice and that it had something to do with me all along, but who knows what's true. I have a hard time believing anything he says anymore."

I paused to bring my head away from his chest. My eyes were moist as tears continued to form. I wiped a few of them away in haste. I'd never told anyone what I was about to tell Ethan. His eyes carried so much concern that it made telling him the rest of the story that much easier.

"We were living together at the time. After being expelled, I came home to find my apartment trashed, and him gone. He was the only person I had allowed inside my heart. He not only shattered it, but he crushed it to pieces. What he did made it difficult for me to find reason in anyone, or anything."

I stopped to drink in his deep brown eyes. They gave me courage, as I bared a side of me that had not surfaced in a very long time. His eyes really were windows to his soul. I stared into them and poured a part of mine into his. Ethan rested his hands along my face, his own filled with compassion. I prayed that he'd understand how deep the damage ran within me.

"After I figured everything out, I started drinking – heavily. Between the large amount of alcohol and my lack of will to survive, I crashed to the floor. I hit my head hard enough on the way down for it to crack open. If Bri hadn't found me, I would've died from the blood loss. I wasn't trying to kill myself. My mind and body broke in every way," I whispered.

Ethan hugged me so tightly that I had trouble breathing. He lessened his grip to bring his lips to my cheek, where he kissed away the tears streaming down. My heart melted at his repeated attempts to ease my pain; the walls around it rattled loose even more. "That's a lot for one person to handle without questioning humanity," he murmured.

I nodded. "It was a really low point in my life. It took me a long time to crawl out of that hole, and I'm still not sure that I'm quite there yet."

He arched an eyebrow. "Where is 'there'?"

My eyes darted across the room. "I want to get back to a point that allows me to believe in people again. It wouldn't be horrible if I found a way to have faith in myself either."

"You carry yourself with such confidence that it's difficult to see that you hold that type of darkness inside of you," he remarked.

"I don't think I'm that confident. I recall having a go-around with you about my attitude on more than one occasion," I joked.

"Will you tell me what got you into such a funk that I had to give you the day off just to get you to lighten up a little?"

I ran my fingers along his jaw while soaking in his wistful eyes. My hands went down his body until I hit his chest where they outlined one of his tattoos. I gave Ethan a playful grin before replacing my fingers with my lips. My tongue licked its way around one of his bigger tattoos. He moaned and pushed me onto my back. Ethan pinned my hands to the side as his lips touched mine. I went wet with the hungriness of his kiss and the roughness of his approach.

"You're really not going to tell me," Ethan growled.

I beamed. "Nope, I think one story is enough this morning – or afternoon. I have no idea what time of day it is because of you."

"Because of me?"

"Yes, because of you. I lose track of everything when I'm around you."

His fingers reached my hot spot and he wasted no time in turning me on. My body buckled to his will. I arched my back and met each stroke of his fingers. I moaned as he switched to an unyielding pace. His lips curled into a sexy grin as he relished his control over me. Our talking had reached its end. Every part of me was more than happy to connect without words.

The sun was starting to set when my brain screamed at me to snap out of it. I needed to get back to reality, or at least check in with it. Bri was probably well past being enraged at me. I looked around his bedroom. Other than the king size bed and Ethan, I hadn't taken the time to observe the rest of it. The bed took up most of the space. The door was in the middle, and to its right, there was a large walk-in closet. Along that wall, there were various pieces of art. Several Celtic pieces caught my eye, as they matched some of the tattoos on his body. The side of the room adjacent to his closet had a huge window. Black drapes concealed some of the sunlight – Ethan had to have shut them between last night and this afternoon. Behind his bed, colorful artistic pieces adorned the wall; more vibrant than the Celtic ones opposite them. The wall across from the window had more Celtic pieces of art with a huge, flat-screen TV. I looked at Ethan, who was flat on his stomach. It appeared that our vigorous afternoon had sated him. I lost track of how many times it had been since we started last night. It must have been enough because he was snoring. I secured the bed sheet around me and tiptoed out of his bedroom.

His place was humungous. My stride slowed as I hit the open space that seemed to be his living room. It had a wide entrance as it sectioned off from the hallway. The room had tasteful decorations, but there was a distance to it. The walls were white, while most of his furniture was black. It gave the apartment a feeling of being sequestered; away from the rest of the world. There was no sign of any pictures of his family or friends. That, coupled with his taste in art only increased the mystery behind him.

My eyes drifted to the wall on the right. It contained plenty of abstract pieces that sucked you in with their complex strokes. The wall on the left was without any adornment, containing only a large flat-screen TV, with a sound system below it. A huge sectional couch cornered off that area with a glass coffee table in front of it. By the looks of the built-in shelving underneath the TV, he had plenty of DVDs to entertain him. I almost walked over to try and get a better idea of him by his taste in movies; however, the wall opposite to where I was standing distracted me. It was a giant window that overlooked the city as well as the lake. I sauntered over to take in the view. The sun was descending and the hues of purple splashed against the caps of the waves. I wasn't surprised that Ethan had selected a place that had such a magnificent view of the lake. It connected with a deep part of him. I wondered if I was the only one that saw that side of him.

"You are," he confirmed.

"Huh?"

"You're the only that knows how much the water means to me."

Ethan brushed my hair to the side and placed a loving kiss on my shoulder. My body fired from the electric current that his lips generated as they trailed along my throat until he reached mine. His mouth urged for me to grant him better access. He was unraveling me again with his torturous lips. I almost gave in but remembered why I got up. "Ethan, I need a moment today that doesn't end in us having sex," I stammered.

"Why? Are you telling me that all I get is twenty-four hours? I haven't even begun to appreciate you, or your body," he growled.

I tilted my head away from him. "I need to check in with Bri. I can't find my purse."

Ethan smirked. "It's not up here. It's in my car along with something else of yours."

"I'm not going down there like this. Do you mind if I borrow your phone? I need to get my car at some point too. A shower might not be a bad idea either," I said, sniffing myself.

"You smell amazing. You can call her from my phone, but that's it. I might be willing to negotiate the shower request as long as it's with me," Ethan replied, nipping at my ear.

I playfully pushed him away and pointed to his bedroom. He strutted down the hallway. I took a deep breath and prayed it would help me to remain focused long enough to call Bri. Ethan returned with his cell. I excused myself for a little privacy to talk to her. I had shuffled past a bathroom on my way to his living room, so I walked back that way. I opened the door and sat down on the ledge of the massive vanity with two sinks. I shifted into a spot in between them. I noticed a glass shower that had multiple showerheads on one side of the room and a large tub that looked more like a Jacuzzi on the other side.

Hmm ... maybe something to consider later, with Ethan.

I broke my attention from the direction of that dirty thought and dialed Bri's number.

"Hello," she answered warily.

"Hey, it's me."

"Mia, where are you?" she asked, downright exasperated.

"I'm sorry Bri. I didn't mean to worry you. It's why I'm calling," I said patiently.

"You're still with Ethan," she said in disbelief.

"Yes, I'm still with him. Who did you think I'd be with?"

She huffed. "Lately, it hasn't been in your nature to linger in bed with a guy."

"I deserve that comment, so I'm going to let it go. I called to tell you that I'm not coming home until tomorrow."

"You're spending *another* night with him. Do you know what you're doing?" Bri yelled. She was so loud that I pulled the phone away to avoid hearing loss.

"Yes, I know what I'm doing. I think," I said, reservedly.

"You *think*. God, I thought it was the alcohol and horniness that did the talking for you last night, but it's not. You wouldn't be willing to stay another day with him if it wasn't something more. Please tell me that you remember what you promised last night."

I sighed. "Yes, I remember."

"Are you sure about that? I've never seen you be so careless," she snapped.

"I'll have a pow-wow with you about all of this when I get home."

"Fine, but tomorrow I want to hash this out with you."

"You have my word. I need to go."

"Oh, and Mia, I want all the hot details too," she said in a somewhat teasing tone.

I rolled my eyes. "Every naughty detail. I promise. I have to go Bri."

I hung up and placed his phone down on the counter. I rested my head on the mirror behind me. My thoughts drifted to all the amazing feelings I had experienced within the previous twenty-four hours. A soft tap brought me out of my daydreaming.

"It's your home Ethan. You don't need to knock," I answered dryly.

He opened the door and poked his head around it. He had changed into a pair of black boxers that brought out all the Celtic tattoos that graced portions of his sculptured chest. My body dampened at the sight of him in his boxers. I sucked in a sharp breath as he sauntered towards me on the vanity. When he reached me, he placed his hands on the sides of my legs. He leaned forward until his forehead pressed upon mine. "You asked for privacy. I was respecting it. You asked me in the club if I respected you and I do. I didn't do a very good job of showing it in the parking lot."

My pulse quickened at the sound of his heartfelt words. His hands slid down my thighs until he reached my knees and slid me to the edge of the vanity. Ethan swept his lips across mine with a hunger. I gave way to the moment before ending it with a delicate kiss upon his nose. "I'm the one that begged you," I pointed out.

Ethan sighed. "I've never met a woman that confuses me as much as you do, but I've found that I like it. Sometimes I can tell what you're thinking by the look in your eyes. Most of the time, I'm sitting on-edge with what you'll do next."

"You do the same thing to me, and it terrifies me. I'm never sure what to expect when I'm with you. I have zero control over my body, making it difficult to learn more about you."

He draped his arms along my backside before tightening his grip. His lips ventured across my jaw before capturing my mouth for a sultry kiss. The hot sparks inside me flickered to life. I fastened my legs around him as my lips became prisoner to his. My teeth grazed along his bottom lip before giving it a gentle bite. Ethan flashed his dimples as I moved away from his mouth.

"See, there you go again."

"What?"

"You know exactly what you do to me when you do it. You seem to understand my body better than I do and it drives me crazy."

His hands glided to my chest where he pulled down the sheet. Ethan came closer as his lips ventured across my breasts before licking their way back to my mouth. He forced open my mouth with eagerness. His tongue commanded mine. A heady burn flared throughout my body. My fingers flitted underneath his boxers before I clasped my hands around his lower back and rocked into him. Ethan groaned as his lips brushed along mine with more zest. Our hands moved all over as our mouths devoured one another. We remained that way until breathing became problematic. I pulled away from him and sucked in a quick breath.

"Before this goes any further, I want to discuss something with you," I panted.

"Make it quick," Ethan demanded.

I pointed to my hickeys with sharpness in my eyes. "Don't do it again."

He shrugged. "I'm sorry. I didn't intend to mark you."

"As long as we have an understanding that it isn't to happen again, I'll let it go."

Ethan nodded. I rocked into him with force. He moaned and tore away the sheet. My hands shoved down his boxers. He kicked them aside. Ethan picked me up and sauntered towards the other side of the bathroom where he pressed me against a set of glass doors as his lips dove into my neck. He licked until he hit the groove of my shoulder where he grazed his teeth. My head tilted to the side welcoming his tongue is it journeyed upward.

"It's time to take care of that shower request of yours," he growled into my ear.

I gasped. "Yes, I do believe that was on the list."

Dressed in a pair of his boxers and a T-shirt, I sat at the end of his bed drying my hair. Ethan was ordering us food from a Chinese place down the road. I tossed the towel to the side and hopped up from the bed to join him in the living room. He was on the couch with his back on glorious display – the tattoos that ran down it were as stunning as the ones on his chest. He had a balance of patterns and symbols with various scripts weaved amongst them. I sat at the edge of the couch, not wanting to bother him as he scrolled through his phone answering emails.

"Hey babe, the food will be here in about twenty minutes."

Ethan spoke with such ease that it made my heart fly out of my body. He sounded like we had been together for ages and tonight was just another Saturday night to lounge around the house with each other.

"Sounds good."

"Is there something on your mind?"

"No," I lied.

Ethan set his phone down and hauled me into his lap. He rested his forehead against mine. I wrapped my legs around him and clasped my hands around his neck. His hands caressed the small of my back. He stared at me, with patience in his eyes, before he took a deep breath. "Please don't lie to me. Let's try this again. What's on your mind?"

"I'm worried about what's going to happen when we step back into the real world. My mind keeps telling me I hardly know you, but my heart feels like it has known you my entire life. It's a very profound feeling that I don't know how to handle," I confessed. My stomach fluttered with anxiety.

His eyes flickered around the room as he exhaled. "I don't know what it is about you Mia. I remember having a bad morning. The softness in your voice made my insides twitch. To be honest, it was unsettling for me. When I looked up to acknowledge you, everything within me shifted." Ethan paused and brushed his lips against mine. My eyes remained wide in astonishment. "I couldn't stop staring at you. I didn't understand how you could make me feel so vulnerable. I had to know what it would feel like to touch you. When our hands touched, it gave me a new sense of being alive. You awakened a part of me that I never knew was dormant."

I placed a soft kiss upon his lips. Ethan gave me a shy smile.

"You didn't hire me because of that, did you?" I whispered with wide eyes.

"You were by far the best candidate that I interviewed. I tend to leave my feelings out of business matters. It was a first to have them crash into each other the way they did in that interview, but I remained professional nevertheless."

I scoffed. "Your behavior with me this last week wasn't very professional."

No wonder we can't seem to stop having sex.

"You set yourself up for that scenario the second you acted like the kiss we shared meant nothing to you," Ethan retorted, his tone lined with resentment.

I softened. "I wasn't sure how to handle you. I'm still not sure."

"You seem to be handling me well so far."

His hand ran underneath my shirt and across my breasts with a wicked intent as he flicked my nipples to a stand. Fiery sensations in my stomach and even deeper below began to explode rapidly. I started cursing under my breath. He had me on my back in a second, with his body hovering over me. His lips ventured along my throat with purpose. It sent another volcanic eruption through me. I tilted my head away to prevent him from taking matters any further.

"I've told you how much that aggravates me," Ethan growled.

I arched an eyebrow. "It bothers me when you turn me on and then slam on the brakes."

"Who said anything about doing that?"

"We have food coming and we aren't done with this conversation yet," I pointed out.

"Fine," Ethan said as he sat up.

I did the same but kept a few inches between us. I propped my elbow on the back of the couch and rested my head in my hand. Ethan shifted towards me with his hands folded on his chest. "I've never felt anything like this before, so I'm at a loss at what's right. Sometimes I wonder if what we're doing is wrong. What happens when work becomes a reality again?" I asked.

I swallowed against the lump in my throat.

What happens when I step back in his company door and become reminded of the reason I ever met this amazing man? What will happen when Ethan knows the truth?

"Why don't we spend the rest of the weekend being just Ethan and Mia? We're a new couple getting to know each other," he suggested.

I grinned. "I think they call that avoidance, but I'm listening."

Ethan moved towards my lips when his intercom buzzed. He got up with an agitated huff to answer it, while I tried to gather the troublesome thoughts that were running through my head. Ethan returned with a sack full of food. He took out several cartons that had my mouth watering with their tantalizing smell. I ran my tongue across my lips in anticipation.

"Don't do that again or we won't get to the food," Ethan demanded.

"Do what?" I inquired.

His husky tone startled me. I gazed into his eyes. They were hungry for more than food. As he passed me a carton, my lips slipped into a sheepish smile.

"Don't taunt me like that when you don't plan on using your mouth on me."

"Sorry."

"You better be. Now replenish your appetite because I plan to work it up again."

Ethan opened the carton in front of him as he passed me a set of chopsticks.

"Are you now?"

"I am. So eat up. You'll need your strength."

Ethan winked at me as he turned on the flat-screen. We devoured the food in front of us. My cheeks flushed as I pondered the thought that we were barely taking time for the basic human necessities like eating. His fingers tingled across my heated face until he rested his palm on my cheek. He flashed a crooked smile that fired up more of my body.

"What has your cheeks turning red this time?"

"This is the first thing we've done today that hasn't ended in us being all over each other."

"Not true. You called your friend. I'd say that counts as doing something else."

"I've eaten, and called home to tell them that a crazy person didn't kidnap me."

"I'm only crazy around you. You bring out my animal instincts. Why do you always think I'm kidnapping you? You've come willingly with me each time," he said with a smug smile.

I grinned slyly. "I had no idea I had such a strong effect on you."

"You know damn well that you do."

"I'm going to have to pay closer attention."

I licked my lips before grazing my teeth across my bottom one. It was fun playing with him for once. He tended to set my body off before I ever had a chance to get to him. Suddenly he faced me ready, to pounce on his prey.

"Don't mess with me Mia," he warned.

"Or what?" I challenged.

"You'll regret that you taunted me."

His voice was low as he crawled closer to me. I repeated my tongue licking antic.

"Remember that you brought this on yourself."

Ethan slid off his boxers and was more than ready for me. He discarded the clothes I had on within seconds. He eased me onto my back with gentleness but then pinned my hands to my sides with more force. I leaned up to trail my tongue down his throat, but he tightened his grip.

"I'm not scared of your threats," I retorted.

"You should be," Ethan whispered sexily.

Ethan ran his hard length inside my thighs. Every part of me quivered, so very eager for him to be inside. I rocked my hips forward, but his hands kept me still in their firm grip. He took my hands and restrained them above my head while pushing roughly against me. I brought my hips to meet his but he stopped me. He kept one hand above my head securing my hands with his while his other hand ventured to my lower body to prevent me from creating any friction between us. I lifted my head to get closer to him, but he tilted away. Ethan moved his hand from my hip and settled into a rhythmic dance between my legs with his thumb and fingers. I moaned as his fingers slickly slid in and out while his thumb brought every scorching sensation to the surface.

"Oh Mia, you're so ready but I'm not," he said in a taunting tone.

Suddenly, I regretted ever messing with him. My body was wet with need, as he drove into me again but didn't allow for any reciprocation. He tucked his head between my breasts where he sucked and bit at my nipple until I screamed out. My loud reaction only increased his efforts as he did the same thing to the other breast. The fire that had settled inside me was screaming for action. He rocked between my legs and I tried in desperation to meet him but he stopped me. He continued suckling across my breasts before making his way to my collarbone. He paused at the marks to place a precise kiss against each one of them.

"I'm tempted to do it again just to piss you off," he growled.

He brought his mouth to mine but kept complete control of the kiss. I tried in vain to get him to open wider. He kept his lips firm and resolved as he continued tormenting me with his fingers and thumb while throwing in the occasional thrust of his hips. My body was approaching its volcanic setting. It wouldn't surprise me if I blew up at any moment.

"Ethan, please," I begged.

My pleading tone only seemed to play into his point. He rocked but kept me from meeting him. I cried out in frustration. He did it again with more ruggedness and nipped at my earlobe.

"Are you sorry?"

"Ah, yes ... I'm sorry!"

He kissed along my throat and neck, not allowing me to participate in any way. His fingers picked up in robustness as they slid in and out. I was ready to crumble at any minute. I whimpered at the thought of what else he might do to my overly turned on body. The inability to do anything to him in return only pushed me that much closer.

"Will you ever do that to me again on purpose?" Ethan inquired seductively.

"No, I won't. I'm sorry. Please let me have you!" I shouted.

Ethan rocked hard and deep within me. The instant friction had me screaming. He drove with force at a rapid pace. He released my hands. I tightened them around his back. I needed every ounce of him to satisfy the hunger within me. Ethan continued at an unrelenting pace. He pushed ahead, not paying much attention to me. I arched my back loving every ounce of what he was doing to me. Ethan continued pushing faster and harder. My body neared its climax but he finished before I had the chance. He pulled out in a flash. My body pleaded for a release as I fell back on the couch chagrined by the ache left inside me. Ethan sat across from me gathering his ragged breaths. I brought myself up and glared at him.

"I can't believe you just did that to me," I snapped.

Ethan smirked. "I told you that you brought it on yourself."

"You're an asshole," I shot back.

He raised an eyebrow. "That may be true, but you asked for it when you started teasing me."

I scowled. "Fine, you've made your point. I get that I affect you too."

He rose from the couch and pulled me along with him. "Let's go take care of you before you end up slapping me."

"It might happen anyway if you ever pull that again," I warned.

I went with him to the bedroom. My body demanded satisfaction to rid the growing ache within me. I loved and hated what he could to me in a matter of minutes. I had never realized it, but he reacted as strongly to me as I did to him. It made me fall even more for him.

CHAPTER TWENTY-ONE
Clarity

The following morning I woke up tangled in Ethan's sheets, thinking about how he had more than made up for leaving me high-and-dry on the couch. For the first time, I was sore from being with a man. He had worn me out, just as he promised. I rolled to my side to find him still asleep. I took in every quiet breath as I lay next to him. Every moment with him was more than I could've imagined. I never thought that I'd let anyone in again, yet here I was lying next to him, and it was more than right. It felt like I belonged with him in every way.

I crawled out from under the covers and went back to his living room to find the boxers and T-shirt he had given me yesterday. I tossed them on and then paused to take in the sunrise as it sprawled across the horizon. My eyes drifted to the opposite hallway that carried on to the left side of his apartment. I ventured in that direction out of curiosity. There were several doors spread out on each side, but I refrained from opening them.

The hallway ended with a top-of-the-line kitchen. It was vast, and contained every accommodation and gadget that anyone serious about cooking could dream of having at their grasp. I shuffled further into it and looked around for a coffee pot. After several sweeps along the granite countertops and steel cabinets, I gave up. I sauntered towards the island in the center of the room and tried to figure out how to jump-start my exhausted body without caffeine.

"I just want a cup of coffee," I muttered under my breath.

"I don't drink caffeine."

Ethan's low voice froze me to the floor as my heart leapt from my chest.

Shit. I can already tell he's less than thrilled with me.

"You've got to stop sneaking up on me," I rasped.

He narrowed his eyes. "I assume you're in here to satisfy your need for caffeine."

My heart beat at an irregular rate. His face displayed that rigid side of him that intimidated me. He continued staring at me as he made his way further into the room.

"Yes, I'm in dire need of it," I admitted.

He beamed. "I know how important caffeine is to you. I had fun cutting you off from it."

"You're an ass for doing that to me," I retorted, and childishly stuck out my tongue.

Ethan chuckled as he opened a cabinet. He placed the coffee pot on the counter and plugged it in before rummaging around in another cabinet to pull out a wide variety of fancy coffee bags. "What do you prefer?" he asked, holding the bags in my direction.

I shrugged. "I don't care as long as it's black."

"You're inability to make decisions about the little things in life drives me about as crazy as when you use your body to tease me. Can you pick one before I end up having to give you another reminder?" he asked, or rather demanded, by his tone.

I pointed to the bag in his right hand. I wasn't about to go through *that* again. We needed to have a day together that didn't end in some sexual act every five minutes. He poured my selection into the pot and leaned against the counter as the coffee stirred to life.

"Why do you get up so early?"

"I don't know."

I sat on a stool at the island hoping he'd drop it, but instead he gazed at me with deep interest. "You really don't know, or you don't want to tell me?" he persisted.

I sighed. "Since Micah left, I don't sleep for long periods of time, but it might go even further back than that. My memories are muddled because of him."

"Micah?"

"He's the ex-boyfriend I told you about yesterday."

Ethan tensed, the veins in his arms protruding to the surface. He folded them over his chest. I wasn't sure what part of my admission had set him off. I continued tracing patterns on the countertop to try and ease my climbing nerves.

"What happened before Micah that made it so difficult for you to sleep?"

I exhaled heavily. "Ethan, what you're asking is a fair question, but I also don't know anything about you. Can I please take a pass on this one? At least for now," I pleaded.

He stared rigidly at me. It made me even more anxious. He ran his hand up his neck to pull at his hair. While we looked at each other, the coffee pot sizzled to a loud squeal. Breaking our trance, he turned around to grab a mug from the cupboard above him. Ethan poured me a cup of coffee and made his way around the island. He stood behind me, with his chin on the top of my head. He placed the cup in front of me, but kept me from going for it as he intertwined both of his hands with mine.

"At some point, you're going to have to let that wall fall too. You promised Mia."

He placed a soft kiss upon my head while tightening his grip. I breathed in deeply at the contact, the request, and the way his voice sounded as he said my name. If Ethan only knew how much I was hiding from him, he'd be less concerned about me putting off answering this particular question. My stomach churned at the thought of what I was really withholding from him. Even worse, how many times I had lied to him. I loosened his grip and turned to face him. My hands went around his waist as I gazed into his beautiful brown eyes.

"I will, but you have to give me some time. Our bodies are miles ahead of what our hearts are ready to divulge. You can't expect so much from me when you offer so little of yourself."

I rested my head on his chest. He settled himself between my legs as his hands slid to my hips. They caressed circles along each side as he took a deep breath.

"What do you want to know about me that would help you share more?"

"Oh, lots of things. Why don't we keep the questions light? It's too early to get into the heavy stuff," I said, stretching for my coffee to take a sip.

"I can do light. What's your favorite thing to eat for breakfast?"

"Eggs and toast with bacon. What's yours?"

"French toast or pancakes covered in peanut butter."

I crinkled my nose. He looked at me confused.

"Really, Ethan? Peanut butter on pancakes? Gross."

"What's wrong with peanut butter on pancakes?"

"Syrup goes on pancakes, not peanut butter," I replied matter-of-factly.

"Don't knock it until you've tried it. Syrup goes on a lot of things."

Ethan looked at me, ravenously sizing me up. I raised both eyebrows before shaking my head.

How can he be thinking about sex when we're talking breakfast?

"I know what you're thinking. The answer is no."

"I can make you change your mind quite easily," he growled.

He lifted me onto the island so that we were at eye level with each other.

"I'm sure you can, but I'm asking you not to right now."

"I've never experienced a yearning like I do when I'm around you Mia," he said, moving his nose up mine. "But I agree. We should do more today. What do you want to do?"

My heart was beating at warp speed as he remained next to me. The desire within me was coming to the surface. It was difficult not giving into it. Everything inside of me squeezed together. I set down the coffee and pressed a soft kiss on his lips.

"It depends. I need to get clean clothes. I can't go out in public wearing what I have on now, or what I had on Friday night."

He blinked with confusion. "What's wrong with what you had on Friday?"

I scowled and pointed at my hickeys. "Remember these?"

Ethan flashed a drool-worthy grin. "I said I was sorry."

My thighs clenched together. It was hard to be irritated when he looked so damn hot.

"I know you did, but it doesn't change the fact that you curbed my wardrobe. It's going to be a bitch trying to find outfits for work."

Ethan pinched my lips shut. "We're not talking about work."

I grunted until he released them. "I need clean clothes, one way or another."

"I don't want to take you home yet."

"We could go get my car. I could go home and get cleaned up then meet back up with you. It's best that I take a solo shower today. I want to get clean this time."

"I didn't hear any complaints yesterday when we were in the shower. I think we got more than clean while we were in there," Ethan said with what I now considered his 'naughty grin'.

"I don't have any," I assured, giving him a peck on the cheek. "I think it might be best if I did that myself today, so why don't you take me to my car."

He stepped away, looking guilty. "I already took care of your car. It's at your house."

"What!"

I hopped to the floor and went to the other side of the island. He was watching me carefully. "I had your keys, so I had a couple of the guys at the club take care of it last night. You don't need to worry about anything being vandalized," he pointed out.

"I'm not worried about it being damaged," I snapped.

"Why are you so angry about it?"

Ethan ran his hands through his messy hair as he stared at me.

"I'm angry because this isn't the first time you've pulled this shit with me. I get that you like to dictate most situations. When you use it against me, it really pisses me off," I shot back.

He took several deep breaths. Either I'd confused him, or he was about to get pissed with me too. It was hard to tell.

"What do you mean that I use it against you?"

"You make decisions without looping me in. It's fine when it comes to your company, but not outside of it. It's my car so you shouldn't have done what you did without telling me."

Ethan grasped his neck. I knew that move. He was working hard to keep his patience with me. I maintained my frustration with him.

"I didn't take care of it to start a fight with you."

"Why did you move it without telling me?"

His face fell, and sadness crept out of his every pore. It chilled my ire with him.

"I moved it because I want to be the one to take you home. I have a bad feeling that once I drop you off that you'll act like this weekend never happened," he admitted.

I felt like I'd been slapped in the face and kicked in the gut all in one shot. My unpredictable actions scared him, and rightfully so, since I didn't know what was going to happen between us. As the grief continued to grow in him, I realized that I didn't want to hurt him any more than I already had with my carelessness. I wanted to throw up. The idea of losing him terrified me. It made every breath difficult. I never wanted to be the cause of that look on his face. I had to give up what Harrison had offered me. I clutched my arms around me to try and shove everything away so I didn't fall apart.

"Are you OK?" Ethan asked as he watched me with worry.

"Yes," I choked out. My voice was having trouble working with the amount of fear running rampant within me.

No, I'm not fricken OK. I'm a horrible human being that deserves every ounce of heartache that's more than likely to come. I'm such a fucking idiot.

"Are you still mad at me?"

"No," I whispered, holding myself tighter.

Ethan made his way over to me. "Are you able to answer with more than one word?"

"Yes," I rasped.

"That's still one word," he pointed out.

He took my hands from around my sides and placed them on his hips. My body calmed with his touch as my heart rate picked up again. I squeezed my arms around him. I was desperate for his touch, if only to ease my aching soul. He settled his hands on my cheeks.

"I'm fine. I'm sorry I overreacted."

"It's OK. You had a point."

Ethan swept his mouth along my lips. He kept the kiss tender, so it was no surprise to me when he moaned loudly after I turned it into a much deeper kiss. I threw every ounce of myself into it. The pain and guilt disappeared, my body fixating on wanting to show him that he was close to getting every part of me. My insides sprang to life, wanting to express how much I needed him. He started moving us but our lips never parted. He set me on the island. I tangled my legs around his waist. His mouth broke from mine to go down my neck to my earlobe where he placed a soft kiss. Our breathing was heading towards an all too familiar place. I pulled his lips to mine for a kiss that left us breathless.

"Wow," I whispered.

"What?" Ethan panted.

"I can go from one extreme emotion to the next in a matter of seconds around you."

"What are you feeling right now?"

"You know exactly what I'm feeling," I husked, running my nails down his back.

"Yes, I do," he groaned, laying me on the island as he got rid of our clothes.

We were lounging in his living room. I was lying on his lap. The TV was on, but I hadn't been paying any attention to it. My fingers were busy outlining his tattoos. I was more alive since meeting Ethan than I had been throughout my entire life. Just lying there, doing nothing, my entire body was humming with a current that made every touch and sound that much more noticeable as I absorbed them. He brought out the best and the worst in me, but I was more at peace with him than anyone. My fingers lowered to his hand. I brought it to my lips for a light peck.

Ethan beamed. "What was that for?"

"No reason. Just couldn't help myself," I confessed.

"What are you thinking about?"

"I'm thinking about how much you consume me. We were supposed to try to get out today, but we couldn't go without getting hot and sweaty long enough to make a decision."

"That's not my fault. You started an argument with me that I tried to end nobly. You're the one that took that kiss to a different level. You can't push my buttons like that and not expect me to take you."

"Here I was thinking that you were trying to see how many places you could have me," I teased.

Ethan had a wicked grin on his face as he moved his hands with dexterity across my body. I melted with his touch. I stopped his fingers from traveling any further south of my stomach. He settled them along my thighs with a gleam in his eye. "Do you still want to go out today? I'm sure we could add a few more places to that list."

"No, I think I'd rather stay right here with you. The real world will be here in a few hours."

He tensed. "Are you saying what's happening here isn't real?"

Here we go. I can feel the fight coming on already.

I shuffled out of his lap and over to his side. "No. Why do you always assume the worst?"

"I can never tell with you Mia. It's how you word things," he shot back.

"Ethan, this is real. It's going to be complicated, but it's definitely real," I reassured.

My stomach knotted at his doubt. The rigid look in his eyes did nothing to ease it.

"Why do you keep referring to everything outside of my apartment as the real world?"

"What do you want me to say? You don't want to talk about work, but that's part of the real world," I defended.

He gave a flippant wave of the hand. "Tomorrow will be fine. You seem more hung up on what's going to happen than me."

His nostrils flared. His fists curled as he worked to keep his breaths even. My temper was on the rise as everything in me constricted with my irritation.

"Bullshit. You believe I'm going to wake up tomorrow pretending like this weekend didn't happen. What do you want me to do to prove that I'm not going to act like that again?"

"I don't know."

His eyes darted away from me. I caught a mixture of emotions behind them before they did. His anger was present, but there was something else that I couldn't place. It made my frustration with him grow even more because he was holding something back.

"Tell me this – how do you want me to act tomorrow? Because I have no clue," I snapped.

"Act like you normally do around me," he said without concern.

"Seriously! Have you thought about how you've been with me all weekend?"

"Yes, of course. It's some of the best moments I've ever had with a woman," he said seductively, trying to steer me in a different direction.

I scowled. "Stop it. Think about what you did on Friday."

"Are you saying that you don't think you'll be able keep your hands off me?"

He leaned closer. I pulled away. He was teasing me, but I found no humor in it.

"I'll be working alone with you for eight hours. It's been a challenge to go a few hours over the weekend. You know what you do to me. That's why you pulled that stunt. I was beyond furious with you. Can't you find someone else now that you have me?"

I didn't want to fight with him, but his strange attitude towards working together was pissing me off. He glared at me, with a harshness behind his eyes that stilled my anger for a second.

"No."

"You admitted that you did it to get me. News flash – you got me. Game over!"

"I said no," Ethan shot back, even more harshly.

I tossed my hands in the air as my blood boiled over with fury. "Why?"

His hand slammed against the side of the couch. "I'm not changing my decision."

"But– " I argued.

"No. End of discussion Mia!" Ethan shouted.

His face was bright red with fury. His fists were curled so tight that his knuckles had gone white. Ethan rose from the couch and left the room in a huff. I laid on the armrest and turned over to see what he had on TV. It was some romantic comedy that made me a little envious. Life was never as simple as what you read in a book or saw on TV. If my life were a movie, the end credits should've rolled with the happily-ever-after the second Ethan and I got together. Being with him just made my life more complicated. I closed my eyes, not wanting to think about it any longer.

I rolled over to find myself in Ethan's bed. He was lying on his side with his head propped up by his arm and his eyes on me. My hands rubbed my tired eyes awake.

"Hey," I murmured.

Ethan ran his hands through my hair in delicate strokes. It made my heart flutter when he was this tender with me. He paused to place his hand on my cheek as a tiny grin spread across his face. "I'm sorry about earlier. I walked away because I was losing my temper. When I came back, you'd fallen asleep. Since you don't do that a lot, I didn't want to wake you."

I sighed. "I was so mad at you."

"I know. Our emotions have the potential of becoming cataclysmic. I realized that when I pinned you against the shelves in the conference room. I was so angry with you. At the same time, I wanted you so much that I had a hard time from not turning you around and taking you right there. Hearing you react to me the way you did only amplified all those urges. I don't always think rationally when I'm around you," he revealed.

"I knew, at that moment, that I wasn't going to be able to deny you any," I admitted.

I rested my head in the crook of his shoulder. His fingers fiddled with the hem of my shirt. "You did?" Ethan asked in wonderment.

"Yes. I was so angry with you, but it didn't stop me from wanting you. It was an overwhelming feeling," I confessed.

Ethan exhaled heavily. "I don't like arguing with you."

His hands wandered underneath my shirt, wreaking havoc with my focus, yet again. "I'm not fond of fighting with you either but it's bound to happen with us," I pointed out as my heart began to flutter.

"Do you really think so?"

He removed my shirt and ran his hands along my sides. With every inch he touched, my skin and everything inside me ignited.

"Yes, I do. We have so much to learn about each other, and we're bound to have arguments. The important thing is that we try to talk through them," I said, attempting to even out my breathing.

"I do like this part of each other that we share. At least when I hold you this close, I can feel your need for me and that eases my mind," he admitted, tugging my boxers down halfway.

"I like that too," I breathed, sliding my hands up to his neck.

"Will you give that to me now?" Ethan asked huskily as his hands found my hot spot.

His fingers and thumbs worked their magic as he rolled me onto my back.

"Yes," I moaned, yanking off his boxers as he hovered over me.

Ethan brought his hand above my eye, letting his fingers trace down my cheek before gently putting it behind my neck. He brought me closer to him and slowly kissed me. Everything was moving at a very deliberate pace, including his hands. I needed him to pick up the pace down there or replace his fingers all together.

"Oh, God ..." I groaned.

I pushed my tongue past his lips, eagerly wanting him to match the frantic beats of my heart with his mouth, but he remained at his measured pace.

"I want this time to be different Mia," Ethan breathed.

He paused at my lips to bring his teeth along the bottom one and gently grazed back and forth.

"Ah, you're going to make me come if you keep doing that," I moaned loudly.

His lips left mine, moving down to my breasts where he began licking and suckling. His mouth focused on one while his fingers did the same to the other. Both nipples were at full attention in a matter of seconds. I was burning everywhere. He successfully sensationalized every part of me.

"I want to leave you with a lasting impression of me," he whispered, nibbling under my ear.

Ethan ran his tongue along my jaw to my mouth and pushed inside as if he was on a mission. My hands found their way down to him where I began stroking him at a quick pace. His breathing picked up, but he made no move to go faster. Ethan restrained my hand from any further action. He kissed the top of it before placing it above my head. His lips went down my neck and trailed down my cleavage to my belly button until they settled between my legs. I didn't care what he did to me as long as he was going to get me to a release soon. His tongue slipped up and down in such an erotic rhythm that I couldn't stop the scream that had built up in my chest.

"Oh. My. God. Don't. You. Dare. Stop."

He continued running his tongue along in a precise pattern while his hands did the same on my hip and breast. My head arched off the mattress as my hands clutched around the sheets. I was so very close, with toxic sensations in so many places. He brought me to the precipice of my climax before changing to an entirely different tempo.

"What are you doing?" I groaned loudly

"You're so ready, but wait," he whispered.

God help me, he better mean he was about to slide into me. I couldn't handle much more before I burst into flames.

"Ethan, please, I need you," I begged in a loud, drawn out moan.

"I need you too Mia," he replied in a reverent tone.

He rested his knee between my legs. His deep brown eyes mystified me. There was so much passion in them. It made my heart beat even faster knowing he was looking at me that way. He shifted my legs apart and positioned his body over me. He situated his elbows on each side of my head. My hands grasped his neck. My fingers tugged at his hair with my desperate want for him. He obliged by sliding into me. I still wasn't sure if it was him, the piercing, or us together, but the feeling was the most exotic thing I'd ever experienced.

"Oh, God ..." I screamed.

Ethan brought his lips to mine. His mouth silenced me as his hips set forth at a studied pace, just like everything else he'd been doing to me. He switched it up with slow, steady thrusts to prevent me from letting go. Every time he started back up at a faster pace. The fire inside me came back stronger; making each move he made so electrifying that I wasn't really sure if I was here with him anymore. My body felt like it had moved on to an entirely different plane.

"You always feel so good Mia," Ethan moaned loudly.

My arms clutched around his back as he penetrated deeper. He switched gears and pushed harder and faster. I let out a long moan, needing us to release soon. I held on tight and clenched my insides to him as he started to get close.

"Fuck, you drive me over the edge when you do that to me," he growled.

He drove into me several more times. I screamed with the immense pleasure of each powerful thrust. It was the most mind-blowing orgasm ever. I continued squeezing around him until he let go as well. As he hit his climax, he moaned louder than I'd heard from him all weekend. He rested his head on my shoulder. Our skin slid against each other with the amount of sweat we'd worked up. After a few minutes, Ethan slid out and rolled onto his back.

"Wow," I panted.

He grinned. "I told you it'd be worth it."

"Yes, it was worth it. I can't say I've ever experienced anything like that."

"Good. That was the plan."

"I need to get home soon."

His face fell and he gazed away. I kept my palm on his check until he looked at me.

"Hey, I had an amazing weekend with you. I'll see you tomorrow," I assured.

He sighed. "I know you need to go home. I just don't want you to go."

"Ethan, I know you're worried, but this weekend is so different from a day of playing hooky with you. This isn't the end of something; it's the beginning."

He beamed back at me. "You can certainly have a way with words when you want to Mia." He placed a sweet kiss on my forehead. "If I have to take you home, I'm showering with you."

"I'm never getting home tonight," I teased.

He picked me up and swatted me on the ass as he carried me to the bathroom. I couldn't admit it to him, but I was terrified of leaving him too. I knew without a doubt that he was my choice. I needed him in my life. I just had no idea how I was going to finagle my way out of everything without hurting him or anyone else.

CHAPTER TWENTY-TWO
Pow Wow

By the time we had finished showering, the sun had nearly set. Since I'd been wearing nothing but Ethan's clothes all weekend, I continued the trend with a pair of his sweatpants and T-shirt. They were huge on me, but they did the job. With his apartment behind us, we were in the hall on our way to the elevator. Ethan was as young looking as I'd ever seen him. He was in a pair of khaki cargo shorts and an olive green muscle shirt. His tattoos flamed up his arms and legs. It made him absolutely delectable.

Christ Mia, you're leaving! Don't even think about it!

Ethan hauled me into his chest. "You really can't help yourself, can you? I've always enjoyed catching you in a stare. It was how I realized you felt something for me too. Well, that and the blushing. I noticed the blushing the first day. It was hard to miss."

He paused to place his hand over my bright red cheek. I grabbed his hand and brought it down to my side as the elevator arrived. As we boarded, I gave it a tight squeeze. We shuffled to the back of the elevator and leaned against the railing, facing each other.

"If I had any control over how any part of my body reacts

around you, I would've exercised it a long time ago."

"I hope it never stops."

He brought his lips so close to me that his heated breath floated across my neck. My breath hitched as my body hummed to life again. "Don't. The parking lot was a one-time thing Ethan," I said hoarsely.

"I'm not doing anything," he disputed.

He ran his nose along my neck with soft brushes of his lips ever few seconds. My stomach clenched along with everything south of me. "Yes, you are, and you know it. So stop."

The elevator reached the garage. I departed as fast as possible. Ethan chuckled, but kept pace with me. We walked with our hands together until we got to his car. Before he opened the passenger side, he pressed his body against mine before bringing his hands to my face and lowering his mouth. We stood there exploring each other's mouths until he ran his hand down to open the door. I was ready to repeat everything we just finished doing in his bedroom.

The bastard turned me on again.

"Sometimes I can't help myself," he declared, helping me into the car.

We made our way back to the suburbs. He slowed to a stop as we hit my driveway. Ethan shifted the car into park and left it running with our hands laced together. I started to untangle my hand from his, but he stopped me by gripping it even tighter. He looked over, with heartache in his eyes that crushed my insides.

"I'll see you tomorrow," I whispered, bringing my mouth to his for a goodbye kiss.

I drove my lips heartily into his and took in every part of him. We did what we did so well with each other and lost ourselves in the moment. As our heated breaths rose, I pulled away and grabbed the handle to open it. Ethan sighed, but let me go. I leaned over for one last kiss to savor his wintergreen taste.

"Bye for now, babe."

"Bye love."

I grinned while getting out. I tapped the window before walking around the car. Ethan waited until I was at the door. To my surprise, it opened and I stumbled through it. It dumbfounded me at first, but I came to my senses fast when I caught sight of Bri behind the door. She was glaring at me with a fiery wrath in her eyes.

"It's about fucking time you came home!" Bri shouted.

"And hello to you too."

"I'm *so* not in the mood right now Mia." She stopped moving us forward and took in my attire. "What the hell happened to your clothes and shoes?"

"They're at Ethan's place."

"Unbelievable."

She yanked me from the safety of the doorway and stormed into the living room. I wasn't sure about going any further into the house, considering the ire surrounding her mood. The fire in her eyes stood a chance of incinerating me if I kept focus with them for too long. I loosened the death grip she had on my arm and settled into the recliner. Bri huffed as she sat down on the couch.

"Where are the guys?"

"I persuaded them to go out tonight so we could talk without them interrupting us. I had no idea you'd wait so long to come home," she snapped.

"I wasn't aware you needed the exact time of my return. I've never had a curfew, so I'm not sure what you expect from me," I retorted.

"Cut the bullshit Mia," she shrieked.

"Where's 'naughty Bri' that wanted to hear all the dirty details?"

"She disappeared when her best friend started making stupid life choices," she snarled.

I inhaled a quick gush of air. "I chose Ethan."

Bri frowned. "Mia, you don't even know him. I know you didn't spend the last two days getting to know everything about him as a person."

"Since when is getting to know someone really well, biblically, such a bad thing. And I mean *really* well," I joked.

She curled her fists to try and contain her exasperation. "There you go again. Cut the sarcasm. You don't know anything about him, yet you think he's everything you need. Please, for the love of God, explain to me how that's possible."

"The way he makes me feel is so different from anything I've ever experienced. It's not just the attraction or the sex. I feel so very alive around him."

I got up from the recliner and headed for the stairs. Bri scowled as she leapt up to follow me.

"Please tell me that you did more than fuck his brains out for the last forty-eight hours."

"Well ..."

I was thankful to be ahead of her on the stairs because if she saw the grin on my face she'd smack me. Bri doubled her pace after I started taking two stairs at a time. I strode into my room and went towards my closet as she sat on the corner of my desk.

"You wanted Harrison's offer more than anything. There's no way you'd throw that all away for a guy you don't even know, so start talking," she demanded.

I glanced over my shoulder to see that she was clearly at her wits end with me. "I don't know what it is, but it's like he came along and awakened me. He makes me so angry at times, but he also makes me feel love so deeply that it scorches my soul."

"Are you sure this has nothing to do with getting over Micah?" she asked skeptically.

I grabbed a pair of mesh shorts and T-shirt and changed into them. I tossed Ethan's clothes towards my desk. They whizzed past her head and took her attention away from picking at her nails, so she could see that she wasn't the only one pissed off.

"If you ask me that again, I might just slap you. This has nothing to do with Micah. If I was so hung up on him, I would've never shared with Ethan what happened last winter," I snapped.

Her eyes bugged out in disbelief. "Did you tell him everything?"

I nodded on my way out of my room. I was starving, so the kitchen was my next stop. If Bri wanted to continue interrogating me, she'd have to follow me there too.

"Wow, I'm surprised you lowered you guard that much. You haven't told anyone about that night in its entirety," she responded, baffled.

I grimaced. "I gave him a summarized version of the evening. I wanted him to understand that I wasn't exactly undamaged goods."

Once we were in the kitchen, I walked over to the fridge and opened the freezer, hoping that there was some food in there. Fortunately, there was a frozen pepperoni pizza tucked away at the bottom. One of us had to have hid it from the boys. Bri took a seat on a stool at the island as I placed the pizza in the oven.

"Mia, you aren't damaged."

I glanced at her to see she had calmed down some. She still seemed pissed, but she was also softening with the more I shared. I jumped up on the counter, keeping an eye on her.

"Yeah, I am. If you hadn't found me, I wouldn't be sitting here. It's just one of the many poor choices I've made over the last few months. I took the offer from Harrison hoping it would get my life back on track. I was desperate for a change, but I made it for all the wrong reasons."

Bri arched an eyebrow. "Can I ask you something?"

I exhaled deeply. "Has it ever stopped you before?"

"Are you in love with Ethan? You barely know him, but you're acting like he's the love of your life, with what you're willing to give up. Whether you want to see it or not, Ethan is part of the problem that Harrison revealed to you."

"I'm not above saying he doesn't have his fair share of secrets," I answered stiffly.

"How can you be with someone that you know could be hiding

such horrible things?"

Bri started to fidget with her rings as her eyes flitted between her hands and me. I rested my head against the cupboard.

"Why do you think I tried to stay away from him? It was because of that very question, which yes I'll admit remains unanswered, but I can't help how I feel. The heart wants what the heart wants, regardless of what the mind tells you is right." I paused to determine if Bri understood me. The hardness behind her eyes remained strong. "I should be scared with my knowledge of how his company operates underneath it all, or the fact that I know very few personal things about him, but I'm not. God knows I'm anything but innocent with all the secrets I'm hiding from people. I can't crucify him for his flaws when I have so many of my own. If I don't take this shot with him, I'll regret it for the rest of my life."

Bri began to loosen up a little. The resistance in her eyes receded as her look became more concerned. "I guess you've put more thought into this than I'm giving you credit for."

"Of course I've put thought into it. I nearly had a meltdown right in front of him. I'm well aware of the mess I'm in right now."

I hopped down from the counter to grab some water out of the fridge. She was right behind me to get a soda. We leaned against the counter, facing each other. She opened and closed her mouth with reservation before she moved forward with her next thought.

"What are you going to do?"

I sighed. "I've made so many mistakes trying to lead a double life. I feel horrible all the time and all I want to do is make it right for everyone that I've wronged, including you. I may not be able to make it right for all the people that are affected by what's happening in his company. I'm selfish enough to want to make it better for all the people that I've hurt in my own life."

Confusion swept across Bri's face. "You haven't wronged me Mia."

I cringed. "Haven't I? I asked you to keep a secret from the man you're in love with. No matter what you say, I have a feeling it's hurt you. When I look at what I've actually asked, I'm disgusted with myself. I should've never put you in that position knowing that it could hurt you. If that's not selfish, then I don't know what is."

"Mia," Bri disputed.

"No, I need to get this out. If there's anything being with Ethan has given me, its clarity. I can't keep hurting the people that I care about. I've hurt everyone in this house. I'm not any better than Micah," I contended.

"You're not like Micah. It's different," Bri argued.

I shook my head. "What makes me any less selfish? When I accepted Harrison's offer, I didn't care if there was a chance of my actions hurting anyone. I did it because that was what I needed for myself. That's selfishness."

"Mia ..."

"You wanted the pow wow Bri. I have no idea how I'll ever be able to hold on to Ethan and get out of this unharmed."

I stepped away from her to get the pizza. I sliced it before grabbing a few pieces. Bri did the same. I took a seat at the island as she sat down next to me with her plate.

"I'll admit it's easier to talk to you when you see reason. You're far more aware than you've been in a really long time, which makes me wonder what Ethan might be doing for you."

"Bri, I've been feeling this way for a while. Do you want to know what made me decide to take the offer?" I asked, in between bites of pizza.

"I've always been curious," Bri admitted before taking a bite.

"I relived that horrible night. I couldn't handle the pain. I gave into that weakness again. I'm a shitty human being. I need you to understand that I'm not overlooking that fact. I fucked up more than once and all I want to do is stop screwing up."

I pushed my pizza away. I was hungry, but my self-disgust had filled me right up.

"You're not a shitty human being. If you were a shitty person, you wouldn't be able to see your mistakes," Bri said quietly.

She pushed my plate forward. I gave her a skeptical look but appeased her by keeping it there.

"I'm a shitty person at the moment," I reiterated.

"God Mia ... I worried about this when you took the offer, but you were so confident that you had it all figured out. I really wish you had considered all of this before you even said yes. It would make everything so much easier now," Bri responded halfheartedly.

Bri finished off her plate and gave me a pointed look to finish mine. I picked up my remaining slice and took a bite. I finished it fast and washed it down with a gulp of water.

"Believe me – I know."

"I can tell I don't need to lecture you anymore on all the points that I had lined up. You seem to have gotten there on your own. I'm not going to push. I don't have any answers for you, but I know you Mia. You'll find a way. You always do."

"It's touching you still have faith in me when I don't deserve it. The truth is that I don't know what the hell to do, but hopefully it will come to me soon."

"As angry as you can make me, I'll always have faith in you. We all will, and you should know that by now," Bri said, trying to contain her scowl.

"Will you please tell me what's going on with you and Trey? I have more than shared. You avoided the question Friday night."

I rested my elbows on the island. Her face paled as she played with the strings on her sweatshirt. She shoved her empty plate towards the middle. When she had ran out of things to fidget with, she redirected her gaze to me. I smiled, encouraging her to tell me.

Bri took a deep breath. "We've been having issues. I think he has a hard time defining relationships in his life. I'm not sure why, but that's what it seems like to me. Who knows? Maybe you can figure it out. You've known him longer than anyone else. The connection you share is different than what the rest of us have with him."

She averted her eyes from me while running her fingers along the edge of the island.

"Bri ..."

She glanced over with hurt in her eyes. It stabbed at my heart that it bothered her this much and she had never told me. I opened my mouth, but her torn expression cut me off.

"I need to know that no matter what happens he'll be there. I don't have that feeling. I need to have that from him."

"I'm sorry," I whispered.

Bri whipped her head in my direction. "Why are you sorry?"

"I just am. I'm sorry for the things I can fix and the things that I can't. I'll talk to him if you want me to. I should talk to him about the standoff he had with Ethan anyway. I have no idea what that was all about," I murmured, running my hands across my face.

"You can talk to Trey, but make it subtle. I don't know what happened when we were in the bathroom, but those two looked like they were ready to beat the shit out of each other. Did Ethan say anything about it?"

I looked away as my neck began to flush. Bri arched an eyebrow.

"Uh ... no ... I didn't give him a chance to either," I admitted.

"I take it I'm not the only one that had a very public display of affection that evening."

My cheeks turned fire engine red. "I guess that's one way of putting it."

She smirked. "I'm ready for all those naughty details now."

We left the dirty dishes behind us and made our way towards The Cave.

"Well, let's just say we made it to his car before I ended up begging."

"You begged?" she asked in a startled tone.

I settled on the couch and looked for the remote. Bri had a smug grin on her face as she sat down in the recliner. I shook my head before rolling my eyes at her. "Seriously, I hadn't had sex in over a month. I couldn't handle it any longer after he marked and mauled me on the dance floor. What would you have done?"

Bri laughed. "Go on."

I glanced at her with a sheepish smile. She laughed even harder, but was eager for more. "We made it to his car. The first time happened so fast that I missed something about him that surprised me later that night."

"What could you have possibly missed that would've shocked you later?"

"He has a piercing," I mumbled.

Bri crinkled her eyes. "What's the big deal? The guy is covered in tattoos."

"He has a piercing down there," I confessed.

Bri's jaw dropped but she snapped it shut as a fit of giggles took over. "How the hell did you miss that? Is he that good?" she asked enthusiastically.

I beamed. "I lose my mind with him every time."

"What draws you more to him? The sex or the man?"

"The man," I answered immediately.

"Really!" Bri squealed.

"Yes. We drive each other crazy, but we also connect in a very powerful way. It's like being together has given us those missing pieces of ourselves that make us whole."

My face exuded the happiness flowing through me. Bri gazed at me in awe.

"Wow, I still can't get past the fact that you two hardly know each other. Do you think he's your soul mate?"

"I don't believe in soul mates."

"You don't?" Bri asked, scratching her head.

"No. I think there are plenty of people that are on this earth that we are destined to cross paths with. I don't think it's limited to a relationship with a man. I think we find the people that we're supposed to have in our lives," I explained.

"Do you think Ethan was supposed to be on your path all along?"

I smiled. Everything happened for a reason. There was a reason I met her so there had to have been a reason that I met him too. "I think that as life steers a new course for you, the people you're intended to meet change with it. I guess if you're lucky enough, you'll get lightning in a bottle with those changes."

"What do you mean?"

"You'll get to meet that person that completes all the parts of yourself that you never knew were incomplete in the first place," I said softly.

Bri sank even further into the chair, completely astonished by my answer. Her happiness for me faded as a significant weight washed over her features. "How are you going to get out of this deal with Harrison without Ethan knowing what you were doing there all along?"

"Bri, I'm trying to figure that out as we speak. All I know is that if I'm not careful, I could bring down a lot of hell around me. I've been careless enough. If danger comes to me, I deserve it. I don't want any of you guys to get hurt," I whispered in fear.

"What about Ethan?"

My heart quivered just thinking about Ethan and how it plays into my mess with Harrison. "The last thing I want to do is hurt Ethan. I'll never be able to live with myself if I don't tell him the truth. I'm trying to figure out a way of going about this that will hurt him the least."

I shoved my worries aside and gave her a wide smile. She eyed me with curiosity.

"Has this pow wow come to its conclusion? I'd really like to break from the heavy stuff and paint our nails while watching reality garbage on TV."

Bri grinned as she leapt from the chair. "I hereby close this summit. I'll get the nail-polish while you find something raunchy for us to watch."

I crawled into bed with a thousand different things running through my head. Most of them revolved around Ethan. A tear glistened at the possibility of him walking away from me. I crept to the end of the bed to grab my purse. I needed a playlist to fall asleep to or I'd be up for hours torturing myself. I opened my purse and grabbed my phone. I plugged it in and it sprang to life. I selected the music icon and went for my playlists. I gasped, seeing a new playlist – 'Ethan's playlist'.

When did he make me a playlist?

I pulled out my headphones and snuggled under the covers. I clicked on his playlist wondering what songs he'd mixed for me. The first song flowed into my ears and my breath faltered. If every song was as thoughtful as this one, then there was no question that he'd fallen for me too. With each one, the walls around my heart kept cracking. My love for him swirled through me with so much intensity that I thought my heart would burst. I swallowed to try and alleviate the lump in my throat, as a few tears cascaded down my temples. I couldn't lose him. There was no way I could go back to a life without him in it.

CHAPTER TWENTY-THREE
Coming Clean

I was more self-conscious about my clothes after this weekend. I'd love to find something that would drive Ethan crazy with want, but that would probably fall under the teasing category. He did bring out a devilish side to me though, so I was considering it. I had a low-cut halter-top in my hand and was digging for a skirt to compliment it.

"Are you kidding yourself? You can't wear that top to his office," Bri remarked.

"Why?"

She rolled her eyes. "If you want to make a spectacle of yourself, by all means wear it."

"What?"

"First of all, you shouldn't try to rev him up when you're around other people. Not until you're out of that place for good. Second, you'll look like a slut if you walk around exposing to the world that you got some over the weekend," Bri reasoned.

"This top isn't that slutty," I defended.

Bri snorted. "It is if you want to show off your hickeys like a proud high school girl."

"Damn it. I keep forgetting about them," I muttered.

Bri started giggling as she walked into my room. I shot her a look to shut her up, but it only made her laugh harder. She grabbed my clothes and tossed them on the bed before pawing in my closet. I flopped on my bed and let her do what she did best.

"Here, wear this pantsuit," she said, dropping the outfit next to me.

"Thanks Bri. Why are you up so early?"

Her face fell. I felt like a jackass for even asking her. "I woke up when Trey got up. He mentioned something about studying for a test. I have some assignments that are due soon."

It was evident that it frustrated her to be up this early for such a mundane reason. I'd have to make a point to talk to Trey tonight. I hated seeing her upset.

"I'm sorry Bri."

"Don't start Mia. I'm going to get started on my papers," she said on her way out.

While getting ready, I contemplated what was going on with her. Her entire demeanor appeared to be anything but her usual carefree spirit. I started wondering if there was something more than just her and Trey that was bothering her, because she seemed on the verge of a breakdown. It was totally unlike her. Bri was resilient, and rarely let guys affect her, so I felt like it was bigger than just Trey. She'd never been in love before though, so maybe this was different. I walked downstairs with those thoughts tumbling around in my head and wasn't paying much attention to anything else. I dug in my purse for my keys but came up empty-handed. I turned to go back upstairs to ask Bri if she had seen them.

"Are you looking for these?" Trey asked, jingling my car keys.

I turned around to see him standing at the bottom of the stairwell. He glared at me as I walked down the stairs. I grabbed for my keys, but he held them in his fist tightly.

"Yeah ... where'd you find them?" I asked, standing across from him.

"I came into possession of them the other night when some random guy pulled up with your car. All three of us were pissed that you'd let some stranger drive your car. We almost beat the shit out of the guy but he said Ethan told him that you had consented to it. Who's Ethan?"

Without a doubt, I needed to talk to Trey tonight. He looked as livid with me as Bri had yesterday. Suffice to say, I was pissing everyone off. The only thing in my favor was my determination to correct it. All the lies had exhausted me, so I opted for telling the truth. "Ethan's new. I met him at work," I replied quickly.

"You never mentioned where you work," Trey pressed angrily.

I glanced at my watch. "Listen Trey, I know we need to talk. Are you home tonight?"

"I have an afternoon class but I'll be home after it. You've been withholding what's going on with you for a while. I've respected it but it's time for you to be honest with me. I've earned it," he demanded.

"I agree. I want to talk to you, but I have to get going or I'm going to be late."

I grabbed at my keys with more force this time. Trey loosened his grip, allowing my keys to fall into my palm. I gave him a halfhearted smile on my way down the last couple of steps.

I arrived at work with about ten minutes to spare. I still didn't know why Ethan was so set on having me work with him. I headed towards his office for what I assumed would be a very long day. I tapped on his door. He opened it with a huge grin across his face. I smiled in return. As I walked through the entryway, he wrapped his hands around my waist. I nearly moaned with how good it felt to have his arms around me again. Ethan kicked the door shut with his foot and spun me around. He pressed my back up against the closed door as if his was on a mission. I was positive my lips would bruise with the force that he put behind each kiss he placed upon them. It blazed me to life. I dug my nails into his shoulders at the frantic way he continued to kiss me. He had more than turned me on, but we weren't in a position to go any further. I unclasped my hands from his shoulders and brought them to his chest to push him away.

"Ethan, stop," I whispered.

"I'd rather not," he said, sweeping his lips back to mine.

"Stop."

I bit down on his lip, hoping he'd get the hint. A low hum rumbled from his chest – not the reaction I had been going for. I ran my hand down to his peck and gave him a titty twister. Ethan flew back instantly, with a scowl on his face as he massaged his chest.

"Fuck. What did you do that for?"

"You left me no choice. You obviously weren't listening to me when I said stop," I remarked, batting my eyelashes.

"So you felt the need to assault my poor nipple."

"It got you to stop, didn't it?"

"Apparently, I'm not the only one that can make an effective point," he muttered.

Ethan stepped forward to close the distance, but I held up my hands. I marched over to his desk and tossed my purse in a chair. I faced him and leaned against the desk.

"I don't want you to do that again. The last thing I need is for someone to find out I'm screwing the boss."

He started walking towards the other side of his desk and sat down in his chair. I did the same with the remaining open chair on my side. Ethan narrowed his eyes at me. I gave him the same determined look.

He huffed. "You kissed me back Mia."

"We need ground rules Ethan. I thought you said you conducted yourself professionally. Because what played out just then is about as far as you can get from it," I snapped, gesturing to the door behind us.

I was beginning to become irritated with his lack of understanding on such an obvious topic. He shook his head before arching an eyebrow.

"Fine, let's talk rules. Clearly, kissing is off the table. Am I allowed to touch you at all?"

I shook my head. "Touching isn't a good idea for us when we're here. It has the potential to get out of control."

Ethan smirked. "You've sucked all the entertainment out of my workday. I had fun touching you last week."

I rolled my eyes. "It was your cockamamie idea to have me work with you. Consider this your plan blowing up in your face. I'm not going to be intimate with you while we're in this building. You're going to have to deal with talking to me all day."

"I can live with that. Occasionally, insightful things pass through those terse lips of yours."

I beamed. "Every now and then I do say something useful."

Ethan batted his eyelashes. "Are you sure you don't want to reconsider touching? I'll keep it innocent."

I scoffed. "No, I don't believe for a second that you will restrain yourself."

"What's so wrong with the idea?"

"It's wrong in so many ways. The answer remains no. What's on the agenda for today?"

My brain had managed to retain an ounce of control. It pushed for me to get into a serious mode with him. I had to do something to get rid of the rising ache. My body didn't give a rat's ass at what my mouth was spewing. If it were in control, I'd be across his desk screaming his name.

"You're kind of on the crabby side this morning. Have you had any coffee yet?"

"No, I haven't," I said softly.

Ethan grinned and pointed to the Caribou coffee cup at the edge of his desk. I smiled shyly while retrieving it. His eyes filled with happiness as I took a long drink.

"Thank you. That was sweet of you."

"How was the rest of your night?"

"It was good. I caught up with Bri."

"Talk about anything interesting?"

"Nope, just some guy. How was your night?"

"Anyone I know?"

Ethan ran his fingers along his desk. I softened, catching him in this vulnerable state. He fidgeted when he was nervous or agitated. It was cute to watch. He captured my gaze with a deep passion behind his eyes. I set my coffee down. It wasn't needed with the warmth catapulting in every direction inside me. I blinked to regain my wits.

"Maybe. You didn't answer my question."

He looked away from me as he settled into a mood that was practically moping. "My night was uneventful compared to the rest of my weekend."

"Sounds like you had a pretty good weekend."

"It was one of the best weekends I've ever had. I was sorry it ended," he confessed.

Ethan focused on me again with a sweltering look on his face. He ran his eyes up and down my body. There was so much desire in them. It made me squeeze my legs together in an attempt to contain the very abrupt flash of heat that coursed through them.

"Me too," I stammered.

"How did you sleep last night?"

"I slept pretty decently after popping in my headphones," I admitted with a shy smile.

He flashed a crooked grin. "Listen to anything good to help you fall asleep?"

"Yes, I had this new playlist that made sleeping easier than it has been in a long time."

"I'm surprised you aren't chewing me out for touching your phone. You're relatively mellow right now. I'm not sure whether that's a good thing or a bad thing."

"It's a good thing," I reassured.

Ethan shook his head. "You flip out when I move your car without telling you but you're fine with me putting a playlist on your phone. You never cease to amaze me, Mia."

I smirked. "I need to keep you on your toes."

"Did you like the songs?"

He was clearly anxious about how I would react to the very intimate and thoughtful songs that he had selected for me. I opened my mouth, but the phone rang. He cursed and picked up the receiver. "Ethan," he snapped.

I watched with concern as he exhaled to calm himself. His intimidating side was starting to rear its head again. He diverted his eyes from me, so I busied myself with drinking my coffee.

"No, I don't think it will be ready by then," he replied curtly.

Ethan banged his hands down on the desk at the next part of the conversation. My eyes drifted around his office. Being in his direct line of vision didn't seem to be in my best interest. It occurred to me that I hadn't really paid attention to what was in his office. I had always been too busy drooling over him.

His large L-shaped teak desk was directly across from the door. Personally, I was a fan of the desk because of its modern flair. If you sat across from him, there was plenty of leg space. What was even better was that one side of it had no back to it so that you could slide right in as if it was your own desk. I settled myself in that spot, suspecting it was going to be my area of his desk indefinitely.

At least the leather chair is cozy. It still irks me that he wants me to work with him, though. I just feel like there's something he isn't telling me. Shut it Mia! You're intuition these days hasn't been on its finest form. Let it go!

On each side of the door there were black leather couches, with artwork on the walls above them. It was the only open wall in his office because the other three contained built-in bookshelves from floor to ceiling, crammed with miles of books. Much like his apartment, there was a very distant feel to his office. There was nothing personal to him. I glanced back to the door to see if maybe there was something that I might have missed on the wall, but it was more of the same. The artwork was amazing. From the quick glance that I took, they appeared to be Irish and Greek pieces. I zoned in to get a better idea but was snapped out of my daze when Ethan slammed his hands down on his desk again. It was so loud that it made me jump out of my seat this time.

"Fine, I'll figure out how to get it ready," Ethan shouted.

I flinched, watching his temper rising. The vein in his forehead was protruding from the skin, as well as several others in his neck. He slammed down the receiver. His hands balled into fists. I focused on trying to breathe without making a sound. It scared me to look at him because of how angry he was. I stopped looking around his office and remained perfectly still. The lines in my hands became the most interesting things in the room.

"We should get to work."

"Sure. What do you need me to do?"

Ethan stared at me with a pain in his eyes that I couldn't place. Everything inside of me wanted to settle myself in his lap to soothe him, but I held back. We became enthralled with each other's eyes. It almost had me drifting in his direction to kiss away his frustrations. I broke our heated connection by pointing at his computer screen.

This is going to be one hell of a long day.

"I'm working on a proposal that needs to be closed soon. We'll work to put together the research from the other departments into a portfolio. It'll represent what our company will do should they select us as investors," he said flatly.

"I'll do whatever you need me to, Ethan."

He rolled his chair over to the other side of the desk and rummaged in one of the drawers. He swung around with a laptop. I took it and hit the power button. I finished the rest of my coffee and looked for a trashcan. Ethan motioned for the cup. Our fingers grazed in the exchange and we inhaled sharply.

This is going to be torture.

I retracted my hand quickly to stop the fire coursing through my body. We knew what direction it would lead in if we let our fingers linger. This was why I had made a rule of no contact. Ethan sat with his eyes closed, muttering under his breath.

OK, I guess that affected him a little more than I thought.

I gave him some space and looked at the computer. I gasped once the desktop emerged and the picture behind it popped out. It was his spot on the lake. The detail of the city appeared in tiny blocks, but the photo was of the lake on a calm day with light ripples running endlessly. I gazed over to him. His face warmed to a bright smile with those delectable dimples. He knew what reaction he was going to get. I swore the man lived for getting a rise out of me.

"There's a file on the Q drive that I want you to look at," Ethan instructed.

I opened the only file on that drive. I examined the contents and dived into editing the proposal. We worked without a word for hours. I wanted this day to be over. I wasn't any closer to telling Harrison that I couldn't do this any longer. The last thing I wanted to do was disappoint Ethan by not meeting his expectations while working on closing this deal. The internal conflict rose to the surface, making it difficult to focus. I was so deep in thought that the knock on his door made me jump.

Stupid caffeine.

Ethan chuckled as he walked to the door. The busty blonde from reception strode in with a take-out bag of food. She paused when she noticed me, but moved past her observation and began openly flirting with Ethan. I literally bit my tongue to refrain from calling her on it. Ethan thought nothing of it as he took the food and dismissed her. I turned to my computer, silently seething. In the past, I'd never been jealous around other women. With him, I suspected it would become a very familiar emotion for me.

"You're cute when you're jealous," he remarked.

Ethan slid a take-out container over to me. I refrained from looking at him. He sat down on his side of the desk and opened his own box of food. My container had eggs and toast with slices of bacon. I glanced at him in awe.

"I thought it'd be a nice gesture since we never got to have breakfast with each other this weekend. It was also the only food I knew you'd eat other than Chinese."

"This looks great. It's no secret that we need to learn more about each other."

Ethan grimaced. "I've always wanted to know more about you Mia. The issue has been more about what you've been willing to share."

I sighed. "I promise to try harder moving forward."

"What are you doing this evening?" he asked.

"I have plans tonight," I answered quickly.

"Are you serious?"

"Yes. I made plans with a friend that I can't back out on," I reiterated.

I didn't care for his sharp tone, or the exaggerated scowl on his face.

"Is this your way of trying to push me away again?"

He stopped eating and stared at me with such anger that it made me sink into my seat. It was enough to get rid of the guilt coursing through me and replace it with my temper. "No. How long do you intend on holding how I reacted after we kissed over my head? I'd like to have a timeline so I can properly prepare for your outbursts," I snapped.

I couldn't contain my agitation with him, nor could I apologize for it anymore. We were going to continue going around in this circle until he got over it. It was easy to spar with him when he brought out this side of me.

"Fuck, you piss me off with your smart-ass mouth," Ethan fumed.

"Duly noted, and the feeling is mutual by the way," I retorted.

He let out a long huff before picking up his fork and taking a forceful bite of his peanut butter-coated pancakes. I lost my appetite with the sudden flare-up between us.

"When can I see you again?"

My head whipped in his direction in confusion. His tone had changed dramatically; quickly losing the venom that it had had a minute ago. He placed his fork into the empty container, closed his eyes and took a deep breath. It surprised me to hear such a shift in him. I was usually the one that went from one extreme to the next, so this was new for us.

"I don't have any plans tomorrow night."

"I'd like to spend it with you, Mia."

"That sounds perfect."

"Good. Are you sure you don't want to reconsider your no touching rule?" Ethan joked.

I sighed in relief that his humor had returned, because his angry side scared me. "I'm going to stand strong on that rule."

"You're going to have to think of a pretty damn good way to distract me," he replied, with a sinful smile.

I grinned. "I'm sure I'll think of something."

We finished the rest of the day without another incident that caused either one of us to lose our tempers. The sun was starting to set, and it was time for me to leave.

"I have to get going, Ethan. It's already well past seven," I spoke up.

Ethan looked up from his screen. I gave him an uplifting smile, rising from my seat. He made his way around the desk. We walked together towards the door where neither one of us made a move to open it. This morning's events flashed through my mind. I blushed at all the sinful desires that ran through me from the thought of it. I grabbed the knob to open the door. His hand came down against mine. He leaned into me. My body jumped to full attention. I resisted at first, but couldn't hold back for long. I wanted everything about him. I craved his body, his scent, and the liveliness he brought out in me.

"Mia, I can't let you walk out of that door without kissing you goodbye."

I separated my body from his and stared, wide-eyed, before my body did all the talking, as my head nodded. His lips crashed against mine. The side of me that I had suppressed all day took over at full speed. When we connected with each other this way, my body surged at a higher level. I opened my mouth and allowed him to take whatever part of me he desired. We remained frozen in time, kissing each other with such intensity that we pulled slightly away, breathless. I lingered near his lips and sucked on his bottom one. He stroked his tongue where my lips dawdled. Before leaving his office, I gave him a parting smile. Ethan looked back at me unhappily. I wanted nothing more than to stay with him, but I also needed the separation.

As I pulled into our driveway, I noticed only Trey's Camaro was parked in the driveway. I was hoping that there would be someone else home to act as a buffer for us. I got out of my car and made my way towards the house at a snail's pace. I dropped my stuff inside the door and prepared myself for what would be nothing short of a colorful conversation. I knew coming clean with Trey would make him so angry that he'd want to punch something. Thankfully, he never hit girls. I reveled in my gender and sat down on the couch across from him. I preferred having the coffee table between us. It was the closest thing to a buffer I was going to get. He was rigid, which was fitting – it matched the fury in his eyes.

"Where is everyone else?"

"Class. Don't even bother with small talk Mia. Who's Ethan? Where are you working?"

I sighed. "Before I tell you, I need to backtrack to my meeting from a while ago."

"I knew you weren't telling me everything that day," Trey snapped.

"The meeting wasn't just with my advisor. The owner of *Inside Out* was there too. His name is Harrison Reynolds. My advisor had given him some of my work. Long story short, Harrison asked me to help him with a major piece he's been putting together for quite some time. He made me an offer I couldn't refuse."

Trey narrowed his eyes. "I'm missing the punch line. Get to the point."

I inhaled deeply. "The way I'm helping him is by being an inside source. I'm trying to gather information that will contribute to what he has already put together so that he can take it to print."

Trey rolled his fingers. "Again, move it along Mia."

I took a deep breath and prayed that Trey didn't blow a gasket. "I'm working at F. F. Sweeney to get that information for Harrison. That's how I met Ethan," I said rapidly.

"ARE YOU OUT OF YOUR FUCKING MIND?"

Trey lunged across the coffee table, slamming his fists against it. His face went from white to bright red. Since he was inches from me, I leaned away from his heavy breathing. "Trey, please calm down. I'm getting myself out of it," I answered quietly.

"*Calm down*. You want me to calm down. The owners of that company are tied to the mob! How could you agree to cross them? Do you have any idea of how much danger you're in?"

He brought up his fist as if to crash it through the table but stopped before the impact.

"I'm trying to get out of it without drawing any attention to myself."

Trey stepped away and clasped his hands behind his neck. He started pacing around the room for a few minutes. He returned his attention to me with rage still in his eyes. "This is because of the guy. You're backing out because of him, aren't you?"

"Yes and no."

My body became anxious as Ethan flowed through my mind. My heart fluttered as my stomach squelched. It was because of him that I was finally able to see the situation for what it was. Part of it was about him, but most of it was about me. I wanted to be better, and being involved with Harrison wasn't going to help me improve on all my shortcomings.

"That's not an answer. Tell me the fucking truth," Trey seethed.

"It is sort of both. After I got involved with Ethan, it made me see that what I was doing had the potential to hurt more than just me. I started thinking about you guys. If something happened to you, I'd never forgive myself."

Trey scowled. "And the guy?"

"It's because of him too. I don't want to betray him any more than I already have. If I stand a shot with Ethan, I need to come clean," I whispered, avoiding his eyes.

"What do you know about him? What's his involvement with the company?"

His eyes told me that his mind was moving a mile a minute. He brought his fists up on more than one occasion as if he was about to punch a wall, or anything in sight. Somehow, he refrained from following through with it. Trey stopped pacing and sat back on the couch again. He remained livid, but he had loosened his fists as his breathing evened out.

"I don't know a lot about him but I'm hoping to have a chance to learn everything. I don't know if he's as bad as the owners of the company. My gut tells me that he's not."

"Your gut. You're going off your damn gut. I swear to God Mia!" Trey barked.

"I'm sorry Trey. I know I've messed up badly," I breathed.

I fought back my tears. This was why talking to your girl-friends was easier than talking to your guy-friends. The tone in his voice was separating me. It screamed at every corner how horribly I fucked up.

"I don't like him Mia. You shouldn't be considering anything with him."

"What happened between you two? You looked like you were ready to kill each other."

Trey frowned. "I knew he was a bad guy. I questioned letting you leave with him. I should've gone with my instincts and kicked his ass so that he stayed away from you."

"I know that you look out for me Trey. You're like a brother to me. I know you won't let anyone hurt me, but you can't keep me from following my heart. I want to be with Ethan, regardless of the things I don't know about him," I whispered, wiping away a tear that slipped down my cheek.

"You shouldn't trust him. He's going to hurt you. How can you not see what's right in front of you? He's part of a bad company. There's no way he's not well aware of the operations that go on underneath the surface. How are you OK with that?"

Trey focused on me with such fury that I couldn't prevent the shiver that ran up my spine. I looked away while taking a deep breath. "I have to follow my heart on this one. You should understand what that means."

Trey did a double take. "What?"

"What are you doing with Bri? You were an ass to her at the club. She's your girlfriend, so you should trust her. You got pissed at her for living a little. What was that all about?"

"We aren't talking about Bri and me," he dismissed.

"We're done talking about me. You have a good thing going with her. Don't be an idiot by throwing it all away because you're scared to admit how you feel about her. If you're going to have her in your life, you have to let her all the way into your heart and trust her," I shot back.

His eyes grew wide with warning. I tilted my head, not fazed in the least.

"You need to call this Harrison clown and get yourself out of this mess."

My temper started to flare. I was just about over his pushiness. I had so many things to figure out before making that call. "Trey, I will call Harrison. I'm not going to do it right now though. I need more time."

His face flushed as his anger came back in full force. "You're making excuses Mia. The longer you let it go; the worse it's going to become. Cut the cord and be done with it. There's going to be fallout one way or another, so you might as well just get it over with already."

My shoulders sagged in defeat. There were times I'd let my stubbornness carry on for hours, but he was right. I needed to accept that there would be a price to pay. "Fine, I'll call him and ask to set up a meeting," I relented.

"Whatever. Make the fucking call already," Trey bit back.

I got up from the couch and searched through my purse to grab my phone. I dialed Harrison's number and faced Trey with my other hand on my hip. We stared at each with the same amount of frustration in our eyes. The line rang several times before dumping me into his voicemail. I left him a message letting him know that we needed to set up a meeting. Harrison was timely with getting back to me so I knew I'd hear from him soon. I tossed my phone back in my purse and glanced over at Trey. He was still far from calm. I slowly walked over and sat down next to him.

"Did Bri know about what you've been up to?" Trey asked angrily.

"Yes, but I made her promise not to tell you or anyone else. I'm sorry for keeping this from you. I hope that someday you'll be able to forgive me."

After a few minutes, Trey pulled me into his arms and gave me a tight hug. Tears streamed down my face as he held me close.

"I'm still really fucking pissed at you Mia. I'm going to need a little time on this one, but I'll always be there for you," he whispered.

I knew he'd be there for me through the good times and the bad times. This happened to be one of the crappier times. All the guilt flowed out of me as we sat there not speaking a word, but saying so much at the same time. Eventually, he released me and left the room. I lay down and closed my eyes. I wanted to be anyone else but me.

CHAPTER TWENTY-FOUR
Six For Six

Several hours later I woke up in my bed. I rolled to my side to see Bri lying next to me. She was sound asleep, so I didn't want to wake her. I crawled out of bed and slipped into some shorts before digging around my desk to find Ethan's T-shirt. I yearned for his scent. There was something about the way he smelled that aroused me about as much as his appearance did. There was a subtle smell of cologne. For the most part, it was a cross of the lake on a hot summer's day and a fresh spring breeze. This, combined with his natural masculinity was toxic to me. I found his shirt, tossed it on, and took a moment more to inhale the smells of him that lingered on it.

I tiptoed from my room downstairs to find my phone. With my cell in hand, I walked back upstairs while checking my call log and texts. Ethan had called and sent a text. I had also missed a call from Harrison, who had left a voicemail. He had instructed me to stop in for a meeting tomorrow morning. My stomach twisted at the thought of what the following days would bring. I redirected my attention towards the idea of savoring every moment I'd have with Ethan before bringing something upon us that would either shatter or strengthen our future together. I sank to the floor in the hallway and opened his text message.

Hey baby! I found something of yours in my car...
Shit.

I had forgot all about that particular lost article of clothing. I could only imagine the dirty thoughts that ran through his mind when he found it. He wanted to be entertained until tomorrow night. I wondered how he'd do with teasing over the phone. I grinned devilishly at the prospect of poking at him.

Hey babe :) Sorry I missed your call – fell asleep. How was your night?

My phone vibrated instantly. I peeked into my room to see that Bri was still asleep. I crossed over to her room. I flipped on the light and was faced with a whirlwind of a mess. I had never seen so many clothes strewn all over. They covered every area of the floor, as well as her bed and desk. No wonder she slept in Trey's room. She probably couldn't find enough space. I pushed aside a pile to lay at the foot of the bed.

I wish you were here right now. I love having you in my bed.

I love that too. Now about that finding, I'd like it back as well as my other clothes.

I'll think about it ;)

I laughed at his playfulness. I loved when this side of him surfaced.

What's to think about? You can't keep them. I'll find ways to get them back!

Oh, do tell. Sounds salacious ;)

There's this spot below your chin that I'd use to my benefit :)

I know what spot you're referring to. Go on...

I'd brush my tongue across it sweeping its way north or south...

You didn't spend much time with your tongue south. Not that I'm complaining with what you did with it because I was more than satisfied.

I blushed at what he was inferring.

You didn't give me much of a chance!

True. Plenty of time for that baby. Patience :)

I'm beginning to hate that word when it comes to you.

So you keep telling me.

I cursed under my breath. He was unable to resist trying to get a rise out of me through any medium. As I went to text him back, my phone vibrated again.

I know you're cussing me out – don't do it again.

I didn't understand this connection with him. My stomach and heart pranced together as one just contemplating it.

I'm not scared of your threats.

You should be. I might have to remind you tomorrow night.

I'm looking forward to it. I should get some sleep.

I'll agree to that. You're going to need your rest. Night love x

Good night babe x

I got up from Bri's bed and switched off the light on my way out. I opened my door and plugged in my phone. I crawled under the covers, trying not to disturb her. I wasn't sure why she was in my room, but she seemed exhausted. I tried for an hour to shake my nerves about tomorrow. Just as I was about to fall asleep, Bri shifted before talking in her sleep.

"Please don't let it be true," she mumbled.

Please don't let what be true. Bri, what are you hiding?

Now wide-awake, I rolled onto my side to face her. She was out, but more restless than when I came in the room. I watched as she moved back and forth, almost trembling at times. Her dark hair splayed across the pillow and moved with her restlessness. Her eyelids twitched every so often, but no more words passed through her lips.

Her face contorted every so often, as if she might say something, but nothing ever came out. It was as if a horrible had dream trapped her and she was unable to surface from it. Everything about her made me wonder even more what was going on. I slid to the end of my bed to check the time on my phone. It was a little after midnight. I couldn't sleep or relax after listening to her slip of the lip. A rush of warmth spread through my heart as Ethan settled back into my mind. I craved to hear his voice. I grabbed my cell and pressed 'Call' on my way back into Bri's room. I situated myself at the end of her bed again.

"I thought you were going to bed," he answered, surprised.

"I wanted to hear your voice. I like hearing it before I fall asleep," I admitted.

"It's shocking to hear you be so honest without having to pry it out of you," he noted.

I sighed. "I'm trying Ethan."

Silence filled the line as we listened to each other's slow breaths. Listening to him breathe made my heart spring to life at a sprint.

"Have you ever heard of six-for-six?" I asked.

"I can't say I have. Where are you going with this Mia?" he asked warily.

"We get six questions. Three of them can be about more serious aspects of our lives but the others need to be lighthearted," I suggested.

My stomach fluttered, hoping he'd agree. The only thing we knew for sure was that we were very drawn to each other and were insanely compatible in bed.

"Is this your version of twenty questions?"

"It's my way of trying to open up to you more," I responded quietly.

"I assume there are rules, so let's have them," he replied, after a moment.

"We have the right to veto at least one question if we don't want to answer it."

"I can live with that rule. Do I at least get to go first?"

"Sure."

Ethan paused and took several shallow breaths. I started nervously biting at my cuticles.

"Where do you feel most euphoric?"

I settled on the bed, letting a smile spread across my face. "It's a point within the old neighborhood that allows you to see all the suburbs and the city as the lake intersects its way through it all. I don't know what it is about that particular place, but I always feel at peace."

"It sounds wonderful," Ethan commented.

"I'd ask you what your place is but you've already revealed it to me. What other companies do you own?"

"Does that qualify as a serious question?"

"Yes."

"I have vested interests in quite a few different businesses. The club is one, so is the pro shop– "

"Seriously? You own that place too? No wonder you were so willing to cover the bill for everything!" I interjected.

"Are you going to let me finish, or are you hell-bent on ranting?" he retorted.

I smirked. "Go on."

"I have a variety of businesses, ranging from restaurants to personal interests. I've mostly invested in areas that I'm passionate about that don't have anything to do with my father's company."

His father's company ... Interesting he doesn't refer to it as 'his' company.

"Have you ever gone skinny dipping?" he asked devilishly.

I giggled. "You have such a dirty mind. Yes, I've gone skinny dipping."

"You made it seem like the other night was the first time you ever did something that shameless in public," he replied, shocked.

"Ethan, we were outside of a very crowded club where anyone could've seen us. God knows how many people heard it. It was a first for me. The times I've skinny dipped were in secluded areas."

"Did you have sex any of those times?"

"Ha! I don't have to answer that because it's my turn."

I attempted to ignore the flashes of heat that started tingling south of me. I wasn't going to let him entice me into phone sex, because his seductive tone implied that *that* was exactly what he wanted.

"What's your favorite fast food chain?" I asked.

My mind had drifted to dirtier thoughts. I focused on willing my body to purge the growing impulse to have hot and sweaty sex with him. Every part of me was alive with a want for him. I tried even harder to stop those feelings before they turned into the familiar ache he creates in me. I never longed for sex like I did with him.

"White Castle," he answered straightaway.

I did little to withhold my gagging, which also helped desensitize my overly turned-on body.

"What's wrong with White Castle?"

"It's right up there with the peanut butter on your pancakes. I don't know if this is going to work Ethan. We have some serious food differences," I teased.

"Your palate is way too limited. I might need to fix that for you."

"I think my likes and dislikes when it comes to food are just fine. If I feel the need to lower those standards, you'll be my first call," I snickered.

"I swear, your mouth kills me at times."

Ethan chuckled then paused, taking a deep breath. I held mine and let the butterflies in my stomach take over.

"What is one of your favorite memories of your past that you feel changed your life?" he asked softly.

I let out a huge sigh. "I'd have to say that it would be my first day of junior high."

"Will you tell me the story and why you feel like it changed your life?"

"Bri and I have been inseparable since we met then. We ended up having lockers next to each other. We quickly came to realize that we were in most of the same advanced classes together and played on the same sports teams. We were both outspoken and a little on the wild side. It was easy for us to get to know each other. She's like a sister to me."

"She sounds like a very important part of your life," Ethan whispered.

"She is, but so are the other people that I live with. They all have a very special place in my heart," I conceded.

I felt a strange sense of peace, sharing this with him.

"It's your turn," he spoke up.

"What's your relationship like with your family?"

I dug my fingers into the comforter. It made me uneasy to ask him at all. Ethan remained silent for a long time before letting out a forced breath.

"It's complicated," he replied in a very strained tone. "My father died several years ago. I never got along with him. I've remained at the company to honor one of my mother's dying wishes."

My heart throbbed, knowing that Ethan had lost someone that dear to him. It was clear in his tone that he held her in high regard and was still mourning her loss.

"Right – same question to you," he probed back.

I dropped the comforter and began twirling a piece of hair. "The people I live with are my family."

"I meant your *real* family Mia," he pressed.

"I only have my uncle as far as bloodlines are concerned," I replied stiffly.

"By the tone in your voice, I assume you're not close."

"No, he took me in out of obligation when I was four. I hardly know the man."

I took my turn before he pried even more. I would veto anything he asked about my parents.

"What's your secret for keeping up that amazing body of yours?"

A hearty laugh rumbled from him. It sent a wave of relief through me. I didn't want to get stuck on a subject that would bring the conversation down. This crazy idea was turning out better than I expected. We were finally learning things about each other.

"I workout every day. I start my day in the gym, whether it is at my place or at the office."

My mind drifted to his naked body. I licked my lips. I was fighting the desire within me as it strongly pressed to be next to him, getting hot and sweaty.

"My turn, and I'm going to play on your sexed-up feelings," he teased.

It frustrates me that he is that in tune with my thoughts. God only knows what he'll ask me.

"What's the kinkiest thing you've ever done?" Ethan asked, and quickly continued, "And you can't use the other night."

I flushed while thinking about my answer. As audacious as my actions were the other night, it wasn't my answer. "I'm going to use my veto on that one, so you'll have to let your mind wander."

"Typical. Do I at least get another question, since you vetoed?"

I rolled my eyes. "Pouting does not become you Ethan, so quit it. I'll give you another question, since I'm sure you are nowhere near done whining."

"How did you know I was pouting?"

I beamed. "What's your question?"

"What are two of your secret talents that you don't share with people?"

"I know how to hot-wire a car and pick any lock imaginable," I confessed.

"Very devious, and good to know," he mused.

"Indeed. Name one thing on your bucket list."

"Joining the mile-high club," he chuckled.

"Interesting ... that's on my list too," I remarked.

"If you could have one superpower, what would it be, and why?" he asked.

"I'd love to be able to control the elements. The possibilities would be endless," I joked.

"In your opinion, what's the difference between sex and making love?" I asked.

He could veto this one or make me decide if it was a serious question. My heart sped up as my mind raced, curious as ever to see what he'd say.

"I've had plenty of sex in my life. I didn't realize there was a difference until this past weekend. I've only made love with one person and the difference can't be measured or described in any words that I know," he answered softly.

My heart seemed to stop beating. It took several seconds for me to comprehend his answer and try and maintain my body's functionality. He took a deep breath, as if to regain his composure from sharing something that deep.

"I guess I'm not the only one that has a way with words. You sure know what to say when you want to, Ethan," I whispered.

"I only say what I mean Mia. If you could pick one song that defines your life, what song would it be?"

A gush of air passed through me. I decided to go with a lighthearted answer. It would give him somewhat of an idea about how I felt about him. It certainly fit our situation. As much as I denied it, I was in love with him. My heart confirmed it by beating even faster.

"Bleeding Love, Leona Lewis," I answered.

"I'm going to have to listen to that one. It's been a while since I've heard it."

"I'm going to ask you the same question."

"Everything, Lifehouse," Ethan said immediately.

"Mia, I know we're out of questions, but I want you to know that you're the only one."

"What do you mean?" I rasped. My voice was unwilling to work as my heart fluttered, sending hopeful waves throughout my entire body. My stomach knotted as I thought about the depth of the lyrics in the song he had selected.

"You're the only girl I've ever wanted to make a part of my life. I don't take chances on people. I'm sure you can relate. But with you, I took a leap of faith. I've watched you from afar, and swooped in at any chance I had to learn more about you."

The walls around my heart rattled even more. Try as I might to keep him out, Ethan had cracked almost all of them in such a short period. I closed my eyes, completely stunned. What did I have that he couldn't get from another girl? He was gorgeous. I was nothing short of a hot mess on a good day. He had no idea what he was getting into by pursuing me.

Why me?

"Did you just ask me why I want you?"

"Uh ... not intentionally. Apparently, my filter is on a sidebar so that particular thought must've flew out," I responded, wholly embarrassed.

"I like when that happens. It's a refreshing change to hear your thoughts as they come. I want you because I love what I see in your eyes and what I hear in your thoughts along with how strongly you carry yourself," he admitted.

"Are you saying I'm yours?" I asked in astonishment.

"You've been mine since the second our eyes met," Ethan responded unwaveringly.

"I remember that moment. Your eyes blew me away. I thought they were an invitation to find out all of life's secrets."

His breath faltered as he asked, "Have you found any of those secrets?"

"I've never seen myself or my life more clearly than I have when I'm with you, so maybe the secret to my life has always been you," I whispered.

My heart oscillated right out of my chest as I gave him another piece of me.

Ethan gasped. "I've never heard you be so open before."

"You asked me to distract you so that you wouldn't touch me. Consider this part of the distraction," I responded wryly.

I listened as he took slow breaths. Whatever happened to us going forward, I had to believe in my heart that sharing as much as we did tonight might just be enough to save us. I wanted to believe it. I was desperate to believe it. I needed him. As I hoped for the best, my cell started to beep.

"My phone is going to die soon. I should go to bed since I need to be up in a few hours."

My stomach twitched, feeling uneasy at the thought of all the things I needed to do when it came to us. He deserved to know so much more about me. We lingered on the line. After plenty of heated breaths, I exhaled slowly and made a move to end the call.

"Good night Ethan."

"I'm glad you called Mia. Good night."

I wanted to stay on the line with him for the rest of the night talking about anything. The walls around my heart had now collapsed. I wanted to tell him everything about me. I didn't want any secrets to linger between us.

CHAPTER TWENTY-FIVE
Tables Turned

The following morning I dressed in a rush, not giving a damn about my clothes. I left the house quickly, wanting to get this part of my day over. I got downtown and found a parking spot without issue. As I walked to Harrison's building I went over my decision in my head from every angle possible. Before entering his suite, I grabbed my cell and selected an application to record our conversation. I pressed record, tossed my phone back in my purse, and took a calming breath before knocking on his office door.

"Mia, come in," Harrison said, in greeting.

My guard went up once I saw him. His legs were on the desk, with his hands rested against the armrest of his chair. The coldness in his eyes made my heart beat insanely fast.

"Thanks for meeting with me on such short notice," I said, taking a seat across from him.

"What brings you to the office – have you found something substantial?"

"No, I haven't found out anything that will help your article," I admitted.

I began to fidget with the strap on my purse just to keep my fingers busy.

"Why did you want to meet today, then?" he asked harshly.

"I'm here to let you know that I'm stepping out. This isn't right for me."

His brow crinkled as his face darkened. My throat tightened in preparation for the blowback. "I see," he said, giving me a calculated stare that sent shivers up my spine.

I should've never taken anything that this man had to offer me.

"I'm very sorry. I don't think I'll raise any flags by leaving their company. I'm sure you'll be able to find someone that's better qualified to get what you need."

My palms started to sweat as my anxiety surged.

"Your apology doesn't really matter. I can't force you to stay, but I'll remind you that I've been privy to everything you've been up to while you were there. It would be a shame for that information to fall into the wrong hands," he threatened.

"What are you exactly saying? Are you going to blow the cover if I walk away?"

Harrison smiled smugly. "You're a smart individual. It's a shame you threw that intelligence out the window when you got involved with a prominent person within the company."

"You're blackmailing me?" I stammered.

I shook my head at my own stupidity. Harrison drummed his fingers against each other. "I wouldn't call it blackmail. Every good executive has insurance Mia. I've had more than one set of eyes and ears in there. It's been curious, the things that you've withheld from me that he's reported."

"I haven't withheld anything from you!" I snapped.

My stomach turned to ice. I hated every ounce of myself for thinking that jumping into cahoots with him would have benefited me. The hard look in his eyes shot straight through me. It made the ice in my stomach spread throughout my body.

"I find it interesting that you didn't admit to spending an exponential amount of time with the senior vice president," Harrison seethed.

"The time I've spent with him outside of that place has nothing to do with me wanting to step out," I said, curling my hands into tight fists.

My nerves were wavering as my temper started to rise. Harrison raised an all-too-knowing eyebrow that sent a combination of rage and fear up my spine.

"I think it has everything to do with it," he argued.

He knows too much about my personal life. How?

"I want to leave because I can't do it. I told you from the beginning that I wasn't sure if I could. This isn't anything new," I disputed.

My anger dissipated as terror began replacing it. I started considering the things Harrison was capable of. He was more deceitful than I imagined. I didn't trust him from the start – I should've gone with that feeling.

"You can't bullshit a bullshitter. This has everything to do with Ethan," he rebutted.

"It has nothing to do with him," I shot back.

"If it had nothing to do with him, you would've mentioned several weeks ago that you overheard a very important conversation. I do believe that we're on the verge of the owners delivering a certain amount of retribution soon, are we not? I hear it happens to coincide with a meeting that will be set up after a proposal is finished."

How the hell does he know that I overheard that conversation?

"I didn't say anything about that because it was circumstantial. I couldn't bring enough of it into context for any of it to make real sense. It could've been them talking about the weather as far as I was concerned."

"I'm not going to sit here and debate this with you Mia. I'll give you a new deal."

"I'm done making deals with you," I said evenly.

Harrison rolled his fingers together with an amused expression on his face. My chest tightened even more. I narrowed my eyes to maintain my composure.

"Oh, I think you'll want to make this deal with me. If you know what's good for you and the people you care about, anyway," he warned.

His tone was similar to the high-pitched laugh of a villain in the movies. Just the mention of my friends being in danger tweaked my terror higher than I thought it could possibly go. It was my worst fears slapping me across my face. My subconscious began poking at every part of my brain. It screamed obscenities at me for not listening to my inner self from the get go.

"What do you want?" I asked.

"I want you at that exchange. I feel that it's the last piece of the puzzle. After that meeting occurs, your obligation to me will be over. I won't interfere in your life again and I won't expose what you were doing for me." Harrison paused, giving me a hard stare. "Should you decide to go against this very generous offer, you'll find that your life will become more miserable compared to anything that happened to you last year, including having your pathetic boyfriend leave you after he destroyed your academic reputation."

Well done, Mia. You aligned yourself with someone who is the devil incarnate. He's nailed you to the wall to get what he wants. Great job!

"You're telling me that if I don't do this that you'll start hurting the people around me? Do you have any more threats for me, or is that it?"

My heart dropped to my knees as my stomach began to churn. Harrison rolled his eyes.

"I know you're recording this so you can just hit stop. Do you really think you stand a chance against a powerful man like me? Your efforts are admirable, but you'll never be able to take me down, so you should stop trying to fight me now," Harrison cautioned.

His eyes came together. They exhibited just how evil he really was on the inside. I pulled my phone from my purse, pressed stop, and flashed it at him so he didn't make any more threats. "You've been using me this entire time. Why?"

He chuckled in a high, maniacal tone. "You had the quality I needed to get me what I want that no other person will ever be able to do for me."

"And what's that special quality?" I asked, irritated.

"Desperation. It's a powerful thing. I offered you something I knew you couldn't refuse. You sit here now with the same desperation. Only this time, you're desperate for the safety of those around you, rather than yourself."

I glared at him. "What if I just walk away? What are you saying?"

"You'll be sorry you ever crossed me. If you think where you're at is dangerous, you'll think again after I'm through with you," he advised.

He gave me a heinous look to drive his point home. It left me trembling in my seat.

"If I make sure I'm at this meeting, you swear you won't hurt anyone. You'll go your way and I'll go mine?" I asked, twisting my fingers to prevent myself from having a meltdown.

"Yes, you finish this out for me, we'll part ways, and you'll never hear from me again," Harrison replied amicably.

"Fine, you have a deal," I agreed, fighting the rising vomit.

The old saying is *true. If something sounds too good to be true, it probably is.*

"Oh, and Mia, please thank your boyfriend for giving me such a wonderful piece to work with when he approached me to help him take down his father's company," Harrison goaded. His eyes twinkled at the pot he was stirring by bringing up Ethan.

My heart dropped, completely taken aback at the idea of Ethan being involved with him. "Why would he do that?"

"I don't ask for those kinds of details from my sources. If you want those closest to you to remain safe, I'd keep this entire meeting between us."

"Did Ethan know all along why I'm there?"

My stomach squelched as my throat tightened. It made each breath a struggle. Between the fear and anger inside of me, my body was ready to explode.

"No, Ethan believes you're there to work for him. The other individual I placed within the company is who he believes is there to collect information for me. He happened to take notice of what was going on with you and Ethan. He kept me abreast of the situation, as well as all the other details you were neglecting to report."

"Why would you put two people in there and not tell him? It doesn't make any sense. What sick and twisted game are you playing?"

"I'm deliberate in everything that I do, as I work for the outcome I envision," Harrison said with a calculated swipe of the hand across his desk.

"All I hear is that you manipulate people in the worst ways to get what you want. Since you are the master manipulator, how do you suggest I get an invitation without tipping them off as to why I want it?" I snapped through gritted teeth.

"I'm sure you'll figure out a way."

"It sounds like you know more than you're telling me."

I hated this man with every fiber of my being. The hate for myself was a close second. I had been beyond stupid to think that something as shady as spying from the inside would ever benefit me. Apparently, I sucked at it more than I thought. I missed the fact that someone else was snooping around too.

"Just make sure you get the invite and that you show up," he barked.

I sat stock still, staring at the artful asshole to try and understand his motives. Harrison was up to something, and his overly cocky stature backed up my suspicions – I was missing something. I clenched my jaw and grabbed my purse. I wasn't about to get any more answers, so getting out of this corner of hell was my last lucid thought.

"Goodbye, Harrison."

"Always a pleasure Mia."

I opened his door, looking back at the evil bastard with so much hate for myself that I could barely breathe. I hit the hallway and ran straight to the bathrooms. My sweaty hands barely managed to open the door. I dropped my purse as my knees crashed to the floor. I lost my entire stomach contents in a matter of seconds. My entire body was shaking as sweat trickled across my brow. My chest felt hollow and tight, like all my breath had been squeezed out. It made each breath that came out a harsh reminder of the severity of my poor decisions. I rested my head against the cool porcelain as the pain coursed through every vein and sliced me to pieces. My body trembled as my concern for those that I loved slashed through my chest, following the same path as the pain.

I just made another deal with the devil. What have I done?

I was standing in front of yet another door, staring at it. I brought my hand up several times but refrained from knocking. I started pacing back and forth. I tried to summon up the ability to act normal around Ethan, so that he didn't see that anything was wrong. I stopped pacing and let my head lightly fall against his door. I fought the nausea creeping inside of me, along with the self-disgust that grew stronger by the minute. As I forced my hand into a fist, a flash of heat spread across my back.

Ethan shuffled us inside. Shutting the door, he pulled me into him, but made no move to kiss me. It surprised me, considering the precocious approach to entering his office. He brought his forehead to mine and stared deeply into my eyes. I wrapped my arms tightly around his waist, in need of his comfort. The sickening feelings started to recede. The disgust I had for myself was still strong, but it moved to another part of my brain as a soothing feeling coursed through me. The smooth pads of his fingers continued to move along my back in light strokes as his eyes sucked me into every part of him. It made me want so much more from him.

"Hey," Ethan whispered.

"Hi," I answered.

I rested my head against his chest and listened to his heart as everything inside of me started to burn at a hotter temperature.

"Why were you pacing outside my door?"

"I'm a little scatterbrained this morning."

Ethan continued to gaze at me with doubt in his eyes. I wanted to wipe away any confusion about us from his thoughts. As his eyes penetrated me, in search for what was troubling my aching soul, every part of me ran rampant with heady desires. My mouth attacked him with powerful force and demanded him to meet every lick I executed upon his lips. Ethan stepped away, but I took a step closer. I needed him just to make it to the next cataclysmic event that was about to unfold around us.

I traced my tongue along his luscious lips. After what seemed like forever, he parted his lips to grant me further access. I took every part of him into my mouth while reaching for his tie to unfasten it. Bringing my hands back to his body, my nails began to outline every inch of his chest before running down to his waistline. I tugged at his shirt so that I could feel his skin on mine. I yearned for the reckless feelings inside of me to grow and take away everything else. Ethan moaned before biting down against my bottom lip. Listening to his soft moans started an intense blaze between my legs.

With each swipe and nip, my breath shortened as my heart raced at a mile a minute. I ran my hands up his neck. I let my fingers appreciate every part of his hair before yanking it as my body begged for more of him. Ethan hissed and stepped away. He looked confused, but shrugged it off. He slowly moved us further into his office. He brought his lips back to mine with an intensity that matched the force I was using. He maneuvered us over to a section of the bookshelves on the right side of his office. His mouth never left mine, as his hand parted from my side and went up to pull down a book. A section of the wall separated and opened to an empty hallway. He picked me up. I wrapped my legs around him. The door closed behind us. He dragged his lips down to my neck. He nibbled at every exposed spot he could find. I leaned my head against the door and banged it as every part of me yearned for him to be inside of me.

"Oh, God," I moaned loudly.

Ethan raised a hand to cover my mouth. I was on fire with my need for him. I ran my hands down to his slacks and unbuttoned the fly along with the buttons of his shirt. My tongue traced the marvelous tattoos that covered his chest. I outlined one of the patterns before grazing my teeth across his nipple. Ethan purred and squeezed me tighter to him. His hardness pressed between my thighs and increased the throbbing that cried for us to shed our clothes.

Ethan took several more steps that further dumped us into an empty room. He shut the door behind us and pressed me into the wall next to it. He brought his hand to the inside of my leg and tore my panties from my body. His long fingers traced along the insides of my thighs until he hit my hot spot, deftly sliding in and out.

"Ethan," I moaned even louder than earlier.

He quieted me with his hungry lips. His tongue commanded mine until I stopped moaning. "You have got to try to be quiet Mia," Ethan said in between heated breaths.

His fingers fell to a meticulous pace that quickly had me close. His tongue swept across my neck and over to my earlobe. I brought my head down and rested it in the crook of his neck. I tenderly bit down to keep from whimpering again. Needing to focus on keeping quiet, my hands travelled to his fly. As I ran my fingers along him, my foggy brain remembered a comment from yesterday. I unwrapped from around him and dropped to my knees. I batted my eyelashes before pulling his pants and boxers down. I gave him one last look before running my tongue along him until I reached his tip. I circled around it delicately before running it along his piercing.

"Fuck that feels unbelievable," Ethan hissed.

His hands went to my shoulders where he kept a firm grip. My tongue went to his tip and piercing each time to swirl and suck before resuming the same course again. Ethan dug into me as his breathing became raspy. I ran my tongue back to his tip one last time before wrapping my lips around him as far as they would go. I sucked and swirled until a loud moan growled from his chest. I sensed him getting close and returned to his tip to lick the soft moisture. Ethan hauled me back up to his chest. His lips crushed mine as he swept me from the floor. He hiked my skirt up before he rocked inside of me.

"Ah, Ethan," I cried.

I brought my hand to my mouth to keep from screaming. My head slammed into the wall as he pumped into me roughly. His fingers squeezed the inside of my hips. My hands clasped around his shoulders. I licked away a trickle of sweat that was glistening along his neck.

Every part of me wanted to find a sense of peace with him, but I wasn't able to with my mind preoccupied with everything else from this morning. I was getting close, but I wasn't able to let go. Ethan continued driving into me with such vigor that I banged my head against the wall in time with him in an attempt to let go of everything. My conscious, however, was alive and well, and refused to do so. Ethan slowed to a stop and held me as his eyes deepened with concern.

"Mia, what's wrong?" he rasped.

"It's nothing. Keep going," I whispered.

All the unprovoked feelings I had for Ethan were there. I thrust my hips hard into his so that he would continue. He twitched inside of me. It made the fire rise higher than before. I focused on it as every part of me began to rely on satisfying that need for him. I rocked against him again. He resumed the pace he was at before my actions had brought us to a stop. He pumped harder. I let go to the moment. He moved us towards the table that was in the room, laid me gently on it, and placed his elbows on each side of me.

Ethan never stopped, but he slowed his pace from the fast way we had been going to an unhurried one. He twisted his hips with each thrust. He discarded my shirt and ran his hands across my chest. Each thrust from him increased the pulsating inside of me. He brought his mouth to my breasts where he began giving me light kisses.

"Ah ...," I groaned.

I swung my hips into his, hoping he'd bring us to a climax soon. Sweat pricked at my forehead as he slid at his precise pace. He dragged my hands to my sides as he continued to rock forward. My teeth gripped my bottom lip to hold back the scream that I wanted to let out as he went deeper. I arched my back to meet him as he started to go faster. I ran my nails up his back as he lowered his head to my chest.

"Ethan ... I'm so close ... please don't let me do this alone," I mewled.

He pushed harder than he ever had before. The love behind his deep brown eyes absorbed me. I climaxed hard around him. Ethan groaned as he released into me. The room was filled with nothing but two hearts beating as one. He slid out and pulled up his pants. I was still trying to come back down to earth from the blissfulness.

He rested his head right next to mine and blew a piece of hair away from my face. "You were dead against touching yesterday but today you come in wanting sex. I can never seem to keep up with you."

I ran my fingers along his rigid jaw, urging him to relax with each stroke. Ethan closed his eyes and took a deep breath. I was a walking contradiction to him. The exalted feelings I had moments before left as the self-loathing returned. I sat up from the table and slid on my shirt. I rubbed my eyes to try and find some clarity again. He left the table and grabbed his shirt and tie. I readjusted my skirt and looked around for my panties.

"The rest of today will be interesting," I murmured, picking up the scraps.

Ethan paused from securing his tie. I waved the scraps at him.

"I can't always control my animalistic urges around you," he justified.

I gave him a full-blown grin and went over to fasten his tie for him. I wiped away the lipstick that was on his collar and along his neck. My hands rested near his heart to take in every beat. "I like that I bring out those urges in you. It evens the playing field for me," I teased.

He rolled his eyes. "The things you do to me Mia. I've never had sex in my car, or this office; and you've managed to cross both off the list in a matter of days."

Before opening the door, Ethan paused for a tender kiss before dropping my hand. The pretense of us just being boss and employee quickly returned as we made our way back to his office. I followed carefully behind him. He ran his fingers along the wall until he hit the latch for the door to swing open. He crossed over to his desk and sat down in his chair. I settled in across from him. Ethan shook his head with a cocky grin. I raised an eyebrow out of curiosity.

"I was going to ask you how you wanted to start this morning, but I guess that question isn't necessary."

"Smart-ass," I retorted. "What time is it?"

"Quarter to ten," Ethan answered smugly.

"Are you serious? Wow, I'm sorry Ethan. I didn't realize that we ..."

I let the sentence trail off as the heat in my cheeks flamed to a deep shade of red. He smiled so wide that his shining teeth almost blinded me. At least he wasn't angry at the loss of hours.

"We should get to work, as most of the morning has slipped by us, among other things..."

I brought up his proposal on the laptop, not bothering to look at him for any direction. His phone buzzed, and he waited, answering it on the fourth ring. Similar to the call yesterday, it was short and left him agitated. I diverted my eyes, not wanting to pry at whatever was pissing him off that much.

We worked in silence for the rest of the morning. I was sharpening the proposal when his fingers ran along the inside of my right hand, pausing in the center. His fingers circled around my scar. It made me cringe. I usually kept it covered up with a watch or a bracelet but must have forgot this morning. I placed my hand on top of his and forced him to stop.

"Don't," I said bitterly.

"I didn't mean to upset you, but it caught my eye. What happened?" Ethan asked quietly.

"I don't know. It's been there for as long as I can remember. I'm assuming it occurred when I was quite young, but I have no memory of it, or anyone to ask," I snapped.

Ethan looked at me, not believing a word that I said by the starkness in his eyes. "How do you not remember something that distinct?"

"I don't have any memory of it because I have absolutely no memories of my parents, or my life whatsoever, before I was brought here. Is that what you want to hear? I'm sure you think this is another thing I'm holding back from you, but I don't fucking know!" I yelled.

I shouldn't be this angry with him for asking, but everything in my life was such a mess that I couldn't contain it. I hated that scar. I had always wondered about it – it was so precise that I found it creepy. It was round, with a center that seemed to resemble some sort of symbol or initial, but it was too marred to be sure.

I caught Chase looking at it over the years. It led me to believe that he probably knew the truth about it, but we never discussed it. Any time that I asked about my past, he would shut me down completely. My entire body shook with the anger running through me. I slid the chair back – I needed distance from Ethan. I got up and crossed the room to even my breathing. The last thing I wanted to think about was that particular part of my past. I gave up figuring out those answers a long time ago.

Ethan rounded his desk and hauled me into him. "Let's go," he commanded.

I stepped away from his embrace. He had switched gears on me – becoming the picture of ease in an instant, not showing an ounce of the distrust he had exhibited a moment ago.

Fuck he confuses me! I wish just once I could follow his train of thought.

"What?" I asked, flustered.

"You need a break. I could use some food, so let's go."

I nodded. He rested his forehead against mine while running his lips across the corner of my mouth. It was exactly what I needed to still everything inside of me.

We strolled at an unhurried pace to the front of the building. Ethan veered off to the reception desk while I kept walking towards the door. I stopped dead in my tracks when a familiar face caught my eye. Needing confirmation, I leaned against the glass wall behind me and squinted to get a better look. My stomach churned when I realized that it was Ian O'Connor. My mind raced to piece together if I'd seen him at all since I started working here. The only thing I could recall was his family's unexplained presence at our house a few weeks ago. If he was at my birthday party, it was more than a coincidence, and it had nothing to do with a damn tweet. I tried to determine if there was any connection to what Harrison was saying this morning, but it was impossible to know for sure if Ian was his other inside source.

CHAPTER TWENTY-SIX
Your Past is Never Far

I rested my elbow against the window to keep my head clear for the drive. What was usually a long journey at this time of day ended up passing quickly. I was in the heart of downtown. Once I had parked my car, I made my way to the address Ethan had given me to meet him at for lunch. As the bustle of the city went on around me, I stared upwards and took in the huge skyscraper that appeared to be my destination.

"Do you want to eat or would rather stand out here on the sidewalk staring?"

Ethan's voice rang above the city noise flooding my ears. He was leaning against the building, watching me.

"Let's eat," I said, walking towards him.

He laced our hands together on our way to the elevators. We boarded an empty one and Ethan selected a floor near the top. As we ascended I felt his eyes on me, but kept facing forward. I'd already given into that side once today. It didn't seem to stop my body from wanting to it all over again. His fingers stroked the inside of my hand, urging me to give in to what he does to me.

The elevator rescued me from succumbing to his tantalizing ways as it stopped and the door opened. Ethan directed me towards a small café. There were no walls, only floor-to-ceiling windows – any seat within it gave the beholder an amazing view of the city. It must have been magnificent in the evening, when the lights from all the buildings downtown sprang to life, preserving their towering presence by illuminating the skyline.

"Two?" a scratchy voice asked, breaking my reverie.

"Yes," Ethan answered, pulling me forward.

We sat in a corner section of the cafe. I continued to stare out the window. I was watching the vehicles travel below. They appeared like tiny Matchbox cars. The pedestrians on the street complimented them by looking like ants. I gazed to my right to follow the view as it sprawled across larger buildings, before fading into the suburbs. I absorbed every angle, taken away by the soft music coming from the cafe's speakers. Ethan's voice brought me out of my daze.

"You haven't picked up your menu."

I brought my attention back to the table and took in Ethan's expression. His dimpled smile graced his beautiful face, but his eyes gave way to his thoughts. My erratic behavior was clearly at the forefront of his mind.

I flashed him a smile and opened my menu. "Do you have any recommendations?"

"I'm partial to the *ravioli a mezzaluna* or the *stracci*. The gnocchi isn't bad either, and you can never go wrong with spaghetti. It's hard to screw up spaghetti," he recommended.

I raised an eyebrow at his many suggestions and scanned the menu thoroughly before closing it, having selected my meal. I avoided his curious stares by gazing out of the window again.

"You're awfully quiet," Ethan murmured.

"I'm enjoying the view. Any particular reason why we came downtown for lunch?"

"It's a great place to free your mind, and the food isn't half bad either."

"It's amazing. I'll take your word on the food. Thank you for sharing it with me. It's going to be one hell of a drive back to the office by the time we are finished here."

Ethan shifted uneasily. "We aren't going back. We're taking the rest of the day off."

"There's no way you can afford to take the rest of the day off," I snapped.

"Don't argue with me Mia. I don't know what it is, but you never seem to relax when you're there," Ethan said, narrowing his eyes in warning.

"If people didn't think I was fucking you before, they sure will now," I shot back.

Before our argument could escalate any further, the server arrived to take our order. Since Ethan was God's gift to women, she directed all her attention to him.

"What can I get for you?" she asked, in a singsong voice.

"I'll take the *pappa al pomodoro* with the *salmone*, along with a Bloody Mary and glass of water," Ethan replied, keeping his angry eyes on me.

She wrote down his order and continued batting her eyes at him. I cleared my throat to get my order out and back to our argument.

"I'll take the gnocchi with a Mojito and a glass of water."

"Oh … yes … right. I'll get these orders in," she replied, giving Ethan a parting grin as she grabbed the menus.

I picked at my cuticles. I didn't know if it was the blatant flirting, Ethan doing yet another thing without telling me, or just the mess my life was, but I was livid. My face flushed as the anger spread out of my pores.

Ethan stared at me in exasperation. "What are you pissed at now?"

"Let's see. It worried me what people would think with me disappearing with you before I started screwing you. Now, I actually am fucking you and you've pulled me out of work *again*. I'm pretty sure that the gossipers around the office are going to have a field day spreading this one along," I hissed.

"This is your last warning – watch your mouth Mia. What's your problem? You're snappier than I've ever seen you," Ethan bit back.

"How can you be so oblivious? I've been dumb enough to leave with you twice during working hours. I never took this job to be the center of attention," I griped.

"Why did you take it? Because I think what you've told me is bullshit," Ethan snapped. His face flushed crimson as he took some measured breaths to prevent himself from completely flipping out. My anger simmered as I tried to find something to tell him.

Shit. I took it too far. I can't tell him the truth. Fuck.

I broke my gaze with him and found a skyscraper across from us to focus on. The guilt settled into a pit in my stomach while my self-hate spread throughout the rest of me. With how things had been going all morning, this was my one shot to switch topics without him pressing me. It was obvious that my mood was bordering on unhinged, so that should be enough for him to drop it.

"How long has Ian O'Connor been working there?" I asked.

Ethan blinked and shook his head in disbelief. I raised an expectant eyebrow.

His eyes flicked around the café as he avoided focusing on me. Apparently, I wasn't the only one with tells, because everything about him indicated that Ian was Harrison's other source. My stomach quailed at the idea of it being true.

"He's been with us around a year and works as an assistant to Sean and Colin. Why?"

I shrugged. "I didn't expect to see someone that I knew working there."

I was beyond happy that we didn't have any food yet because that admission was a bit more than I could handle without throwing up. I plastered on a fake smile. Ethan looked at me for more, but I narrowed my eyes to discourage any further inquiry. He cocked his head, doing nothing to hide his growing agitation with me. He opened his mouth to speak, but I cut him off.

"I need you to explain more about this deal. I'm under the impression it needs to be wrapped up well ahead of schedule, yet here we are skipping out on work. Either it's not that important or you're not telling me something. Which is it?" I asked punitively.

Ethan huffed, crossing his arms over his chest. He stared me down, trying to pick me apart, but I remained unwavering under his scrutiny. "It's important for the company because it is a multimillion dollar deal. Sean and Colin want it closed soon so that another investor doesn't sweep in and steal it. It's important to me for other reasons," he answered squarely.

My insides swirled at the mention of *other* reasons. Ethan gave me a hard look that left me squirming in my seat. His jaw tightened as his forehead creased. It made him morph into the version of himself that left me a little afraid. It was enough for me to give up asking any other questions along those lines.

"You mentioned playing sports last night. What sports did you play?" Ethan asked.

I reveled in the light topic of discussion. He seemed to need it too as he took measured breaths to regain his composure. "I played soccer, basketball, and softball."

He smirked. "Were you any good?"

I beamed. "Ever heard of the Miracle Maker?"

"Are you serious?"

I nodded as his jaw dropped. Our server was back with our drinks. I took a long sip of mine. Ethan picked up his glass and mixed the contents before bringing it to his lips for a drink. I watched his lips caress the edge of his glass and had to blink several times. My body jolted out of the unease, right into a dull ache to have those lips all over me. The look of awe he was giving me revved up every part of me.

"Stop looking at me like that. It wasn't that big of a deal, Ethan. I had awesome teammates that were just as talented. Bri and I worked really well together in basketball. We used that to our advantage. I played for fun."

His eyes had a lingering interest. "How did you get so good?"

I sighed. Who knew that he'd get fixated on such a mundane topic? At least it was something I could deal with that didn't send my mind into a tailspin. "I gave every sport my best effort, just as I did in school. I probably had a slight advantage growing up with a bunch of boys that never went easy on me. Those boys never treated me like a girl. I had to learn to hold my own and get better than they were if I didn't want to be knocked on my ass."

Ethan continued to stare at me with awestruck eyes. Our server broke the connection when she came over with our plates. The food steamed with the delicious scents of pasta and fish, making my mouth water. We picked up our silverware and dived into our meals.

"Did you play any sports in high school?" I asked, around a mouthful of pasta.

Ethan drove his fork into his salmon. He chewed slowly while assessing me. Coolness washed over him. It made me wonder why that would set him off.

"Yes, I played rugby, football, and basketball."

"Were you any good?"

"I wasn't nearly as good as you. I played for an escape."

His face tightened as he took deep breaths. His eyes were full of pain. I felt sorry for him, but I wanted to know what he meant by 'an escape'. I wanted to learn more about the mystery behind him. "Elaborate, please," I said softly.

Ethan gave me a hard glance before taking another bite of food. He chewed for a minute before returning his attention to me. I finished off my plate while I waited for him to answer.

"It kept me out of the house for longer periods, and prolonged the inevitable with my father. He had a precise plan. I played sports to spite him."

"I see. We all play for different reasons."

I had figured he harbored some disdain for his father, but that just confirmed it. In fact, the entire answer he gave was rather cryptic. While I contemplated whether to push for more, Ethan stunned me by giving my hand a gentle squeeze. I looked at him with wide eyes. He took a deep breath and I caught a glimpse of his tortured eyes before he closed them. The torment behind them struck at every part of me.

"Mia, my Dad was a ruthless prick that went out of his way to make my life miserable. He cheated on my mom and beat the shit out of us. As I said last night, my relationship there is complicated. In time, I'll explain more, so please let this be it for now," he pleaded.

I felt my eyes begin to moisten at the agony in his voice. It was obvious that his childhood experiences rivaled my own when it came to misery. I nodded, suppressing my tears, and he tightened his hold on my hand. He opened his eyes and let a small smile grace his torn face.

Pointing to the plate between us, I asked, "Did you order that to let it go to waste?"

His brow crinkled in displeasure. "No. I'm not sure why our appetizer came out with the entrées. It should've been here earlier. I'll have to take that up with Benny at a different time."

I raised an eyebrow and picked up a piece of the flatbread. I dipped it in the marinara sauce. It tasted remarkable. I titled my head, fully catching his comment. "Is this another one of your business ventures?"

Ethan smiled proudly. "Yes, I'm a silent partner. It was hard not to invest. There aren't many cafés that are over a thousand feet above everything else, with one of the best views you can have while enjoying a good meal."

I grinned. "Sounds like you're a savvy businessman."

His face lost its zest as he gazed away. "I endeavor to be."

He placed his fork down on his empty plate and took a long drink. I finished off my cocktail and grabbed my water to wash down the lingering taste of alcohol in my mouth. I wished it could wipe away all the other feelings inside of me. The more I learned about Ethan, the more questions I had. I saw how much everything outside of his father's company mattered to him. He didn't want to be associated with that place any more than I did. Pain cut through me at the thought of sharing that sentiment with him but not being able to tell him. I halted dwelling any further so that I didn't start crying.

"It looks like we've finished everything. Do you want to do us a favor and bat your eyes so that our server comes back with the bill?"

He cocked his head to the side. "You don't strike me as the jealous type. Why do you let the way that women react to me bother you?"

"I wouldn't say it bothers me, per se – it's just an annoyance."

Ethan huffed. "You don't think it pisses me off to watch countless men check you out on a daily basis, with no shame as they do it?"

I scoffed. "I think we need to get your eyes checked because that never happens."

"The hell it doesn't. You really don't see it, do you?"

"See what?"

"How beautiful you are. You're every guy's fantasy."

Ethan waved his hand to bring the server over. We stared at each other without a word. The glimmer that lingered in his eyes entranced me. He shut them and exhaled slowly. Ethan set his drink down on the table. He opened his eyes with his head shaking back and forth. I loved getting to him. It warmed every part of me.

"Don't," Ethan said, barely above a whisper.

"What?" I asked, trying to control my breathing.

"Stop giving me that look," he demanded hoarsely.

"What look?" I taunted.

"Don't tease me Mia. You know how it will end," Ethan warned.

"I'm sorry. Sometimes you provoke a side of me that loves pushing your buttons. You do it to me all the time so I take the open windows that come to me."

Ethan opened his mouth to answer but our enthusiastic server was back with our check. He handed her his credit card without looking at her. His eyes burned into me with so much desire that my heart rate became supersonic. Our server let out an irritated huff and stormed off to run his card. His lips curled into a cocky smirk. I raised an eyebrow at his smugness.

"You were right. It isn't a good idea for us to work together alone. I guess you're going to have to learn to have some self-control."

Like I'm the only one that struggles with control. Arrogant ass.

"At least I got you to admit that I was right about something. It must have been hard for you," I retorted.

A light chuckle escaped from his chest. "I should've never told you that it was OK to drop your filter. Your mouth pushes my buttons more than anything."

"I didn't hear you complaining about how I used it this morning," I sniggered.

Ethan bit his lip to hold back the smile that was spreading across his face. The server returned with his card and receipt. He scribbled his name across it without giving her the time of day. He clutched my hand and pulled me out of my chair. I squeezed his as we walked away. I couldn't resist the urge to gaze back at our server, who stood frozen as she watched Ethan pull my hand up for a gentle kiss. I gave her a parting smirk before leaning into him. For the moment, he was mine. I wanted to rub it in the face of anyone that saw us. I held on to those happy feelings as we walked out of the restaurant.

Once back down on the street, we stopped outside of the entrance to the building. Ethan brought both of my hands to his chest and bent down for a loving kiss. I released my hands from his and rested them around his hips. His hands drifted to my face where he held my cheeks. He parted my mouth and drove his tongue inside, kissing me with no regard for everyone walking past us. The wind swirled around, bringing up leaves from the sidewalk. People continued walking by, with an occasional whistle ringing out for our passionate embrace.

After a few minutes Ethan slowed his lips. I took in every ounce of love that was pouring from his eyes. I loved him more than I could express. I didn't know it was possible to feel this way about someone else. He released his grip from my cheeks and closed his eyes. He opened them moments later with such bliss that it sped up my heart.

"I'll never be able to thank the universe enough for bringing you into my life," he murmured.

"Me neither," I choked out.

He was going to make me cry if he kept saying such damn sentimental things. I stared at him and fought the tears of joy that wanted to break free. I tugged him with me towards the direction of my car.

"Where are you going?"

"To my car, seeing that's how I got here and all."

"Where did you park?"

"I'm in the ramp. Where did you park?"

"On the street."

"Of course, why would we park in the same place? For as synched as we can be, we go in opposite directions more often than not," I pointed out, dropping his hand.

"I'm not letting you walk to your car by yourself. I'll walk with you," he said sternly.

Ethan took my hand; his determined expression told me not to argue with him.

"Why? I walked up here by myself. I'm not some damsel in distress, Ethan," I replied, utterly annoyed.

He didn't give me a second glance as he moved forward. I scowled, but continued walking. "It's not up for discussion. I'll walk with you before I get my car. You agreed to spend the evening with me so we'll be going to my place now. You can't get there without directions. If I were you, I'd swallow this one," Ethan advised.

"Fine; but you can be such an ass," I shot back.

"If that means making sure you stay out of harm's way, I'm fine with it."

Ethan grasped my hand as he strode along the sidewalk. His marching pace had leaves flying all over. I was barely able to keep up with him in my heels, but I wasn't going to say anything. In retrospect, I probably shouldn't walk anywhere alone with a malicious bastard watching my every move. Having a man hell bent on protecting me wasn't the worst thing in the world.

"It's over there," I whispered, pointing to my car in the corner of the garage.

It *was* a tad on the eerie side – a loud crash on the other side of the garage made me jump. Ethan looked at me, not hiding his confusion with my reaction to the noise.

Yeah, it's a good thing he came with me. My subconscious is on high alert.

When we reached my car, I wrestled my hand out of his to rummage through my purse for my keys. As I dug, Ethan interrupted my focus by resting his hands on my hips. He moved his thumbs closer to the inside. My breathing faltered as the rest of me became red-hot. I shot him a warning look. His eyes danced, knowing that he had got to me.

I found my keys and unlocked my car. Rather than release me, he continued the circular motions with his thumbs. He pressed me up against my car; his hands trailed a blaze as they went up my sides. He was going to get me completely turned on, just to leave me high-and-dry. I bit my lip to keep from moaning. When his fingers ran across the bottom of my bra, I brought my hands up to stop him, but they had a mind of their own. They ran up his chest when they should've been grabbing his hands. With my last rational thought, I tugged on his tie.

"Stop," I groaned.

The act only encouraged his advances as his lips captured mine. He pinned me to the car and parted my mouth with a hunger for every part of me. I met each lick with every ounce of what he gave me. He continued at a sensual pace before we lost our breath. He placed a soft kiss on my lips before stepping away.

"Are you calmer?" Ethan asked, as he straightened his tie.

"Calm is not exactly how I'd describe what I'm feeling," I said, with aggravation.

"At least you're calmer than you were a few minutes ago," he pointed out, flashing his dimples.

I both loved and I hated it when the dimples made an appearance. I ended up forgetting why I was irritated with him. "Yes, I'm calmer, among other things. Can you text me your address?"

"Your wish is my command, my dear."

I giggled at his upbeat mood. I wasn't sure what he had in store for the rest of the day, but I'd take it if it meant he was happy. As he searched for his phone, I saw some movement at the opposite end of the row of parked cars. It sent a chill down my spine to think that someone might be watching us. I didn't have time to dwell on it. My ringtone kicked in with the arrival of his text. Ethan looked at me in shock as it played the lyrics of "With Me" by Sum 41. I smiled as my cheeks filled with color. He ran his finger along the spots that had reddened before placing his palm on my face.

"Is that my ringtone?"

I nodded, not being able to find my voice with the look of amazement he was giving me.

He beamed. "I love that song."

I smirked. "I know. It was on my playlist."

He raised an eyebrow. "It's not the song you picked that defined your life."

"I have a variety of songs that can define my life, especially when it comes to you."

Ethan ran his hand down my cheek before letting go to pick up mine. He placed a kiss on the inside of my wrist, near the scar that I screamed at him about earlier. He opened my door to help me into the car. As he was helping me in, a flash of light came from the corner of the garage that I had been looking at earlier. Several more flashes followed it. Ethan let go of my hand and ran halfway across the garage before doubling back to me.

I rolled down my window and waited for some sort of

explanation. His face was hard with anger. He slammed his fists on the top of my car. I flinched as the bang echoed throughout the garage. I listened as he took deep breaths to try and calm down. Ethan gripped the side of the car before leaning his head through the window. I was already as far back in my seat as I could go, but the look on his face made me want to crawl into the backseat. His eyes were full of so much fury that whoever had made him that livid should have been terrified, because I sure was.

"What was that all about Ethan? Why were they taking pictures of us?" I rasped. My voice wasn't working because of the anxiety running through me.

"Not now Mia. Go to my place and park in the garage. The stall is in the text. Wait for me to get there before you get out of your car," Ethan instructed in haste.

"But– " I continued.

"Damn it, Mia. Please, just this once, can you do as I ask without questioning it?" he snapped.

"OK," I whispered, against the lump in my throat.

He released his grip from my car and took a few more steps back as I started it. As I was about to pull out, he came back to my window. I shook my head, completely confused by his actions. He leaned through the window and grabbed my face. I gazed at him with wide eyes.

"I'm sorry. I'm not angry with you, Mia. Please drive carefully. I'll see you soon," Ethan said softly.

"I will," I confirmed, just as softly.

The words barely made it past my lips. His mouth caressed mine until I parted my lips. It was a brief kiss, but full of apology. I reached over to touch his cheek. "I'll see you in a few minutes."

Ethan nodded as he backed away. I threw my car into drive and updated my GPS with his address. Not a second after I finished, my phone started ringing again. I picked it up to see a new text message. Because the traffic was thick, I refrained from opening it and kept my eyes on the road. After weaving through the traffic for several minutes, I hit a stoplight. I grabbed my cell and opened the message to see a picture of Ethan and I. It was one of our more passionate embraces from the garage, with a message:

I have eyes everywhere Mia. Remember what you committed to this morning.

Fucking Harrison.

My hands gripped the wheel in frustration as the light turned green. I accelerated faster than that I should have on a side street. I wanted nothing more than to be in the sanctuary of Ethan's apartment. The self-loathing from this morning resurfaced. My hands slammed against the wheel. It made me furious that I had no way out of this mess.

CHAPTER TWENTY-SEVEN
Killing Me Softly

Taking the rest of the day off ended up being the best idea that Ethan had had yet. His agitation with the incident in the garage was still present when he arrived at his apartment. I decided against asking about it because he was beyond irate. We spent the rest of the day exploring areas of the city that were significant to each of us. How much of the city you could cover when you put your mind to it was surprising. We stuck to mundane topics of conversation, with each of us treading with caution because of each other's unpredictable mood swings. By the time we got back to his apartment that evening, we were talking with our bodies rather than our mouths. Every part of me felt sated by the time he wrapped me in his arms to sleep for the night. Without knowing, he had given me exactly what I needed to make it to the next day.

I woke him up before sunrise the following morning and took him to my favorite place in the world. I needed to share mine, since he had taken me to his. Watching the sunrise was breathtaking. The tender look upon his face as he sat with me made every part of my heart swell. He was elated that I shared this part of myself. I hoped it would be enough when the time came for me to tell him the truth. We had plenty of time before we needed to be to his office. He drove us back to his apartment in no hurry along one of his favorite scenic routes by the lake.

As we were pulling into his garage, his cell rang. He glanced at the screen before taking the call. His entire body went rigid. It made me tense up just as much as him.

"What do you want Sean?" Ethan asked harshly.

He parked his car and kept his gaze from me. It frightened me to be around him whenever he spoke to Sean or Colin. Between the other day and today, it was apparent that he despised those two about as much as his father. I stared at my hands, doing my best to keep them from shaking with the anxiety that was seeping into every nerve-ending. Sean went on for several minutes, which only served to enrage Ethan even further.

"It's none of your fucking business if I take the afternoon off," Ethan snapped.

I glanced at him, and felt the color in me drain. His face flamed, and his knuckles turned white from his grip on the steering wheel. I knew our absence the day before wouldn't have gone unnoticed. A wave of terror rolled within me as I contemplated what Harrison might do with that information. My self-disgust distracted me so much that I almost missed the end of his conversation.

"I'll have a rough draft up to you today," Ethan said icily. He glanced at me, trying to seem like he was fine. "I don't give a flying fuck what you and Colin demand. I'll give you what I have and you'll wait until I'm finished before you finalize the meeting date."

The whole conversation had made my stomach curl together. I didn't have all the details, but there was enough for me to believe that Ethan had some involvement in this mysterious meeting. I swallowed repeatedly to prevent myself from getting sick. He listened to what Sean had to say for a few more minutes. Ethan banged his fist on the dash before hanging up his phone. I refused to look at him; I knew he'd see right through me. I needed to get upstairs to collect my purse and get home without breaking down. I went to open the door, but he grabbed my arm. His hands sparked the usual slow burn within me, but it mixed with the overwrought feelings from his phone call. I paused to look at him and prayed in the hope that my face wouldn't betray me.

"I'm sorry Mia. I didn't mean to scare you," he said quietly.

His eyes widened at my indifference. I blinked, and gave him a slight headshake. "I'm fine. We should get upstairs so we can get to work," I whispered.

I got out of the car so he didn't have a chance to say anything further. He met me at the front of his car with his hand extended. I grabbed it and pulled him away. We walked in silence to the elevators, where I let go of his hand. I needed every inch of distance for the ride up to his apartment. Being in an enclosed space with him when I was even slightly aroused was dangerous. Every part of me was more than eager to forget our problems by doing what we do best. He broke from brooding and gave me his naughty smirk. I tucked myself into a corner on the other side of the elevator. He chuckled as we watched the floors pass beneath us. The elevator stopped on his floor. We stepped into the hallway.

I started experiencing every inappropriate feeling imaginable as we neared his apartment. We stopped at his door. I took a deep breath to try and beat down my wayward desires. His lips slipped into a half-smile as he unlocked his door. Ethan swept me into his arms as we crossed the threshold. I squealed in shock as he marched straight to the bedroom room where he set me down, lowering himself over me. Ethan took my hands and secured them above my head. He was being more forceful and demanding than he ever had been before. He kissed me fiercely while his hands ran across every inch of my body before he pulled away.

"I know what you're about to say but this time I need you," Ethan pleaded.

I looked into his eyes and recognized the desperation behind them. I nodded and bit my lip. His lips dived back to mine roughly. He continued at a feral pace before switching over to my neck. He hit my collarbone and started sucking as his hand disappeared, making quick work of my bra and shirt.

Once my clothes had vanished, he discarded his own whilst making sure his lips never left my body. My back bowed as he hit my breasts where he sucked hard. I gasped as he bit forcefully down against my nipple before he settled into a soft suckling between both breasts. His hands went in opposite directions. One settled on the breast not occupied by his lips, with the other hitting the spot I needed him at the most. His fingers dipped in and out ferociously. I was so close, with everything he was doing to me. My stomach clenched along with everything south of me as I tried to refrain from falling apart. I screamed out from the amount of pleasure he was giving me. I moved my face closer to him to bring his attention back to me, but he didn't budge, carrying on at a ferocious pace.

"Fuck!" I shouted, climaxing hard against his fingers.

He pushed forward even faster and ran his lips up my chest before kissing the sides of my neck. He settled on the spot under my earlobe that drove me nuts. The embers remaining from the orgasm he had just given me burned red-hot while he bit down under my ear. Ethan slid his fingers out and ran them along the inside of my thigh before he pushed my legs further apart to settle himself between them. His eyes met mine, creating a headiness that had me rocking against him. Ethan drove into me roughly. He took no time whatsoever to claim what was his as he pushed deeper once inside. He continued, at an unforgiving rate, with each thrust of the hips. His hand came tenderly up to my face, as his eyes implored me to stop trying to figure out what had led him to this. I closed my eyes and gave in to him. He twisted his hips and drove faster. As he got closer, I tightened around him. I was still out of breath from my first orgasm, but my body built right back up for another. His breathing increased as he rocked harder for his release.

"I love when you squeeze against me," Ethan hollered.

He penetrated even deeper. I consumed every part of him, but he carried on relentlessly, like he wanted even more of me. Ethan getting close brought me to the brink too, as I clenched around him even more. He released my hands. I dug my nails deep into his back. He groaned and slammed harder as he climaxed. I exploded right along with him. He lowered his head and lay in the crook of my neck as we panted together; utterly breathless and satisfied. I ran my fingers through his hair as I wondered why – this was not something I had expected from him. It worried me that something had brought his guard down this much. "Feel better?"

"Not quite," Ethan panted.

He was hard again as he started to grind slowly against me.

"Again?" I sputtered.

I bit my lip and met his measured rolls of the hip.

"Yes," he grunted.

He lifted his head and rested on his elbows, rocking harder. I grabbed the blanket beneath me. My insides started to spark and flame. He drove deeper with each push. If this was what he needed, I wasn't going to stop him. All I wanted was to help him relax, because he was starting to freak me out.

It didn't take long before he was completely hard, and clearly on a mission. He drove against me, at a pace even more rapid than earlier. I grasped his chin, willing him to look at me so I could try to figure out what was going through his head, but he brushed my fingers away and kissed my hands as he brought them above my head again. My breathing hitched as I stared at him.

Every part of me was at his command. I wiggled my hands to

free them, but his clasp on them strengthened. His eyes drifted to mine with desire, but there was something else. Something terrible was bothering him. It crashed with the heady feelings within me. I was with him physically, but my mind was focused on what was going on in his head.

His lips came down against mine again, begging for response. I gave it to him. As we explored each other's mouths, he slowed his rapid thrusting and switched to gently twisting his hips. I stared at him, trying to figure out what was troubling him. It distracted me so much that he slowed to a near stop.

"Let it go," Ethan demanded.

"What!" I cried out.

My mind drifted from the room, but my body trembled with the loss of friction.

"You're not here with me right now. Your mind is wandering. It's like yesterday. Either push it aside or tell me to stop because I won't do this with you when you're mind is elsewhere," he demanded.

"I'm here with you," I yelled.

The roughness he exerted when he started pushing again brought every part of my attention back to him. My mind no longer had any room to think about anything other than the dull ache he was intensifying with each thrust.

"Then be here with me, Mia. Stop looking for answers and be with me *right now*."

"Oh God, I'm here with you. Believe me, I'm here with you," I shouted.

"Good," Ethan groaned.

I raised my hips and met him as he slammed against me. Ethan carried on, driving us to our release. My hands throbbed from the pressure of his grip. He looked me in the eyes, silently demanding that I do this with him. I nodded, as if to show that he wasn't alone.

He drove as hard as he could, and my body welcomed the pleasure. I screamed out as I found utter bliss once again. The deep ache within me flamed out, as an intense ecstasy took over every nerve-ending within me.

"Fuck," Ethan shouted, as he climaxed.

"I think we accomplished that in spades. Anything else you want to do today," I joked.

His lips came down to silence me. He remained inside of me as he attacked the inside of my mouth before partially separating himself from me. A bead of sweat prickled on his forehead. I wriggled my hand free from his grip and wiped it away.

"You're going to have to move eventually," I observed.

"I don't see you fighting me on it," Ethan retorted.

He deliberately rolled his hips, stirring me to life for more. I threw my head back into the pillow to try and find a rational thought. "You have a deal to finish. I promise I'll make it up to you. I'll show you all the ways I can make you crumble with my lips alone," I reasoned. I ran my eyes down his chest so that he fully understood what I was implying.

"You drive a hard bargain."

Ethan slid out while I continued to catch my breath. It made me happy that he agreed to my suggestion without getting pissed at me. I loved losing my body to him in this way. It was indescribable, but giving into that side of us was becoming increasingly difficult, with everything unspoken between us. I could only forget the world outside of us for so long before it penetrated my skull again. I scanned the room for my clothes so I could get home then to his office. What I wanted more than anything was a shower. I craved to wash away every part of the meeting with Harrison. I hated myself so much for falling prey to him.

Yeah, I want a shower. At least the water can clean everything on the surface. I need something about me to be fresh and untainted, because my soul is black enough from the lies.

I dressed and found my purse on his dresser. He lay on his back on the bed, still coming down from our heated romp. I sat down on the edge, near his face. I leaned down to give him a chaste kiss, but had to squirm away from his arms before he had a chance to pull me back down for another round.

"I'm going to head home to shower and change. I'll see you in a bit."

Ethan nodded, as he got up to walk with me. He placed a soft kiss on the back of my neck before guiding me further down the hallway as he veered into his bathroom.

"Take your time getting in today. I want you there in one piece, so don't worry about being late," he said over his shoulder.

I grinned on my way out of his apartment. It dawned on me that the things he had said or done from the very beginning had indicated that he had deep feelings for me. He was always worrying about my well-being. But as with most things these days, the warmness within me didn't last – as I opened my car door, my cell phone buzzed with a text message.

I suggest you go to work Mia. You're pressing your luck. You'd better get an invitation to this meeting by the end of the week or I'll show you just how malicious I can be. I expect you to confirm this much by Friday afternoon.

I tossed my purse inside as my stomach contents splattered across the concrete. I held on to the car door to keep from passing out. My knees started to grow weak with the terror that raced along every nerve-ending. I rested my head against my door and took a few deep, deliberate breaths. I didn't doubt Harrison in the least. He had already proved that he had eyes watching my every move.

No one was up when I got home. I quickly took a shower, wishing I had more time. I sorely needed it, if only to wash the self-hatred from my body. I got ready in a flash, to get to work as instructed by my text message. I hated that Harrison had such a deep level of control over my life. On my way to the office, I struggled to breathe against the deep pressure in the center of my chest. I had never experienced an anxiety attack, but was fairly sure I was starting to know what one felt like. I focused hard on anything but my life to ease the pressure. As I pulled into the parking lot, I had calmed myself enough to be presentable in front of Ethan. I strode into his office without bothering to knock.

He was already at work, but paused to give me a warm smile as I sat down. His earlier mood seemed to have lightened. I focused on the laptop that sat open, ready for me, and located the proposal on the Q drive. His upbeat mood drifted into my thoughts; and it brought a smile to my face, thinking what it takes for either one of us to relax.

"Care to share what you're thinking?" Ethan asked.

The corner of his eye was on me, but his attention was on his screen.

"I remember asking you how things would be if we worked this closely together. I knew how difficult it would be to have restraint. Even though we laid out the rules, we suck at sticking to them."

"I'm following your lead, my dear. You tend to set the mood, whether you realize it or not."

His eyes twinkled, but he kept focused on his computer.

"Can you clarify something about this proposal?"

"Sure," Ethan responded as his face became unemotional.

"Why is this deal important to you?" I asked, with caution.

Admittedly, I was curious because any phone call he took about the deal left him in an angry state. The proposal was up on my screen for me to pick up where I'd left off. I continued editing, while waiting for his answer. I was unsure of who had typed it up, but it was very half-assed at best. I pulled some other files to insert the spreadsheets, graphs, and tables that each department had compiled for the pitch. As I went to open them, other folders that weren't on the drive before caught my attention; specifically ones assigned for Sean and Colin. For the hell of it, I clicked on Colin's. It opened, to my surprise. Inside was a document, updated within the last few days that looked relevant to this mysterious meeting. I went to open it, but it was password protected.

No shock there. I know Jayden would look at this and lick his lips at the challenge of breaking into all the data on this computer. Gah! No, Mia. You have enough problems.

I continued scanning until I saw another file that was similar to the last one, but it had been over a year since it had been updated. I tried to open it, only to run into the same issue. There was not a chance in hell that any file pertaining to illegal activity within this company would be wide open for anyone to review. Ethan drummed his fingers along the desk. I peeked over to see his face spreading into a sly grin.

"If it closes without issue, I'll be able to leave the company."

"I see. What– "

"No more questions for you. My turn," Ethan interrupted.

He pinched my mouth shut. I grunted, and tilted my head away from his grip.

"Will you come to Atlantic City with me?"

His eyes were full of hope. He slid his fingers across the top of mine to still them from typing. My heart skipped a beat at the question, because it had a chance of being the invite that I needed to get Harrison out of my life.

"Umm ... when?" I inquired, with my stomach somersaulting.

"It'll be when this deal closes. We're trying to agree on the day. There's some other business to tend to out there apart from this deal.

Sean and Colin want to get it all done in one trip. It's why they're pressuring me so much. It agitates me because I have my own plans."

The pressure in my chest started to rise, as if a cinderblock was sitting on it. This had to be my invite. It would be one hell of a coincidence if it weren't it. I pushed aside the icicles coating my veins. I was a horrible human being for agreeing to his request, because it was purely for selfish reasons. It had nothing to do with him and everything to do with my mess of a life.

"Sure," I whispered.

Ethan jumped up and grabbed me from my chair. He brought his hands to my cheekbones as his lips immersed mine. I hardly had time to react, let alone participate in the kiss before he stepped back to look at me. His eyes were full of so much joy that it broke my heart. I never deserved to find anyone like him, yet here I was agreeing to things without telling him why I was so keen to leave with him. His kiss left me barely breathing, but my own self-disgust had already knocked the wind right of me. I tried to move away from him, but he held me close. His fingers grazed along my cheeks. Part of me wanted to fall into his tender embrace and be happy with him. The other part of me needed separation. Each stroke he gave me sent shards of pain throughout my body.

"The life I've wanted for myself will be possible when this is over. And I'll have you with me when I start that new chapter of my life," Ethan whispered.

I wiggled out of his grasp and fell into my chair. He returned to his seat.

My entire body felt like a bomb had blown through me. It took every part of my insides with it as it blew out the surroundings. I had to tell him. There was no way I'd let him think that I was everything he had ever wanted to start a new life with, when I haven't been completely honest with him. As I opened my mouth to tell him, my friend's faces started flashing in my head, in perfect sequence like a home movie. My mind flashed to every happy memory, from the time Trey and I were children. It crossed over to the times I shared with Bri and Shane. It drifted to my first day of classes at the university and every moment on campus I spent with Jackson. It wrapped up with the last few months, with all of us together at our happiest.

I snapped my jaw shut and focused on handling the twists of pain that were growing inside of me. My eyes went back to the laptop so that I could distract myself. I took in every ounce of agony that sliced through me; all the while working on the proposal that would be everything Ethan needed to start afresh. I peeked at him, only to see a huge grin on his face. My heart sank even more. I stared blankly at the protected file for a while, before moving more graphs into the proposal.

The rest of the day was very productive. It turned out that we could work well together when we focused. The only words between us were about my opinions on changes. Occasionally, he would ask for my thoughts on the actual pitch he was going to give with the proposal. I had no clue why he even asked at all – he didn't need my help. Ethan had one of the sharpest minds I'd ever known. If I were to estimate his IQ, I'd say he was maybe a few points shy of a genius. He had an uncanny ability to recall data and numbers that blew me away. I'd offer suggestions on different word choices, but that was about it.

I glanced at the clock and noticed that it was well past six. We hadn't discussed spending this evening together. Frankly, I wanted to spend tonight alone. I wasn't ready to have his hands all over me. My body was far from finding neutral ground; I needed more time to silence the voices within my head that screamed every self-loathing thought imaginable. I deserved every one of them, so it didn't seem right for me to escape it quite yet without some penance for my deceit.

It terrified me that I was capable of this level of selfishness. I refrained from thinking about telling him anything because it only amplified every other feeling. I had no idea if he would want me after the truth came out. The prospect of being without him devastated me as much as the idea of any harm coming to my friends. The inner conflict of the two slashed at every part of me.

I peered over at Ethan as he clicked across the keyboard, only stopping every few seconds to move the mouse to another area on the screen. I hated interrupting him when he was in this mode. I quietly cleared my throat. Our earlier discussion was still gnawing away at me. It had left me feeling raw and ripped open, so basic mannerisms were a struggle.

"Are you finished for the night?" Ethan asked. He gestured towards my unmoving hands on the laptop.

"I'm sorry, but my brain has more or less shut down. I'd rather be done than start putting in half-assed work that I'll just have to correct tomorrow. I'm going to head home, but I was wondering if you wanted to have dinner tomorrow night with some of my friends."

"Yes, I think dinner tomorrow would be fine. I wish you'd consider staying with me tonight," Ethan stated, with a crooked grin.

I forced a smile. "I need to go home tonight. Thank you for agreeing to dinner. I'll talk to Bri and Trey to see if they can make it work in their schedules. I'll have more details for you in the morning," I answered, rising from my seat.

"I could spend the evening catching up on Sports Center. I've fallen behind on my teams," Ethan replied as he joined me.

"Why did you fall behind?" I asked, amused.

"I've been wrapped up in some girl. She's been taking up all my time even when she's not with me."

I winked. "Some girl huh. Anyone I know?"

"No, she's exquisite. I doubt *you'd* know her," he teased.

I poked him in the side, but he grabbed my hand and placed a soft kiss on top of it. He was certainly a gentleman. It made me feel even guiltier for lying to him, because for the way he treated me, he didn't deserve to suffer my deception. His happiness with my agreeing to go to Atlantic City was all over his face. It made the pit in my stomach stretch from my heart to my knees. I had no doubt that this trip coincided with the meeting Harrison expected me to be at, especially since it was on the east coast and Ethan admitted that Sean and Colin had other business to tend to out there aside from finalizing this deal. Given the shadiness around here and what Harrison had already reported on the east coast mob and the connections to our metro, it would be stupid of me not to assume that this was my meeting invite. I still didn't understand why I was being blackmailed to be there, but I wasn't in a position to dig for the answers. It'd only promised to bring my loved ones and me a world of hurt. I stood on my tiptoes to give him a brisk kiss before leaving.

"Until tomorrow babe," I whispered, fighting off the tears.

"Bye, love," Ethan said softly, as he let me go.

CHAPTER TWENTY-EIGHT
A Night To Be Normal

I spent the evening filling in everyone at home on the new situation. Trey urged me to follow Harrison's instructions, since he had proved that he had far more power than I ever anticipated. Jackson disagreed, instead endorsing the idea having Jayden dig deeper. Shane was stuck in the middle of the two of them. In the end, he agreed with Trey, saying I should stick it out without bringing any unnecessary attention to myself. It almost brought the three of them to physical blows with one another. Each of them agreed on one thing – they were all pissed off at me for hiding this from them. I didn't blame them. My hate for myself was far greater than any of the frustrations that they might have. I cut my time with them short and spent the rest of the night with Bri.

My recap with her was very different. It terrified her that I had no way out from the situation. We mulled over whether there were any ways to get out of this ordeal without hurting someone, but came up with nothing. I had been out of my league with Harrison from the beginning. It became more obvious as each day passed. She considered calling her father, who was a senator, but I told her not to involve him. I wasn't sure how he would be able to assist until she revealed that he had people within his office that specialized in unorthodox matters. I didn't buy it, until she admitted that she had found out that her father had had an illegitimate child years ago. His office made sure nothing came to light during his last campaign. It shocked me that she had never shared that with me, but I let it go. I pressed, looking to find out what else she was withholding about herself, but she shut me down every time I brought it up. Instead I asked her about joining Ethan and me for a late dinner Thursday night, but it didn't work for her schedule. Friday worked better, so we planned on that evening.

Thursday and Friday at the office went by without any issues between Ethan and me. We made it through both days without a fight while working on his proposal. Spending Wednesday night at home had helped me to manage the massive amount of emotion coursing through me. I eliminated any further threats from Harrison by calling him Thursday morning to tell him that I had secured an invitation to go to Atlantic City that coincided with the finalization of Ethan's deal. He confirmed that it was the meeting invite he wanted me to obtain. He followed up with his other source to verify my claim. He demanded that I keep my mouth shut, stating that he still had an eye trained on my every move. I still didn't understand why my presence at this meeting was necessary and figured that there was more to the entire matter, but I let it go. I had enough problems.

It was evident that Ethan suspected that something very big was going on with me, but for some strange reason he held back on asking me anything. It made me want to come clean even more. I still hadn't asked him about why he became so angry when we were photographed. Granted, I knew who was behind it, but I wanted to know more about Ethan's place in this whole mess. I was very close to telling him the truth just so I could find out more about his own involvement.

Bri convinced Trey to join us for a late dinner on the Friday night. According to her, it took some fine motor skills before he agreed. I needed them to see what I saw in Ethan, and to help me figure out if clueing him in was a good idea. I had very few days left where I'd be able to keep my wits together without going off the deep end. I fell in love with him more each day, so the idea of lying to him was close to shutting down all my vital organs. Ethan suggested a pizzeria he favored that was near his place. I planned to stay with him that evening, since I had spent the prior two evenings at home. I missed him, but the space became more important to sort out the ramblings in my head.

Suddenly, Friday night was upon us. We walked into the pizzeria with our hands laced together. It was the first time that we were out together, and were both dressed very casually in jeans. Ethan had on a white button-up shirt with sneakers. I went with a dark red three-quarter shirt and boots. As we walked in, I looked around to find Bri and Trey. It didn't look like they were there yet, so it was up to us to grab a table.

Since it was later in the evening, it was a 'seat yourself' type of atmosphere. The place itself was set up as a cross between a bar and an old-fashioned diner. The artwork and ambiance were true to all the landmarks of Chicago, with specific homages paid to the many successful sports dynasties that the city had seen over the years. There were booths that lined the walls with plenty of tables scattered throughout the place. As you walked through the door, a large bar was across from you. There were hidden nooks off to both the left and right sides that had pool tables and darts. They purposefully took you away from the hustle of the rest of the pizzeria. It was still busy, given the time of night, so we had to walk for a bit before we found an open booth with enough room. Ethan went up to the bar to get us a pitcher of beer. He returned rather fast and filled two glasses.

"Who else will be joining us tonight?" Ethan asked, passing me a full glass of beer.

"It'll just be Bri and Trey," I answered before taking a long drink.

"I'm looking forward to meeting them," Ethan replied, with a mischievous grin.

He ran a hand down my thigh and let his fingers inch far too much to the inside. My breath hitched and I shook my head to admonish any further course of action that would result in his hand going further up my leg. His eyes danced at the silent reprimand. It was as if he got off on it. It was either that, or he loved pushing me to my limit in any way possible. He never failed to keep me guessing at what ran through his astonishing mind.

"I'm glad you're happy to be here. I wasn't sure if I'd have to bribe you to agree to it."

Ethan retracted his hand and took a sip of his beer. "Why would you think you have to bribe me to spend time with your friends?" he asked, obviously offended.

I flinched at his tone of voice. "I didn't mean it in a bad way. It's just the age difference between us. Sometimes it sticks out."

As I was bringing up my glass to finish my beer, his hand capped it and urged me to put it back on the table. I set it down and gave him my attention. Ethan ran his hand along my jaw, keeping my head still as he gazed at me, with significance upon his face. "I may be a few years older than you Mia, but you're far older than me in ways that you don't even recognize. I don't know why you can't see that in yourself, but I'll do everything I can to show you," Ethan declared. He paused and tenderly stroked my cheek with his other hand. I softened at his touch. "I've never saw you as a partying college girl. You have far too much passion in you. It's one of the reasons I'm drawn to you," he confessed.

He released his grip on my face and picked up his beer to finish off his glass. I was in shock from the amount that he saw into me. I had hardly scratched the surface with him when it came to the deep stuff. What he just said made me believe that he might have sensed some of the deeper parts without me saying a word. My lips crept into a timid smile as I tried to keep from crying. I was about to respond when my phone vibrated. I moved closer and gave him a gentle kiss on the lips before I left to get Bri and Trey.

I smiled, seeing them. She was fiddling with her long layered silver tassel necklace. Trey was whispering into her ear. She cuddled even further into him with a soft smile. He stood behind her with his hands wrapped around her waistline. She kept his gaze intently fixed upon her, as she flirtatiously batted her eyes at him after something he commented on towards the bar. His face relaxed as he gazed at her while she continued to tease him. He stopped her fidgeting with her necklace by taking her hand and placing a soft kiss upon it. She rested her head against his chest as they continued to keep in quiet conversation with each other. I liked seeing them this happy. I almost felt bad for interrupting them when they appeared so synched.

"Hey guys, thanks for coming out tonight," I greeted, with a genuine smile.

Bri straightened up and gave me a wholehearted smile. Trey made it very clear that he was still less than thrilled with me. Bri pushed him forward, since he made no move on his own. It was fine that he was irate with me, I thought, but if he could sideline it for the evening, it would be wonderful. He shrugged at me. I scowled at his inability to meet me halfway. Rigidness spread throughout his body. Bri sensed it as she wiggled out of his grasp and stepped between the two of us. I continued to glower at him, with my arms crossed over my chest. Trey stared me down with his stink eye. Bri whipped her head back and forth as we stared at each other like the two hotheaded kids that we were years ago. It was as if we were seven again and fighting over toys. She shook her head and urged us to move from the doorway.

"The tension between the two of you calls for a round of shots, so that we can actually *look* like we're all friends," Bri said, eyeing us cautiously.

"That's a damn good idea Bri," I agreed, taking her hand on my way to the bar.

I placed an order for another pitcher of beer and a round of tequila shooters. The shots lined the bar within seconds for us to grab. I motioned for them to pick up the shots. They grabbed them and we tossed them back without a word. The pitcher of beer quickly followed. I took it and laid the money on the bar and led them back to our table. When we were near the booth, I sighed at the hardness that still lingered upon Trey's face. It would be a long night if he didn't lighten up at some point. He brushed past me, with Bri at his side. She shot me an apologetic glance as they slid in across from Ethan. I loved and I hated that kid at times. When he wasn't happy with a situation, he had no problem sharing it with anyone around him.

I set the pitcher down on the table and slid in next to Ethan. He stretched for my hand to intertwine it with his before bringing them to the table. Trey studied our hands, seemingly deepening his irritation with me. He filled a glass of beer for Bri and then one for himself. As he poured, I downed mine and grasped the near empty pitcher to fill it back up.

"Ethan, this is Bri and Trey," I said, pointing to each of them. Bri gave Ethan a warm smile. Trey forced a thin one. "I know that you met in passing at the club, but I never formally introduced you," I continued nervously.

Bri stared at me, with a warning to settle down or I was going to make it overly awkward for everyone. I brought my beer back to my mouth to keep it occupied.

"Do you come to this place often Ethan?" Bri inquired.

She ran her eyes along the menu with a nod of approval. Trey wasn't as hospitable. He kept his eyes forward, unwilling to converse with anyone. I gave him a swift kick under the table. He scowled at me and picked up a menu, skulking behind it like a toddler. It made me want to punch him – I swore he was doing it to piss me off.

Rather than go down the immature route, I looked at Bri and begged with my eyes to have her do whatever she could to get him to switch gears. She gave me a wily grin and slid her hand underneath the table. A minute later, Trey grunted and brought the menu down.

God bless her gifted fingers, hands or whatever the hell she uses to get him to do what she wants. She has more control over him than anyone.

"I've never been to this place. How did you find it?" Trey asked cordially.

I mouthed a silent thank you to Bri before leaning towards Ethan. I was just as eager for his answer. He seemed to find all the gems in the city, and this was no exception. Ethan tilted his head towards me, with a look that indicated that he was well aware of what was going on around him. I pleaded with my eyes for him to not say a word about it. Ethan gave a headshake in amusement before focusing on Bri and Trey. I let out a huge breath of relief.

"I found this place in college. The pizza here is astounding and the beer is cheap. It's a great place any night of the week," Ethan stated. I looked at him in wonderment. Before I had a chance to voice my question, he spoke up. "No, I don't have an interest here. It's a stomping ground of my past that I wanted to share, since it's too amazing to keep to myself."

He kept his focus on me with every word he said. I fell into the sparkle behind his eyes. He smiled softly as he wiped away some beer from the corner of my mouth. My breathing wavered at his tender touch. I blinked a few times before tearing my eyes away from him. I didn't want to be caught up in him. I peeked at Bri and Trey. They were motionless as they stared at us. Her lips curled into a huge smile. Trey seemed to relax some more.

"Do we want to order some pizzas for all of us or are we going Dutch?" I asked.

The three of them gave me a round of shrugs. I wanted to kick Ethan. All of a sudden, he had jumped on the bandwagon of indecision. I squinted at him with daggers in my eyes. It was unbelievable that he was even trying to pull this with me. He tried to stifle his laughter. I could have sworn that any way that he could mess with me, he jumped at with the enthusiasm of a child. I dug my nails into his hand to drive my point home. Bri was watching me closely. By the twitch of her lips, Ethan pressing my buttons entertained her.

"The pizza here is extraordinary, so I'm fine with doing a group order if that works with everyone else," Ethan spoke up.

"That works," Bri and Trey said as they set down their empty cups.

"Perfect. Why don't you and Trey head to the bar to get the order in with another pitcher of beer? Bri and I are going to excuse ourselves to the ladies room."

"What do you want on it?" Ethan asked with a crooked smile.

"Trey knows what we'll tolerate on a pizza. My advice is to get two. Get one that you two will agree on and one that Trey knows that Bri and I will eat."

"Well said, Mia," Bri agreed.

She made her way out of the booth. Ethan slid out so that I could go with Bri while they went to the bar. As we walked, I hissed, "Do you think Trey will play nice while we're away from them?"

"If he knows what's good for him, he will," Bri muttered as we entered the bathroom.

We strategized a way to keep Trey cordial for the rest of the night, because it was clear that Ethan suspected something was up. We didn't come up with much other than her continuing with her handiwork whenever she had a chance. I wasn't opposed to her dragging him away entirely to ensure he remained civil. It frustrated me that we were even talking about it. If one more thing popped up regarding my mess with Harrison, I was coming clean with Ethan.

I opened the door for us so that we could get back to the guys. Before we reached the table, Trey cut me off by grabbing my arm, towing me in the opposite direction. He gave Bri a quick peck and whispered in her ear. She nodded with alarmed eyes and made a beeline for the booth. Trey took us over to the side of the bar, out of sight of Ethan.

"What Trey?" I asked, loosening the grip he had on my arm. Trey pointed to the opposite end of the bar. Micah was there with Ian O'Connor. "Fuck. What the hell is he doing here?"

The sight of those two together sent an icy chill throughout my entire body. It was beyond troubling to see Micah with Ian. I believed that Ian was Harrison's other source on the inside. Seeing Micah with Ian made me wonder if he was part of Harrison's circle. I clutched my arms around myself to push my thoughts in a different direction. I didn't have time to dwell.

In that instant, the whole evening took a turn for the worse. They didn't notice us as we watched them from across the bar. After several minutes, Ian got up and went for the door. I pulled on Trey's arm so that we could get away without Micah seeing us. The effort went unrewarded as Micah spotted us. He made his way over to our side of the bar. As he closed the distance, I saw that there were no signs of him being high, so that was a point in the plus column, for now.

"Mia, we need to talk," Micah spat.

Trey took a protective stance against his tone. "Don't demand *shit* from her, or I'll beat your ass again," he warned.

I patted his arm and took a brave step closer to Micah. It was so strange being terrified of someone that had brought you nothing but comfort in the past. I inhaled deeply to squash the fear that was attacking me. "I know. How about we meet at O'Reilley's next week?"

"Why are you here with that asshole?" Micah asked, nodding his head towards Ethan as fury swept across his face.

Trey leaned in to Micah, giving a clear indication that he had better not start shit. Micah took a step closer towards Trey to show that he wasn't going to back down. I stepped in between them with my hands on each of their chests. To my relief, touching Micah for the first time in almost a year had no effect on me whatsoever. I could've been touching the bar because there was nothing there. It made more than happy to know that he no longer had that hold on me. The rest of me felt like tornado was whipping around within. My veins sliced open with the residual pain, anger, hate, and love that I had for Micah. Every inch that the funnel cloud hit stirred a different memory of him. It was difficult for me to breathe.

"Stop. We're not going to get tossed out of here, so let it go. Both of you," I demanded.

"You didn't answer me. Is that piece of shit your new boyfriend?" Micah questioned.

His face went wretched as the words passed through his lips. Trey scowled as his arms folded across his chest. I glanced towards our booth, but didn't have a clear view of it. We were out of sight so hopefully Ethan wasn't watching this or I'd have one hell of an issue on my hands if he came over here. I let go of his reference to Ethan. I wasn't going to let my temper get mixed up in the raw emotions circling through me. I directed my attention to Micah, who was shaking with the amount of rage running through him.

"I just started seeing him."

"You won't even give me a chance to explain anything to you," Micah fumed.

"I'll talk with you next week. I moved on a long time ago, Micah," I answered.

I looked him in the eye so that he wasn't the least bit confused about us talking. As he gazed at me, there was no question that he understood that this wasn't about us getting back together. Our time together was over. Everything upon my face reinforced that. Micah's face started to turn red as his temper started to climb.

"I'm still in love with you. Fuck, Mia! We were together for over five years and you act like it meant nothing to you," Micah shot back.

"I'm not getting into that shit with you right now. I suggest you give me a day next week for us to meet so we can talk," I snapped.

Micah settled down a bit when he heard the ire in my voice. He knew not to push me. The mess running rampant in me would be enough for me to blow up.

Micah huffed. "Fine, can we have lunch next Thursday at Lockharts?"

I nodded and motioned for Trey to come with me. "I'll meet you there at one. We have to get back to our evening. I'd appreciate it if you left us alone. I agreed to what you wanted, so give me this in exchange. It's the least you can do."

Trey grimaced as he walked over to my side, not saying a word to Micah. Though it was what I asked, it made the heavy pressure in my chest increase as the pain tore through me. I finally realized that Trey would always be at my side. He'd never have the friendship he had with Micah and it was because of me. He made a choice and he wouldn't waver from it, even when he was furious with me.

Micah watched him close the space between us. He came to the same conclusion. He let out a forced breath and pushed off the bar. "I won't bother you. You look happy. That's all I've ever wanted for you," he stated.

He gave us a heavyhearted look on his way to the door. He paused for a moment to glance at me before leaving. His eyes were full of so much hurt that I had to look away. I knew that our brief conversation had torn him up. It mixed me up too. It was the last thing I needed, but that seemed to be my luck these days. I leaned into Trey for support, so I didn't fall over. Trey placed his arms on my shoulders and gave me a gentle squeeze.

"You did well," Trey remarked.

I turned to face him. I wasn't nearly as content about this exchange as the tone in his voice suggested. I stepped towards the bar to order another pitcher of beer. I needed to have a decent excuse as to why we had disappeared for so long. I wanted to rid myself of every raw emotion that Micah brought to the surface. I ordered a round of shots for us. I pushed one towards Trey and picked up mine. I slammed it down and savored the burn as it trickled down my throat. It helped squelch everything else within me. Trey did the same and placed the empty shot glass upside down on the bar. I grabbed our pitcher of beer. We made our way back towards our table.

"I'm sorry, Trey," I said softly.

"You have nothing to be sorry for Mia. Micah made his choices. After he destroyed you, it wasn't that hard for me to dismiss him. I'd given him plenty of breaks, far too many times," Trey replied earnestly.

We walked the rest of the way in silence. When we got to the booth, it was empty. I set the full pitcher of beer down and looked around the bar. Ethan and Bri were at the opposite end of the place and engaged in an intense game of darts. I took comfort in her quick thinking with Micah's unexpected presence here tonight. She had cornered them into a section in one of the nooks that was out of eyesight of the bar. Trey let out a soft laugh as he came to the same conclusion. He walked past me. Before we reached them, he rotated to face me – it was tight with worry. The unease in my stomach grew as he stared at me. "Did you know that he was involved with Ian?"

"No, I had no idea. I believe Ian also works for Harrison, and that makes me question everything that much more," I answered quietly.

The look in his eyes grew distressed. I nodded, feeling the same way about the idea of those two working together. We didn't have time to figure out why Ian and Micah would be together. We knew that it was bad, anyway that you sliced it. It looked like Micah and I had one hell of a discussion ahead of us. It was also the last straw for me.

CHAPTER TWENTY-NINE
Revelations

Ethan and Bri broke from their game to acknowledge our arrival. Bri gave Trey a swift kiss before stepping up to the line.

"I'm kicking his ass. It's great to play someone that I can beat. You two never give me a chance in hell at winning," Bri said, with a cheerful grin.

Ethan strolled over to me. "I'm letting her win. She's horrible at this game. Where were you? You left with one friend and returned with the other."

I wrapped my arms around his waist. My hands grazed up his back until they hit the tips of his hair. Ethan slid his hands down my sides. He entwined my hands with his and leaned against the wall.

"We got sidetracked at the bar. We grabbed another round. It turned out to be a good decision, since you two finished off that pitcher. After you wrap up this game, we can play in teams. I'm sure Trey and I can show you a thing or two about darts," I said spiritedly.

I nestled my back into him. With our hands around my stomach, Ethan let out a peaceful sigh. Trey nodded at the idea with a cocky smirk. Bri shoved him while looking at me nothing short of annoyed. She realigned herself to throw again.

"You two are so damn arrogant at times that I want to smack both of you," she huffed.

Bri threw a dart at the board, not hitting a number in sight. Trey refrained from howling with laughter. I tried to suppress my own laughing, but the redness in Trey's face pushed me too far. I started chuckling as she collected her darts. It caused Trey to join in with me. Ethan tilted his head to me with a raised eyebrow.

"I grew up in a bar, so naturally I'm good at darts – and pretty much any other bar game. I've been playing them since I was old enough to know the rules. Once I figured it out, I started challenging my friends. By the time we were teenagers, we were pretty lethal at most of them," I clarified.

Trey gave me a heartfelt grin. We learned a lot, playing countless bar patrons. Trey pulled Bri closer to calm her irritation. He swept her in for a deep kiss to try and make the scowl on her face disappear. Bri beamed at him before she turned to me with a less amused look. Out of the corner of my eye, I saw the bartender placing our pizzas at our booth.

"Looks like you two caught a break tonight. Our food is done," I pointed out.

Ethan fell in step with me as Trey and Bri followed behind us. As they neared the booth, Bri yanked Trey towards the bathrooms. She gave him a salacious grin as they strode away. Trey licked his lips while grabbing her ass. They hurried along, having no shame in what they were about to do. I slid into the booth and grabbed my cup as Ethan settled in next to me.

"Do you intend on sharing anything tonight, or am I supposed to draw my own conclusions as to where those two are off to now?" Ethan asked.

I filled our glasses with beer before taking a piece of the pie. "I don't think where they went or what they are doing requires an explanation. It's quite obvious," I answered around a bite of pizza.

Ethan was not wrong. The pizza was mouthwatering. He had already devoured two slices of the pie he was sharing with Trey. A crumb fell to the corner of his mouth. His tongue slid out to lick it away. My body jolted at the action with a variety of desires. It longed for his tongue to work its magic on me. I shook my head and tore myself away from staring at him any longer. My thoughts were heading towards to a very dirty place, and this wasn't the time for that. It didn't stop my eyes from darting towards the bathroom. I forced myself to focus on my food. It was the only thing to distract me from giving into the strong urge to do exactly what Bri had done with Trey. I finished off my slice. My beer was at the bottom, so I grabbed the pitcher to replenish it. I glanced over at Ethan while filling up my glass. He was staring at me with a mischievous grin.

"What?"

"I was just thinking about where your friends disappeared to, and where you more than likely picked up your openness in public places."

I kicked him, to deter him from taking the conversation in that direction. It wasn't helping my body calm down in the least. I suspected that he knew what he was doing to me, too. Ethan flashed his signature smile as he polished off another slice.

"Are you having a good time?" I asked, picking up another slice.

"I am. Bri seems like a lovely girl. It's obvious Trey cares very much about her, and you. I already knew that about him from the other night."

"I've been meaning to ask you about that little exchange. What happened?"

"I could tell that he didn't like the idea of you leaving with me. It's clear he's very protective of you. He wasn't going to get in my way, so I made sure he knew it."

I didn't have a chance to ask anything else. Bri and Trey were back. They kept their eyes from mine. It made me even more entertained at their behavior. Her neck and cheeks were a deep red. Trey had a smug grin on his face. He picked up a piece of pizza from the pie Ethan had been eating from, while Bri grabbed a slice from the other. They reached for the beer pitcher to fill their glasses at the same time. Bri pulled back and let Trey fill their cups. I rested into Ethan's side. He draped an arm around me. When Trey finished pouring, I picked up the pitcher and topped off our glasses before taking another drink. Ethan released my arm and snatched the empty pitcher.

"Be right back," he murmured. He swept in for what I thought would be a brisk kiss. To my surprise, he made it much more intimate and longer than I preferred, when in the presence of other people. My body had just cooled down. He swept his tongue across the top of my mouth. I squeezed my thighs as every part of me quickly developed a wanton ache for him. My face heated to a boil as he gave me a crooked grin and walked away.

Bastard. He knows exactly what he is doing.

"Wow! At least we excuse ourselves when we want a moment like that with each other," Bri exclaimed clearly entertained by what she had just witnessed.

My attention wandered back to the table as they stared at me. "It's a lot easier to roll with the punches than try to figure out what he will do next," I admitted.

I rested my elbows on the table before glancing over my shoulder to confirm that Ethan was out of earshot. Bri placed her pizza down as Trey waited for me to speak up.

"I want to tell him the truth tonight."

"I don't know Mia. Are you sure you trust him not to interfere in the ways that Harrison believes he might if he knows the truth?" Trey asked. He glanced at Bri protectively. She had her attention on me, as a serene look ran through her green eyes.

"I think you should tell him, Mia. After spending time with him, it's clear he will do anything to protect you. If you tell him to sideline it until you get out of this with Harrison, I'm pretty sure he will without question," Bri stated. She grasped my hand and gave it a tight squeeze. "It's going to kill you if you continue to keep this from him. The conflict is in your eyes – it's eating you alive. You have too good a heart to live a lie," she finished softly.

A large clap of thunder boomed in the sky, almost shaking everything around us. The rain started to come down in sheets as it hit the windows of the pizzeria. Lightning filled the sky, causing the lights to flicker for a minute. It made what I was discussing with Trey and Bri all the more eerie. She gave my hand another soothing squeeze before picking up her pizza. Her eyes remained on Trey as she urged him to agree with her. He ran his hand along the side of her cheek and tucked a few hairs behind her ear. She smiled at him encouragingly.

"Tell him, but be careful is all that I ask," Trey said, not nearly as convincingly as Bri.

I understood why he was skeptical. I nodded and watched the rain pour down.

Maybe it's a sign. It looks dreadful out there. This storm has spine-chilling timing.

"I know what you're thinking. Let it go. Just tell him," Bri reiterated.

Ethan approached the table with another full pitcher of beer. It was hard to tell if he caught the tail end of our conversation. By the wicked grin on his face, I'd say not. His mind appeared to be savoring our over-the-top display of affection. "Tell me what?" Ethan asked curiously.

Bri shoved a bite into her mouth. Trey took a long drink of beer. I gave them a slight shake of the head before giving Ethan a delicate smile.

Smooth, guys. Very subtle.

"Tell you how hopelessly attracted I am to you, but I think that ship already sailed."

Ethan looked at me with skepticism but was wise enough to let it pass. I stretched for the pitcher to pour myself another beer but he kept it out of reach. "I think you might have had enough to drink tonight. You're actually being sweet with me. That never happens," Ethan teased.

I poked him in the ribs to hand it over. He rolled his eyes and passed me the pitcher. I filled up my glass and did the same for him. "I have no idea what you're talking about. I give you plenty of compliments and I'm always sweet. It's not my fault if you miss it," I contended.

Ethan snorted. Trey and Bri watched us, amused as ever with our bickering. The stare-down I had engaged in with Ethan had them chuckling. "What the hell are you giggling about?" I asked.

"Well, you don't compliment easily, Mia. You always have your guard up," Bri said, trying very hard to keep a straight face.

"So I'm not Susie Fricken Sunshine. I do say nice things from time to time," I retorted, sticking out my tongue at them.

Ethan joined in with the growing laughter. I scowled at all three of them. He pulled me towards the edge of the booth. He grabbed his drink and motioned for me to grab mine. I did as he asked of me before sliding out. Trey and Bri did the same as they hopped out of the booth to follow us. "I want to play darts. I'm intrigued to see you live up to your words," Ethan badgered.

Trey's smile lit up. I smiled cockily in return. Bri huffed as she brought up the rear. She knew exactly why we were more than happy to engage in a game. At least we wouldn't be playing on the same team. We were lethal when we played together against others.

"It's your funeral, Donovan," I jabbed.

"Watch it Ryan. I might have a few tricks up my sleeve that I haven't shown you yet," Trey responded, with as much cockiness in his tone as was in his face.

"Enough, you two," Bri jumped in and separated us as we neared the board.

Ethan passed us each a set of darts. "Let the games begin …"

We played darts for a couple of hours before calling it a night. It was long enough for us to switch over to water so the guys could drive without feeling affected by the beer. Bri and I were in great spirits as we held our respective men on our way out. We shared the same silly grins and sang softly to the song playing on the radio. Trey and Ethan rolled their eyes as they hauled us through the door. We had forgotten that it was raining out, so we ran towards the parking lot in a rush. Trey dragged Bri towards the safety of their car. The wind howled as the rain continued to pelt us. Ethan and I made our way towards his car. The rain was drenching us, but he prevented me from getting in.

"Ethan, we're getting soaked out here," I whined.

"Let it pour on us. I don't care how wet I get. With you next to me, I couldn't care less what happens around me," Ethan responded with reverence.

He pushed a strand of slick hair back before grabbing my face as he lowered his mouth to brush his lips against mine. I struggled to keep my eyes open against the rain coming down. He pressed against my lips, subtly requesting deeper access. He got it immediately. Thunder clapped around us and the wind whipped through us but it didn't slow our kiss. We stood frozen in time, exploring every ounce of each other. My insides started to liquefy with the heat that each swoop of the tongue intensified. He kissed me until I started to shiver from the cold. Before Ethan pulled away, he let his top lip linger on my lower one to keep it from quivering.

"Thank you for tonight. I'm glad you let me in to another part of your life," he whispered.

Ethan escorted me inside the car and crossed over to his side. We left, not saying a word to each other. I looked at the clock and saw that it was almost one. I closed my eyes, feeling exhausted but knowing our night was just beginning. He rested my hand on his thigh. I opened my eyes and caught the sparkle in his as he weaved through the streets. Once we had parked at his place, he brought my hand to his lips for a sweet kiss. He got out and came over to my side to open the door. I exited the car and we walked hand-in-hand towards the elevators.

Once inside, I separated myself from him by going to the opposite side. He snickered but let me have my distance. I wanted to reveal the truth the second we were back in the comfort of his apartment. I wasn't about to be sidetracked by sex. After we were upstairs, I grabbed my bag to change. I went to the bathroom to freshen up while he went towards his bedroom to get settled in for the evening. I set my bag on the vanity and opened it. I picked up a piece of lacy lingerie I had had for a while, but hadn't worn in quite some time. I changed and set my bag on the floor. I inhaled deeply on my way into his bedroom.

Ethan was in the middle of the bed in a fresh pair of boxers. My breathing dwindled as I took in his beauty before crawling into bed next to him. He pulled me tight to his chest as his hands ran up and down my body. He leaned in for a quick kiss before trying to free me of my attire. I grabbed his hands so that he would stop.

"What?"

"I've wanted to ask you something for the past couple of days," I murmured.

I shimmied to the head of the bed so we could talk. Ethan grunted, but sat up.

"What do you want to ask?"

"When someone took pictures of us the other evening, you got very angry but you never explained why. I want to know, because you scared the hell out of me at one point."

Ethan let out an agitated breath as he swung his legs over the bed. He placed his elbows on his knees as his hands supported his head. He rubbed his face a few times before sitting up straight with his back to me.

"It's complicated," he whispered.

"I'm sure I can follow," I answered.

He glanced at me with an aggrieved look before facing forward. I sighed, not liking his expression, so I crept over to him. My fingers made delicate strokes along his tattoos.

"It's part of my exit strategy. Part of what I promised my mother is that I'd take down the empire that my father built. It's far too late to get into the details about why I'm doing it," Ethan replied in pained tone. I continued tracing along the patterns of his back.

"I gave a top-notch magazine owner inside information so that he could build an article that wouldn't be able to be disputed by anyone," Ethan admitted. He stretched for my hands so that he could secure them to his stomach. "I got angry because I've had my suspicions about him. He's the only person I can think of that would want to photograph me. I don't know what game he's playing right now. I've nearly lost my mind trying to figure it out. I'm sorry I took it out on you. I never meant to scare you."

I hugged him tightly and took a huge breath. It was now or never.

"Ethan, I have to tell you something, but I need you to promise me two things."

I had never felt this terrified in my entire life. I thought I knew my worst fears, but I was wrong. I felt like I was in a plane preparing to jump without instructions on how to open my parachute. It fit the situation at hand, since heights petrify me. My heart was beating so fast that I was afraid it might stop. I kind of longed for the plane scenario versus the next five minutes of my life. It would probably be easier.

Ethan released my grip around him as he turned around to face me. He picked me up and positioned me on top of him. My legs straddled around his hips. His hands tightened around my back. He saw the panic in my eyes. It was difficult to hide since my entire body was on the verge of shaking. He brought me even closer to him.

"Tell me, Mia. Whatever you need me to promise you, I promise," he choked out.

"I know you're talking about Harrison Reynolds. He handpicked me to work at your company as a mole. I never supplied him with any information. I was never able to find anything out and what I did hear I never shared with him. I didn't see any potential with it." I waited for any reaction from him, but he remained stone cold, not displaying any emotion. "I tried to back out of the entire arrangement earlier this week. Harrison made it clear that if I didn't get myself involved in this meeting in Atlantic City that he'd start hurting the people in my life. He told me not to tell you anything. With how deeply I feel for you, I had to tell you the truth. I'm so sorry," I whispered.

Tears started to stream down my face. Ethan remained a silent statue. I prayed that he'd give me some sort of reaction. He continued to hold me tight, but he didn't speak. I heard his heart beating in his chest, or maybe it was my own – I wasn't sure. The terror inside me ran ahead at full speed, not allowing much room for anything else. The pressure in my chest began to suffocate me. I thought it would lessen, but his lack of response intensified it so much that every part of me constricted. I didn't know if he'd keep to an unspoken promise. The thought of anyone being hurt because of me stopped my breathing altogether. I started to drift onto another level, listening only to the beats of the rain that came down in the stormy skies above us.

Ethan gave me a gentle shake to bring me out of my daze. "Breathe, Mia."

"I need you to say something," I rasped.

"Calm down," Ethan demanded. He ran his nose along mine to get me to relax. My breaths continued in spurts. "Damn it, Mia. You're going to pass out if you don't settle down."

I gasped. "Please tell me what you're thinking, because I can't get any of this under control until you give me some sort of reaction."

"This is huge, Mia. I asked you on more than one occasion why you decided to work at the company. You lied to me the entire time. I can't say I'm not upset with you or that I won't second-guess you going forward. I'm glad you told me the truth though. I understand how much it scares you to open up that way. I'm glad you trust me enough to do it. It makes your behavior at times that much clearer," he stated quietly.

"I'm so sorry," I wheezed.

"I know why you're scared of Harrison. He's a ruthless bastard that instills fear around anyone that he can manipulate, which is why I went to him. I knew he would get the job done. I imagine he offered you something pretty extraordinary to suck you in to his ploy," Ethan murmured.

"He offered me a chance to get back into journalism by waving the chance to become the chief editor of his European circuit under my nose. I was foolish enough to believe him. Truthfully, I was so lost when the entire offer came about that I took it for all the wrong reasons. Then I met you and my life changed completely. I saw everything in a new light," I mumbled.

"He's well known for over-extravagant offers to get what he wants. I'm not sure why he preyed upon you when he already has Ian there. I don't know what game he's playing, but I will find out," he professed.

I panicked. "Ethan, please no. You can't let him know that I told you. Harrison warned me that if I crossed him it would be even worse than whatever Sean and Colin could do to me. I'm begging you not to do anything until I go to this damn meeting that he wants me at so badly. He's convinced that if you know the truth you'll stop it."

Ethan placed me on his side of the bed, and averted his eyes from me as he got up. He paced around the room while running his hands through his hair as he cursed. I focused on keeping my marbles so I didn't pass out. Ethan paused in front of the window right as a flash of lightning lit the room. It displayed the rage in his face. He continued to pace as I sobbed into the pillow. After a few minutes, Ethan returned to the bed and coaxed me out of the ball that I had curled into.

"Look at me Mia," he directed. I opened my blurry eyes. He grasped my face and placed a soft kiss on my lips. "I won't do anything to put you, or the people you care about, in danger. You can trust me."

I tried to relax into him, but our uncertainty loomed over me. Another sob escaped my chest at that thought. Ethan brought me even closer to him. He pulled the covers over us as we faced each other. "What?" he asked, perplexed.

I wiped away the tears that were drying out. "I'm scared that any second you'll push me aside; and how could I blame you with everything I withheld from you."

Ethan cupped my cheek and took a deep breath. "I've been waiting for the right moment to tell you Mia. As heavy as this moment is between us, it seems like the best possible one."

My eyes grew wide at the prospect of anything else coming out tonight. I doubted that either one of us would be able to handle it. "I'm not sure I understand."

He rested his forehead on mine. "I love you. I've been in love with you since the second I saw you; maybe even before that, without my heart realizing it."

I lost my breath, for an entirely different reason this time. Ethan watched me with worry as I struggled to find it again. "I love you too. I didn't know it was possible to feel this way about someone else. It's all happened so fast, but I can't picture my life without you in it. I'm so sorry I didn't tell you sooner," I confessed.

The depth of love behind his eyes mesmerized me. He closed them for a moment, then opened them again with such a beam that it almost blinded me. I cuddled into his body.

"I'm still waiting to collect on what you promised me," Ethan said with a sinful smirk.

And just like that he switched gears on me. He jumped from one emotional extreme to the next in all the same ways that I did. We had to have been made for each other. Everything turned out better than I could have imagined. I resented not telling him sooner. It was like we finally had a chance to begin with each other.

He grabbed my ass and slid me onto his hard length. I let out a low moan as his hands discarded the scant lingerie covering me. His hands journeyed over to my breasts. They brought each nipple to attention as he stroked his long fingers along them.

"I thought you wanted to collect on my promise," I groaned.

Ethan removed his fingers and replaced them with his tongue. His lips kissed along a trail before his teeth grazed along the same path until he hit the center of my nipple. The swivel of his tongue and teeth along each nipple sent everything inside me to another level. It turned every part of me completely on. My frail insides shifted to a fiery burn. I tried to shuffle down his body to make good on my promise, but he held me still, not allowing me to move an inch. He slid my legs around his sides as his hands went from my chest to my face. He framed my cheekbones tenderly before pulling me into him for a scorching kiss. He twirled along the sides of my mouth, until he consumed every part of my tongue so that it twisted along with his until we were breathless.

"I don't doubt that you are good for it, but I'm busy," Ethan husked.

He pressed his chest into mine and lifted me so that he could thrust forward into me. I gasped as he entered hard at first but slow and deliberate with each push thereafter. Ethan brought his forehead to mine and ran his hands along my back. I fell into an easy rhythm with him. There was no urgency, distraction, or lust between us. It was raw and emotional. Every inch that his hips rocked into me was with a reverence for this connection we were sharing with one another. I returned each thrust with the same devotion. I clasped my hands around his neck and ran my fingers through his hair. He raised his hips even higher and it drove him even further within me. I arched my back and cried out from the intensity of it. His grip strengthened as he did it again.

"Ethan ..." I cried out with God-like praise.

Everything about what was happening between us was so intimate that I didn't have words for how it all felt as it happened inside me. My heart had already left my chest with everything I'd admitted to him tonight, including that I was in love with him. He jerked his hips harder into me. I met him with just as much robustness as we continued at a slow, steady pace. Ethan buried his head into my shoulder. My hands wrapped snugly around his back.

Every part of me was alive and welcoming everything he was giving me. Every wanton feeling that I had always had around him ran throughout me, but in such a different way than it ever had when we'd been together before now. I got lost with the man I'd handed my heart over to, for what I hoped was forever.

Ethan shifted us as he laid me down on my back, but never stopped our movement. His hands journeyed along my sides. His lips met mine for a soft kiss. He pressed on at a measured pace before he came to a stop. I moved forward with my hips, but Ethan kept me still as he grabbed my hands and put them above my head.

"Don't panic. I want to take this slow with you Mia, so you know how much I love you," Ethan groaned as he twisted his hips.

He gave my neck gentle kisses before bringing his mouth to my lips for a soulful kiss as he began moving again. I gave way to his change of direction, not being able to fight it for a second. Everything about this time was different for us.

"I love you too," I panted.

Ethan resumed at a steady pace, before shifting into a relentless one that I welcomed. He continued pushing faster and harder. I met each thrust and clenched even tighter around him before I couldn't hold back any further. He quickly followed once I had let go. He released my hands. I wrapped them around him as he buried himself into me.

Ethan brought his head up from my chest and rested next to me on the pillow. We stared at each other, completely lost in the love that had been unspoken until now. I ran my finger along his brow to wipe away a bead of sweat that was about to trickle down. He clutched my hand after I finished. I cuddled into the crook of his shoulder. I wanted nothing more than to be as close to him as possible for as long as he would have me.

I awoke the next morning to open blinds and the sunlight flooding in around me. I went to reach for Ethan but came up with nothing but the cold side of the bed. I sat up in a panic. My chest tightened as I whipped my head around the room. He wasn't here. I looked around his room for any signs of where he might be, but I came up with nothing. I gave up in the bedroom. Against my better judgment, I snooped around the rest of his place but it was empty.

The frail edges of my heart began to splinter at the idea of him leaving me. It was déjà vu. With each step I took along the cool tiles, my heart began to tear open. The agony seeped into every vein and travelled into every part of my body. My eyes watered on my way back to his bedroom. He had left me. I went into the bathroom to collect my things and get the hell out of here so that I could have the proper meltdown that my body demanded.

I barely made it to the bathroom without falling over. I gripped the sink as I started hyperventilating with the uncertainty of what this meant. He said he loved me, but followed it with a disappearing act. The pain subsided after I let the terror of what this meant for my life creep in. If he had betrayed me, Harrison would start executing his threats. I slid to the floor as tears streamed down my face. I should've never told him, but I did because love blinded me, yet again. I crawled over to grab a pair of jeans and a T-shirt. I couldn't be here any longer. I staggered to my feet and over to the vanity to retrieve the rest of my things. On my approach, I caught sight of the envelope taped on the mirror.

Mia

*I'm sorry for leaving you alone this morning. I need a little space. It doesn't change my feelings for you, but I need to come to terms with the fact that you lied to me. I can't be without you. I'm asking you for time. I need some time to determine our road together. I stress **our** road. I won't do anything to jeopardize your situation with Harrison. I would never do anything to bring harm to you or your loved ones. You must trust me when I say that, but you also need to know that I'm not a man that will let anyone dictate my life. I need to determine why he preyed on you. There is a ticket inside this envelope. I've taken the liberty of planning your weekend for you. I know how much you hate when I do this but believe me when I say that it is for your own good. I don't want you to sit* *around becoming deranged because I need some time away from you. Bri will meet you at the airport. Appearances need to remain in place so you will return Sunday evening so you can be in the office Monday morning. I'm not leaving you. I love you. I'm not sure if you believe it as you read this, but I hope you give me the benefit of the doubt. I'll be in touch.*

Ethan

My hands shook nonstop as I read. My heart twisted with the uncertainty while the rest of my body dealt with the continuous waves of agony shooting out from every direction. As with everything with him from the very beginning, my heart believed he wouldn't do anything to hurt me. I believed that he wasn't evil like Sean and Colin. As my breathing evened out, I worked to control the tears that refused to stop. I didn't have a lot of faith in this letter, but then he knew me well enough to know it was exactly how I'd feel.

I wanted to curl up on the floor and let the overwhelming ache in my heart win. I managed to find the last shred of strength in my feeble bones to get away from his apartment. I gathered the rest of my things while wiping away the tears that continued to cascade. With each swipe, my wrath surfaced and replaced the ache. On my way out of the door, I opened the envelope and looked at the ticket information. My anger radiated through me at the thought of even entertaining what he wanted me to do. Curiosity got the better of me. I wanted to know where he planned to ship me off to while he ran around doing God-knows-what as he took his "time".

Hmmm ... Now that is one place I can get on board with to disappear to for the weekend. If he wants time, he has it. He just might not have me when he returns.

EPILOGUE

Two months ago I set out on a path with a desperate need to have a *plan* for my life again. I had experienced unfathomable pain that almost took me out of this world. My body remained, but my insides were dead. I hit rock bottom, with no direction on what was right or wrong. I stopped caring if my actions could hurt people. In my search to find purpose, I settled on a path that threatened to take my last few morals from within me.

I never believed that one person could shake you to the core; until he came along. Ethan turned my world upside down. He breathed life back into me with a love that scorched my soul. In a short amount of time, he stole my heart in every way. He made me realize everything; from the depths of deception to how much I love my friends. Ethan did it all while remaining the biggest mystery I'd ever come across in a person. His soul was pure. The depth of love in his deep brown eyes tugged at my heart, even now. They were always pushing me to believe in him.

Faith was difficult to give someone that you hardly know, especially when it was more than your own life on the line. The people I was fortunate enough to give all my faith to were the same people that stood to suffer because of my poor choices. I had a letter asking me to hand over that same faith. It was hard without knowing him. Faith and love were two *very* different things. It was possible to have one without the other. I learned that today.

Forgiveness was an even harder thing to come to terms with after this year. I didn't deserve to be forgiven for my recent actions. Was it better to forgive and forget? Was it better to keep things buried, so that you didn't end up revealing too much of yourself to be betrayed? I didn't have any of those answers. In the loneliness of this hallway, I fell even deeper into the abyss. I welcomed the emptiness that spread throughout me.

The *secrets* and *lies* that dictated my life almost made me miss out on a life-changing love. Walking away, I wanted to believe in the power of love, but my mind was full of doubt. In falling for him, I learned how very dangerous living a lie could be, and that secrets do nothing but shatter your world in the end. Ultimately, it now all came down to one question.

Is loving someone with every fiber of your being enough to save you?

To Be Continued...

ACKNOWLEDGMENTS

First and foremost, I have to say thank you to Nikki. Mia's story would not have made it to paper if it hadn't been for a good kick in the ass from you. You've always believed that I could do something like this even when I didn't. You and your family have changed my life beyond measurable words. I will forever be grateful that I kicked that trashcan in your direction our freshman year. Who knew such a simple act would be life-changing?

I have to give a huge shout out to my very first reader Teri. Bless your heart for taking this story in its rawest form and reading it and not smacking me over the head with all the errors. Your feedback, suggestions, thoughts, opinions and support got this book to the finish line. I truly believe that the path life takes us on dictates the people that we meet within our lives. I am so grateful that our paths intersected leading to a wonderful friendship. I have learned so much about life, love, strength, courage, and faith through you.

To my second reader and dear friend, Maureen, thank you so much for everything. As you know, I was absolutely terrified to give you my story. You are a bright, intelligent, and well-read woman so I knew it had to be up to par to put into your hands. The feedback and encouragement you gave me has been invaluable. Most importantly, you gave the untitled book a title that I still absolutely love. I cannot express enough thanks for your support and countless hours of listening to me ramble. It is truly difficult to come up with enough ways to say thank you for all that you did for me on this journey.

To the first part of Sassafrass, Emily, I am truly blessed to call you a friend. You have one of the kindest souls I have ever met. We are alike in so many ways yet different in all the ones that help make me a better person just by knowing you. I cannot thank you enough for listening to me go on about this crazy little idea of writing and giving me your support. Our friendship is one that I will always cherish.

To my first work wife, Amber, I am so grateful that we met each other. You are one of the sweetest, kindest, funniest, and carefree spirits I have encountered and I'm so happy we have remained friends all these years. Thank you for all your thoughts and enthusiasm with this story. It has helped more than you will ever know. The biggest thank you is for giving me the gift that keeps on giving – Marley. He is my everyday example of unconditional love.

To my second work wife, Siobhan, I am glad you got over your aversion to me quickly so that we could become the amazing friends that we are now. I have never met anyone that compliments my personality as much as you do. Thank you for being one of my beta readers and boosting up my confidence on the days that I needed it and tearing it down on the days I needed a reality check.

To my dear friend Sam, thank you so much for taking me into your family. It's rare that we get to meet people that understand exactly what we mean when we tell a story from the past. There are so many things that I've been able to share with you that have helped me heal and for that I am so grateful. You have helped me out so much over the years and a thank you will never be enough. I appreciate everything you have done for me more than you will ever know.

To my counterpart mole at work, Kelly, thank you for keeping me sane at the place that pays the bills. I am so grateful that we met and that we have maintained a friendship with one another even though we never see each other. Your support throughout this adventure of mine has been so important. It's another fine example of how life leads you to the people you're supposed to have in your life. I'm thankful our paths crossed.

I need to recognize three of my favorite little kids in this world, Jakob, Kade, and Kali – thank you so much for touching my heart in so many ways. There is nothing more wonderful than seeing the world through the eyes of a child. Thank you for inspiring me everyday with your innocence and brilliance.

I must give a huge shout out for Tom at tgh writing services. It's terrifying as an author to hand your work over to someone that will dissect it and point out all your shortcomings. I can honestly say that you took my novel and made it so much better. Your editing is phenomenal. You preserved my voice and writing style throughout the process and made corrections and suggestions to the story that made it that much better. I feel so very fortunate to have found you, not only because you've made me better as a writer, but because of your professionalism, quick turnaround, and superior service. I have done nothing but sing your praises to those around me. Any author would be lucky to have you work on their novel. Thank you for all your hard work and dedication on this book!

Finally, I have to give a huge thanks to L.J. at Mayhem Cover Creations. You created a cover that truly speaks to my characters. I am ecstatic with it! I cannot say enough how much I appreciated your patience and the collaboration to get the design exactly the way I wanted it. Your service and quick turnaround are by far the best in the business. Thank you again for all your hard work and patience!

The greatest thank you goes to each person that gave this novel a chance. Please know I share your love for a good story. I truly hope that you were entertained and thank you from the bottom of my heart for taking a chance on Mia and I.

ABOUT THE AUTHOR

Photo Credit: Amber Eckman

M. M. Koenig, a graduate from the University of Minnesota, has remained in the Twin Cities area with her loving dog Marley. She is a passionate person with many interests. The greatest of those is a good story accompanied by a killer soundtrack.

Find M. M. Koenig online to stay up to date on news, teasers, and deleted scenes on the Secrets and Lies saga:

Visit her website http://www.mmkoenig.com
Follow M. M. Koenig on Twitter: @M_M_Koenig
Follow Author M. M. Koenig on Facebook:
https://www.facebook.com/pages/Author-M-M-Koenig/734651516551415?ref=hl

Made in the USA
Charleston, SC
02 March 2015